The
Thirteenth
Pillar

J.L. O'Faolain

Dreamspinner Press

Published by
Dreamspinner Press
382 NE 191st Street #88329
Miami, FL 33179-3899, USA
http://www.dreamspinnerpress.com/

The Thirteenth Pillar
Copyright © 2011 by J.L. O'Faolain

Cover Art by Paul Richmond   http://www.paulrichmondstudio.com

ISBN: 978-1-61372-221-3

Printed in the United States of America
First Edition
November 2011

eBook edition available
eBook ISBN: 978-1-61372-222-0

To Margaret, who knew.

Chapter One

COLE suspected every morgue in the world carried a chill to it.

As a sidhe, he wasn't susceptible to temperatures the way humans were, but the subtle changes in climate were something he remained aware of regardless. It was currently February, and outside in the bleak darkness, New York City was currently facing a maelstrom of winter snow. The heavy clouds churning with white flakes had blanketed half the country, spreading out as far south as Texas and the Gulf Coast.

Cole had walked out in it alongside his partner and superior, Inspector Joss Vallimun, as the two had been called down to the morgue to inspect another body. It hadn't bothered him to walk outside while the flakes continued to pelt the ground. Joss had been shivering the whole time, but Cole was perfectly comfortable. Then they had entered the hospital morgue, and for the first time that day, Cole had shuddered involuntarily.

His left hand was twitching now. It always responded when there were a number of dead bodies in the area. His Hand of Power, the Hand of Cold Death, could summon anything cold and dead up to obey his every command. It had been called a weak, shameful power in the land of Faerie, but here amongst mortals, where he now worked as a special detective, the Hand had its uses.

The morgue, of course, reeked with the stench of formaldehyde. The smell of it was making Cole's nose itch as Joss spoke with the coroner. The man didn't look as though he was particularly happy to see him, and Cole suspected he knew why. They had been to this morgue before and each time had needed a moment to themselves in order to "examine" the body. That was the official story, at least. In reality, Cole didn't enjoy being gawked at while he questioned the deceased. It made him uncomfortable, a rare thing among his kind. Plus, the screaming and pointing from other humans in the room got old after a while.

Cole waited while Joss sorted things out with the head of the department, making sure all the paperwork had been filed and whatnot so they could carry on with their investigation. Meanwhile, the coroner's assistant, a young woman with olive skin and dark hair, kept shooting glances his way every few seconds. She had pretended to be busy sorting files, but when several fell out of her hands, the facade was pretty much blown. Cole waited while she picked them up, then caught her attention for a second. As Joss came over to fetch him, Cole gave the woman a wink and smiled as she blushed.

"Having fun?" Joss's voice carried a thread of jealousy far beneath the mirth on the surface. "We can go inside now. They've got the body already laid out for you."

"Right." Cole said nothing more, following after Joss as he led them across the room into another area, one filled with drawer after drawer of dead hosts. One was already pulled out and waiting for them. Cole felt his left hand twitch with nerves as they entered, begging for the power inside it to be released.

"Name?" he asked, as the coroner lingered.

"Aaron Hoover," the coroner replied. "The body was found in an alley. Someone had called their landlord about a bad smell coming through their window."

The body in question was of a young boy around the age of ten with dark hair and blue eyes, having a light-colored skin. Cole knew this because he'd read the report. Had he not, there would have been no way of figuring that out, going by sight alone. The body had been burned to a crisp. The whole surface was burned from head to toe, except in places where it looked like chunks of flesh had been torn away.

"What about the wounds?" Cole asked, looking the body over. "It looks like they were caused by teeth."

"Official report says the same thing," said the coroner. "It looks like the body was burned first and then torn up afterward. There's also evidence that he was held prisoner in a very cramped space before dying."

"Just like the other two," Joss commented, keeping his voice even and neutral.

"I'll leave you two alone," the coroner said, walking away now. "Just knock when you're finished doing… whatever."

Cole waited until the door shut before speaking. "There may be more," he reminded Joss. "The first one we spoke to said that he'd been held prisoner in a dark place and that he'd heard other children talking."

"The report said that the body had been held in a cramped space before dying," Joss mused quietly to himself. "That corroborates with what the first one said, and the second one talked briefly about being in a cage."

"The first one said that he'd been held in a cage," Cole reminded. "The second one mentioned a tiny space before it got really hot."

"It fits with the killer's MO." Joss nodded, keeping his face relaxed. "Good thing you told me to ask the coroner to check and see if the bodies showed signs of being imprisoned before they died."

"It was just a hunch. Shall we get on with it, then?" Cole stretched his left arm out over the corpse and let the power burst out of his hand. "It was Aaron Hoover, wasn't it?"

Cole released enough power to summon three or four bodies at once. It was needed, however, to shift the dead body back to something resembling a human form. There was no way the deceased could speak with a body charred so badly. The Hand of Cold Death could temporarily fix a damaged body with no life in it, but this required a little extra effort. Cole took several deep breaths as the form recovered some of its former youthful beauty and blinked up at them.

"Aaron Hoover," Cole said slowly. "I want you to listen very carefully to me."

The corpse blinked again. "Where's my mom?" it croaked. "I want to see my mom."

"Aaron," Cole said sharply. "You are already dead."

Joss gave Cole a look, but Cole ignored him. "You've been dead for a few days now," Cole explained. "I have awakened your body so that we can ask you some questions about how you died. Once we are done here, you will be laid to rest again, and your spirit can finally move on."

The boy didn't stop looking terrified by this news, but with each word Cole spoke, the tension in his body seemed to lessen.

"Good," Cole said, smiling now. "Now, do you remember where it was you were being held prisoner?"

The body of Aaron Hoover tried to swallow and found that it couldn't. "It was dark," it whispered hoarsely. "I couldn't see anything."

Joss looked across the slab at him. "Just like the others," he said softly.

"Do you remember who kidnapped you?" Cole asked.

The body shook its head slowly. "I don't remember being kidnapped. I was walking home from the bus stop. The next thing I knew, someone had put me in a cage, and I could smell something baking in an oven."

"Baking," Cole repeated, looking back at Joss. "Didn't the others mention they smelt something?"

"Maybe," he said with a nod.

"What did it smell like?" Cole went on. "Was it a bad smell?"

"It smelled good," the boy who had once been Aaron Hoover replied. "It reminded me of when we used to visit Grandma's house. It almost smelled like cookies, but better. I could smell it the whole time."

Cole took a deep breath. "Here we go," he warned Joss. "Aaron, do you remember how you died?"

The corpse didn't answer at first. Cole wondered perhaps if it hadn't heard him when the body suddenly shook. It almost rocked itself off the slab and onto the floor, but Cole forced it still by pushing his will into it through his Hand.

"They came for me," the body cried out now, panicking. "I could feel them grabbing me with their sticky hands. They were taking me somewhere, and it was small and tight. I couldn't breathe!"

Aaron Hoover's corpse gasped, his breath rattling like a clanging bell in his lungs. "It was too small. I couldn't get out, and it was getting so hot!"

Cole tried to will the body to stay calm, but it was reacting like the others before had. The more Cole tried to force the panic back down, the more it fought.

"It's not supposed to react like this," he growled, steadying his power and feeding more of it into the body. "Aaron Hoover, I command you to be at peace!"

The body went still at once, but the corpse began screaming. "*I want my momma!*" it shouted, the voice echoing off the metal drawers surrounding them. "*I want my momma! Momma, help me!*"

"Cole, turn it off before the whole department hears him," Joss ordered.

Cole made a fist, shutting his power down at once. The corpse rattled for a bit as the air was expelled from the lungs, making a loud whistle. Stepping farther back, Cole waited as the deceased form went back to being a lifeless burned shell.

"Just like the others," he commented. "They all died horribly, and under such traumatic circumstances that raising them for questioning is nearly impossible."

"Held in a cage," Joss said, thinking the words over carefully. "Then put inside a cramped space where it got hotter."

"A furnace," Cole said, feeling certain of his answer. "Or an old-fashioned stove."

Joss nodded. "A kiln could have the same effect. I've seen some of the bigger ones up close. You could stuff a dead body his size in there no problem. As hot as they get, it's a wonder there wasn't just bone left."

"The sweet smell, though," Cole pointed out. "They all smelled something, and this one said that it smelled like his grandmother's house. That's why I think it was an oven."

Cole was silent for a moment. "Should I try again and ask if it remembers seeing her?"

Joss shook his head. "We tried that last time and the poor kid kept right on screaming. I don't think this is her handiwork."

"Me neither," Cole admitted, turning away. "But it was worth a shot."

None of the people in the main area would look at them as they left. Everyone, including the coroner, was entranced by the floor or their own shoes. Cole ignored this and marched out the front door, timing his steps to where they fell in alongside Joss's.

"I think the sound of dead bodies screaming is beginning to affect them," he remarked once they were safely outside the hospital.

"You think?" Joss asked, cocking an eyebrow at him.

"It's just a theory at this point."

Both men climbed into Joss's car and got comfortable. The snow had let up for a few minutes, but Cole could sense it was just a temporary reprieve. Soon, something much bigger would be slamming against the city with full force. It was lucky he had the very best that money couldn't buy in central heating. Otherwise, he might have wound up freezing his ass off like so many who lived here.

"Come over to my place tonight," Cole asked as Joss pulled out of the hospital parking lot into traffic. "It's warm, and you can take a hot shower for as long as you like."

"Sounds good," Joss replied. "I could use one after today. They've had us running all over this fucking town looking for leads on this killer."

"While we're supposed to be out looking for clues to where Naryssa is hiding," Cole pointed out. "How did this case get dumped into our laps again? Shouldn't it have been something for homicide to deal with instead?"

"I guess the department thought it was weird enough," Joss said, shrugging. "I really don't know, but my guess is they're swamped too. Budget cuts were not kind to those people."

"They haven't exactly been the Spring Faerie Falls for us, either. Speaking of which, has there been any word about getting some more people transferred to our division?"

Cole and Joss both worked in the same department, a clandestine undercover group called Section Thirteen. It had originally been started back in the fifties by a group of mortal cops who specialized in occult crimes and the supernatural. The city had disbanded them sometime during the seventies after too many of their reports read like acid-rock poetry. One month ago, roughly, the city agreed to bring the Section back into business after a mad half-sidhe hag by the name of Naryssa had gone on a murdering spree and kidnapped a number of half-fey children. Cole had gotten dragged into the mix and was now working with the police as an officer of the law to bring her in.

Cole often found himself repeating that statement to himself. Even now, it sounded too weird.

The Section had started off with the two of them and one other homicide cop, a man who had been Cole's contact when he worked as a police consultant. These days, he and James Corhagen didn't speak with each other much. It was just as well, especially considering Cole had moved on in his life, away from James and his problems.

Working in the Section had given him a whole new set of problems, and those were more than enough. When Cole had first signed on, Joss had brought in several members of the city's vice squad to help out. Two weeks later, following an incident in the sewers, where they had been chasing after a large gelatin cube, every member of vice had pleaded with the brass to be taken back to their old assignments.

Dealing with the supernatural underside of New York was not something for the weak of stomach.

So it ended up that the Section was stuck with the three core members and no one else. No one else wanted to come close to them, and no matter how much Cole claimed he didn't care, they were only three men. The Section had jurisdiction across the whole city, meaning they got called out several times a day to examine a crime scene just to clarify that it had been caused by something mundane and not a rampaging orc.

"I want to take my car home first," Joss said, breaking up his thoughts. "Since there's no place to park outside your place."

"Let me have your cell phone, then," Cole said, holding his hand out. "I'll go ahead and call a cab for us so it can be waiting when we arrive."

Joss fished his phone out of the back pocket of his pants and tossed it to him. "We really need to get you one of those. It's difficult enough getting hold of you when you're not on duty."

"That's the whole point," Cole replied, punching in the number. "Hey, Crystal," he said into the phone. "Yeah, it's me again. Can you have a cab waiting for us at the usual place? Right, we're a good fifteen or so minutes away, maybe more now that traffic has picked up again. Just tell your man to park outside the apartment, if you wouldn't mind. Thanks!"

Joss shook his head. "I think she's starting to wonder."

Cole handed the phone back to him and stretched comfortably, gazing out the passenger window. "I love it when it snows here," he said softly. "It reminds me of home."

"I hate it," Joss grumbled. "Give me spring any day. Before long, summer will be here and it'll be too hot to breathe."

Cole kept his thoughts to himself and allowed Joss the silence he needed to make it home quickly and efficiently. Soon, they were pulling up into the driveway of the inspector's apartment, a shabby but neat building that Cole had been a guest at several times since he had joined the police force. The cab he had called for was waiting for them with the motor, and probably the meter, running. Joss parked his car; then they both rushed out to jump in the back of the waiting vehicle. The driver didn't so much as comment, pulling out into the street without a backward glance at them.

They reached Bowling Green Park a little bit later. Cole already had his money out and passed it up to the driver before hopping out.

"Keep the change," he said, slamming the door shut behind him.

"I'm surprised you can afford to keep doing this," Joss remarked as they wandered through the entrance together.

"I just have to pay for food," Cole reminded him. "The sithen provides me with everything else."

"Lucky bastard."

Cole laughed as they came up to the fountain. The jets had been turned off due to the weather, yet the water inside the basin had yet to freeze. People surely found this strange but were too busy with their own lives to investigate the cause. Cole snapped his fingers, then waited as the entrance to the world below rose up in front of them. As the doorway formed from the water's surface, Cole brought his arms around the inspector's waist and squeezed.

"Whenever you are ready," he whispered into the mortal's ear.

The first time they had gone through this door together, there had been an uneven flight of stairs leading down into a dark corridor. The sithen had been under Naryssa's control back then, but after Cole had defeated her with Joss's help, he'd taken up living in it. Naryssa had escaped, and now her home was his to do with as he pleased. Cole had gotten rid of those blasted steps first.

There was only a step or two down now. Joss went through first and removed his shoes at the landing. Cole came in next and waited as the door slid shut, sealing them off from the mortal world.

"Everything okay?" he asked.

"Fine," Joss replied nonchalantly. "No strange visions or unusual colors. I had worse side effects from walking into my roommate's dorm in college."

"I simply wanted to be sure." Cole had brought Joss here several times already, and each time, they'd stopped before going too far in to check and make sure the sithen wasn't playing tricks with Joss's mind. Legends spoke of the Faerie mounds giving mortals the odd turn now and again.

The ceiling was high, held in place ostensibly by a long row of columns that had tree roots wrapped around them. Halfway down the stone path was a stone fountain, the water of which splashed merrily, welcoming them home. Cole could hear laughter coming from it and waved at the pixies playing there as he walked past. They had once lived in a storm drain in Central Park, but after he had moved into the sithen, Cole had invited them along.

Above the fountain were two ghostly figures. The bean sidhe who guarded the entrance had taken to avoiding their posts whenever Cole brought Joss home. Cole suspected they were jealous and knew what he would do to them if they tried anything on Joss.

Smart ladies.

"Welcome home, Master Colewyn," a voice said.

Cole looked to the source as a short man with a balding head materialized. "That way," Mal, the ghost and operator of the sithen, said, gesturing. "Right through the door. I've already gotten your bed ready, and the bathroom water is nice and hot."

"Thanks, Mal," Joss said as they entered the double doors he'd been pointing to. "He's really taken to this whole 'butler' role, hasn't he?"

"I think he finds the role amusing," Cole replied. The sithen had already changed itself around, as per Mal's instructions, to take them directly to Cole's private chamber. It was just down the smaller hallway now and to the left.

"That makes me worry," said Joss in a grave voice as they entered the expansive room. "If what you told me is true, why would the ghost of a former sorcerer condemned for practicing black magic find being a butler amusing?"

"He was trapped in a book for centuries," Cole pointed out, directing them both to the bathroom. "Mal is probably relieved to be out and doing anything now."

"Good point."

The sithen, with Mal's help, had constructed a spacious room for Cole that was decorated in brown paneling with cobblestone floors covered by thick rugs. The bed was by far the largest piece of furniture in the room, but the cabinets, shelves, and desk were all massive and varnished a deep brown color to match the walls. It was the sort of room he'd always dreamed of having.

Off to the side was the bathroom. Cole entered first and began shucking his clothes as Joss came up behind him and did the same. As usual, Cole had worn all black while on patrol. His leather pants and long vest were far from regulation, but since Joss had insisted that Section Thirteen be a plainclothes operation, there was very little the higher-ups could do. Plus, as Cole himself had pointed out, a uniform would do very little to help him blend in.

Joss, unlike him, had dressed for freezing weather. His knee-length coat was the first thing to go, followed by the cream-colored button-down shirt. Cole was already naked now and stood there enjoying the view. Joss took a moment to slowly draw the undershirt over his head, knowing how much Cole liked to watch. His abs and chest came into view, covered in a natural rug of curly hair. Cole sighed, feeling a low moan rising up from his throat. He loved running his fingers through that carpet and did so at every chance. When Joss dropped his pants, the underwear came with them, and his shaft stood upright and rigid.

It was as big as a baby's arm.

The head was leaking precum now, causing Cole's mouth to water. Once Joss had stepped out of his clothes, Cole wasted no time in dragging both of them into the shower. The water kicked on immediately, and true to Mal's word, it was at just the right temperature. Joss groaned as the three showerheads above them sent jets of steaming liquid onto his back, pounding the stress of the day out of him. Each head was shaped like a theater mask: one frowning, one grinning, and one trapped in between.

Cole seized Joss by his thick mane of wet blond hair and pulled him in close for a kiss that ended with their tongues dancing around one another. His own cock was stretched as far as it would go, almost to the point of pain, as their arms encircled each other. Cole could feel Joss's hands all over him, and he moaned his pleasure down the mortal man's throat.

Cole began kneading the knots out of Joss's back as he nuzzled the man's ear. "That feels so good," Joss breathed, kissing Cole lightly on his shoulder. "Don't stop, please."

"Never," Cole cooed. "Let go. I've got both of us now."

Joss went silent for a moment as Cole continued to massage his back in time with the water. "That boy," said Joss softly as Cole worked lower. "He couldn't have been, what? Ten years old? Somebody baked him alive."

"We'll find them," Cole assured him, not letting up. "And when we find them, we put a stop to it."

"You make it sound simple," Joss groaned, running his own hands up the slicked surface of Cole's back. "It's never that simple. Being a cop is anything but simple."

"I'm not really a cop," Cole reminded him. Seizing the man by the hair, he gently pulled until Joss's eyes were facing his. "I am a sidhe warrior. You brought me into the NYPD, but at heart, I will always be who I was raised to be. No amount of paperwork or procedure will change that."

"I shouldn't let you say things like that," Joss mumbled. Their foreheads pressed together under the jet stream. "We're supposed to catch the bad guys, not execute them. But after what I heard those kids say...."

"One thing at a time," Cole said, shushing him. "For now...."

Joss looked at Cole when he didn't finish.

"I'm going to fuck you silly," Cole whispered into his ear before spinning Joss around.

Joss brought his arms up to brace himself against the slippery wall of the shower as Cole reached his hand out. The sithen was always quick to respond, and this time was no exception. Before Cole's hand could touch the wall to the right of Joss, it opened up a hidden compartment to reveal a small bottle of golden liquid.

"Last time, it was under the frowning shower head," Cole noted, pouring some of the fey lubricant onto his fingers.

Joss merely grunted and steeled himself as two of Cole's fingers were inserted into his ass. Cole quickly flexed and wiggled the tips as he felt them brush across Joss's love nut. Joss's cock jumped at the stimulation and began drooling. The rough and rugged male grunted as another finger joined the others. His asshole was opened slightly, but it was still tight and snug as Cole began to gently fuck his digits back and forth.

At the same time, he managed to dribble a little bit of the oil onto his other hand by tilting it slightly. It wasn't easy, and he wound up with more than was needed, but the glass bottle didn't slip out of his fingers once. Cole placed it back into the slot in the wall, snapped the cap back into place, and watched as it disappeared once more. Satisfied, he used the oil smeared all over his left hand to slick his cock up as Joss began moaning with pleasure.

"Here it comes," he warned, pushing the head of his dick up against Joss's entrance.

"Umph!" Joss grunted as the head popped past his sphincter. "Ohhh, yeah!"

"Get ready." Cole braced himself, getting a nice grip on Joss's hips as he drew back slightly, then drove himself forward hard. The head of his cock plowed into Joss's innards, tearing a path that made the rough-and-tumble man moan.

"Fuck, yeah," Joss breathed as the steam built up around them. "Fuck me, lover."

"You want that?" Cole began to pick up speed as he slapped his hand across Joss's ass cheek. "Your ass is as tight as I've had in a long time. It's hotter inside of you than in this shower. I'm going to enjoy fucking the shit out of you."

"Just shut up and fuck me!" Joss replied.

Cole was a sidhe warrior, and despite his svelte frame, he had the strength of ten muscled men on crack. It was very important for him not to forget how delicate Joss was by comparison. The mortal would not have liked hearing that, but of the two of them, Cole was actually the more durable. Yet the two had been on the move for days, tracking a killer who seemed even more elusive than the one they'd come up against a month ago. In that time, they'd barely had the chance to share a private conversation that didn't involve the more unpleasant aspects of their work. As such, Cole found himself throwing aside some of his restrictions now. As Joss's moans filled the steamy air surrounding them, Cole's hips picked up speed, and he began to really pound into his man.

Joss tossed his head back and howled as his canal was savaged. Water from the showerhead splashed down into his face and mouth. Even then, he didn't stop yelling for Cole to fuck him harder.

Cole was happy to oblige. As he kicked it into high gear, Cole felt his balls begin to draw up. Cum churned inside them, ready to unload down the dark tunnel of Joss's ass any second. Joss's own balls were already swollen and ready to burst. Cole grunted right along in time with his lover and steeled himself. Both of his arms snaked around Joss just below his hairy chest. As Cole was getting ready to bust, a voice rang out in his ears.

"*Tuulois MacColewyn!*"

"Shit!"

Cole gasped and leaped backward, drawing his dick out of Joss's asshole as the air around them swam unexpectedly. Joss glanced back in confusion, still pulling at his dick as Cole leaped out of the shower in a panic.

"What happened?" he moaned. "Why did you stop?"

"Tuulois MacColewyn!"

"Never mind that! Turn the water off and get your clothes!"

The sithen was already two steps ahead of him. The shower heads shut off immediately, and Cole suddenly found their clothes much closer than where they'd left them. Amidst the pile were their weapons, which to him was much more important. Cole could already feel the spell beginning to take hold of him.

"Hold on," he ordered, snatching their things up off the floor and jumping back in with Joss. Joss, however, had gotten the wrong idea and seized his cock, jerking it back and forth.

"I didn't mean that!"

"Tuulois MacColewyn!"

Cole turned sideways next to Joss and felt his cock jerk hard as his balls were drained of their essence. Joss's own cock was already exploding in the same direction. Something was pulling both men upward through what felt like a wet rubber tube as they shot their loads into clear space. A sense of displacement followed, and Detective Corhagen was abruptly standing in front of them with two separate loads dripping down his face.

Joss still had a few good shots left in him, it turned out. A whole rope of cum landed on Corhagen's long coat, and another from Cole splattered across his tie. Corhagen's eyes went wide from shock to disbelief as he took in the sight of both Cole and Inspector Vallimun standing together naked inside the summoning circle he'd drawn.

"Well," said Cole, dripping wet. "This is a new twist."

THEY were standing in what looked like an open-ended alley. The circle used to summon him and, by extension, Joss, was smoldering now around their feet. Cole didn't recognize the place, but he assumed Corhagen knew where they were.

Corhagen was wiping the remains of both money shots off his jacket and tie with a clean handkerchief while Cole attempted to dry both him and Joss off with his sacred weapon, Aed Deigh. The double-headed bladed weapon had been tucked away inside his bundle of clothes along with Bandersnatch and Jabberwock, his specially made twin guns. One end of the hilt contained a blade endowed with the icy touch of coldest winter. However, it was the other side that interested Cole at the moment. It held a blade that constantly glowed red hot.

The blade was intended for use as a powerful weapon, but Cole was applying it in a much more practical fashion at the moment, using it to heat the air surrounding their bodies. The moisture that lingered on their skins from the shower quickly vanished, leaving Joss dry but shivering.

"Quick," Cole ordered, handing Joss his clothes. "Put them on before you catch a cold."

Joss was quick to comply. Cole pulled the glowing red blade back into the hilt with but an effort of his will, then made to dress himself. He was far more comfortable being nude, but the mortals living in New York had made their feelings on the matter clear long ago. Besides that, Cole suspected Corhagen hadn't dragged them out of their nice hot shower just to say hello.

He rarely spoke to Cole these days.

"You missed a spot," Cole said, pointing to a place on Corhagen's tie.

Corhagen looked down and saw it. Cole received a nasty glare for his trouble as Corhagen began furiously scrubbing at it. Corhagen's effort nearly saw him strangled for it, as he was so intent on rubbing the jizz off that he yanked too hard on his tie. The tan-colored noose pulled tight around his neck, causing him to gasp. Cole sighed and reached over to help his comrade in arms out, still shirtless, but Corhagen jumped away from him.

"Whatever," Cole said, leaving Corhagen to choke to death. "Do you have any idea why he brought us here?" he asked Joss, who was finishing up. "I'm under the impression that this wasn't a social call, but until he's done wrestling with his tie, we'll never know."

"There's been a murder," Corhagen choked out, yanking his tie loose.

"That's not new," Cole replied casually. "This is New York. Hundreds of people get gunned down every day. Nobody cares about it unless one of the numbers in that statistic is important."

"It's our job to care," Joss reminded him.

"Oh yeah."

"The man was a schoolteacher," Corhagen went on, his voice still slightly rough. "He taught at one of the private schools here on Staten."

"Staten?" Cole interrupted. "You brought us all the way out to Staten Island?"

Corhagen pretended not to have heard him. "The victim's name was Melvin Jagger. He was in his midfifties and taught economics at a local private school. Unmarried, but had several relationships over the years with a number of coworkers, and he was in no way related to the lead singer of the Rolling Stones."

"Well, that's good to hear," Joss said.

Corhagen seemed to acknowledge that the inspector had spoken but was avoiding any eye contact for the moment. "The chief sent me out here while you guys were working the serial killer angle," he said, clearing his throat. "I don't know why, but it looks like this guy was important. The chief made it clear I was to drop whatever I was doing and haul my ass out here."

"Maybe the victim really was related to Mick Jagger?" Joss offered.

"Why was the chief so convinced this man's death concerned us?"

Once again, Corhagen didn't acknowledge that Cole had spoken. "The natives here have held the crime scene open for us. CSI has already gathered forensics, so there's nothing left but for us to go in and have a look-see."

"You didn't answer his question," Joss said pointedly.

"Don't worry," Cole replied, stepping forward. "I do not require the assistance of anyone to make myself heard."

Cole stood right in front of Corhagen and stared him down. At one time, a long time ago, they had been friends. Corhagen had been running from his attraction to Cole and ended up married to an already pregnant wife whose third child was on its way. Cole suspected Corhagen had guessed the nature of his new relationship with Joss Vallimun. It had been Corhagen who introduced them.

"James," Cole said in a very level, even tone. "I asked you a question before. Why would the chief believe a deceased teacher from Staten Island concerned us?"

Corhagen looked as though he was going to fight Cole but backed down suddenly at the last second. "I don't know," he said in what nearly sounded like a sullen tone. "The chief just called and ordered me out here. I don't know if the man's death had anything to do with the supernatural community or Naryssa. I haven't gone over to the crime scene yet."

"Why?" Joss wondered.

Corhagen's mouth twisted upward in a frustrated smirk. "They weren't very happy to see me. I told them I was here on orders of the chief of police, but none of them were willing to share much information."

"They never are," Cole said, sighing.

"Let's find out what's going on," Joss said, motioning for them to fall in line behind him. "I want to know what was so special about an economics teacher from a private school."

Cole was already listing some possibilities. "Maybe the private school was the police chief's alma mater?"

"Don't know," said Joss. "But we'll find out soon enough."

The crime scene was easy to spot. There was still police tape sectioning the area off, along with several lingering cars that still had their strobes on. Cole, Joss, and Corhagen all ducked under the tape and headed toward the spot where Cole smelled blood. Almost immediately, someone jumped up to stop them, spilling coffee onto the freshly fallen snow in the process.

All three of them had their badges out before the officer reached them. "Section Thirteen," Joss announced in an authoritative voice. "The chief of police sent us."

"Oh," the young man replied, shaking the hot coffee off his hand. "Right. Go on then, I guess. The body is that way."

Cole could have led them without directions, but Joss nodded his thanks anyway. A moment later, they were staring down at what had once been a human being. Something had gotten hold of the victim in a bad way, to the point that it looked like his whole body had been carved up by dull knives.

"It looks like something with claws mauled him," Corhagen noted.

"Obviously," Cole replied.

"They'll probably run a match to see if the claw marks match anything in the police system's database," Joss pointed out. "My gut tells me this wasn't an ordinary animal, though."

"Not unless a tiger from Prospect Park got loose and decided to take a tour of the island for some local color," Corhagen joked.

"This wasn't a tiger," Cole stated. "Look at how deep the wounds are. And look at the incision. The length is all wrong too. I suspect that's because at least some of the damage was done by fangs. Something with shorter claws but much more adept at using teeth than a tiger attacked this man. Also, going by the position of some of the wounds, it looks like whatever did this was taking its time."

Both Corhagen and Joss looked at him.

"What makes you say that?" Joss asked, interested.

"There are more than enough wounds on the body for the victim to have bled to death," Cole explained, pointing at one in particular running vertically on the lower abdomen. "This man's abdominal aorta was cut open. That should have been enough, but it looks like the attacker kept going. A human will bleed to death from a severed abdominal aorta in a matter of minutes."

"His throat is slashed too," Corhagen said quickly, pointing. "On both sides, no less. That had to open the jugular."

"The arms, the legs, the ribs...." Cole pointed to each one. "This man was sliced up, but if whatever did this was quick enough to go for his vulnerable regions, why not stop there?"

"What does that say to you?" Joss asked.

"That whatever did this knew the man," Cole replied. "And probably hated him."

"This was a hate crime?" Corhagen looked confused now, even as he resisted looking at Cole directly. "It doesn't look like the guy belonged to a minority."

"I said that the perpetrator was probably someone that hated him," Cole explained. "That doesn't mean that whoever did it hated him because of his ethnicity or nationality."

"As if we didn't have enough on our hands already with the serial killer case," Joss groaned, marching around the body in a circle. "Now the chief wants us to find out why this poor bastard got fucked up."

Nobody said anything for a moment. "Can you talk to him?" Joss asked Cole after a moment. "Raise him to get some answers for us?"

"Sorry," Cole replied without looking up. "Even in this weather, the body is still too warm. It just isn't dead enough." Cole tilted his head to the side as he observed the deceased further. "Ironically."

"How long?" Joss pressed.

"Tomorrow," Cole assured him, backing away from the corpse and the smell of spilled blood. "Or the day after. We'll get some answers then. In the meantime, I don't see any point in hanging around here longer. There doesn't seem to be...."

Cole froze and felt the skin on the back of his neck crawl. Sniffing the air, he whirled, kicking up snow and slush all around him as his nostrils flared.

"What?" Corhagen wondered.

"I smell something," said Cole, on full alert now. "It smells like...."

Cole breathed in deeply, cycling through each scent brought to him by his nose, searching for the brief glimmer he'd picked up on before. At first, it almost slipped through his grasp, but Cole hadn't been one of Titania's Wolves for nothing. Opening his eyes, he grinned long and hard before pointing further down the street.

"That way?" Joss asked, looking. "You sure?"

"I can smell them," Cole insisted. "The trail is faint. It was hard to pick up at first because of the blood and smell of other people running around all over the crime scene. I can't be sure, but it almost smells fey."

"Fey?" Corhagen groaned. "That's just great."

"Almost," Cole reminded him before giving his attention to Joss. "I think I can track it."

Joss looked down at the snow-covered ground all around them. "There aren't any tracks," he noted.

"Some fey know how to move through snow without leaving tracks," Cole explained, already taking off his vest and shirt. "No matter how hard they try to disguise their scent, though, I will find them."

"Go," said Joss, reaching for Cole's clothes. "We'll borrow a police car and catch up to you later."

"You're going to let him strip right here in the middle of the street?" Corhagen interrupted. "While it's snowing?"

As if in answer, one of the officers standing by the car let out a whistle. "They should be paying me to see this," said Cole. "If any of them see something they don't like, it isn't my fault."

Joss snatched Cole's leather pants out of the air as Cole placed the leather holsters for his guns and Aed Deigh back on his body. The officers farther back were watching now with incredulous looks, no doubt wondering why a member of the Section had stripped down in below-zero weather.

"Hurry," Joss said. "The scent will fade if you wait too long."

"Don't worry," Cole swore. "I'm not about to lose my prey now. Let the hunt begin!"

The catcalls abruptly fell silent as Cole loped off in the direction of the trail. There was about half a second as the change took hold where his hands were pressed down into the snow as he prepared to leap. Then the change came and Cole was in his wolf form, a massive solid-white wolf with the same three-ringed eyes of gold, copper, and topaz he had been born with. Everything shifted with him to a new perspective, but Cole had long since gotten used to that and was ready to trace the scent back to its source.

Snow flew behind him as he raced off after his intended prey.

The snow had done its job of concealing the trail, but Cole had been born partly of the winter court, and he knew intimately how to read between the layers of ice. Deeper still lay secrets most would never think to look for, and his nose was able to separate them out. Like a blind man sweeping his hand across a Braille page, Cole tracked the elusive scent through the streets and over rooftops. The longer he gave chase, the more convinced he became that the elusive scent belonged to one of the fey. Though Cole was having trouble working out which one, he knew he would soon have the answer.

The straps hanging across his back and sides were chafing, but

Cole endured it. Years ago, he'd had the leather belt custom made to hold his weapons while he shape-shifted so he would never be without them. Crossing a stretch of rooftops, Cole began to suspect he would need them shortly. The trail seemed to end just up ahead at what looked like a private boarding school. It was harder to tell in this form, but that turned out to be a moderate concern.

Something leaped out of the shadows at him while he was still several feet in the air. Cole had smelled his assailant coming, though, and quickly turned in midair to grasp the other wolf by the scruff of the neck with his jaws. One quick toss of his head and the smaller wolf went flying. Cole landed, shape-shifted back to his sidhe form in the process, and looked forward at a sign, bolted to a length of iron fence, that immediately caused his skin to crawl.

"Sir Frances North Academy," he read aloud as several more wolves began gathering around him in a circle.

"You are trespassing," a voice growled at him. "Leave now."

"I am looking for someone," he declared, raising himself up to his full height. "This is my hunt. What purpose do you have here?"

"That is not your concern," replied the alpha of the pack, sniffing Cole disdainfully from several feet away. "Fallen sidhe. Why did one who was cast aside by Oberon come here?"

In answer, Cole drew out Aed Deigh and brandished the frost-covered blade. Swinging it forward, he crouched down to where he was eye level with the alpha and at the same time got a good whiff of who he was dealing with. In the process, Cole received two shocks. One was that he recognized the scent of the creatures surrounding him. The second was that a wave of icicles as big as his forearm went flying out from the blade. The fey wolves jumped out of the way in time, causing his unintentional attack to slam into the iron fence behind them.

"That was a surprise," he said, glancing around as they moved in closer. "You're Cu Sith, aren't you?"

Some of the wolves hesitated.

"Why are you guarding this school?" he pressed, keeping both eyes peeled for an attack. "What is so special about it?"

"Silence!"

Cole was ready for the attack and struck out with his foot, sending the Cu Sith wolf back the way he'd come. Two more came at him from behind, forcing him to dodge out of the way in a roll and come up with the red-hot end of his weapon at the ready. The heat coming off it was intense, forcing some of the snow around him to melt slightly. Cole could have ended this with a few shots and one or two strokes. It wasn't as though the Cu Sith posed a severe threat to him. He wanted answers more than anything. Keeping the Cu Sith alive for the moment was more important. Of course, that didn't mean they felt the same way about him.

And at any rate, he was reluctant to harness the full power of Aed Deigh, since it was behaving so strangely all of a sudden.

Without warning, something landed softly behind him. Cole stiffened, as much in shock as anything. He hadn't sensed anyone nearby save for the wolves. There weren't many who could boast of sneaking up on him in such a way.

The wind shifted, and Cole knew at once who was behind him by their scent. Looking back, he saw a figure wrapped in an old cloak that smelled like it was made out of burlap. The figure was tall, though a head shorter than him at least, and a pair of athletically trim legs poked out from the lower half of the cloak.

Surprisingly, the Cu Sith seemed more perturbed by this new presence than his. Several leaped into the air, intending to attack his prey and catch her off guard. Cole rolled forward out of the way, which turned out to be a wise call. No sooner had he moved than the figure flipped over onto her shoulders and spun around like a break dancer. Her body was a cyclone of feet, fists, and claws as blows exploded across the bodies of the fey wolves, sending them flying.

Cole caught a glimpse of two perky breasts as she slowed down. The girl was indeed naked under her cloak and didn't look very old. Her hair was clipped short and spiked outward away from her head. It was also colored an unnatural shade of green. Unnatural, at least, for a human.

Cole could see the claws coming out of her hand. With the cloak's hood pulled back now, the girl's pointed ears stood out prominently. Her feet looked to be padded like a cat's. Her eyes were slanted like a cat's as well, save that they had turned a deep purple.

The girl was a changeling.

She was also the suspect he had tailed here.

The girl turned at the same time he did, hearing the sound of approaching sirens. Giving Cole one last glimpse of her face, she leaped up into the air as the Cu Sith charged for her. Cole raised his blade and charged it, hoping to cut them off and stop her at the same time, but a police car roared up from around the corner at the last second and blocked his line of sight. The Cu Sith weren't hampered by its presence and leaped right over.

The changeling girl was long gone.

"What was that all about?" Joss wondered, looking off in the direction where the wolves had gone.

"I don't know," Corhagen mumbled, staggering out of the car with both hands over his eyes. "I had my eyes covered the whole time. Let me know when he's less nude, okay?"

Joss ignored Corhagen and came forward with Cole's clothes. Since Corhagen had his eyes covered, Cole greeted his lover with a kiss before taking the pants from him.

"What did we miss?" Joss asked.

"A lot," he replied. "This new case that the chief of police dropped into our laps?"

"Yeah?"

Cole gave him a look before pulling his shirt over his head. "It just got really interesting."

Chapter Two

CORHAGEN waited in the backseat as Joss left to speak with the police officers still on duty. None of them would come near the car after seeing Cole sitting in the passenger seat, so the man in charge was forced to step forward as Joss approached. He didn't look especially happy, but someone needed to inform them that the Section's investigation of the scene was, at least for the moment, over with.

Cole found the whole thing amusing.

"You'd think they had never seen someone strip down and shapeshift before," he said mockingly.

Corhagen didn't respond.

"You're taking this much better than I expected you to," Cole went on, sensing the tension building up. "Although I thought you would have realized it by now. Incidentally, what exactly is it that you have against me showering of late?"

Corhagen shifted in his seat and let out a long sigh.

"I just hope Joss doesn't catch pneumonia," Cole added in a serious tone.

"Yeah."

The weight of that one word made Cole sigh himself. "I waited for you," he pointed out. "I waited for over a year to hear from you. I admit that the last time we spoke did not end well, but I'd thought we might talk again after a while."

Corhagen was back to not speaking.

"You chose your wife and kids," Cole said. "I respect that. I still don't think that was a smart decision, and I sure as hell don't trust

Sarah not to screw you over in the end, but doing this for your children is a very noble thing. However, even if what I'd said all this time was out of line by human standards, you have no right to be mad at me for moving on."

The silence in the car became overwhelming.

"Did you really think I would just wait for you?"

Corhagen opened his car door and nearly leaped out in his desperation. However, the seat belt he'd worn was still fastened securely to the clip, holding him down. The strap caught him by the throat as a result, and Corhagen gagged for several seconds before locating the release. Free at last, he jumped out of the car and slammed the door shut under the pretext of lighting up a cigarette.

Cole watched from his seat as his former friend and fellow Section member puffed furiously on the cancer stick as Joss wandered back their way.

"Brrr!" the inspector groaned, sliding back in behind the wheel. "That went well."

"I could see from here," Cole noted. "Did you tell them what we found?"

"Eh, some of it." Vallimun reached for the knob that controlled the car's heater and turned it to full blast before continuing. "I gave them the abridged version, as usual. They didn't sound thrilled."

"They never do."

"True," Joss agreed. "Give me your assessment of the situation right quick before we have to turn the car back over to them. It'll give me time to warm up."

"I think the girl who showed up to help fight off the Cu Sith was a changeling," he explained as Joss held his hands in front of the vents. "She might have seen the attack on the teacher. That would make her a witness to the crime."

"That's good news," Joss reasoned. "Any chance you'd be able to locate her?"

"It's possible," Cole said, thinking. "She looked to have been on the run for a while. This is just a guess, but she might have a hideaway somewhere near here. If it's in the area, I should be able to locate it. It's just going to take a little time. Her scent is remarkably vague."

"What is a changeling exactly?" Joss interrupted, his brow wrinkled in concentration. "I think I've heard the term before."

"It's a word humans once used to describe a baby human that was taken by the fey," he explained. "Most children who are taken choose to remain in Faerie. Some because it is all they've ever known, and some because they don't have any choice in the matter. Every so often, though, a taken child will escape for one reason or another and return to the mortal realm. The problem with this, however, is that being inside Faerie changes you, if you aren't already fey."

Joss looked at him thoughtfully. "Changes you how?"

Cole squinted as he struggled for a way to explain. "Faerie affects mortals differently," he said. "The changes are never really consistent, but the longer a human stays inside the boundaries of Faerie, the more it begins to affect them. The real problem, though, is when a human tries to pass through the Hedge."

Joss was completely lost now.

"The Hedge is what we call the border that keeps Faerie isolated from all the other realms," Cole added quickly. "It's like a maze, except that it really isn't a maze at all, but a lot of people who've traveled through it perceive it as such, so the thought basically settled into everyone's brains to see it that way."

Cole smiled at the look on Joss's face now. "It's okay to be confused. A lot of people have trouble understanding that. The Hedge isn't really something that can be described in mortal terms."

"Did you go through it?" Joss asked. "When you were banished, I mean?"

Cole shook his head uncomfortably. "I wasn't banished that way," he said quickly. "Nobody goes through the Hedge willingly unless they have to. Oberon put me on a skiff and sent me from one shore to another. He's the King of all Faerie. That sort of thing is something he could do in his sleep."

"But this changeling girl went through the Hedge," Joss went on, catching on now. "And it brought her here to New York?"

"It could have taken her anywhere." Cole shrugged, grateful to be off the subject of his banishment. "She could have come to New York afterward. When you travel through the Hedge, though, it changes you.

No one crosses it unscathed."

"How?"

Cole hesitated before answering. "The Hedge tears away at a mortal's… mortality. It strips a human of what it means to be human. That's why so many of the sidhe and other fey think of escaped changelings as abominations. There's rarely anything left of them that could be called human, but there was never anything fey in them to begin with, so they can't come back to Faerie. Not unless someone from there offers to take them, which doesn't happen a whole lot."

"How often?"

"Never, really," Cole admitted. "To my knowledge, at least."

Joss thought on that for a long time as, outside the car, Corhagen pulled out another cigarette. One of the officers from earlier was wandering over and quickly made a motion with his fingers to bum a smoke. Cole observed the exchange for a moment.

"Why would that girl have left?" Joss asked, causing him to look away quickly. "Do you know?"

Cole shook his head. "It could have been for any number of reasons. We don't know that she was taken in the last fifty years. She could have been in Faerie for centuries and not aged, and who knows what the Hedge would have done to her when she escaped."

"Did she kill the man?"

"Oh, no," Cole assured him. "No, the man was most likely murdered by the Cu Sith."

"Okay, so what are these Cu Sith? I probably should have asked you this before."

Outside, Corhagen laughed unexpectedly at something the other officer said. "Nice that he's taking part in this investigation with us," Cole muttered.

"Yeah," Joss said, and he sounded highly annoyed now. "What's his problem, anyway?"

"He's pissed because he found out about us."

Joss frowned. "Why should he care?"

"It's complicated," Cole admitted. "To be frank, I don't understand it myself. When we used to be friends, he had a hard time dealing with the fact that he was attracted to me. After a while, it got bad enough that it was causing problems. You know I didn't care, since the sidhe don't judge attraction that way, but James could never get past it. I sometimes wonder if that didn't have something to do with why he ran back to Sarah so fast."

"Hmm," Joss mused. "So what business is it of his now?"

"I don't know." Cole shrugged. "And frankly, I don't think I care anymore. He had the chance for a while and never took it. Maybe he thinks I should feel bad for moving on."

"That's his problem, then," Joss replied adamantly. "We've got a serial killer to catch and a murder to solve. I'd say the plate is full already."

"I would agree with you."

"Corhagen!" Joss barked, pressing the button to roll down the automatic window. "Get your ass in the backseat. We've got work to do!"

Corhagen jumped and quickly extinguished his cigarette before climbing back inside. The officer gave a wave as he walked back toward his comrades.

"Okay," Joss said once Corhagen had shut the door. "Detective MacColewyn here thinks the changeling he tracked to that school witnessed the murder. When we locate her, she'll probably be able to tell us more about what happened."

Corhagen snickered. "It'll be interesting bringing her into the interrogation room."

"What will be even more interesting is trying to charge the actual murderers with something," Cole countered. "Somehow I don't think a jury will be pleased to sentence a bunch of fey wolves to twenty-five years."

"The wolves did it?" Corhagen asked, clearly surprised. "The same ones that nearly hit us?"

"Okay, explain to both of us what Coo Scythe are," Joss cut in. "Now that Detective Corhagen has decided to join us."

At least Corhagen had the decency to look properly chastised. "Sorry about that, sir," he said, lowering his head a little.

"It's Cu Sith," Cole informed them. "And like I said earlier, they are fey wolves. Many of the noble houses used to train them as guards.

The Cu Sith I fought tonight said that I was trespassing. I think they were guarding that school."

"Okay," Joss said thoughtfully. "We've got a dead body, a changeling witness, and a private school being guarded by the murderers. What was the name of the school again?"

"Sir Frances North Academy," Cole said, thinking hard now. "I've heard that name before."

"Sir Frances North Academy was where our murder victim taught school," Corhagen informed them. "Sorry, I forgot to mention that."

"This is no coincidence," Cole said.

"No," Joss stated, agreeing. "I don't believe so."

Everyone was quiet for a moment. "So who ordered those wolves to kill that man?" Corhagen wondered aloud. "If they were protecting that school, why would they have murdered someone who worked there? Didn't you say that those Cu Sith were once used as guards?"

Cole nodded. "The school could have ordered it," he said thoughtfully. "If that is the case, then logically, whoever is in charge of the school was responsible."

"Who would have a bunch of fey dogs guarding a school, though?"

"Wolves, not dogs," Cole corrected, shooting Corhagen a dirty look. "I don't know, but you said it was a privately run school. I think we'd better have a talk with whoever is in charge of the place later on."

"That goes without saying," Joss said. "For right now, though, I want to get back and catch some shut-eye. Today has left me beat."

"Same here," Corhagen said, observing his shoes now. "Are you both going back together?"

Joss didn't answer.

"I mean," Corhagen stumbled. "Do you need me to send you back through the circle together?"

"Yes," said Cole. "We do."

"I tried calling your cell phone," Corhagen said, stumbling over a drift of snow as they made their way back to the alley.

Cole noticed a few officers from the crime scene lingering around. A few of them sent looks their way as they crossed the street. Before the three of them were too far out of sight, he shot the finger at one that was openly staring.

"The mayor called after I got out here," Corhagen went on as Cole looked back. "He wanted to know why I was the only one that responded. I had him chewing on my ass for ten minutes before he would let me hang up. That was why I used the summoning circle."

"This smells of something fishy," Cole said, getting into the circle with Joss. "Why would the mayor of New York and the chief of police care so much about one economics teacher at a private school biting the dust?"

"Hopefully, we'll have some answers tomorrow," said Joss, holding onto Cole for good measure. "And speaking of which, tomorrow we are going to buy you a cell phone."

"No."

"Too bad," Joss said as Corhagen pressed his newly cut thumb against the circle to activate it. "I'm getting tired of not being able to get in touch with you when there's an emergency. At the very least," he added in Cole's ear, "we'll have a heads-up the next time he tries something like this."

"But that's the fun part," Cole teased as Corhagen began to chant.

"From whence they came, return them now.

From whence they came, return them now.

From whence they came, return them now!"

Joss winced in pain as both he and Cole were again forced through what felt like a wet rubber tube. In a flash, they were standing back in the shower together, fully dressed.

"We never did get to finish that shower," Cole mused, stepping out into the bathroom.

"Tomorrow," Joss said, looking nauseous. "Does it always feel like that?"

Cole nodded. "If you think you're going to be sick, head for the toilet."

"Nah," Joss insisted, still looking a little pale. "I'll be fine. Just give me a minute to recover."

Cole waited beside the shower as his lover regained control of his stomach. Once Joss was sure he wouldn't hurl all over the floor, the two left the bathroom, each with an arm tossed around the other's shoulders, and made for Cole's bed. The covers had already been turned back.

"What's this?" Cole asked, stepping out of his pants.

"Hm?" asked Joss, looking up. "What's what?"

Cole held up the cell phone that was resting at the corner of the nightstand, as though someone had left it there for him. "Is this yours?" he asked.

Joss shook his head and frowned as he lifted the bedsheets. "Mine was in my pants pocket, remember?"

Curious, Cole flipped the smart phone open and waited as the screen came to life. "Oh, brother," he groaned once the logo came into place. "I don't believe this."

"What?" Joss was holding his arm out while sliding under the covers. "Let me see."

Obligingly, Cole passed the phone along so Joss could see for himself. "Sidheular Wireless," he stated as Joss's mouth turned up in an amused smirk. "The sithen made a cell phone for me, and it looks like it's inherited some of Mal's sense of humor too."

"Well," Joss said, passing the phone back to him. "That's one problem taken care of!"

Cole grumbled as he climbed into bed and cuddled up alongside him. "That thing had better have roll-over minutes."

MORNING came far too quickly, as it was prone to. Cole was noticing that more and more, now that he had to be up at the crack of dawn with the rest of New York. One small bit of thanks was that living inside the sithen meant he didn't have the sunlight shining in his face.

Of course, being that the sithen shared some of Mal's humor, the lights going on and off when he didn't rise out of bed right away was just as bad.

"All right," Cole moaned when the lights began blinking faster. "We're getting up."

"Does it do that a lot?" Joss muttered, stretching his body up against Cole's.

"Oh yes." Cole snaked an arm around his lover's warm body and snuggled in close. "Let's just stay in today. We could spend the whole morning fucking our brains out."

Joss smiled. "Sounds good," he said sleepily. "But there are bad guys to catch. I took an oath, remember?"

Cole grunted. "That pesky little thing."

Joss snickered as he turned to look at Cole warmly. "*You* took an oath, as well."

Cole frowned. "No, I didn't."

"Yes, you did," replied Joss, throwing the covers off them. The room was thankfully at a comfortably warm temperature, though Cole could sense the temperature was slowly beginning to drop. Another hint from the sithen to get moving.

"You were sworn in to serve and protect this city and its citizens," Joss went on, scratching his left cheek as he stood up. "The same way I was."

"I never showed up for it," Cole revealed, following suit. "I just picked up the badge when you offered it to me, and that was it."

"When you picked up the badge, it was implied."

"Oh." Cole stopped and thought for a moment. "An implied oath has many loopholes to it, just like swiss cheese."

"Come on!" Joss insisted, though he never lost the grin plastered over his face. "Let's get moving."

Joss convinced Cole to hurry up by offering to share the shower with him. Cole spent the entire time under the water trying to make out with him and tugging on the inspector's balls.

"You owe me," he insisted when Joss tried to pull away.

"How's that?" Joss grabbed the shampoo bottle from the shelf that appeared and began applying liberal amounts to his head. Not so long ago, while trapped inside an enchanted sleep with Corhagen and Cole, Joss had come into contact with some powerful fey magic delivered in person by the Queen of All Faerie herself. As a result, he had gone from being a candidate for Rogaine to having a full mane of golden locks that would've made a romance-cover model burn with envy.

Cole's hair was just as long. When standing together, they looked like members of an '80s hair metal band. Some of the people down at the precinct liked to give them hell, but Cole didn't care, and Joss turned out to be a good sport about it in the end. More times than not, they would have fun attracting attention from female pedestrians while the other officers watched.

Cole massaged the soap into Joss's head as he spoke. "We never got to finish what we started last night," he reminded him, letting his fingers run through the length of Joss's hair.

"We finished," Joss disagreed. "We finished all over Corhagen, in case you'd forgotten."

Cole snorted. "Yeah, we did. But I had been hoping for a little more."

Joss waited until he'd rinsed the shampoo out and cleaned his face. "So was I," he confessed. "But we'll have a chance to soon."

Cole pulled Joss in for long, deep kiss. "How soon?" he whispered.

Joss kissed Cole lightly on the lips. "Soon," he promised. "I'm going to have a word with some of the brass soon. We can't keep the Section going with three men. We've been running ourselves ragged ever since the boys in vice went back to the squad."

"Tell me about it," Cole groaned, stepping out from under the jets. "One living gelatin cube in the sewer system and they get all bent out of shape."

Joss chuckled. "I think it was more the fact that the cube in question was absorbing and dissolving people. Remember, one guy nearly lost an arm."

"He shouldn't have stuck it down that pipe in the first place." Cole busied himself by drying off with a towel while Joss finished rinsing the soap off. "I don't know that sending more men to us will solve the problem, though. You and I, and even Corhagen, have gotten by so far because we've dealt with the supernatural before. Truthfully, I trained Corhagen on how to deal with some of this stuff before I met you, and surprisingly, it managed to stick in his brain."

Joss let out a breath between his teeth as he climbed out of the shower. "And it isn't like any of us have the time to train a new batch of men," he admitted, reaching for a towel of his own. "Those vice boys were having a hard enough time."

"So what do we do?"

Mal suddenly appeared a few feet away. "Sorry to interrupt," he said in a very formal voice. "I put your and Inspector Vallimun's clean clothes on the bed."

"Thank you, Mal," Cole said. "I appreciate it."

"Not a problem," Mal replied. "Your badges have been polished, and I left your new cell phone on the bed next to your guns where you won't forget it."

"Thank you," Cole repeated, much more sarcastically this time. "You are really getting into this butler role. I guess that cell phone was your idea."

"I overheard Master Vallimun mentioning you should get one a couple of days ago," he admitted. Mal was unable to keep the grin off his face now. "Also, you should go down to the end of the hallway. There's something behind the door there you should see."

"Mal," Cole warned as the former sorcerer dematerialized right in front of them. "Mal, what is that supposed to mean?"

Joss was laughing. "I guess we'll find out soon enough."

Cole finished getting dressed, feeling the little knot in his stomach grow each minute that went by. Since fusing with the sithen, Mal got a kick out of being the caretaker of the place. Every so often, though, his mischievousness came through and he would pull some sort of elaborate prank. Cole had learned that whenever Mal withheld information, it usually meant something was up.

"Ready to get this over with?" he asked when Joss clipped his badge into place.

"Ready," said Joss, holstering his gun. "Time to catch the bad guys."

"Who cares about the bad guys?" Cole retorted. "I meant, were you ready to see what Mal is up to this time?"

"No," he admitted, laughing. "But let's get that over with too."

Cole led Joss down the hall to the very end, where a door that hadn't been there before was waiting. Cole had grown used to this sort of thing after living here for a month. The sithen was always changing itself around. Usually, the entrance stayed the same, but hallways and passages would switch around, or one set of stairs would lead to the

kitchen and the next week to a room full of chamber pots that Cole
hadn't been able to locate since.

Cole wasn't sure if the sithen did this on its own because it liked
to change positions or if it was because Mal enjoyed screwing with his
head.

The door opened by itself before Cole could reach for the handle.
On the other side was a garage setup, totally empty except for a solid
black car. Cole felt the air around him ripple as he stepped through.
Joss came after him and shivered slightly.

"I can't get used to that," he said, looking back as the door shut
itself. "So what is this place?"

"I've never seen it before," Cole replied, looking around
cautiously. "Where did this car come from?"

Cole wasn't asking Joss but the sithen itself, assuming they were
still inside it. The lights came on at once, however. Cole took a step
toward it, and the car started on its own.

"Did the sithen steal a car?" Joss wondered jokingly. "Are we
going to have to arrest your home?"

Cole was deep in thought. "When Mal overheard you saying that I
needed a cell phone the other day, did you mention anything about me
getting a car?"

Joss looked at the car then. "Do you think the sithen made you a
car?"

"It made me a cell phone," he pointed out. "Why not a car?" Cole
placed a hand on the hood. "In the old days," he explained, "in the
stories I've heard about the sidhe who lived in Ireland, there were
vehicles created for nobility. The hollow hills fashioned war chariots
and, later, carriages for those in need. Most of them were alive and ran
with the wild hunts."

The engine revved at those words, flashing its headlights on and
off once. "The stories say all the old carriages of the wild hunts
disappeared."

Joss stood next to Cole now. "Maybe they just left," he offered,
looking the car over. "Until someone came along who was worthy of
driving them again."

The driver and passenger doors swung open for each of them. "I think someone wants us to take it for a ride," said Joss. "Do you have a license?"

Cole had to think for a minute. "I think I got one back in the sixties. Speaking of which, I wonder whatever happened to it? I know I had my license on me when I drove down to Florida in the sixties."

Joss was giving Cole a look now.

"I hate driving," he said defensively. "You know that."

The door to the driver's side slammed shut. "That's different," Cole said, rapping his knuckles gently against the hood. "I don't like being in big chunks of metal, plastic, and glass with tanks of combustible fuel loaded into the back."

The driver's-side door opened up once more. "What kind of car is this?" Cole wondered, climbing in. "Is it a sports car?"

"It's a Camaro Black model," Joss replied, strapping himself in as the seat automatically adjusted itself. "I think. Never seen a model like this that had four doors, though. If we're seen driving this thing around the precinct, people are going to start thinking one of us is working for Chevy on the side."

"Their problem, not ours," Cole said while the garage door opened. "And since we're on the subject, which problem do we tackle first?"

"I want to wrap this serial killer case up," Joss said as Cole rolled evenly into traffic. "But with the mayor and the chief breathing down our necks, it looks like we're headed out to Staten Island to check out the private school."

"Works for me."

The sun was just beginning to rise over the Manhattan skyline as they made their way through the busiest section of town. Joss was helping to navigate, since Cole wasn't used to being behind the wheel, and though it took longer than they would have liked to get to Murray Hill, it was still early when Cole brought the car to a stop outside Corhagen's apartment building.

"It has been ages since I came this way," Cole said, looking around at the neighborhood. "I can remember when this whole area was reserved for ritzy old people. Now it looks like a college town."

"I still don't get how he can afford this place," said Joss, resting his elbow on the door. "It isn't as expensive as it used to be, or so I hear, but on a cop's salary, things would be tight."

"I wouldn't have found the place if you hadn't given me directions," Cole confessed. "I haven't been out this way in years. Corhagen lived in a different apartment when I first met him. He and his wife and kids must have moved here sometime afterward."

Corhagen was coming down the stairs now.

"What does he see in her?" Cole wondered, catching a glimpse of Sarah leaning over the top railing, yelling.

Joss shook his head. "Don't know. I guess she must be good in the sack."

Corhagen stopped a few feet from the car as he caught sight of Joss and Cole sitting inside it. Cole pushed a button to open the back door for him. He stood in front of it for a minute or so before finally climbing in.

"Morning," he said in a surprisingly chipper voice. "What's this all about?"

"It's Detective MacColewyn's new car," Joss said as a smile yanked at the edges of his mouth. "Apparently, Santa was good to him this year, if a little late."

"Don't ever trust gifts from that fat friar," Cole warned, shifting gears. "I'm not going to tell you what sort of stuff that guy is into."

Cole brought the car out into the street and made tracks for the Brooklyn-Queens Expressway.

"Have we got time to pick up some breakfast?" Corhagen asked. "I didn't get a chance to eat this morning."

"Was that what Sarah was yelling at you about from the railing?" asked Cole, making a turn as Joss pointed.

Corhagen didn't answer.

"I was thinking we could pick up a few bagels," Joss suggested. "I think there's a shop near here."

"Sounds great," Corhagen said, ignoring Cole. "Let's hit it."

Cole came up to the bakery a moment later and zipped into an empty space right in front, beating out a Ford full of what looked like college girls holding Starbucks cups.

"Sorry, ladies," Cole said, flashing his badge. "Official police business."

"No way are you a cop," one taunted from safely behind her windshield.

"Seriously," Corhagen pressed as Joss climbed out of the car to the sound of catcalls coming from the Ford. "Where did the car come from? It kind of looks like this sweet Camaro I saw in a display window not too long ago, except I don't think the Chevy company makes these kinds of cars with four doors anymore."

"You'd have to ask Joss," Cole replied. "I've never been one for motor vehicles myself."

"Why did you get one, then?" Corhagen pressed. "And since when could you ever afford something like this? You barely made ends meet back when you were living in that loft."

Cole said nothing.

"Have you gone out to visit her grave yet?" James asked quietly.

"What would be the point?" Cole spotted Joss exiting the bakery and pressed the button to open the door for him. "Nothing is out there but a dead body. Katalina is gone."

"Here you go," Joss said, passing a bag to Corhagen in the back. "I got three for each of us."

"It's something we lowly mortals do as part of the grieving process," Corhagen explained, pulling a bagel loaded with jelly out of the bag. "Visiting a grave helps us to appreciate things and move on from our sorrow."

"I'm aware of that inane ritual," replied Cole, digging into his own bag. "I just don't see the point."

"I think you should go," Joss said as cream cheese dribbled out the sides of his bagel. "It might help to see her."

Cole gripped the steering wheel with one hand as he pulled out of the parking space. "Could we discuss this later? I thought the point of climbing out of bed this morning was finding the creep we've been chasing for two weeks now and make painful things happen to them."

"We can," Joss said quickly. "We're just worried about you, is all."

"Swell."

It was quiet in the car for a long while. Corhagen saw fit to end the silence, however, as they came up on the Verrazano-Narrows Bridge. "You never did answer my question," he said around the bite of bagel still in his mouth. "Where did the car really come from?"

UNDER the harsh light of day, Sir Frances North Academy didn't look the least bit inviting. As he climbed out of the car, Cole gave a shiver that had nothing to do with the new batch of snow that had decided to fall on their way here. Neither Corhagen nor Joss looked thrilled by the sight of the school. All in all, Cole thought it resembled a kind of prison.

"Do all schools for human children look like this?" he wondered, walking up the steps alongside them. "No wonder so many students leave. And this is supposed to be one of the places parents pay to bring their kids to?"

"Maybe we should do the talking?" Corhagen suggested.

"Yeah," Joss admitted before looking toward Cole. "Why don't you look around and see if you can find any of the wolves from last night?"

"Don't I need a permit for that?"

"You won't be looking around inside the school," Joss clarified. "Just check the area and see if any of them are still guarding the place. We'll be back in a few minutes. Have you got your cell phone turned on?"

Cole reached into his pocket and fished it out. "It's on," he said. "I'll call if I find anything."

"Have you got our numbers?" Corhagen asked.

It took five minutes before Cole found the right button to push that let him program Corhagen and Joss's phone numbers into it. By that point, they'd each given theirs to him three times.

"Blasted infernal device," Cole grumbled. "They should use these things as a form of juvenile punishment."

"Now that I'm thinking about it," Corhagen said, pulling his own. "Give us your number right quick."

Fifteen minutes later, Cole was walking back down the steps to the school, growling under his breath. Joss and Corhagen had snickered the whole time he had wrestled with his phone, trying to locate where the number was stored. The little icon on the screen seemed to be mocking him as he stuffed the beeping thing back into his pocket.

The further away Cole got from the Sir Frances North Academy, the better he felt. Everything about the island he'd seen so far, save for the school itself, was rather cozy and exuded a warmth that belied the frigid month they'd had so far. Cole might have mistaken the area for an idyllic town nestled around a thick forest were it not for the Manhattan skyline visible in the distance.

Nearby, he could hear a dog barking restlessly. Cole rolled his eyes at the sound, then paused as a thought occurred to him. In all likelihood, it was just a coincidence, yet Cole couldn't help but wonder if the animal hadn't been spooked by something else. And a pack of Cu Sith in the area would definitely put most creatures indigenous to the island on edge.

Cole wandered across the street toward the noise, keeping his eyes peeled the whole time. Snow had hit the island just as hard as anywhere else. As he rounded a corner, Cole happened to glance down a narrow passage made by a tall picket fence just a few feet shy of a three-story brick building. Halfway down, a lone figure in a burlap cloak had her hand out. The Cu Sith she was petting remained perfectly still as her fingers danced lovingly between its ears. Cole stepped back out of sight and peeked around the corner, watching, as low to the ground as he could get, as the changeling girl began to fumble with something on the wolf's neck.

The wolf let out a pitiful whimper, as if in pain, but the changeling didn't let up. Several frustrating minutes went by, which saw the girl growing agitated and the wolf stumbling back and forth in pain. Just when Cole was beginning to wonder if he shouldn't make his presence known, his ears picked up a faint *click*. The wolf sniffed and made a grunting noise that sounded like relief before licking the girl's free hand. The other one clutched something that looked like a black ring, big enough to fit around the Cu Sith's neck and be concealed under the fur there.

The girl tossed the ring away without a word and patted the wolf on the head again before running off in the opposite direction from where Cole was hiding. Quickly, he threw a net of glamour over himself as the wolf leaped up to the roof of the building. Once the coast was clear, Cole climbed the picket fence to retrieve the black ring. A moment later, he found it sticking halfway out of the snow quite a ways from the border where the fence was. The changeling, it seemed, had a very good arm on her.

The ring was part plastic and part metal. It didn't contain any iron, however, which struck Cole as odd. The interior was nothing but exposed electronics, some of which gave Cole a nasty shock when he prodded it with his finger. Unsure of what it meant, Cole carefully gripped the ring with one hand and leaped back over the fence.

There were four Cu Sith waiting for him when he landed on his feet on the other side.

"Return it to us," one growled angrily. "Or suffer the displeasure of our master."

"Why did you kill that man last night?" Cole demanded, rising up to his full height. "What did he do to you?"

No one answered at first. "We were ordered to," the one on his far left said, whimpering.

"Quiet," the lone female in the group ordered, snapping her jaws angrily. "He doesn't need to know."

"He got one of the rings off," the other on the left insisted. "He could take ours off too."

"I didn't," Cole said, hooking the ring to his belt. "Someone else did it. What is so special about this thing, anyway? Do you all have them?"

"If you didn't take it off," the female growled, "then we have nothing further to discuss. Our master sent us to retrieve the ring and learn who was removing them. Give it to us!"

The female lunged for Cole's midsection, but he was already armed with Jabberwock, his silver custom-made gun. The she-wolf's jaws clamped down on the barrel of the gun. Their eyes met while Cole brought down the hammer.

"If I fire," he said calmly, "your brains will paint the brick wall of the building behind you."

"No bullets could stop us," one wolf insisted, though he made no move to attack.

"These are specially made bullets," Cole said. "My gun was

forged using one of the long-forgotten Chalices of Dagda, which came straight out of the Cauldron itself. I will never run out, never need to reload. You can attack me all day, and I'll just keep right on firing."

The she-wolf's eyes rolled down to the gun currently lodged in her throat.

"And before I forget," Cole added, "these are enchanted iron bullets."

The male wolf on Cole's left began to crawl forward in submission. Before he reached Cole's boot, he had turned over onto his back to expose his belly.

"Please," the Cu Sith pleaded. "We have so few females left."

"Why did you kill that man?" Cole demanded. "Who was he to you? What is the name of the master that you serve?"

"Our master," one of the two in front whispered, his head sinking low, "is the Lord of All Fey."

Cole blinked and, in that instant, made a crucial mistake. The wolf that had been resting on his back suddenly leaped up. The jaws closed round the black ring and yanked it off his belt just as the she-wolf released the gun barrel from her mouth and backed away. Cole had less than a second to make up his mind which way to fire. Drawing Bandersnatch, he looked straight ahead and aimed both guns in opposite directions while squeezing the triggers.

The remaining two were on him in a second.

Neither gun went off. Cole didn't want to risk firing while his arms were pinned down. One wolf was snapping its jaws in his face while the other worried his shoulder. After a moment, the two jumped back and were off like a flash in either direction. Wincing as he rose, Cole gripped his shoulder where it was bleeding, cursing angrily.

He'd let his guard slip and lost the only lead they'd found so far on the murder case. Today was turning out to be just perfect.

Chapter *Three*

THE walk back to the school was uneventful. Cole was on edge the entire time, but nothing out of the ordinary happened. More than once, he spent several embarrassing seconds aiming Bandersnatch at a clump of snow that had fallen from a rooftop to the ground. Knowing he had screwed up so royally was humiliating.

No one tried to stop him when he entered the building. Coming back to it, Cole thought it looked more like a prison than ever. The building was a solid, dull brick color. The only decorations were two crosses on the windows of the front doors. Cole suspected this had to do with the school's status as a private organization.

The main office was just up ahead and to the right, so Cole stepped inside and walked up to the woman behind the counter, who drew back in shock at the sight of him.

"Are Detective Corhagen and Inspector Vallimun meeting with the principal?" he asked in a calm tone.

Most of the bleeding had stopped, but the Cu Sith had taken a chunk out of his shirt, leaving the marred skin exposed. The woman's eyes kept darting to it, away from Cole's face.

"Ma'am," he said a moment later.

"Oh," she gasped. "Um, yes. I believe they went in there a little while ago. They haven't come out yet, though."

"I'll wait," Cole replied, and took a seat directly in front of her next to a couple of young kids who didn't look happy to be waiting there.

Both of them were watching Cole the whole time, and they drew back slightly when he sat down next to them. One kept looking at the spot on his exposed shoulder where the teeth marks were healing. The other seemed fixated on the guns he wore on his thighs. After a moment, he risked clearing his throat. "What are you doing with those?" he asked in a meek voice, pointing.

Cole looked at the kid, then glanced down at where he was pointing. "Those are mine," he explained, drawing them out. "This one is called Jabberwock."

He held the silvery gun up so they could both see it clearly. "And this one," he said, showing off the other, "is named Bandersnatch. I had them forged over ninety years ago."

The second child, a dark-skinned boy with green eyes, looked at him skeptically. "You don't look that old."

"No," Cole admitted, smiling as he put both guns away. "I imagine I don't."

"Are you a cop?" the first one, a pale boy with soft curls, asked excitedly.

In answer, Cole whipped out his badge for them to look at. "Special Detective Too-lowiz Mac…."

"Too-loose," Cole pronounced for him. "Tuulois MacColewyn. Most people who know me call me Cole. And it's okay. A lot of people can't pronounce it right."

"Why are you bleeding?" the second boy asked, running a finger in the air just above his wound. "Did you get into a fight?"

"Yeah," he admitted. "I did."

"Sir!"

The woman behind the counter was glaring at him sharply now. "Yes, madam?" Cole answered, feeling mischievous at the moment.

"Was there a reason you needed to speak with the detective and inspector?"

"I'm here with them," Cole replied sincerely. "They rode here with me in my car."

The woman didn't look like she believed a word of it, so Cole stood up and showed her his badge. "We work in the same unit," he explained, enjoying the look of surprise on her face.

"I see," she said, inspecting the badge closely for any sign that it was a fake. "Were you working undercover before you came here?"

Cole was wearing his standard black leather boots, rocker T-shirt, and belt with silver buckle today. "Ma'am," he said, never losing his smile, "if I were, I couldn't tell you."

The woman appeared offended now. "I don't know when the principal will be finished talking with your... with the detective and inspector," she said. "How long do you intend to wait?"

"Until they are finished with him," he said, turning back to his seat. "Oh, but just to clarify, these are my regular clothes."

The boys were snickering as he sat back down. "Lesson one, boys," he whispered. "If you want to confuse an adult, the truth always works better than a lie."

Meanwhile, the mystery woman behind the counter was edging her way over to the door on her left as quietly as possible. Cole heard Joss and Corhagen's voices coming from inside as she cracked it.

"Excuse me," she whispered, though Cole could hear her perfectly. "I'm sorry to interrupt, Principal McGregor, but there is a man out here who claims he knows the detective and inspector."

"What does he look like?" Corhagen's voice drifted out into the main area.

"He is dressed in black," she replied, glancing over her shoulder at him. "And he's bleeding."

Cole could just picture Joss and Corhagen turning to one another. A second later, he heard them standing up and moving toward the door frame. The woman backed out of the way so they could peek around the side. As she did, an odd fragrance drifted out of the office to tickle Cole's nostrils.

Joss's eyes widened when he got a look at Cole. "Thank you," he told the lady before looking back into the office. "Principal McGregor, could we pick this back up in just a second? I need to have a word with the detective out here."

The woman looked surprised at the word "detective," even though she must have seen it printed on Cole's badge.

"This won't take long," Corhagen assured the invisible principal who remained hidden in his office.

"Billy Thorton and Bobby Higgins," the woman said, motioning the boys forward, "why don't you go inside and speak with Principal McGregor while he has a moment?"

Cole gave the boys a quick wink before ducking out the front door. Once all three of them were in the hallway, Joss rounded on Cole and stared at his wound, which was nearly closed up by now.

"What happened?" he asked, his voice thick with worry. "These look sort of like the marks that were on that stiff we were called in to look at."

"They are," Cole said. "I made a rather large error."

"You came back to a private school covered in blood with your shirt halfway torn off," Corhagen stated, glaring. "For once, I believe you."

Cole quickly filled the two in on the details. "I don't know what made me trust the Cu Sith," he said, feeling furious with himself now. "Before I knew it, he had leaped up off the ground and snatched the ring right off my belt. The other two were on top of me before I could stop him."

"Do you know who they were talking about?" Joss asked, brushing a thumb over the exposed flesh. "This 'Lord of All Fey', I mean."

"It was one of the names Oberon was sometimes called by," Cole admitted. "Though I haven't heard that particular title used to describe him since I was a child."

"Oberon," Corhagen repeated, eyes growing wider. "The same guy who kicked you out of Faerie."

"Yes," Cole said, glancing around. "But it's highly unlikely that he is here on Staten Island or has anything to do with the teacher being murdered."

"Oh," Corhagen breathed out. "Good."

"Very," Cole agreed, nodding.

"Someone calling themselves the Lord of All Fey ordered the Cu Sith to murder an economics teacher?" Joss didn't sound convinced. "That sounds...."

"Stupid," Corhagen finished.

"Very stupid," said Cole. "But it fits. It looks like the Cu Sith are under the control of someone else. Why that someone wanted the teacher killed, I don't know, but I think if we snoop around here for a little while longer, we'll be able to find out."

"We would need the cooperation of the school in order to do that," Joss said. "I'll see about getting us a search warrant and try to explain to the principal why we think his school has some connection to the murder without revealing that a shapeshifting cop's nose led us to their doorstep."

"I'd love to find out how the changeling fits into all of this," Cole said to himself. "She was obviously trying to help that one wolf, but why not take the rings off the others? And why did she help me last night?"

Corhagen shrugged. "Can't say. I never understood what women saw in you."

"Likewise," Cole retorted before looking to Joss. "So what's the game plan?"

Joss closed his cell and looked over at them wearily. "We have to go back into the city and see if we can't find another lead on the serial killer. In the meantime, I want you to stay here on Staten and see if you can't track down those Cu Sith wolves. They're probably still somewhere close by. I suspect the school is tied into this somehow, though how far is anybody's guess at this point."

"Will you be taking the ferry back to Manhattan?" Cole asked as Joss and Corhagen turned back to the office together. "Or hailing a cab?"

"Shit, that's right!" Joss swore, pressing a hand to his forehead. "We took your car to get here. Crap, I still haven't wrapped my brain around the idea of you driving."

"I don't think I've ever seen him drive before today," Corhagen added.

"How about the two of us go back into the city and Corhagen stays here to hunt for the Cu Sith?" Cole offered. "Doesn't that work out better?"

"The Cu Sith are more likely to trust you than either of us," Joss replied. "They'd tear Corhagen to pieces."

Cole smiled.

"We're not leaving Corhagen here," Joss said adamantly. "Start looking for them. We'll figure out what we're going to do once we're done here with this asshole principal."

"Why can't we just take your car?" Corhagen insisted. "Both of us have more experience on the road than you."

"And how many car wrecks have you been in since the state of New York granted you a license?" Cole bit back. "Besides, the car is a product of the wild hunts. I'm not sure what would happen if either one of you got behind the wheel."

Corhagen flinched at this bit of news, which made Cole smile. Nevertheless, it didn't look as though Corhagen was convinced.

"The seats could theoretically swallow you whole," Cole elaborated threateningly. "And you'd be trapped inside of it, forever a part of the car and unable to get out."

Corhagen swallowed and leaned back away from him.

"I've told you this before, James," Cole went on. "Faerie magic is something you don't want to fuck around with."

Corhagen looked to Joss then. "I guess we're taking the ferry."

"Don't bother," said Cole, taking his phone out. "I'll call a cab for you. I still have a little extra cash left, so it should be okay."

"Thanks," Joss said meaningfully as he rubbed the side of his head. "Man, sometimes I really hate this job."

"I wish I had thought to bring an extra shirt," Cole told him, hoping to lighten the mood. "With the hole in this one, it's getting a little drafty."

That won him a smile, at least. Giving a two-finger wave, a habit he'd picked up recently, Cole headed out the doors again and looked around. Getting an idea, he sniffed the air and began walking in a circle around the outside of the iron fence surrounding the school, careful not to get close to it. The metal made him uncomfortable, but Cole dealt with it as he came up to where the fence stopped. A solid wall of concrete greeted him where the iron fence came to an end. Turning around, Cole retraced his steps and wandered back in the opposite direction, this time casing the other side. It was the same thing there.

The school grounds were surrounded on three sides by iron fencing. The back wall was nothing but concrete, and almost the whole area smelled of the Cu Sith. It wasn't unexpected, since the Cu Sith had been guarding the place. Tracking one of them from here would be impossible because the many different scents had mingled together for so long, which was why he hadn't bothered the first time. It looked like the Cu Sith had been camped out here for a while now.

The sixty-four thousand dollar question was: on whose orders?

Thinking for a moment, Cole decided to try a different approach. After wandering back to his car, Cole hopped in and started the machine, letting the roar of the engine run through him. None of the nervousness that came with riding in these blasted things bothered him this time. It was as if he and the car were made for each other, and knowing the sithen, that was a possibility.

Cole turned onto the street and drove down a little ways. Once he found a turn, he circled back and followed the road he'd walked down earlier, keeping his eyes peeled. It was a long shot, possibly even a wild goose chase, but for the moment, he had no better ideas.

The locals were keeping themselves busy and warm by fighting a losing battle with the snow. Armed with shovels and snow blowers, they attacked the frost that clung to the sidewalks and edges of the street with a vengeance. A few actually paused to look up and wave at him. Cole was taken aback by this and too stunned to return the favor. Generally, people regarded him the same way the lady behind the receptionist's desk at the school did: as something to be feared or treated with suspicion.

Thinking it over, Cole brought his car around and went back to the corner where one woman in her forties was helping another man clear the sidewalk. As he pulled up alongside the road, the man raised his head slightly and watched Cole through narrowed eyes. The woman saw him and hesitated a moment before approaching the rolled-down window.

"Can we help you with something?" she asked in an unconvincing tone.

"I'm Special Detective MacColewyn, ma'am," he said politely, holding his badge up for her to see. "We're working with the Staten Island precinct on a case, and there may have been a witness to a crime in the area. I was wondering if anyone in the area has ever mentioned seeing a young woman wearing a robe made out of burlap."

"Burlap?" The woman looked back to the man watching them by the sidewalk. "In this weather?"

"We suspect she may be homeless," Cole elaborated. "She looked to be in her late teens."

The man on the sidewalk had been listening in, apparently. "Is this about that streaker we had a couple of months back?" he shouted to her.

"Oh, that's right," the woman said, turning back to Cole. "There was talk about this girl running around in the street at night naked. Some people say they saw her in this area." The woman was nodding now, very excited. "My husband said he saw her. And yeah, I think he did mention she was wearing some sort of cloak over her, but nothing underneath."

"Did the reports stop?"

"Mm," she said, nodding faster. "About a month or two ago. Right around the time people started saying they heard wolves at night."

Now Cole was interested. "Wolves?"

"Well, it was mostly just the little kids," she confessed. "Some of the five- and six-year-olds were saying that they could hear dogs howling at night. It was actually the older people who said that they were wolves. My husband's grandmother talked about it right before she died, in fact. We get a lot of odd stories every so often, though. Most folks just ignore it now."

"Of course."

"But people actually saw the girl I think you're looking for," she added. "Not recently, but she was lurking around here somewhere. Say, is this about that dead body people say was found near the private school last night? St. Frank's, or something?"

Cole hesitated, then nodded. "Yes, ma'am," he admitted. "But I'd appreciate it if you kept that to yourself. We don't want people to panic unnecessarily."

"Right!" The lady actually put her hand over her mouth for a second. "Of course not."

Cole put the car back into drive and started to pull away.

"Did that girl really witness the murder?" the woman asked quickly, ducking her head down lower.

"We believe so."

"That poor thing," the woman whispered. "She must be frightened out of her gourd, and all alone in the middle of this weather, to boot."

"I'll find her," Cole said, pushing the assurance in his voice out to brush along the lady's skin. "Trust me."

The woman's eyes seemed to flutter for a moment, as if she were just waking up from a nap. "Of course," she said. "Please be sure to get her some help. I've felt so sorry for her."

Cole nodded and pulled away, watching in his rearview mirror as the man she'd left by the sidewalk began speaking to her in what looked like a hushed manner. The interaction between them was curiously interesting, so much so that Cole almost didn't realize it when he came to an intersection. Instead of turning right like he planned, however, the steering wheel seemed to turn to the left on its own. Cole held on to keep the car from spinning out of control, though the wheels had amazing purchase against the slick asphalt.

At the next junction, Cole went left again. The car seemed to know where it was going, even if he didn't have a clue. This part of the island looked slightly more run-down, though it paled in comparison to some of the places the mainland had to offer. Cole turned right sharply at the car's prodding. He was just beginning to wonder if getting out and sniffing around was a good idea when something landed hard on the hood. Cole slammed on the brakes without thinking and sent the car into a skid. Whatever was there was flung sharply off into a pile of snow as the vehicle came to a stop. Product of the wild hunts or no, it was still bound to the laws of vehicular science while in this form. At least the suspension was proving to be top-notch!

Cole got out and surveyed the damage as the figure in the snow pile struggled to get free. "Hey!" Cole shouted angrily. "You scratched my car!"

The figure stood up, and Cole had to hold onto the door to steady himself. The girl from last night, the same one he'd witnessed taking that black ring off the Cu Sith's neck not long ago, was looking up at him now, wearing an irate expression. Twisting the burlap cloak around, she leaped up out of the snow and went racing down the road.

"Come back here!" he shouted, jumping back inside the car and giving it a tap on the dashboard. "Let's get her."

The car roared to life and was off down the road after the changeling girl before he had time to grab hold of the steering wheel again. Turning to the right, Cole spotted her up ahead, above the power lines, swinging on tree branches and leaving a trail of scattered snow on the road below. After losing her again, Cole caught sight of her out of the corner of his eye, perched on a magnolia tree that was covered in icicles. The moment he turned toward her, she leaped off and went running across the row of front yards.

It went on like that for several minutes. Each time Cole was afraid she had given him the slip, the girl would conspicuously appear again and guide him along for another block or so. When Cole thought they were getting close to wherever she was leading him, he pulled the car over to the side of the road and got out, waiting. It took a moment, but she finally made an appearance behind a snowman one of the neighbor's kids had constructed.

"You might as well come out," Cole said in an even tone, confident she could hear him. "I know you're there. You have a talent for giving me the slip, I admit, but if this was about getting away from me, you'd have been long gone before now."

Nothing was said in return.

"You really did a number on the hood of my car," Cole went on, glancing over at the marks that were now fading. "It's brand new, in case you didn't know."

Still nothing.

"There are easier methods of communicating with someone," he said, growing exasperated. "Cell phones, for one thing. I understand text messaging is the new thing amongst girls your age. What say we give that a try, since I happen to have my cell phone with me now, and you're in no mood to talk back."

Someone tapped him on the shoulder. Cole turned, expecting to see an annoyed neighbor wanting to speak with him about talking to himself on a public street and frightening the local youth. Instead, he found himself face to face with the purple-eyed girl.

Cole blinked. "You are amazingly good at that."

Cole blinked a second time, a mistake on his part, as the girl was gone again when he reopened his eyes. "How does she do that?"

Something tapped on the window of his car. Cole whipped around sharply to find her sitting in the passenger seat, looking through the window at him expectantly.

"I hope your feet weren't on the upholstery," he mumbled, storming back to his still open door.

This time, he had to start the car on his own. Cole punched a button on the dashboard that he somehow knew controlled the heating and cranked the knob all the way up so that the inside would be toasty warm.

"Put your hands up next to the vents," he instructed, pointing at them. "If you're cold, that is."

The girl obediently did as he bade and smiled, as if savoring the sensation of warmth. "Was there anywhere in particular you wanted to go?" he asked, pulling back into the street.

The girl sat in silence until he came to a stop sign. Cole watched as she pointed ahead at the street farther down, looking anxious the whole time. Thinking it over, he obliged and continued on until she gestured for him to turn right. Cole followed the girl's directions, which almost came too late at times from her not wanting to pull her hands away from the dashboard.

"I don't suppose you would be willing to just tell me where we're going?" he offered, before it came to him. "You can't speak, can you?"

The girl shook her head sadly.

"It's okay," he assured her. "I know someone like that. His older brother says it's because his tongue is too big, but personally, I suspect the goblin was just born without a voice box."

The girl acted as though she didn't know how to react to that, and kept looking out through the windshield at the passing buildings. Up ahead was an old factory, clearly abandoned, which she began pointing toward as they came up closer to it.

"Here?" he asked, pulling into what might have been the parking area at one point.

The girl jumped out of the car before it came to a stop. Cole parked it and got out as quickly as he could, yelling at her the whole time. Feeling his temper beginning to flare, Cole tried to hold himself in check as he removed Aed Deigh and ran through the partially opened door after her.

The interior was deserted. It looked like the main part of the building had once been filled with machinery, though for what purpose, he didn't know. Now, spare parts were strewn across the floor. Cole was careful not to step on anything that might be made of iron and headed toward the back. He hadn't seen the girl go that way, but there was nothing in this area big enough for her to hide behind. At this point, he didn't think she was interested in hiding from him anymore. The girl had clearly brought him this far for a reason. Now he just needed to find out what that reason was.

And keep his head on his shoulders at the same time.

At the far back was a set of carpeted stairs that led up. Cole could smell her distinctly. Whatever power she had to mask her scent, it wasn't affecting him now. Cole followed until he reached the upper level, an area that had clearly been marked for the management at one point. Now, it was nothing but a set of empty rooms spread out along a vacant, dusty hallway. Cole sniffed the air and continued on until he came to the very last door at the end. It was already open for him.

Just as Cole nudged it open wider, there was a flash of something that might have been lightning. Aed Deigh was drawn and at the ready as something small and furry slammed against the wall just a foot or so to the right of Cole's head. The wood goblin landed in a heap on the carpet a second later, swearing and smoking up a storm.

"Blasted thing's still not cummin' off!" it growled furiously. "You sure you know what you're doin'?"

The changeling girl didn't answer, of course. She regarded Cole almost beseechingly where he was standing now in the doorframe.

"Him?" the wood goblin exclaimed. "You brought a sidhe here to help us? Girl, you must be outta yer mind."

Cole was looking down at the still-smoking fur ball curiously. "Bugbear?" he asked. "Is that you?"

"Huh?" The wood goblin glared up at Cole in surprise. "How'd you know my cuz?"

"Bugbear and Bugaboo are your cousins?"

The wood goblin squinted even harder at Cole, until his eyes were little more than narrow slits. "What if they are?" it bit back. "How'd a sidhe such as yerself come to know them, anyhow? I thought us folks were beneath you, exiled or no."

"Bugbear and his little brother work for me some of the time," Cole replied. "I thought you were Bugbear, since his brother doesn't talk. You do sort of look like him, actually."

"Yea, right. I hears that a lot."

The changeling came forward and gently placed her hands on the wood goblin's back. "I'm good, girl," he said in a gentler tone. "Ya just knocked tha wind outta me, is all. Believe me, after wha's been goin' on around here, that ain't nuthin'."

"Have you got a name?" Cole asked, kneeling down beside them.

The wood goblin considered him for a moment. "Boogaloo," he said by way of introduction. "Jus' Boogaloo, like the song. Why do I get the feelin' I'm speakin' to the Fallen Sidhe himself? Word is you sold yourself out to be a slave to the humans."

"You are correct," Cole replied. "As far as me being who you think I am, but I am no one's slave. No one commands me but myself."

"Yeah, right," Boogaloo muttered.

Cole decided to let the remark slide. "Any particular reason you happen to be squatting inside of an abandoned factory?"

Cole got a good look around and saw one or two other goblins huddled together. The rest of the group seemed to be composed of wolves, along with what looked like a dryad lying on a makeshift pallet in the corner.

Boogaloo saw where he was looking and shook his head. "Nuthin' to be done about that 'um," he said sadly. "One ah them black rings was placed around the trunk ah her tree. She couldn't go near the darned thing after that. It's been too long. She'll be dead soon, we're thinkin'."

Cole went over to the dryad, who flinched as he knelt down. "Do you want me to sing to you?" he whispered softly in her ear. "I can sense it won't be long now, but I can make the journey easier for you."

The dryad seemed to think it over, then nodded weakly. Cole closed his eyes for a moment, summoning his will, and began humming.

Soon he formed words in the language of his people, the language of Faerie. A spring wind kicked up around him, pushing back the cold that leaked in from the winter outside. The room was chilled but warmed slightly as his song picked up. His hair began to rise and fall with the gusts. Light from underneath his skin shone against the darkness. It was like moonlight.

The dryad gasped and rose up off the pallet. Her hand grasped his as she sang along with him. Neither of them knew the words, but the song came from their hearts, woven together by the power Cole carried over the long dead and the life she had brought to the tree that had been her home and soul over the years.

When it was over, the dryad lay back down and fell silent. The air was still as her body began to transform into dust. Soon, there was nothing left on the blanket but dirt and brown leaves. Cole picked one up and carefully placed it in his hair.

"May you find peace in your next life," he whispered softly. "And in the Summerlands as you wait to be reborn."

None of the others spoke for a moment. Boogaloo was the one who finally broke the silence. "Think you could git dis thing offa me?" he asked, pointing at his throat.

Cole looked at the black ring digging under the wood goblin's fur and into the flesh underneath. "What is that thing?" he asked, taking a closer look.

"Dat punk who calls himself da Lord of All Fey made 'em," Boogaloo explained, wincing in pain as if the ring sent a small shock through him. "They control us. Make us do wha'ever he want us to. None ah us here knew how to take 'em off until she showed up."

Boogaloo jerked a clawed thumb toward the changeling. "Only dis 'un ain't cummin' off fer sum reason."

Cole raised Aed Deigh up and brought out the frost-covered blade from the hilt. "I think," he said slowly, "this will work."

Cole held the tip of the blade against the black ring, careful to not let it touch Boogaloo's fur. The wood goblin whimpered nonetheless when the ice began to spread, though it was difficult to tell whether the noise was one of pain or relief. Cole withdrew the blade a second later and observed his handiwork.

"Got it," he said, gripping the black ring carefully. "It should come off now. Ready?"

Before the wood goblin could answer, Cole yanked hard. The place on the ring where the ice had frozen through snapped. The metal and plastic came apart at once in his hands, and Boogaloo collapsed to the floor in a heap. Some of the Cu Sith barked in congratulations, but Cole's attention was drawn away from that to the sound of the ring giving off a loud beeping.

"Whadaya waitin' for?" Boogaloo snapped, rising up. "Git rid 'ah it!"

Cole took aim and tossed the black ring out a broken part of a nearby glass window. Everyone ducked as an explosion rattled the whole building, sending jagged pieces of glass flying off the windowpane.

"They 'splode sometime if ya ain't careful wit 'em," Boogaloo explained.

"So I see," replied Cole as his cell phone rang.

The caller ID on the screen said it was Joss. "Hey, lover," he said softly into the phone. "I hope your day is going better than mine so far."

"It is," Joss answered, stretching out his words with a smug drawl. "We just got an anonymous tip on our serial killer."

Cole paused. "From whom?"

"Don't know," Joss admitted. "It came through on my cell phone, but the phone didn't recognize the number. I tried calling back and got a voice message that said the number was not in service. It must have been one of those disposable phones. Either that or a cloned number."

"So what do we do about it?"

Joss sighed. "Normally, I would chalk this up as another wild goose chase. The tabloids have been sniffing around recently, so I shouldn't be surprised that this happened. To be honest, though, I'm ready to get this case over with."

Cole nodded, even though Joss couldn't see him. "Where does the trail of bread crumbs lead us?"

"A house in Murray Hill," said Joss. "Not too far from where Corhagen hangs his hat, in fact. Corhagen is going nuts, trying to get hold of his wife so she can warn the kids."

"Ever the family man."

"True, but after what was left of those other kids, I can't make fun of him for it." There was silence on the line for a second, during which it sounded like he was listening to someone standing next to him. "Corhagen wants to get a warrant and check the place out, maybe see if we can't get some backup."

"I can be there in thirty minutes or less," Cole promised, moving toward the door. "How long will it take for you to get a warrant for us to search the premises?"

"Less than an hour," Joss said, sounding worried now. "But you're all the way over on Staten Island still, aren't you?"

"Don't worry," Cole teased. "I'm a cop now. It's okay for me to break the speed limit."

"Speed limits are one thing," Joss warned, his voice growing more worried by the minute. "Playing demolition derby with New York traffic is another matter altogether. Please tell me you aren't actually going to try and get here in a half hour."

"I found a lead on our enigmatic Lord of All Fey," Cole told him, changing the subject. "And the changeling girl from last night."

Joss sounded excited now. "Have you gotten anything out of her yet?"

"She can't speak," Cole said. "But there's an abandoned factory where some of the fey she's helped have taken refuge. I think this Lord the Cu Sith spoke of has been controlling the locals with some sort of shock collar, which would mean the Cu Sith murdered that man against their will."

Joss sighed. "It's never something simple, is it?"

"I'm afraid it's only beginning. I haven't worked out how the school fits into it yet, but somehow it fits into this."

"What? Are ya blind?" Boogaloo snapped loudly. "Dat's wher da Lord of All Fey hangs his hat usually!"

"Who was that?" Joss wondered.

"Nobody," Cole said quickly. "Should I follow up here or meet you guys in Murray Hill?"

Joss sighed deeply again. "We could use you. Call me crazy, but something in my gut tells me that this wasn't a crank call. I'll feel stupid for being wrong, but we were caught with our pants down before."

"I like you with your pants down," Cole teased.

"I'd rather not have a repeat of what happened in the sewers before the vice squad boys split," Joss went on, ignoring him, though Cole thought he heard the inspector's breathing speed up slightly.

"See you soon," Cole promised, hanging up.

The others were watching him with leery expressions now. The ones that didn't show their loathing outright averted their gazes whenever he glanced at them. Cole turned to the changeling girl and approached her very slowly. She never flinched once.

"I need to go take care of something," he told her, offering his hand. "Do I have your permission to return later? I would like to help."

Boogaloo snorted. "A sidhe askin' fer permission from a lowly changeling. What's the whole world cummin' to?"

The girl nodded, however, and gave his hand a squeeze before releasing it.

"I will come back," he promised the others. "This isn't over. When I do, I will need you all to tell me everything you know about the Lord of All Fey and what has been happening on this island for the past few months."

One or two nodded their consent. Boogaloo didn't look happy, but he said nothing as Cole made for the door. The changeling girl followed him, keeping in step with him the whole time. Her footfalls made no sound at all as they crossed the main area of the factory together.

"Be safe," he told her. "I don't like what's going on here. Something is very wrong."

The girl's eyes softened for a moment at those words, and for a brief second, Cole thought she looked heartbroken about something. The moment passed, however, and he dipped his head once in salute to her before leaving out the front door. A set of locks on the other side he couldn't recall ever seeing before fell into place the moment it closed. Heading for his car, Cole pressed the unlock button on his key chain and looked out in the direction where Manhattan was.

He had a bad feeling.

THE building had a brick exterior. There really wasn't much else to say about it. For a home in Murray Hill, it looked painfully generic. Cole thought that someone must have erected it back in the nineteenth century and left it there until a troop of renovators came through and decided to add a little exterior flavor. The result was, sadly, not a success. It was still just a generic two-story brick building with windows and a front door tacked on as though they had been afterthoughts.

Cole had spotted Corhagen and Joss waiting outside across the street from it, and spent the next several minutes locating a parking place so he could join them.

"Are you sure this is the right place?" he said after giving the building a once-over from their position.

"We'll find out in just a sec," Joss replied. "We're waiting on our backup." Joss waved the warrant in front of Cole's face. "So while we wait for them to get here, tell us about what you found over on Staten."

Cole filled them in.

"Something's not right," said Joss, deep in thought. "I get the feeling we're missing something really big."

"If there's someone running around with the power to stick shock collars on lesser fey and make them do whatever," Corhagen protested, "what would they be doing on Staten Island, of all places? And in a private school, to boot! How does someone get hold of that sort of tech in a place where they still teach economics?"

"For once, I think Corhagen has it right," Cole agreed, looking toward Joss. "I think we're missing something, and everything so far seems to suggest it has to do with that school. We need to find out more about it."

Joss nodded, then turned to Corhagen. "See if you can't dig up some stuff on it once we get through here. I don't want to go back to that place without something to confront that bastard they've got running the place with."

Corhagen looked past Cole and Joss at the parking spot across the road. "Looks like our backup is here," he said. "Let's get this show on the road."

Cole frowned as the quartet of uniformed officers climbed out of the vehicle. "How come they get to park on the curb?"

Both Corhagen and Joss stopped to look at him. "Because they're cops," Joss said in a very obvious tone. "The same way you and I are. We're allowed to do that sort of thing when we're on duty."

"Oh." Cole suddenly wished the earth felt up to swallowing him whole. Corhagen was snickering very loudly at him now. "I forgot," was all he could come up with.

Joss patted him on the back as they continued on. "You'll get used to it."

Joss immediately gave orders to the uniformed officers to spread out and case the area. One of them Cole couldn't help but notice as they headed up to the front door. The man stood out because he was so much shorter than the others. Cole might have mistaken him for a high-school student were it not for the NYPD badge he was sporting. The uniform helped add a couple of years to his face, but he still looked impossibly young for a cop.

The guy's ears stuck out from his head slightly. On another body, they would have been normal sized, but on him, they added to the impression that he was a big dork. The lines on his youthful face suggested he spent a lot of time smiling. The expression he wore now was impish, and his eyes lingered on Cole for a moment longer than necessary. It was those eyes that really gave away his age. They looked too knowledgeable.

Cole reasoned the man had seen a little too much and turned away to focus on the task at hand. The unnamed officer and one of his fellows disappeared around the corner and out of sight. Joss was ringing the doorbell now and already had the search warrant in his hand. Cole sensed everyone was nervous.

He felt like a trick-or-treater on Samhain.

A very pretty blonde girl answered the door a moment later. Her eyes widened sharply as she looked up at Cole and Joss standing side by side.

"Wow," she breathed. "Um, I mean… can I help you?"

Cole smiled. The girl looked like she was ready to melt. "I'm Special Detective MacColewyn, and this is Inspector Joss Vallimun."

"Detective Corhagen," James announced loudly from behind them in an irritated voice.

"We received an anonymous tip earlier today concerning a case we've been working on," said Joss, showing her the warrant. "I'm afraid we're going to have to search the premises."

The girl glanced at the warrant and frowned. "Okay," she said, backing out of the way. "Come inside."

Cole nodded his appreciation to the girl, who immediately blushed when he walked past. Corhagen frowned at the gesture and pushed past him once they were out of the foyer.

Despite the building's initial impression, the house was well furnished. Cole would never have expected such an impressive layout, were he human. The furniture looked old, but in a well-kept sort of way that companies today often attempted to emulate. A stairway was located directly in front of them, leading to a second floor that was partially visible through a railing.

"Is there something I could help you with?" the girl asked nervously. "The owner is downstairs, I think, if you need to speak with him."

"You rent the house?" Corhagen asked, looking around. "Are you a college student?"

The girl nodded to both questions. "My name is Amber," she said. "My friends and I found a flyer last year advertising the place. The rent was really reasonable, and we've lived here ever since. The owner mostly stays down in the basement. It's where he lives."

"Could we speak to him?" Joss asked, stopping beside her.

Amber frowned again. Cole couldn't help but notice that her lower lip puckered out slightly when she did that. It made him think she was a very good kisser. "I don't know," Amber said, looking embarrassed now. "None of us have seen him for a while. The basement used to be a bomb shelter, and there's a whole kitchenette and shower set up down there, so he really doesn't come out much. In fact, I don't think I've seen him in the last few weeks. Maybe one of my roommates have, though."

All three of them looked at one another. "Do you have a key to the basement?" Joss asked her.

"We're not supposed to go down there," Amber admitted. "But I do kind of know where one is. It's upstairs, though."

"We'll wait," Joss assured her.

Joss watched Amber head up the stairs with an appreciative look smeared all over his face. "Nice," Cole remarked, looking right alongside him.

"Indeed."

Corhagen gave a cough that sounded almost like a snicker. A moment or two later, Amber returned with the key in hand.

"The basement is this way," she explained.

Joss was following her. Cole started to follow, but then paused and looked up. Four girls standing in a row along the second floor railing were staring down at him.

"Are you guys really with the police?" one asked. "You and the other one, I mean."

Cole smiled and nodded in the affirmative as, behind him, Corhagen swore softly under his breath. "Don't worry," Cole told them in a calm tone of voice. "I don't think we're here to arrest you."

"You could arrest me," the one on the far end said hopefully. "You could arrest me all you want!"

The others started snickering as Cole waved goodbye. "You can arrest me all you want?" he heard one tease as he made his way to the back of the house. "Please!"

"It was all I could think of!"

"Nobody believes you're really a cop," Corhagen noted as they turned a corner together. "I can't say I'm surprised, what with the long hair and the black leather. At least you haven't managed to turn Vallimun all the way over."

"Turn him over how?" Cole asked, stopping.

"You know." Cole stood there waiting as Corhagen stared at him expectantly. "You two are supposed to be bosom buddies now, right?"

"We're sleeping together," Cole stated. "Assuming that's what you mean. I haven't 'turned' Joss over to anything, though."

Corhagen didn't look like he believed him.

"Joss still finds women attractive," Cole elaborated, feeling like he was explaining something very simple to a confused child. "So do I. Nothing has changed concerning our personal likes or dislikes. He's still the same man he was before."

"Except for feeding it to you up the ass," Corhagen replied dryly.

"And me 'feeding it to him up the ass', as you put it," Cole retorted. "In case you've forgotten, you had that pleasure yourself not so long ago, so I wouldn't point fingers."

Corhagen was already moving past Cole in an attempt to leave the conversation behind. Cole sighed and rolled his eyes heavenward for a moment before following after.

Joss was waiting on the both of them with Amber, who had the door to the basement open. "What kept you?" he demanded, looking angrily between the two of them.

"I had to convince some of Amber's roommates of my status as a law man," Cole explained as Corhagen went down the stairs. "We're ready now."

Amber watched as Cole and Joss headed down the steps after Corhagen. "You know," she commented thoughtfully, standing behind the half-opened door, "you really don't look much like a cop."

Cole didn't bother stopping. "I've never heard that one before," he called back over his shoulder as Joss reached the basement floor.

Joss was chuckling as he added, "He really hasn't."

The basement wasn't crowded, but every available space had been used to its maximum potential. There was very little room for getting around. Post-it notes and diagrams were stuck on everything from the walls to the furniture and even one of the empty glasses that were in desperate need of a good scrubbing.

"What is all this stuff?" Corhagen wondered, squinting to read the fine print on a Post-it note.

"Do you recognize any of this?" Joss asked, turning to Cole.

"They look like…." Cole stopped in mid-sentence as he examined a long strip of paper that had a number of formulas scratched in pen around archaic symbols. "Don't touch anything," he warned. "This looks like…."

"Quit keeping us in suspense," Corhagen complained. "What is it?"

"Alchemy," Cole said, rising back up. "These are all alchemy equations. The man that owns this building must be an alchemist. Either that or he dabbles, but this looks way too complex to be the work of an amateur."

"What do you know about this stuff?" asked Joss, picking up a small stack of pages that'd been scattered on the floor.

"Not much," Cole replied sadly. "I know a few people who might be willing to interpret it for us, but they're pretty reclusive, and they don't talk to the police. Ever."

Another stack on top of a desk caught Cole's eyes. Joss was talking again, but Cole barely heard. The diagram on the top page was of a human figure, specifically a female. It had been outlined with various alchemic symbols, and the whole outer edge of the sheet was filled with equations. Farther up on the desk, above the mess he had been looking at, were a bunch of photographs. Cole took a closer look and felt his stomach churn.

"We need to get the guys down here," Joss was saying in the background. "This stuff needs to be bagged up and cataloged. We'll go through it back at headquarters."

"Are we sure this has to do with our case, though?" Corhagen pointed out. "I mean, this guy is a wacko who likes to dabble in spells and whatnot, but that doesn't necessarily make him a homicidal maniac."

"Guys," Cole said, waving to them, "you want to come look at this."

"What?" Joss asked, hurrying over at once. "What'd you find?"

"These pictures." Cole pointed. "They're of the girls living in the house upstairs. Some of them have been cut up, too."

"Cut up?" Corhagen was looking over the inspector's shoulder now. "Cut up how?"

"He took pictures of them," Cole explained, showing him. "Then cut them up into pieces and arranged them back together. Also, this diagram here on the desktop? I think it's a formula for making golems using alchemy."

Corhagen frowned. "I thought alchemy was all about turning lead into gold?"

"Only amateurs bother with that," Cole said dismissively. "Most alchemists are all about knowledge. They love knowing how things tick. That is why they used to refer to it as the Great Art. It wasn't about getting rich or living forever, the way most movies portray it."

"This guy was trying to make golems," Joss said, thinking hard. "Like those scarecrows we saw in the hospital a month ago?"

"I don't know." Cole sighed and glanced around. "But the diagram and the photos make me think he had something else in mind. I think we need to find this guy whether he has anything to do with our case or not. It looks like he was planning something serious before he disappeared."

"It's never a slow day," Corhagen groaned. "Okay, I'm going to bring down the boys upstairs so they can start loading this crap up."

Corhagen turned sharply, his eyes still glued to the photograph of Amber in his hand. Not paying attention, he caught his knee on the lower half of the desk and swore loudly. The desk shifted slightly from the jarring, and Cole thought he saw the side panel near where Corhagen had bumped it open slightly.

"Is everything alright?" Amber called out from the top of the stairs. "I thought I heard yelling."

"It's fine," Joss assured her. "Detective Corhagen was just demonstrating to us some of his finesse."

"Do you need anything?" Her voice sounded closer this time. "Is there something I can help with?"

"Don't come down here!" Joss barked. "I mean, just stay up there for right now, please. We don't want anyone disturbing the evidence."

"Oh, right." It sounded like Amber was moving up the stairs again. "Sorry, I watch reruns of *Hill Street Blues*. I should know things like that."

"Thank you." Joss turned back around to find Cole kneeling on the floor next to the desk, staring at the crack between the panels now. "Find something else?" he asked, leaning over.

"You might say that," Cole said, giving the panel a gentle pull. The piece of plywood swung back on concealed hinges to reveal a secret compartment. "Yes," he affirmed. "I have definitely found something. Or rather, Corhagen did."

Cole moved back out of the way so that Joss could see. "I think Corhagen just found out how this basement fits in with our serial killer," he said as Joss got an eyeful of row upon row of thumbnail photos. "It looks like our anonymous informant was on the money after all."

Joss's mouth was drawn up in a thin line like he'd tasted something bitter. Quickly, his eyes swept the photo collage of young boys, all within the age range of the murder victims. Joss pointed at one.

"Aaron Hoover," he said. "And look down there at the bottom. It's Samuel Richenstein, the first victim."

Cole nodded. "We finally found our killer."

Chapter *Four*

IT TOOK a while to get everything loaded up. Cole had hoped they could keep all the files and notes together, but it came down to not understanding the kind of system their perp had used in the slightest. No matter which way Cole turned, it all resembled one big mess, the answers to which made sense to one man and one man alone.

Specifically, one Robert Foleman. Apparently, the home had belonged to his grandparents, and he had inherited it upon their deaths several years ago. Foleman had rented the house out to the troupe of college girls in order to help with the upkeep while he lived in the bomb shelter working on who knew what. Cole was really at a loss for the moment as to what the man had been trying to do. Alchemy just wasn't a strong suit of his, and being in the dark was frustrating.

Fortunately, there was some good news.

It had taken until they got back to Joss's office with all the boxes of stuff in Foleman's basement home, but Joss had phoned ahead for someone to see if there was information in the police database. Cole reminded him to pull info on the Sir Frances North Academy as well, and it was waiting for them on his computer screen when they sat everything down.

"According to this, he's been marked before," Corhagen told them, scrolling through the file. "There were three different cases where allegations were brought against Foleman for sexual assault of a minor."

"It fits so far," Cole mused, opening the box that contained the photographs of the college girls. "Anything else?"

Corhagen hesitated. "Yeah," he said, as if waiting to deliver a blow. "This Foleman guy was once a schoolteacher. He switched districts several times, and usually due to someone accusing him of child molestation. No official charges were brought against him, so it looks like the school dumped him somewhere else to avoid a lawsuit and bad press, but get this. One of the schools Foleman had to leave was the Sir Frances North Academy on Staten Island."

Joss's eyes widened. "You're not serious."

"Very," Corhagen replied. "There's very little detail as to what happened, but the kid who made the accusation was named Daniel Whittaker. This was just a couple of years ago, in fact. The kid might still go there."

"Check the academy records right quick," Joss ordered as Corhagen began punching keys on the keyboard. "If the kid still goes there, he'll be listed in the student records."

Corhagen moved the mouse around to bring the file up. "Not much in here so far," he said, staring at the screen. "School was founded in the early twentieth century by a private organization. Hold on just a sec."

Cole leaned forward to peer at the screen as Corhagen hit a few more keys. Corhagen leaned back slightly, as if unnerved by the sidhe's closeness. "Daniel Whittaker is listed as a student there," he said after a moment, nodding. "According to this, he's in sixth grade."

"What's that?" Cole pointed down at the bottom.

Corhagen moved to the right slightly as he brought the mouse over the tab and clicked on it. "It's another article," he said, bringing it up. "It's a bundle of insurance reports."

"Accident reports," Cole clarified, scanning the title. "According to these, that school has seen a number of incidents in the last few months."

"They were all reported as accidents," Joss read. He was standing behind Corhagen now. "But in each case, someone died."

"It says most of them were students," Corhagen added. "And they go back several months."

"Someone could have staged them to look like accidents," Cole pointed out, moving around to stand by Joss now. "It wouldn't be impossible."

"No," Joss agreed. "But what about the economics teacher that was murdered? Why kill him and not conceal the crime?"

"Unless his death was some kind of message," Cole said, his mind racing. "The others may have just been convenient ways of disposing of the students, but the schoolteacher needed to be killed in a way that would draw someone's attention."

"That's just speculation at this point," Joss said, cutting him off. "We need proof before we go chasing after anything like that."

"Yeah," Corhagen replied. "And I'd rather get this serial killer case wrapped up before we go snooping around that school again."

"We're going to," Joss assured him. "I've got Foleman's financial records right here. There's one other place that's listed under his name, and it's a business in Murray Hill."

Cole climbed on top of Joss's desk as the file came up. Joss had moved in closer now so he could see. They both stared in shock as the name flashed up on screen.

"I don't believe it."

"Me either," said Cole.

"We were just there this morning."

"THIS is like one of those random coincidences you read about in mystery novels," Cole commented as they stood outside the bakery.

"I know," Joss said, pursing his lips. "Maybe we should recruit Angela Lansbury into the Section."

"Nah," Corhagen joked, standing behind them. "I'd rather have Kristen Bell."

The bakery wasn't crowded for the moment, which was a good thing. Joss had already gotten an arrest warrant ready, so all that remained was catching Robert Foleman and getting him to confess. Cole hoped it would be that easy, yet his bad feeling from before was coming back in spades.

Several patrons looked up as the bell over the door dinged loudly. "Can I help you?" the girl behind the counter asked.

Her eyes already looked wary as Joss approached her. "My name is Inspector Vallimun," he explained, showing his badge. "I need to speak with the owner, Robert Foleman. We have reason to believe he might be here."

"I'm sorry." The girl was obviously unnerved now. "Um, you'll have to speak with the manager. I just started here a few months ago, so I don't know anything about the guy that owns the place."

"Is your manager here right now?" Joss pressed.

"He's in the back," she said, pointing to the swinging door behind her. "I'll go get him if you can just wait a second."

"Not a problem."

Joss put his badge away as Cole stepped up alongside him. "She's hiding something," he whispered.

"I think so too," Joss replied. "But we'll give it a minute and see how this goes. If she's smart, this doesn't have to go badly."

The three of them stood there waiting. Cole kept an eye on the clock hanging on the wall behind the cash register. Just when it looked like the girl had run out on them, the door swung open and out she stepped behind a balding man with a round belly leading the way. The man didn't look thrilled by their presence, yet he spoke in a very calm, pleasant tone. "Can I help you gentlemen?"

"We're looking for Robert Foleman," Joss said. On cue this time, both Cole and Corhagen flashed their badges beside Joss's. "According to police records, he owns this building. We were wondering if you've seen him recently."

The man shook his head at once. "The owner hasn't been this way in a month or so. Last time I saw him was when he came in one night to check the books. That's the last I heard from him. You might want to check upstairs, though. The whole building is registered in his name."

"What's upstairs?" Cole asked.

"Just some old apartments that used to be rented out before this place became a bakery," the man said, shrugging. "I think they belonged to Mr. Foleman's grandparents, but he had them shut up after they died. Now he just uses them for storage."

All three were interested now. Joss leaned forward slightly and said quietly, "Is there a key?"

Cole kept an eye on the girl as the manager went to the back again to fetch the key to the upstairs. Her eyes kept drifting toward him every few seconds, like she couldn't look away. Cole checked to make sure neither Corhagen nor Joss were paying attention, then cast a drop of glamour her way with a flick of his wrist.

The girl's eyes never left his as he moved in closer. "What is it about the upstairs?" he asked her in a smooth, seductive tone.

The girl whimpered, then answered him. "I hear noises sometimes," she confessed. "It sounds like someone is in pain, but the manager tells me to ignore it. He said the owner gave orders for no one to go up there for any reason. It scares me."

"Don't worry," Cole told her, releasing the girl from his hold. "I won't let anything happen to you. We're here to take care of it."

The girl visibly relaxed as the glamour faded.

"What's your name?" he asked.

"Cindi," she said, looking a little dazed now.

"Beautiful name," he told her as the manager returned. "Why don't you wait here while we have a look at what's going on up there?"

The manager led them out the front door and around the side. Apparently, the entrance was up a flight of stairs in the back. Joss held back slightly as Corhagen walked ahead of them.

"Should I pretend I didn't notice what just happened?" he hissed, gripping Cole's wrist.

"She was worried," Cole explained. "I think the bald guy up ahead has been threatening her. She asked one too many questions before."

"That's not the point," he insisted. "We're the police. We can't go around using magic to coerce people into telling us things, no matter how much easier it might make our job."

Cole didn't argue but wasn't entirely convinced as the manager opened the door at the top of the stairs for them. The steps themselves resembled a fire escape and had seen better years. With all four of them standing there, Cole wondered if the rickety frame of rusted metal would collapse while they were still standing on it.

"Help yourselves," the manager said. "I'm assuming you boys have a warrant for this sort of thing. Probably should've asked earlier, but nevertheless."

Joss was already pulling the warrant out to show him.

"Right." The man nodded. "I'd best be on my way, then."

"This explains a lot," Corhagen said after the manager left. "All of the deceased said they remembered smelling something baking in an oven. If they were held hostage here before being murdered, the smells from the bakery downstairs would've drifted up to this floor."

"We thought something like this was the case," Joss said, entering the building first. "We just couldn't narrow it down without anything else to go on."

Cole sniffed the air upon entering. "I smell burned flesh," he told them. "The scent is stale, and it's faded some, but there is no mistaking it. Someone was burned alive here."

"Probably three someones," Joss corrected, holding his gun up. "Maybe even more. We only found the three bodies so far. Who's to say there weren't more?"

Cole sniffed the air again as Corhagen shut the door behind them. "That way," he said, pointing. "Through the corridor on the left. The scent is coming from that direction."

"Okay," Joss said, taking a deep breath. "You go first, then, since you'll be able to tell us when you've found the right room. We'll cover you."

"Don't let anyone shoot me," Cole asked, taking the lead now. "I really hate it when that happens."

The hallway was mostly a stretch of narrow space littered with boxes. The first two doors were located on the left. The rooms were empty save for some old furniture. The third door, this one on the right, led into what was once a bathroom, now blocked off by more boxes stacked high on top of one another. Cole tried to peer around them but didn't see anything of interest. That and the fact that the smell was coming from farther down made him keep going.

The end of the hallway met with another one on the right, forming a kind of upside-down L shape. At the end of it was a set of stairs leading up. Just off to the side, however, was the room the smell of charred human remains was coming from. Cole pointed as he raised both his guns up at the ready and motioned for Joss and Corhagen to stay close.

Inside the room was a furnace. Cole could tell even from a distance that it was old and made out of iron. Stepping aside, he pointed the two men to it. "I can't touch it," he whispered. "It's made of iron."

Joss nodded and moved on. Corhagen gave Cole a look as he maneuvered past, but Cole ignored him. The furnace door had been left open slightly, and as Joss swung it back, they could all see what was left inside.

It was another body, one that looked impossibly small crammed into the tiny black space. Joss kept his face perfectly neutral as he inspected the remains. Corhagen looked as though he was going to be sick.

"I can't raise it," Cole informed them quietly, keeping his distance. "It's still too fresh."

Joss rose and wiped his hand clean on his pants leg. "We're going to put an end to this," he said. "Let's see what's upstairs."

"I'll go first," said Cole, taking the lead again. Joss started to protest, but Cole quickly pointed out, "If this guy is here and he's armed, my body can take more punishment than yours."

Joss didn't look as though he liked the idea, but he relented in any case.

"I smell something else coming from upstairs," Cole told them, climbing up a few of the carpeted steps. "It smells like human waste."

"Maybe he forgot to put the seat back down," Corhagen offered. "Sarah is always yelling at me about that."

Cole glared back down at him.

"Now's not the time," Joss warned easily. "Keep going, Colewyn. He was just trying to lighten the mood a little."

"I didn't only mean feces," Cole explained, going further up. "Although there is that. It smells like a human who hasn't bathed in some time. I think someone is being held prisoner here."

"Let's go, then," Joss ordered, moving faster. "It could be more kids."

There was another hallway at the top of the stairs. It, too, veered off to the side in an L shape like the one below. Cole sniffed the air again as he continued on, this time with Joss moving closely beside him. Corhagen was bringing up the rear and pointing his gun behind them.

"This doesn't feel right," Cole said. "I keep smelling something. Something besides human waste and burned flesh. It smells like old candy wrappers."

"We're above a bakery," Corhagen reminded him.

"It smells stale," Cole explained, for once not being sarcastic. "And it's coming from up here. It kind of reminds me of a box of donuts you used to keep in the back of your car."

Cole waited, but Corhagen said nothing. "Corhagen?" he said, turning around.

There was no one behind him and Joss.

"Great," Joss muttered.

"That isn't right," Cole said, looking around. "Did you hear anything?"

"I'm right here," said Corhagen, sticking his head out of a doorway on the left. "You guys should come in here and see this. It's just like the basement of that house."

Cole looked around the minute he entered the room and shook his head. "This is much worse than the basement. I'd say we just found out what Foleman was doing with those photographs of the girls living there."

This room had crates instead of boxes, and they were filled with body parts. The stale sweet smell inside of this room was overpowering. All over the wall were alchemy diagrams and figures. Some of the same emblems were sketched onto the surfaces of the arms and legs sticking out of a nearby crate. Cole leaned down to inspect it and received a shock.

"These aren't real body parts," he said, sniffing to confirm.

"What?" Joss asked, turning around.

Corhagen looked surprised too. "It's food," he said, picking a piece up to lick it.

"Cole!" Joss exclaimed.

"I'm serious," he said, holding it out. "It's got sugar and cream in it. Maybe flour, as well. All of them are like this."

Corhagen peered through one of the boxes with bemused interest now. "This one has a couple of heads in it," he told them. "They smell like peppermint and chocolate. It's like a box of mannequins."

"Except for them being edible," Cole agreed. "This guy has been trying to make golems."

"Out of confectionery?" Corhagen was looking skeptical again. "Why would anyone make a golem out of sugar and flour?"

Cole had no answer for him.

"This is the weirdest thing we've seen so far," Joss said, putting his gun away. "What sort of psycho is this guy?"

"Maybe he played with Barbie dolls as a kid," Corhagen suggested. "I hear that messes little boys up when they get older. All of these golem parts are female."

"This case just gets stranger by the minute," Joss said, looking around. "Let's finish searching the place and then call it in. It's beginning to look as though Foleman isn't anywhere in the building."

"Can we help you, sirs?"

Cole turned at the voice that came from the doorway and stepped back slightly at the sight of the two young women there. Two young women, he noticed, who were impossibly disproportionate. The air smelled stale and sickeningly sweet as they came forward.

Joss and Corhagen were transfixed. "They're golems," Cole warned, moving away. "Just like in the hospital. Don't let them get too close."

"They're really hot golems," Corhagen noted, looking around him. "You never told me they could look like this. I think I like these better."

One of the golems giggled. "You're so sweet," she said, reaching a hand out toward him. "I've never met a man who was so flattering before."

Joss kept his distance, but his eyes never left the second one. "They seem human enough," he pointed out. "Are you sure?"

"You know those movies where robots look and act just like humans do?" Cole reminded him. "The principle is the same."

"Why are so many of the bad guys we fight able to make golems?" Corhagen interrupted. "Is this some new fad going around?"

He hadn't moved near the one motioning to him yet, surprisingly.

Cole noticed he was, however, dancing back and forth on his feet. "Oh well," Corhagen went on. "At least these are better looking than the scarecrows."

"We're not scarecrows," the first one said, laughing. "Our father made us."

"Your father," Joss said, fully alert now. "Richard Foleman?"

The second one nodded. "He made us. We serve him as a way of showing our appreciation."

"Would you like to meet him?" the second one added.

"Certainly," Joss said, keeping his eyes forward as he bowed ever so slightly. "If he's available, that is."

Both girls smiled and motioned for them to follow.

"Does it feel like we just stepped into the plot of a Cinemax movie?" Cole wondered, reluctantly heading after them.

"Who cares?" Corhagen replied.

"Don't let your guard down," Joss warned as they maneuvered down the hallway. "They could still be dangerous. There's something about those two I don't like."

"Well, you've ruined him forever," Corhagen moaned.

"You are becoming an even bigger jerk than Heisen was," Cole bit back as they came upon a spacious room. The hallway split in two just before reaching the entrance, and the other half led to another room roughly the same size, but completely dark. Through the inky blackness, Cole could make out cages the size of chairs. It took little imagination to picture what might have been inside them at one time.

There was only one piece of furniture in the room the golems stood in, a single cage big enough to hold a tiger from the Bronx zoo. Inside wasn't a tiger, though. A man gazed up at them as they stepped inside. His face was sallow and he looked pale. His fingers looked like they were caked in grease and some kind of dried fluid. The cage itself reeked of human waste, which explained where the stink had been coming from. It hadn't been cleaned out in a very long time.

The man's eyes blinked as they stared through the bars at them. It was there that most of the damage was located. They looked haunted. Richard Foleman shook uncontrollably as his gaze moved past Corhagen to Joss before landing on Cole.

At once, he began to scream.

"Father," the first golem said, speaking loudly over him, "these men have come to see you."

"Take them away!" Foleman screamed, shaking the bars of his cage. "Let me out of here! Do you hear me? Let me out!"

"We can't let you out of there, Father," the second golem chided as if speaking to a child. "You'll just run away again. Haven't we been taking care of you like you told us to?"

"He's one of them!" Foleman continued to scream. "He was sent by them! I told you they would find me, but neither of you would listen. He's come to kill me!"

Corhagen looked around Joss at Cole. "I think the man means you."

"I agree," Cole said. "The question would be why, though."

"Anyway," the first golem said, speaking in an exasperated tone now, "this is our father. He was the one who made us."

"Using alchemy," Cole clarified.

Both golems shrugged. "He made us," they repeated together. "He's our father."

"I have to ask," Joss interrupted as Richard Foleman continued ranting. "Do you know this guy?"

"No," Cole answered, unperturbed. "I didn't know who he was until today. Do either of you know why he seems to think I've come to kill him?"

Neither Joss nor Corhagen had an answer. "Excuse me, ladies," Joss said when Foleman's ranting had slowly subsided to whimpers and quiet pleas. "Would either of you care to explain why Mr. Foleman is inside that cage?"

"He tried to run away," the first said, frowning as Foleman kept on sobbing. "Fathers should never run away and leave their daughters. We knew this already, but one of the boys said it too."

"Boys?" Cole was sure Corhagen hadn't meant to ask. The look on his face said he was regretting it already.

Unfortunately, the golem sisters had heard him. "We bring father boys," the second explained. "Father always liked boys. We were the only people he could share that with. When he tried to run, we had to put him in a cage. He told us he needed food, so we thought he would like boys to eat."

Corhagen looked sick. Joss wasn't doing much better, though he hid it well. Cole couldn't blame either of them.

"He said he didn't like them at first," the first added thoughtfully. "We thought it was because we let them cook for too long, but after a while, he said they were fine. He kept asking to be let go, though."

"That reminds me," said the second one, giving all three of them a stern look. "You aren't the bad men he kept saying would come and kill him, are you?"

"We really should have asked them that before," the first said, giving her sister a reproachful look. "Next time company comes over, be sure to ask if they've come to kill Father before you let them in."

"I didn't let them in," the second one replied defensively, looking at her. "I thought you were the one who let them in."

"How could I have let them in?" the first one countered. "I was with you when we found them."

"Oh yeah." The second one paused. Cole's bad feeling was getting a lot stronger, and he quietly slipped Aed Deigh free.

"Does that mean they're burglars?"

"I was just starting to get a good fantasy going with those two," Corhagen grumbled. "Now it feels like I'm back home with my kids again."

"We're cops," Joss said very gently. "We've come to take your father away to a safe place so none of the bad men will get him."

Joss started to move toward them, but Cole seized his arm and shook his head. Before the inspector could protest, Foleman started screaming again.

"They're lying!" he yelled, tugging desperately at the bars. "They can't be cops. *He's* with them! They sent him along to kill me!"

"This is starting to make me feel self-conscious," Cole mused, eyeing both golems carefully. "If either of you ladies make a move, I will have to hurt you. I don't want to, but I will."

The first golem looked indignant now. "He just threatened us!"

"Get him!" the second ordered.

Cole extended the blade that glowed red-hot as the golem sister flung herself at him. Cole swung, remembering what had occurred before with the wolves outside the school, this time willing it to happen. Fireballs erupted from the blade as he swung it sideways with a whoosh. The balls of flame caught the golem in the chest, abdomen, and part of her face, flinging her backward. Her sister screamed as she splattered against the wall.

"What have you done?" the golem cried as her sister began to melt.

"No running... in the halls," the golem mumbled as her body dissolved. "The secret password is swordfish. The album comes... out next... utensil."

The room was filled with the smell of melted butter, nougat, and burned gingerbread. The remaining golem was shrieking at the top of her lungs while the fragrance blended with the other smells in the room.

Corhagen was as eloquent as ever. "Yuck!" he spat.

"It doesn't have to be this way," Cole warned the surviving golem as she fell silent and glared at him. "I don't want to do this, but if you leave me no choice, I will kill you."

The golem was already charging at him. Joss and Corhagen had their guns up and were firing as Cole swiped Aed Deigh down vertically. The bullets struck her just a few feet from them, stopping her in her tracks and causing her to jerk uncontrollably. Less than a second later, Cole's attack cleaved her in two, causing both pieces to fall to the floor in opposite directions.

The golem's head snapped free as the half it had stuck to crashed. Before it had finished rolling over to Foleman's cage, it was already melting along with the rest of the body.

"Give me all your pudding," she mumbled as the peppermint eyes rolled out of their sockets. "I am not... shazam."

Steam drifted up off the blade as Cole retracted it back into the hilt. "This has been one very weird day," he stated.

"It has," Joss said, looking over to where Foleman was huddling up in a far corner of the cage. "And it isn't over yet."

"Keep away from me," Foleman begged. "Don't let him come anywhere near me. He's going to kill me!"

Joss and Corhagen eyed him. Joss, at the very least, looked apologetic. "Fine," Cole said, turning around. "I'll wait downstairs. I didn't relish sticking my hands anywhere near that cage anyway."

He could hear Corhagen speaking as he traced his steps back down the hall. "Maybe we should bring him back. I really don't want to do this either."

Cole slowed his pace slightly. "Get going," Joss ordered, making him smile. "I'll call it in."

"You always call it in," Corhagen grumbled. "When will I get promoted to inspector so I don't have to do this?"

"When you stop insulting my boyfriend," Joss answered with a hint of a warning in his voice. "And implying that I'm anything less than a man behind my back."

Cole didn't wait around to hear Corhagen's feeble protests. He was still laughing as he exited the building and walked down the rickety metal stairs. Outside, the winter snow that had plagued New Yorkers so far was suddenly looking quite beautiful to him.

RICHARD FOLEMAN wound up going to the hospital first instead of the police station. He was suffering from malnutrition and had several infections as a result of living in his own filth for weeks. It looked like he had stayed alive this long by eating the burned corpses of the children the golems had brought him. Richard declined to comment the whole time he was being loaded into the ambulance, insisting he speak with his lawyer.

Corhagen made sure to read the man his rights before the medics took him away. Joss was adamant that they not let him slip through their fingers now that they'd finally found the man responsible.

"He made the golems," Cole assured them, sensing their inner conflict. "He might not have ordered them to murder those boys, but they were acting on his impulses. You can't build golems and give them human traits to emulate behavior without putting yourself into it."

"A jury will have a hard time buying that, though," Joss said, looking out at where the ambulance had driven off. "The man was held prisoner for months. I want to blame the guy, but the golems weren't obeying his orders anymore."

"I know what you mean," Corhagen said, grimacing. "I don't want to, but a part of me feels sorry for the guy."

No one said anything for a minute. "I will never understand human morality," said Cole finally. "The man probably violated a number of boys over the years and only escaped punishment because of bureaucracy. If anything, this is what you would call divine retribution."

"He was held prisoner, though," Joss countered. "A part of me wouldn't wish that on even him."

Cole was confused now. "He will be a prisoner again," he pointed out. "Assuming he is convicted."

Silence fell again. The cold air felt uncomfortable as snow began to drift down in heavy flakes once more.

"I don't relish being the one who has to type up the report," Corhagen said after a moment. "If you don't mind, I think I'm going to find a cup of coffee and maybe something to eat."

"I'm surprised you can eat after dragging him out of that cage," Joss remarked.

"I'm going to wash my hands first," Corhagen explained, walking away. "Maybe my face, too, and arms. In fact, I think I'll run home and take a long, hot shower. Tell my kids that I love them."

"I could use a shower," Joss said quietly as Corhagen disappeared from sight. "I really don't want to type up a report for this, even though I'm glad it's over."

"Can it wait until tomorrow?" Cole asked, rubbing a hand up and down Joss's spine.

Joss groaned at the contact. "I guess so. It's not like the chief will want to hear about how we had to melt two gingerbread girls before we could pull the guy out of his cage. Explaining that part away is going to be rough."

"We'll worry about it later," said Cole, pointing him in the direction of his car. "Let's go home. There is a long, hot shower waiting for you there. If we hurry, we can make it back to the garage before the snow gets bad."

Cole was able to lead Joss to his car without a word of protest from the inspector. Joss leaned back in the seat as Cole started the car, and dozed during the drive. It was already starting to get dark by the time they made it out of Murray Hill. Cole figured the two of them had been on the job for twelve hours now. It felt like it as he continued across Manhattan to the sithen. Though his sidhe body did not feel fatigue as fast as a human's would, emotional weariness could plague his kind far worse and for a much longer time if something were not done. Cole felt he had been hit hard by the day, and there was still the business on Staten Island to make sense of.

Cole wasn't even sure where his garage was, but the car seemed to know. Joss was stirring as they made their way down Fifth Avenue.

"I can't believe the garage is somewhere around here," Joss muttered, gazing out the window at the bright lights.

"People don't expect it to be here," Cole explained. "Therefore, they don't see it. It might surprise you to learn just how much of glamour involves playing with people's expectations."

The garage door was nestled between two inconspicuous buildings. No one driving past gave any kind of notice that they even saw the car sliding inside. Cole pressed a button to bring the door back down, then climbed out.

"We're home," he said.

Relief washed over him as he and Joss opened the door that led back to the sithen. Rather than being in the same hallway they'd left in that morning, though, they found that the sithen had shifted itself around so that the door opened into a back corridor leading into the kitchen. Joss looked around, bleary-eyed, as the lights flickered on overhead.

"Sit down," Cole suggested. "I think I'll make something up for the both of us. You're probably hungry after everything that happened."

"Not really," Joss replied, though he pulled up a chair. "After yanking that fat bastard out of the cage, I lost my appetite."

"It will come back," Cole said. "Besides, you should eat something to keep up your strength."

Joss didn't protest as Cole located a skillet buried under several pots in the cabinet below the stove. Next, he fished out some garlic panini bread and began throwing together a sandwich using lunch meat. The skillet on the lit stove began to sizzle from the butter Cole had placed in it as he slathered one slice of bread with mayonnaise.

"No mayo for me," Joss requested. "It makes me sick to my stomach."

"I remember," Cole replied, slathering the other half with mustard. "No mayo and no onions for you. This one will be mine."

Cole made his first, then threw together one for Joss and tossed it into the skillet. Placing a lid over the top, he stood there for a moment, counting silently to himself as the sandwich heated up.

"You move around like a chef," Joss noted, watching Cole closely. "I've never seen a single man work around a kitchen the way that you do."

"I worked in a deli for a brief period of time," Cole said as the countdown in his brain reached zero. "That was where I developed a taste for these things."

Joss waited a moment as Cole flipped the melted sandwich up into the air and onto a plate. "You worked in a deli?" he asked disbelievingly. "I find that hard to accept."

Cole spun the plate around on his finger for a second for show, then tossed it down on the counter in front of Joss. "It was only for about three months," he explained, doing the same to his own next. "I was low on cash, as usual, and work with the fey had dried up. This was back before I ever got started using a website to keep in touch with clients, so dry spells weren't all that unusual. I had to take a job just so I could keep myself afloat."

"What happened?" Joss asked before biting into his meal.

"The manager's wife was in charge of the shift I worked on. She started flirting with me, and after a while, her husband caught on. He changed the schedule on me deliberately so I would miss my morning shift, then called to tell me I was fired."

"That sucks."

Cole shrugged. "He was an asshole. Right afterward, I found some work for a dryad who was being harassed by some gung-ho lumberjacks upstate."

"How was she?" Joss asked after a moment.

"The dryad?"

"The manager's wife at the deli," Joss corrected, licking some of the mustard off the sandwich's edge. "Was she worth getting fired over?"

"Oh." Cole shook his head as he sat down. "I never touched her, at least not in the way you're implying."

Joss mumbled something around the bite he was chewing as Cole began eating. "What was wrong with her?" he repeated after swallowing.

"Nothing. She and her husband had been having problems for a while, from what I had seen. I didn't want to get mixed up in it and become a part of their drama. Also, although someone had already assured me that being a cantankerous small-dicked midget troll with a receding hairline wasn't a sexually transmitted disease, I really wasn't willing to risk it."

The two ate in silence together for a bit. As Cole was finishing his dinner, Joss pushed his plate aside. "I can't eat anymore," he groaned. "That was a big fucking sandwich you made me."

"I'll eat it," Cole said, sliding the plate toward himself. "Was it just not good?"

"It was great," Joss insisted. "I just couldn't eat anymore. Honestly, I don't see how you are able to put so much away and stay so thin. If I ate like that, I'd balloon up like a whale."

Cole shrugged. "Thank you for what you said to Corhagen today," he said quietly after a moment. "It meant a lot to me."

Joss frowned. "What?"

"In the third floor above the bakery," Cole explained. "When you told him to shut up and called me your boyfriend."

Joss's eyes widened as he shook his head. "Wasn't a big deal, really."

"It was to me," said Cole, putting his food down. "I've never been called someone's boyfriend before."

"Really?" Joss looked genuinely surprised to hear this. "From another man, or in general?"

"Anyone in general," Cole clarified. "Most humans prefer not to stay close to me. The ones who found me attractive quickly decided I wasn't worth having around full time. There was always something about me they found off-putting. Women were drawn to me, but they didn't want me to stick around and complicate their lives. I would get calls to come over late at night while their husbands or fiancés were traveling. They would wax poetic about my skills in bed, but when that was all over, I was shown to the door."

It didn't look like Joss believed him.

"My kind are more primal, I suppose you could say," Cole tried, hoping he could explain better. "We share a close affinity to nature and all that it represents. Making love with a sidhe can be quite passionate and powerful, but most humans find it a harrowing experience at the same time. No one wanted a steady diet of it. That," he added, embarrassed, "and the fact that apparently, in comparison to human males, I rank more than a little above average."

Joss chuckled. "I've been there before. Lots of girls in college loved having me on the side, but they wouldn't dump their boyfriends to be with me full time. I was just their sex toy. It was fun, at least in the beginning, but toward the end there I found myself getting sick of it."

Cole had to laugh. "Bitches," he said, holding his fist up in front of Joss.

"You ain't lying," the man replied, rapping knuckles with him.

Cole finished off both their dinners quickly, ending with a reverberating belch that seemed to flicker the lights. Once they were done, he left the dishes in the sink for Mal and pointed to the door.

"I'm surprised Mal didn't offer to make dinner," Joss mused, following after Cole so as not to get lost. "He gets such a kick out of playing Jeeves to you."

"He knows I like to cook for myself every so often," Cole explained while the sithen shifted around them to lead them into the bathroom. "Ready for that shower now?"

Both of them took their time letting the hot water run over their bodies. Since the sithen didn't have a problem with keeping the water warm, Cole thought they should take advantage of it. When the two of them emerged, dripping wet, their clothes had vanished from the pile on the floor. In their place were two towels, each big enough to lie on.

Their guns, badges, cell phones, and Aed Deigh were lying on top of the chest at the foot of the bed in Cole's chamber, once they had dried off. Cole made sure his phone was turned off before stopping Joss as he reached for some underwear that had been laid out for him.

"Leave them," Cole said, taking Joss's hand. "Come here for a minute."

Cole crawled on top of the bed sheet, pulling Joss gently behind him until he had stretched out naked on his belly. Straddling the man just below the buttocks, Cole began to knead his fingers into the surface of Joss's back. Joss began to moan as Cole worked the taut muscles beneath the weary flesh, pushing the stress of the last several days out of his lover.

Cole worked steadily for a half an hour, first working the outer layer of muscles before pushing farther in to the deeper regions buried around the spine. Joss kept making sounds that were a mixture of pain and pleasure, yet he never asked Cole to stop. Cole began using his index and middle fingers together to form circles counter-clockwise down both sides of Joss's backbone. As Joss began to relax further, Cole reached the curve just above his ass and pushed in hard.

Joss bowed his back slightly as the aching pain shot through him, followed by a sense of tranquility that almost felt foreign. With his thumbs now, Cole was pushing his way back up farther out near the edges. Before he got to the shoulder blades, Joss was panting.

"Turn over," Cole commanded in a soft voice.

Slowly, reluctantly, Joss did as Cole said and looked up into the face of his otherworldly lover. Cole stared down at him for a moment, taking in the face of the man he had found himself loving in such a short time. It felt alien to be in love with a mortal again after so long. Cole tried to keep the invasive thoughts about how this would never last at bay. Joss was mortal, and he would never age the way mortals did. Cole would still look the same after Joss's body had been lowered into the ground.

Cole took a long steadying breath and ran his thumbs over Joss's erect nipples. The sidhe, as a rule, didn't have much in the way of body hair. Joss was covered in it, a fact Cole found fascinating. Leaving the man's nipples alone for the moment, he began to play in the thick patch of fur nestled between the small mounds of chest muscle. Cole ran his fingers through the curls and savored the feel of it. It was his favorite part of Joss's whole body.

Well, one of his favorites, at least.

Leaning forward, he captured Joss's mouth with his own as his fingers raked down the flat expanse of stomach where the hair was even thicker and curlier. Up and down he played as Joss kissed him back, enjoying the thrill Cole seemed to get from this part of his body.

Joss began to run his hands up Cole's toned arms. His own larger biceps flexed as his fingers reached the sidhe's shoulders and worked their way down to Cole's own developed chest. Joss squeezed and played there, digging his fingers into the smooth expanse of marble-colored skin. Cole's flesh began to glow like soft moonlight as Joss first pinched his nipples, then moved down to lightly brush across the thin treasure trail just below the sidhe's navel.

It formed a path to Cole's crotch, where his cock was standing erect and ready. Cole kissed Joss again, then stretched out on the bed beside him, his head pointing toward Joss's feet. Cole grasped the thick baton that was Joss's cock in one hand as his tongue licked out over the tip like a kitten's. Joss groaned, his hand moving back and forth in a steady rhythm over Cole's pale dick, causing precum to ooze out.

Together, the two went down at the same time to suck on the thick head of each other's cock. Cole's tongue was still rolling around the plum-sized head, digging into the piss slit as his arm looped around Joss's raised leg to give him better access. Joss did the same and pushed the long cock all the way down his throat in one gulp, choking on it.

Cole took the mortal's dick more slowly. Joss was nothing to sneeze at in the phallus department, having both length and girth on him. Cole didn't mind, however, as it gave him plenty to work with. Using his free hand, he jacked the man off while working more and more of the enormous dick down his throat. He had to breathe through his nose now, and each exhalation caused the hairs on the man's prize-bull-sized balls to wave.

Cole began to finger Joss's ass as he increased his tempo. Joss abruptly leaned forward, shifting his weight until he had rolled over on top. Cole went with the movement, as it gave him access to more of Joss's big cock and put them at an angle where it would slide right down his throat. Cole had managed over half by now and was determined to get the whole thing before the night was over.

Pulling back, he took a moment to catch his breath while Joss kept right on blowing him. The cock in front of his face was covered in saliva. Cole let some dribble down to his finger and applied more spit before pushing the finger back into Joss's ass. Joss grunted as Cole got past the second knuckle and then rose up suddenly, gasping for air.

"Holy fuck!" Joss cried out as a second finger went in. "You are so much better at this than Allen ever was."

Cole paused for a second. "Allen?" he asked, rubbing his fingers along the spot inside Joss that made him grunt and whimper.

"My buddy," Joss said as Cole tortured him. "We messed around a little when we were teens. I never told anybody about it."

Cole remembered something Joss had said when they had been trapped in an enchanted sleep. "That was what you meant when you said you hadn't done this since you were a kid."

Joss whimpered again as Cole added a third finger. "Sorry I brought it up," he whispered. "That feels amazing."

"Don't be," Cole replied. "I like hearing about your life." Cole roughly pushed all three fingers in at the same time, causing Joss to gasp. "But now really isn't the time," he teased, slowly drawing them out. "I have to do something to make you think of me instead of Allen when we're together."

Joss all but collapsed on top of him. "Way past that," he grunted, looking through the tiny crack formed between their bodies. "You're glowing again."

"I glow during sex," he said, bringing Joss around for a long, passionate kiss. "You know that."

Joss moaned into his mouth. "I like seeing it," Joss explained. "It's interesting."

There was a bottle lying on the night stand next to the bed. Cole couldn't remember seeing it before, but it was there now. Joss reached for it and applied a liberal amount of the oil to Cole's cock. Lubing up his ass, Joss then placed the glass cap down on the top and tossed the bottle aside before aiming Cole's erect dick at his ass. With one swift lunge, Joss impaled himself.

"Fuck!" he cried out long and slow.

Cole could already feel his balls beginning to draw up as Joss rode him hard, like a rodeo cowboy. "I'm not going to be able to hold it," he warned, feeling the first wave of orgasm hit him.

"Don't," Joss said between gasps. "I want you to cum in me."

Cole grabbed Joss by both hips as the man flogged his almighty johnson while slamming his ass down. Joss's face was screwed up in pain, yet he didn't let up even a little as Cole continued skewering him.

Joss let out a cry as Cole pulverized the man's love nut with his cock. Cum went flying everywhere, some of it landing on Cole's face as Joss climaxed. Joss's ass ring gripped Cole's cock tightly, forcing him over the edge next. Cole howled like the wolf he sometimes was as Joss's ass was filled up with sidhe cum.

Joss fell forward, but Cole caught him in a bear hug. Together, they nuzzled one another on the rumpled sheets as Cole's seed leaked slowly out of Joss's asshole, coating his low-hanging balls. Joss began to kiss him and ran both hands through Cole's hair as his erection grew again. Joss's dick was soon pulsing between them. Cole felt Joss rise up, and released him. Joss was panting now as Cole's cock fell out of his ass.

Cole watched as Joss pushed his legs up and slid between them. Joss's man meat was pushing against his hole now, and he whimpered slightly as the head popped through the first ring. It had been a while since they'd done this, and Cole wasn't as stretched out as he usually was. It still felt amazing going in.

Cole reached up and captured Joss's lower lip between his teeth, pulling him back down for another kiss. Joss's own mane of golden hair fell around them, reflecting the light that was coming from underneath Cole's skin. The two kissed each other hard as Joss pushed his horse cock all the way into the sidhe's ass, one inch at a time. Cole couldn't stand it anymore and let go of Joss's mouth, throwing his head back and howling as those last few inches made their way into him.

Joss began to move then, slowly and tenderly, as Cole brought his legs up to wind them around Joss's back. Each time Joss drove his cock into him, Cole pulled with his legs to make sure every last bit of that enormous dick went into him. When it did, Cole let out a gasp and bucked his hips. He expected Joss to speed up, but Joss was taking his time.

They stayed like that for hours.

Joss rocked back and forth in the ancient rhythm of lovers as his dick plunged into Cole. Every so often he traced patterns along Cole's neck and jaw with his lips, nibbling and kissing a path that ended each time with Joss's long tongue running up Cole's throat. The light from Cole's skin cast shadows all over the wall as the sithen responded to their lovemaking. The room faded away; the bed beneath them ceased to exist as Joss finally increased his speed a little.

Reaching up, Cole dug his fingers into Joss's developed chest and held the flesh there as power built up between them. Joss felt it run through him sharply, like a blade. The unexpected sensation sent him into overdrive. His cock thrust forward hard with one smooth stroke that pierced Cole all the way to his center.

"Oh Goddess, lover," he gasped, arching his back up. "I can't take much more of this. Fuck me hard!"

Joss was all too happy to do so. His cock was throbbing and as large as it would ever get. Cole's ass had finally adjusted to the cudgel as it pounded him relentlessly.

"Fuck!" Cole swore as he felt himself being hammered.

"Just like that," Joss breathed into his face, pressing his forehead down into Cole's. "Just like that, huh?"

"Always," Cole cried, feeling his balls churning again. "Fuck me like that! Oh lords above us, make me cum. Make me cum, lover!"

Joss came. It felt like a dam had burst open and flooded Cole's ass with hot thick seed. Joss roared his pleasure into the air, and the sound bounced off the walls of the room they had somehow returned to. Cole howled right along with him as he felt his own release paint his stomach and Joss's thick, bulging arms. The hair on Joss's body was plastered to his flesh now as sweat from the both of them soaked into the sheets. Cole felt Joss pull out of him and lay his body down next to him.

Reaching over, Cole used Joss's rising and falling chest as a pillow. The light from his skin was fading as the room went dark. The sithen was still active, though for the time being, it felt far away from them. Sleep claimed Cole as three words fell softly from his lips. Joss never heard them.

"I love you."

Chapter
Five

COLE awoke the next morning and slipped out of bed without waking Joss. The man looked exhausted and needed some extra sleep after the last few days. Mal was kind enough to block any incoming messages to his phone and move the bathroom farther away so the running shower water wouldn't wake him up. Cole left instructions when to wake Joss up and slipped out to the garage, intent on learning all he could about the mysterious events on Staten Island.

It took over an hour to get there that morning. More snow had fallen earlier, it seemed, and it was getting worse by the minute. The roads were filled with honking cars and angry drivers yelling and shaking their fists. The black Camaro jumped forward several times like an antsy animal, hoping to nudge its way through the maze of vehicles.

"Easy," Cole warned when its engine revved all by itself. "We'll get there."

Things improved once they were on the bridge. Cole couldn't quite take his eyes off the island as he drove toward it. People were outside again today all around, shoveling snow and fighting the bitter chill of the morning to walk to work. It looked as though the local residents weren't willing to risk spinning off onto the shoulder just to stay warm today. The roads weren't nearly as good here.

Cole drove past the private academy and continued on down the path he'd taken yesterday to get to the abandoned factory. It took one wrong turn and the car correcting him before he made it, but the place looked deserted. Cole wondered if its inhabitants hadn't made tracks for parts unknown already. Getting out of the car, he took a quick look around before sliding up to the front door.

The door was hanging off its hinges. It looked as though something had forced its way inside. Cole shook his head to clear away any lingering images he had of a similar time he'd come upon a scene like this and drew out Bandersnatch and Jabberwock together. Kicking what remained of the door away, he eased in ever so slightly and looked around.

The place didn't seem different from the last time. Cole thought that someone relying solely on their eyes would mistake the place for normal, but his senses told him better. Cole could smell the Cu Sith, far more than had been here before. The rest of the pack still under the control of those strange black rings must have returned. He felt his stomach churn slightly at the thought that they could have been following him.

Something moved behind him and farther up as he entered the building all the way. Cole whirled around and brought Bandersnatch up, preparing to fire, but what he saw there made him pause. Unfortunately, the changeling girl from yesterday had no power to alter her course once she was airborne. The girl slammed hard into him and sent Cole flying backward onto the floor. Sprawled out on his back, he glared up at her through narrowed eyes as she looked down at him sheepishly.

"I suppose a home security system is out of the question," he grumbled, waiting for her to get off.

"We wasn't sure if you wuz one ah 'em comin' back for seconds," said Boogaloo, stepping out from his hiding place behind a stack of boxes. "What took ye so long, anyways?"

"I had to help catch a serial killer," Cole replied, getting up. "But I'm here now. Were all of the others taken?"

Boogaloo turned away. "Ev'ry last dang one. Damn Cu Sith with them collars still attached to their necks broke in an' started roundin' everybody up. Wuz a nightmare!" Something flickered across Boogaloo's face then. "An' before ye start getting' any ideas, sidhe, I woulda stayed and fought 'em off wit the best ah 'em. She made me hide on account ah somebody needin' ta be here if you decided ta cum back!"

"I said nothing," Cole answered pointedly. "Certainly nothing to suggest that a wood goblin wasn't a suitable fighter."

"Okay, right." Boogaloo nearly looked grateful for a moment. "Like I wuz sayin', what kept ya so dang long?"

"As I said previously," Cole repeated, keeping his tone of voice neutral, "I was called away to catch a killer. Section Thirteen has other cases besides just what has been going on here. When did the collared Cu Sith show up?"

"Las' night." Boogaloo stared at the floor as he nervously scratched an arm. "We'd jus' finished discussin' what we'd do if ye never came back and had decided on getting' sum shuteye when they trashed the downstairs. They took hostages, an' she tried to follow. I shuddn't be surprised at where they were dragged to."

Cole started to ask, then guessed correctly. "The Sir Frances North Academy," he said aloud. "What is it about that place?"

"It's where the Lord of All Fey lives," Boogaloo said, glaring. "I'd've figured you to have gotten that befer now!"

Cole turned to the girl, who had stood off to the side, wearing her cloak up over her face. She looked frightened now and was visibly shaking. Cole approached her cautiously and placed both hands on her shoulders. The girl didn't move away. "I'll get them back," he swore. "Can you show me who this Lord of All Fey is?"

The girl didn't move for a moment. Then she quietly shook her head.

"She's been decidedly quiet on tha' particular subject," said Boogaloo, moving in closer. "I dunno why, but it must be serious."

"How come she never talks?" Cole asked, rubbing the girl's shoulders gently now.

"Sumthin' happened ta her back when she wuz trapped in Faerie," Boogaloo explained, sitting down on the concrete floor to pick at his toes. "I dunno what. She won' talk 'bout it. I not even sure of whether it wuz that specifically er jus' movin' thro' the Hedge fer so long."

"Can you write the name of the Lord of All Fey down?" Cole asked her, to which the girl shook her head again.

"Can't read er write," Boogaloo explained, sharpening his claws now. "She wuz taken long befer she could learn how to."

"And I'm guessing she doesn't have a name?"

"It's Jynx," said the wood goblin. "Jus' Jynx."

Cole let go of Jynx's shoulders and pulled her around to face him. "I'm going to take you someplace safe," he explained softly. "You'll be taken care of and no one will hurt you. Once this business with the so-called Lord of All Fey is done, it will be safe for you to leave if you want."

Jynx's eyes teared up as she raised her head to meet his gaze. Throwing her arms around him, she gave Cole a long hug that felt desperate. Cole patted her head tenderly, then gently but firmly pulled her away. Jynx was wearing a resigned look now. Whatever had been going on in her mind had reached a resolution somehow. Now she almost seemed to be waiting for the worst to show up.

"Wut 'bout me?" Boogaloo snapped sharply, giving Cole's leg a poke. "I dun't suppose you gots some place I could crash, huh?"

"What about your cousins?" he asked, jerking his leg back. "Couldn't you stay with them?"

Boogaloo glanced away again. "We dun' exactly get along," he admitted. "Cuz of account that I rescued a human baby once. They'd said I went soft on 'em. Mostly Bugbear, but Bugaboo always did go along wit whatever Bugbear saids. Guess it's cuz Bugbear wuz da olderest."

Cole debated for a moment, then nodded. "Come on, then."

It was a long drive back to Manhattan. Cole was getting sick of making these trips. Traffic was still bad, yet the car seemed to have a better time maneuvering through it now. Cole sat back and just let it guide him through the narrow gaps between vehicles. The car seemed to know what it was doing, so Cole wasn't going to fight it.

"I just hope you don't require regular fill-ups," he said.

"I haven' seen one ah these things in years," Boogaloo said from the back seat, patting the leather with his claws. "How'n Danu's titties did ya come across it?"

"It was waiting for me in the garage yesterday morning," Cole replied, turning off the bridge into Brooklyn. "I didn't ask too many questions. A lot of the artifacts and beings from the wild hunts tend to take offense to that sort of thing."

"Tell me 'bout it," Boogaloo grumbled. "So where're we goin'?"

"My place."

Cole had thought they would be heading back to Fifth Avenue, but the car veered sharply to the left once they were away from the congested area surrounding Verrazano-Narrows. Just up ahead, he spotted a familiar-looking garage door nestled between two buildings. The door opened automatically, and though the exterior looked run-down, the inside was exactly like the one he'd left through that morning. It seemed the garage entrance to the sithen could move around. Cole didn't complain, since he'd been dreading the thought of going back and forth again all morning.

"Dis is pretty swank digs," Boogaloo commented as he and Jynx followed after Cole. "How'd ya cum across somethin' like this?"

"It belonged to a murderous psycho before Consort named me the true inhabitant and she was flushed out into Bowling Green Park."

"I'd heard 'bout sumthin' goin' on out dat way a month er so ago," said Boogaloo as they entered the sithen. "That wuz you?"

Mal appeared suddenly a few steps in front of them. "That was me," he said, smiling. "Master Colewyn, I regret to inform you that Inspector Vallimun wishes to have a word. He seems a little upset over the fact that you didn't wake him up this morning."

"Is he back?" Joss's voice echoed down the hall behind Mal. "I'm going to kill him."

Cole went on ahead and found Joss coming around the corner. Whether this was the sithen's doing or just good timing, he didn't know. Joss opened his mouth to say something as Cole walked up to him. Before a word could come out, Cole captured his mouth and kissed him long and hard.

Joss broke free a minute later. "I hate it when you do that," he growled.

"I missed you too," Cole said. "It looked like you needed the extra rest, so I just let you lie in. I've been over at Staten Island trying to work out what's been happening there. Our witnesses were taken captive, just so you know, but two of them managed to find me."

Joss looked past Cole to where Jynx and Boogaloo were standing with Mal. Boogaloo was sniffing Mal's leg curiously. The ghost of the former sorcerer didn't seem to notice, not even when Boogaloo hiked a leg up.

"Not on the floor," Cole warned threateningly. "We have a lavatory for that."

Mal looked as if he wouldn't have cared. "Master Colewyn brings home the most interesting guests," he noted, looking down at the wood goblin. "Will they be staying for the time being? Do I need to make a few extra rooms?"

"Jus' point me ta the kitchen," Boogaloo replied, walking off. "Jynx 'ere can take care uh herself. She eats like ah bird anyhow."

A copy of Mal appeared in front of Boogaloo, stopping him. "The kitchen is this way," he instructed. "And I've moved the bathroom for your convenience."

"Great service," the goblin said happily. "Think I'll stick 'round here forever!"

"Not on your life," Cole mumbled, turning to the other Mal, who was still waiting beside Jynx for instructions. "See if she wants a shower," he said. "And then maybe some food, as well."

"I've still got a report to submit," Joss was telling him. "The chief was on my butt this morning about how I hadn't filed it yesterday. He seems anxious to read about all the crap he doesn't believe in for once."

"Truly a remarkable man," Cole replied sarcastically. "Why don't you have Corhagen do it?"

"Corhagen is taking the morning off," Joss replied. "He's been working just as hard as we have, and I can't let all my men drop dead of exhaustion."

"I could use your help working the Staten Island case," Cole admitted, following Joss back to his private chamber. "Something big is about to happen there. I can sense it."

"I can't," Joss replied, and he didn't sound pleased. "I'm due in Interrogation Room D once the report has been filed. They want me there to help drag the truth out of that crackpot Foleman. He keeps demanding to speak with a lawyer, saying we're holding him against his will without charge. Last night, he kept insisting someone was going to kill him. The man switches songs real quick, it seems."

Cole hesitated a moment. "Can't you get someone else to do it?" he pressed. "This isn't like me, but I can't take on whatever is happening by myself."

Joss looked back at him as he looped his tie through the open knot. "You've handled worse than this solo. I thought you liked working on your own."

"You're better at dealing with humans than I am," Cole stated unabashedly. "I think the person behind the murder and enslavement on Staten Island is human, and they are using the private school as a cover. It could be that the perpetrator is one of the instructors there."

"That could get sticky," Joss agreed. "I'll call Corhagen and arrange for you to pick him up later on. Can you be outside his apartment after noon?"

Cole frowned but nodded.

"We have to do something about this mess," Joss said quietly. "The city is going to work us all until we're dead on our feet."

Cole eased up behind Joss and wrapped both arms around him. "We'll take care of it," he said, nuzzling Joss's ear through the curtain of hair blocking it. "It will all work out one way or another."

"I wish I believed that." Joss sounded positively defeated. "It's only going to get worse before it gets better."

Cole moved away and ran his fingers lightly through his lover's golden hair. "Come back to the sithen tonight," he whispered. "We can take a nice long hot shower together without worrying about running the water bill up or it turning ice-cold on us."

Joss made a sound at the idea.

"I can make us both something," Cole offered, rubbing Joss's shoulders now. "We'll come back here where I can rub your back and shoulders. And other things."

Joss didn't reply.

"You could just move in here," Cole offered tentatively. "There is plenty of room. I'm not certain, but the sithens of old were said to contain whole worlds inside them. There is probably enough space for Mal to make one more bed."

Joss stood there silently as Cole ran his hands up and down over his thick chest. "You could have privacy, and we would be closer together. Didn't you say that your apartment is freezing this time of the year?"

"I don't want to be a kept man," Joss said, turning around slightly. "I appreciate the offer, but...."

Cole waited, but Joss didn't elaborate. "But?"

"I don't know," he admitted finally. "Something about it doesn't seem right just yet."

Cole looked down as Joss bumped their foreheads together.

"It's not that I'm saying never ever or even no outright. I just don't think now is the best time. I learned the hard way a long time ago about making snap decisions while under stress. I'd like to think it over. Plus," he added as they backed away slightly, "we've only known each other for a month."

Cole looked at him. "It feels longer somehow."

"That's the life of a cop," Joss explained, laughing. "Time drags by the longer you stay on the force."

"That just makes me want to keep you down here forever."

Cole ended their discussion by kissing Joss hard on the mouth. This turned into several minutes of touching and groping, which culminated with Cole stroking Joss's hard, thick shaft through the fabric of his pants. Joss finally pulled away when Cole started to get down on his knees.

"I have to get to my office," he protested, stopping Cole before he could yank down the zipper. "And you need to get back to Staten Island. Don't forget to pick up Corhagen on your way."

Cole pulled himself back up the length of Joss's body, stopping to rub his face into the crotch of his slacks for a moment. Joss sighed as his cock throbbed, yet he reached down to pull Cole the rest of the way up. Cole kissed him hard again, wrapping both arms around the mortal's neck.

"Come back tonight," Cole pleaded. "I'll be lonesome here without you."

Joss hesitated. "I'll try," he said. "The weather may be bad, though. If that's the case, I'd rather go straight home and not risk getting into a car accident."

"I could come pick you up," Cole offered. "I have a car now, remember?"

Joss chuckled at that. "It is going to take some time getting used to that thought. Okay, since you have a car now, meet me back at the station once you get done going through the school. I'll want a briefing on what you find anyway. I'll even let you drop me off, since you'll be needing to go get Corhagen anyway."

Cole smiled, having gotten his way, and complied by releasing Joss so he could straighten himself out again.

"Speaking of the school," Joss added, "we have a warrant to search the premises. I didn't want to run the risk of that school principal giving you a hard time. It's waiting for you at the precinct."

Joss checked himself in the mirror to confirm he was presentable and headed out. Cole checked with Mal first to make sure their guests were resting comfortably, then headed to the garage. Joss was already waiting impatiently beside the car.

"I am not looking forward to this," mumbled Joss as they wound their way into the maze of city streets. "Something tells me this interrogation is going to go to hell fast."

Cole linked his fingers through Joss's. "How long can we officially hold him?" he asked, turning the wheel one-handed. "Will his lawyer post bail for him?"

"Bail hasn't been set yet," Joss said. "The judge is shuffling back and forth on the issue. For some reason, this guy is making people nervous."

"What for?" Cole glanced in Joss's direction before making a sharp turn. "Isn't the case fairly solid by human standards?"

"The photos that were hidden inside that secret compartment are what really clinch the deal, and with Foleman's history of charges for child molestation, it doesn't look good. Of course, the hard part will be convincing a jury that two gingerbread girls had been holding him hostage in a cage per his programming."

"Yours is a strange world." Cole brought his car around to the parking garage and spotted an empty space just up ahead.

"This one is going to be a mess."

Joss was wearing a sour expression as Cole brought the vehicle to a stop. "Everyone is going to want me to explain this, and the only thing I have to offer them is the truth. I'm afraid what will happen is that Foleman is going to plead no contest by way of insanity. If he starts talking about alchemy and candy-cane robots, the jury will sympathize."

"As long as he's off the streets and under guard, does it matter?"

Joss thought about that for a moment. "I don't know."

Deciding he didn't need to know any more details for the time being, Cole wandered in and went to collect his warrant before leaving again for Murray Hill. Corhagen was outside near the edge of the sidewalk, waiting with a brown paper bag in hand. As Cole pulled up, he thought he saw someone watching from behind the curtains in Corhagen's apartment window. Corhagen, meanwhile, wouldn't look Cole in the face as he climbed aboard.

Something told him that Corhagen's wife hadn't been thrilled to learn who was picking her husband up. A quick sniff confirmed it.

"Peanut butter and tuna fish," he mused, pulling out into the street. The aroma from the bag grew stronger as Corhagen dropped it down in the slot between them. "You had a fight with her again before lunch?"

James's face turned sour for a moment as he glared out the front windshield. "I told her I would get my own lunch," he grumbled, more to himself than Cole.

"Was that before or after you two argued?"

Corhagen didn't answer. Cole was getting used to it by now and focused his attention on avoiding the other maniacs driving all over the road. It was a long and uncomfortably silent drive over to Staten Island. Cole found himself missing the company of Boogaloo, strange as that was.

"I have a warrant to search the school premises," he said almost as an afterthought. "Joss said something about you two having some problems with the principal. I guess he assumed this would make things go quicker."

Corhagen didn't respond.

"What happened in that office yesterday?"

James made a sound like he was clearing his throat. "Not much," he said quietly. "The principal was just being a jackass. He didn't want us making a scene at the school and scaring any of the students."

Cole frowned. "That doesn't sound right. From what I've seen, school is about instilling fear into the hearts of your youth."

Once again, Corhagen sat in silence without responding. Feeling frustrated, Cole turned on the radio to at least fill the void. When he spotted the school in the distance, it was a relief.

Cole saw a number of children on the playground to the right as they entered through the front gate. Almost at once, two of them pointed in his direction and came running. Cole remembered them as the two from the receptionist's area yesterday morning and quickly passed the warrant on to Corhagen.

"Go and show this to the principal so we don't have any more problems," he said. "I want to have a word with these two in private."

"You aren't going to whisk them off to some far corner of fairyland, are you?"

This time, Cole ignored him and threw the warrant into his face. "Billy Thorton," he said, pointing at the pale boy with curly hair. "And Bobby Higgins."

"You came back," Billy said excitedly.

"And you're not bleeding this time," Bobby noted, pointing at Cole's shoulder. "Did you catch the bad guy this time?"

"That is why I'm here, actually," Cole told them. Quickly, his eyes swept the area. "Is there a place where the three of us can talk privately? I'd like to have a word with you about something that happened the other night."

Billy looked nervous now. "We're not in trouble, are we?" he asked. "Is this about why we had to go to the principal's office, because that was just us messing around."

"He's not here over that," Bobby snapped, giving his shoulder a thump.

Cole couldn't help but laugh. "It isn't that," he assured them. "I wanted to ask about one of your teachers, so long as it doesn't get you into trouble."

Billy and Bobby both shook their heads in unison. "Ms. Thatchell is supposed to be watching us," Bobby explained. "But she's down around the side of the building smoking cigarettes with Mrs. Ettkins. They won't come back until just before the bell rings. No one will notice if we're not there."

The three of them wandered over to the front steps of the building. Corhagen was watching them from behind the window of the front door, as if waiting for Cole to do something wrong. Cole stared at him until he went away, then turned his focus back to the two boys. Each had taken a seat on either side of him. Billy was showing a renewed interest in Cole's guns, while Bobby stared closely at Aed Deigh sticking out from the horizontal sheath strapped to his back.

"Be careful," he warned in a friendly tone. "Anyone who tries to wield Aed Deigh will either be burned horribly or frozen to death."

Bobby's eyes widened. "How come?" he asked skeptically.

"It was made for me," Cole explained. "No one else."

"Can I touch your gun?" Billy asked timidly, pointing to Bandersnatch strapped down in the holster on his right leg. "Will it hurt me?"

Cole moved his leg closer to Billy in answer. "Go ahead," he said. "It won't hurt you. Just don't take it out of the holster."

Billy pressed his finger against the butt of the gun, then jerked it away quickly and smiled as though he'd done something incredibly brave. Bobby just snorted and shook his head like he knew better.

"Let's see," Cole said. "This is probably the point where I am supposed to work in some type of moral about gun control. Since I'm in a hurry, though, and the detective who rode here with me will be back soon to make sure I didn't sell you both into fey servitude, let's get this over with."

Neither boy said a word. They were both watching Cole like he might sprout a second head at any moment. Luckily, he was cut from a different mold than that. "Can either of you tell me about a teacher named Jagger who worked here?"

Both boys looked at each other. "He's dead," Billy said simply. "He died the other day. They held a memorial service for him."

"We had to go," Bobby added. "All the other teachers said it was man... detory."

"Mandatory," Billy corrected. "They said it was mandatory."

"Right." Bobby nodded.

"And no one wanted to go?" Cole asked, looking from one to the other. "How come?"

Billy fell silent. "Nobody here really liked Mr. Jagger," he explained finally. "He was mean."

"He was an asshole," Bobby said without remorse. "Some of the other kids threw a party in an alley not far from here after school yesterday. We weren't invited, but it was to celebrate him being dead."

That sounded highly unusual to Cole. "He was that bad?"

Billy nodded emphatically. "Once he made this kid in our class who failed a test write each answer a thousand times. He only failed by two points, and the test had over a hundred answers. He was given two days to finish it on top of all the other homework assigned for us and having to study for a makeup exam the next day."

"He liked to walk around with a police whistle," Bobby added. "If he thought you were doing something bad, you'd get a whistle blown right in your ear."

"Remember the time we had Mr. Jagger for study hall?" Billy asked, speaking to Bobby again. "Mr. Jagger was the substitute teacher for study hall one day. He caught this girl doing homework and made her stand up in front of the whole class and tear each sheet up one at a time. She was crying for the rest of the afternoon."

"Mr. Jagger didn't like students to do homework during school hours," Bobby explained. "If he thought you were doing homework during school, he'd confiscate it."

"He caught this one boy out in the hall without a pass. His teacher had sent him to get a garbage bag out of the storage closet, and she forgot to sign a pass for him. Mrs. Lumis found him standing in a corner with tears going down his face. Mr. Jagger had paddled him for five minutes straight and then left him there.

"He was a monster," Billy finished off, looking up at Cole gravely. "People here had nightmares about him. I asked my mom twice if she would let me change schools so I didn't have him as a teacher anymore."

For the next few minutes, Cole was entertained with stories of life under the iron fist of Melvin Jagger. Before story time was over and the bell signaling the end of recess sounded, Cole found himself longing for the times when he'd been at the mercy of Lord Oberon. Going by what the two boys had just told him, Oberon was quite pleasant when compared to the mortal Jagger.

As the children were being lined up, one boy in the group who was holding a rather thick book peered over the head of the girl in front of him and stared at Cole for a moment. Billy and Bobby were both pushing him along as the line began to move forward. Turning around, Cole went inside to avoid getting caught up in the crowd and headed for the main office. He had briefly entertained the idea of going to look for Corhagen but quickly dismissed it. Cole had the feeling the investigation would move a lot faster without the mortal keeping himself underfoot.

The receptionist was absent this time. Cole glanced around for signs that she would be right back. Finding none, he decided to take advantage of his good fortune and swiftly ducked around the counter and through the slightly opened door to the principal's office. This room was deserted as well.

Cole shut the door behind him and began looking through the room. On a whim, he decided to cast his magic out and see if it reacted to anything. It was a futile effort, since his power only worked in such a manner on the long-deceased. It seemed unlikely that the ruler of this academy would be hiding a corpse anywhere close by. The smell would have alerted him before he could locate it using his personal power, and Cole's glamour had always been very short-range and only able to twist the minds of people one at a time.

So it naturally came as a huge shock to him when he struck gold. His glamour rebounded off something almost immediately, causing his head to throb. Staggering slightly, Cole looked around sharply for the source. Tentatively, he probed again and found it to be resonating from inside the bottom drawer of the large desk that took up most of the room. Cole walked around to pull it open at once. What he found in there made his heart grow cold.

It was one of those collars from before. A black ring.

JOSS didn't answer his phone until the fifth ring. "It's about time," Cole told him, moving down the hall quietly. "What kept you?"

"I was in the interrogation room," Joss answered, sounding unhappy. "Trying to crack a very stubborn nut."

"Try a hammer," he suggested, turning a corner while keeping both eyes sharp. "Listen, I found a black ring inside the drawer of the principal's desk. I need you to tell me everything that happened when you and Corhagen spoke with him."

"He wasn't very helpful," Joss responded, his tone turning serious now. "You might say he was being a jackass, in fact. Corhagen and I spent most of the time trying to convince him to let us search the school before you showed up. He didn't see the point in it. And they wouldn't let me bring a hammer to the interrogation. Something about civil rights."

"Talk to me about civil rights when people constantly deny your existence," Cole retorted. "If the principal was hiding something, that ring may be the concrete evidence we need."

"He's our killer?"

"I think he may have set the Cu Sith on that teacher, yes," Cole replied. "A couple of students told me a very interesting story before I found it. It seems our deceased economics teacher was not very well liked at the academy."

"Why would the principal have killed him, though?"

"Good question," Cole said, coming up on another turn. He had been peeking through the narrow windows in the classroom doors the whole time, hoping to spot Corhagen. So far, there was no sign of him or Principal McGregor. "Maybe Jagger just pushed him too far?" Cole offered, slowing down as he approached a line of students outside what looked like a cafeteria. "Or the guy could have been sleeping with his wife?"

"Ain't no telling," Joss said. "Look, I've got to get back in there and see if Foleman has decided to sing a different tune."

"I'll call you once I have something more," Cole said. "Right now, I may have made a huge mistake again."

"What?"

Cole hesitated. "I sent Corhagen into the principal's office to deliver the search warrant while I questioned those two boys. Neither one was there when I went inside."

Joss wasn't happy. "Why didn't you keep him close by you?" he demanded. "The whole idea behind having a partner is for you to watch each other's backs."

"Old habits," Cole answered. "Plus, he was being a dick."

Joss groaned into the phone. "Find him. Make sure he's alright, and don't let him slip away from now on, no matter how big of an asshole he is being. Understood?"

"I will find him," Cole promised. "Over and out."

"You just wanted to say 'over and out' on your new phone!" he heard Joss yelling as he hung up.

Not having any luck locating Corhagen the human way, Cole decided to forgo it and trust his reliable nose to lead him. Unfortunately, there were quite a few humans in the building. It was one thing when Cole was leaping over rooftops in downtown Manhattan. There was nearly always a breeze to carry the scent toward you, and the area wasn't so densely packed. Still, Cole had known the detective for several years now. If he could not track Corhagen's scent, no one could.

A few minutes later, Cole had backtracked down a different hallway and traveled nearly all the way back to the front of the school. The trail had led him to a door marked as the entrance to the basement. Corhagen's scent was coming from there, along with the cheap cologne he had taken to wearing as of late. Cole pulled and, finding the door was locked, gave it an extra-hard tug. The lock screamed in protest as he forced it open.

The air was stale, and at once Cole recognized the musky scent that hit his nose. Drawing out Aed Deigh, he checked to make sure the coast was clear before stepping into the room. It sounded like there was a boiler running somewhere past the foot of the stairs. A row of pipes blocked his view as he descended the first few metal steps. At a gap, Cole peered through and spotted Corhagen lying on the floor.

He was clutching one of his arms, which looked as though it had been bitten. Surrounding him was a small pack of Cu Sith. He could hear them growling over the noise of the machinery. Standing back several feet away was Principal McGregor, holding a crystal in his hand.

"Take great care with this one," the man instructed. "He has the Sight. It will be of greater use to us once we learn how to enthrall him."

Cole continued down the steps until he came to the point where the pipes ended. Grabbing hold of one, he used it as leverage to draw himself up over the railing. Cole jumped down to the dusty concrete floor with both blades out and ready. Before his feet hit the ground, he thought he saw movement from behind a row of boxes beside the hot water heater. The Cu Sith, however, turned around and faced him, growling, the moment he landed. Standing, Cole brought his weapon up into a swing.

A row of icicles shot like missiles through the air toward the fey wolves. Each one scattered out of their path before they could connect. Some moved to attack, but Cole shoved the tip of his ice blade to the ground and froze it. Ice spread all over the surface, causing them to slip. The principal staggered, bringing up the crystal in his hand as if to defend himself with it. Cole saw and launched a volley of fireballs his way.

With a path cleared, Cole charged forward to see about Corhagen. "What kept you?" the mortal grumbled, trying to stand. "I thought you'd never get here."

"Nice to see you too," he retorted. "Your arm doesn't look too bad. Can you stand up?"

"Get him!" McGregor cried out.

Cole swung Aed Deigh around as Corhagen slowly climbed to his feet. "You can't use that thing down here," James protested weakly. "You might start a fire. There are children inside this building."

"Very well," Cole said, switching to the other blade as Corhagen nearly lost his balance on the ice.

"That's not what I mean."

"Tear the courtspawn sidhe apart!" the principle barked as the Cu Sith drew closer. "But leave the mortal alive for me."

"In your dreams," Cole sneered as the first Cu Sith made his move. "I've been waiting for this."

The first fey wolf that jumped at Cole found himself seized by the back of the neck. Cole kicked another in the stomach, then brought his leg around to swipe at a third while his hand felt beneath the matted fur of the one in his grip. Sure enough, he felt metal pressed next to the skin. Bringing the Cu Sith around, he dug his fingers underneath the black ring and pulled as hard as he could. The wolf choked, needing air to stay conscious but not to remain alive, and gasped as the tip of Aed Deigh's red-hot blade slid underneath the ring. Cole jerked the hilt back as two more wolves jumped at him, and used the Cu Sith in his grasp to bat them away.

The black ring clanged to the floor. Cole tossed the freed wolf aside and kicked the ring away from him as it began beeping loudly. The other wolves scattered, their claws digging into the icy floor for traction as the explosion knocked them to their sides. The nearest one whimpered as Cole brought his blade in closer.

"It will all be over soon," he whispered, slicing the ring neatly away.

Thankfully, this one didn't explode. Principal McGregor was watching in shock and fury as Cole raised his sword up high.

"I did not come here to slay you," Cole shouted to the room. "Those of you that wish to be free from this madman, come to me now."

"Silence!" The principal raised the crystal up as it began to glow. "You all belong to me!"

"The hell they do," Cole replied, drawing Jabberwock out.

McGregor let out a high-pitched squeak and ducked as the bullet Cole fired missed him by just an inch or two. The crystal in his hand fell to the floor and rolled out of the way. The squat man chased after it, keeping his head low the whole time. Cole got off a few more shots before holstering his gun. The real threat at hand was the Cu Sith. So long as they remained under the principal's control, he and Corhagen were outnumbered.

Corhagen, meanwhile, had torn the sleeve of his shirt off and was using it to bandage his arm. Seeing McGregor duck down to retrieve his precious control device, Corhagen threw caution to the wind and took a flying leap at him. The room wasn't especially big, and Corhagen managed to cross the space between them with no problem. Just as McGregor rose with the clear glass object in hand, Corhagen slammed his whole body into him. The resulting crunch sounded like something one might hear at a Giants game.

McGregor, however, was not to be taken so lightly. Corhagen found himself flying through the air into a wall. McGregor had used James's own momentum to roll backward and flip the much heavier man off him. With the crystal in hand, he once more stood up, leering triumphantly.

"I've got it!" he crowed. "Come to me, my wolves. Tear this mortal bastard apart!"

Nothing happened.

"Ahem," Cole said mockingly. "I already removed all the rings from their necks."

McGregor looked over to where Cole was standing with Aed Deigh in hand as the remaining Cu Sith gathered round. The rings that had been controlling them were now scraps of metal frozen solid on the floor. The ice Cole had summoned to freeze the ground underneath the Cu Sith had disappeared. The wolves glared across the space between it, them, and McGregor, baring their teeth. McGregor gulped as he tightened his grip on the crystal in his hand.

It shined but could do nothing now.

"I'm curious to know how that crystal controls the black rings," Cole said, watching as the Cu Sith moved slowly toward McGregor. "But it looks to me like these guys want to have a word with you first, and I doubt any of them could be dissuaded by me. Plus, there is also the matter of you knocking my partner unconscious."

One of the Cu Sith snapped its jaws hungrily. "Assault on an officer of the law isn't a good idea," Cole went on. "Imprisoning the Cu Sith against their will is just plain stupid."

"You can't do this," the principal reasoned feebly as the wolves closed in around him. "You're with the police!"

"They don't exist," Cole reminded him coldly. "Neither do I, according to popular opinion, and you just knocked out your only eyewitness to the crime."

McGregor turned toward Corhagen and began shaking his motionless body as one of the wolves licked her chops eagerly.

Corhagen didn't stir. Soon, McGregor gave up and backed away into a corner.

"Don't hurt the other one," Cole told them. "He's with me."

"We won't," one wolf swore, not looking back.

"I can give you answers," McGregor pleaded as one wolf seized him by the leg. "Arrggh!" he cried out as the wolf worried it. "You want to know what this was all about, don't you?"

McGregor was cut off as his body began to jerk spastically. None of the other Cu Sith had touched him yet, however. The one with its jaws attached to his leg was thrown off with a sharp yip. McGregor howled in pain as his body convulsed for a moment. "I'm sorry!" he screamed. "I'm sorry!"

Cole watched through narrowed eyes as the Cu Sith kept a slight distance between them and their former master's body. One sniffed the air near McGregor as he calmed down.

"Forgive me." Cole wasn't sure who the man was talking to now. "I'll never do it again."

Cole watched as McGregor gasped for breath. The Cu Sith were moving in close again, though much less eagerly now. McGregor didn't act like he was concerned with their presence for the time being. His eyes were fixed on Cole. "There is one thing you should know," he said breathlessly.

"What's that?" Cole asked, standing perfectly still.

McGregor grinned then. "What's behind you!"

Something closed around Cole's neck with a snap. Cole thought he heard movement behind him as his fingers brushed over a thin strip of metal that circled all the way around his throat. He started to turn, but pain shot through his body before he could complete the movement, and the world faded into a haze of nightmarish pain.

Dimly, he could still feel Aed Deigh in his hands. One thing he had learned early on when being trained as a sidhe warrior was never drop his weapon for any reason. Cole gripped the hilt tightly as though it were his only saving grace from the agony coursing through his veins. It felt like hot iron and glass shards were being piped into his bloodstream now. The room had ceased to exist for him.

Forcing his eyes open, Cole looked down at himself and saw his skin turning gray. The pain had struck him so hard that tears were rolling down his face. Cole squinted through them and saw the discoloration for what it really was.

There were rolling clouds under the surface of his skin. Cole thought he might have been mistaken, but the swirling gray didn't dissipate when he gripped his wrist. It was just underneath the surface, spinning and spiraling as unseen wind and lightning rippled through it. His thick mane of hair had fallen to the sides of face. It was as black as soot.

The black ring was changing him. Cole tried to think through the pain, but it only grew with each attempt to force it away. The ring pulsed against his skin with each frantic beat of his heart. Whatever it was doing to him had sped up. He could feel it growing more powerful.

There was still earth beneath him. Cole felt it as he sank to his knees. Gripping Aed Deigh, he brought the hilt up and forced words from his lips.

They were little more than a whisper. *"God and Goddess,"* he hissed weakly. *"Help me, please!"*

All strength left his arms. Both fell to his chest, his hands still clutched around Aed Deigh as one of the blades automatically sprang out from the hilt. Cole felt the tip of it press to his throat, and through the vague awareness that was left in him, the intense heat burned his skin. Opening his eyes, Cole fought to raise his arms just a fraction higher.

The effort made his lungs seize up. Gasping, Cole began to cough as though his chest was caked with sulfur. His head jerked forward, and the tip of the blade pierced the metal ring digging into the flesh there. At once, the heat intensified. Cole managed to push the blade in just a little bit farther.

With a gasp from Cole, the ring snapped. Cole jerked his head up, sending the black ring rolling down his back. Air filled his lungs, sweet winter air of February blowing down from somewhere off to the side. Snow blasted his face, snapping him out of the drunken daze of pain. Cole looked around, confused by what his senses were telling him.

It did not take long to figure out what had happened.

There was a gigantic hole in the wall. More accurately, the hole was more like a trench leading diagonally down into the basement. It looked like a blizzard had invaded the space, coating everything in a thick layer of snow. Cole stood in the middle of a circle, the only space left in the whole basement where the concrete was still visible. Directly above him was another hole, this one roughly the same size as the circle he was standing in. It looked like a miniature tornado had sprung up around him and blasted through to the floor above.

Snow was slipping down through the opening there, leaving Cole with a very bad feeling. A Sir Frances North Academy student peered down through it tentatively, as though frightened by what he might find.

The black ring that had been fitted around his neck was not far away, sticking out from the mound of snow. It hadn't exploded. In the corner where Cole remembered seeing Corhagen last were the Cu Sith. They had piled on top of him when the disaster struck.

Principal McGregor, as well as his mysterious ally who had slipped the ring around Cole's throat, were nowhere to be seen.

Cole sighed, hanging his head low. "I'm really going to hear it over this one."

Chapter *Six*

THE wolves cleared out of the basement before the humans could take notice of them. Cole left them with instructions to find a place they could hide out in. He promised to come and find them just as soon as it was all over. None of them looked particularly comforted that he gave his word. The word of a banished sidhe, after all, was worth nothing. Still, in the end, they agreed that leaving before the humans saw them was a good idea.

Corhagen had to be taken to a nearby hospital so he could be patched up. Cole was surprised at how grateful he felt that the man was alive. It seemed his old friendship with the mortal ran deep in spite of their current bitter streak.

The doctor was curious to know how Corhagen had received what looked to be a wild animal bite on his arm during what was already being reported as an unexplained burst of snow and wind over the school. The humans were chalking it up to the unpredictability of Mother Nature. Cole had informed the good doctor that it was police business and on a need-to-know basis only.

Once Corhagen was patched up, Cole finally answered his cell phone. It had been ringing for some time. The caller ID showed it to be Joss.

He was not happy.

"I would just like to go on record as saying that this incident was not my fault," Cole said, finishing his report.

"How did whoever put that ring on you manage to get so close?" Joss wondered. "I've seen you in a fight before, and you're usually much more alert than that."

Cole paused. "I've been wondering about that. Corhagen was already knocked out, so there is no way he would know. It must have been another fey under McGregor's control. At least we know who is doing this now. I just wish I understood why."

There was silence on the other end for a moment. It sounded to Cole like his boyfriend was chewing on something. He suddenly had an amusing mental image of Joss munching on a bagel with cream cheese.

"How come that ring couldn't control you?" Joss asked once he had swallowed. "It worked on those wolves. What did you say they were called again?"

"Cu Sith," Cole answered. "And the wolves are lesser fey."

"How does that matter?"

Cole chose his words carefully. This was likely something that a human would take offense to. "There is a reason the sidhe rule over all of Faerie," he explained. "We might be smaller in number, but our power is far greater. All the different races have their magic, but ours was said to be the most powerful when we first came to the Goddess seeking asylum."

Joss was chewing on his bagel again. "Sorry," he said between bites. "Could you repeat that?"

Cole held the phone between his shoulder and head as he fished his car keys out of his front pocket. Corhagen had already been released and was waiting by the car. "It isn't a well-known fact," Cole said, pressing the unlock button on his key chain, "but the sidhe weren't created by Danu. She took us in when we had nowhere left to turn. Consort agreed to it if we would swear fealty to them and all their other children. Over time, the sidhe began to mingle in with the other races and eventually took over."

Corhagen had already climbed in. His bandaged arm wasn't slowing him down so far.

"Lesser fey are, in reality, the closest to Danu and her Consort that anyone could hope to get. The sidhe are much more devious and tricky. We got into Faerie, took over, and subjugated the other races through control of their crafts."

"Your lot sounds like a wonderful bunch of people," Joss mused.

"I am sidhe," Cole stated proudly. "But I have no court to speak of anymore. Whatever sins they may have committed cannot touch me. That whole banishment thing works both ways."

"I see." Joss sounded as though he didn't know what else to say. "Can you and Corhagen swing by the precinct so I can confirm you're both all right?"

"I was going to come by anyway," Cole reminded him, getting in. "You're still coming over tonight, right?"

Corhagen stiffened but didn't say anything. For once, the silence felt like less of an insult aimed at Cole's relationship with the inspector. The detective clearly hadn't come to terms with it yet, but going by his body language, he wasn't going to make a big deal out of it right now.

Strangely, Cole felt a pinch of gratitude.

"I don't think I'm going to make it," Joss was saying. "The day still isn't over for me, and I'm exhausted. I think I'm just going to get one of the guys to take me home once this is over with and hit the sack."

"Oh." Cole was fighting his disappointment, but he'd been hoping to spend another night with Joss in his bed beside him.

"We'll make it work," Joss said, and Cole knew he wasn't speaking solely of this one night. "Come to the interrogation room once you get here."

"You still haven't made any headway on Foleman." It wasn't a question. "It's strange that a human could stand being locked up in such a small space all day."

"He's not happy," Joss affirmed. "He hasn't had anything to eat and is making his displeasure over the fact well known. We've had numerous threats from him to sue for police brutality once his lawyer gets here. Speaking of which, he called the guy last night, supposedly, but no one has showed up to defend this bastard."

"Maybe the lawyer got a better offer?"

"It was the number for a real high-price firm," Joss said. "So that is possible. I wonder what made Foleman think he could afford a group like that, though. He's got money, but not enough for these guys."

Cole thought of something then. "Let me talk to him."

Joss said nothing.

"You want me to come down there anyway," Cole pointed out.

"We know Foleman is afraid of me. He tried to rip his way through the bars of his cage when he first saw me."

Joss was considering it now.

"I should have thought of this before," Cole added. "I've wanted to know since then why he acted so terrified. I think I may be getting old."

Joss chuckled softly then. It wasn't a happy sound, though. "Hurry up and get here," he said. "If Foleman doesn't break down and tell us something soon, we'll have to put him back in his cell."

"I'm on my way."

Corhagen was watching Cole as he hung the phone up. "News?"

"Maybe," Cole said, starting the car. "Joss wants us back at the precinct. He needs help cracking a nut."

"He should use a hammer."

It was the first time in a long while that Corhagen had made a joke while alone with him. The shock took a moment to wear off. "That was what I said to him," Cole replied. "More importantly, though, where was your sense of humor hiding when you found it?"

Corhagen laughed, though only a little. "Can I ask you a question?" he asked after some hesitation.

"You just did."

"Right." Corhagen sighed. "What do you know about dreams?"

Those words carried a heavy weight to them, along with a foreboding sense of déjà vu. "You've asked me that question before," Cole said with a hint of caution in his voice. "I told you the same thing before. Dreams were never really my specialty."

"I remember." Corhagen said nothing for a moment. "I've been having them again," he confessed while the car moved along through the falling snow.

It was dark now, and almost impossible to see the road. Had Cole been in any other vehicle, he would have been fighting off panic.

"You should speak with someone who understands dreams," Cole advised. "I told you that last time as well. Your dreams have foretelling properties to them. If you've been having *those* types of dreams, it must be for a reason."

"That's what I think." Corhagen seemed to be deliberating over something. "I'm okay with you and Joss," he blurted out. "Really, I am."

The vehicle turned onto the main road with Cole barely gripping the wheel.

"No, you're not," Cole said it in a matter-of-fact tone. "Everything about you lately says you aren't okay. I'm sorry if it is something you can't accept. I'm sorry that the fact I don't share the same beliefs and wasn't raised under the same moral umbrella as you were bothers you so much."

Corhagen looked like he had been bitten again. He was clinging to the door now as though ready to barrel-roll out of it any second.

"I'm sorry that you wanted me out of your life," Cole went on. "I didn't ask to be a part of Section Thirteen, though. I had no plans of becoming a cop."

"You could have said no." Corhagen's voice was bitter now. "You didn't have to agree to do it."

"I had my own reasons for doing it," Cole countered. "Whatever they are, you don't need to know. As Joss already said, it isn't any concern of yours."

Feeling like he had just lit a stick of dynamite in the seat next to him, Cole pressed the radio button and cranked up the volume to block out Corhagen's presence. When they finally reached the precinct garage, the snow had gotten worse. It was nothing compared to the storm raging in Cole's heart. He could almost see the same clouds whirling underneath his skin that had been there before, when the black ring had snapped around his neck.

Cole didn't wait for Corhagen. The mortal would have only slowed him down.

Joss was waiting for him outside the interrogation room along with a couple of guards. "Where's Corhagen?" he asked as Cole stormed up to him, his skin giving off a faint glow.

"Later," Cole replied. "Is Foleman still in there?"

Joss nodded. "He still won't talk. He hasn't said much in the last hour or so, unless you count the number of times he's complained about how cold it is. I was getting sick of hearing the same old song, so I came out here to wait on you."

"Let's go."

Cole opened the door and stepped through, his eyes staring straight at the spot where he knew Foleman would be sitting. Foleman's eyes widened sharply and nearly popped right out of his head the moment he laid eyes on him.

The man handled Cole's entrance well, considering.

"Let me out of here!" Foleman screamed, fighting to yank his fat hands out of the handcuffs. "I mean it. He's come here to kill me. You can't do this. You're the police!"

"I wouldn't tell them how to do their jobs if I were you," Cole warned, taking a seat at the opposite end from where Foleman struggled. "They've had a long day."

Foleman was paying Cole no heed. He had yet to stop panicking. "I'm serious!" he shouted at the guards standing in the door frame. "If you let him kill me, that's a dereliction of your duty!"

"Give us a few minutes," Joss told both guards, who were watching as though they weren't sure if the scenario was funny or dangerous. When neither one of them moved, Joss pointed to the hall behind them. "Move it," he ordered. "I'm staying here to make sure nothing happens to the guy."

With that reassurance, both officers left without argument. Foleman really started to lose it then. Someone had handcuffed his arms behind his back and, it looked like, through the rungs of the chair. Meaning that Foleman couldn't so much as stand at this point. Someone had evidently gotten very frustrated with him.

"You look as though you've been there for a while," Cole noted. "That cannot be comfortable. Were I human and in your position, I would be grateful for a chance to get those handcuffs off and stretch a bit."

Foleman grew quieter. "You're going to let me out?"

Both Cole and Joss snickered. "Not on your life," Joss answered.

Foleman planted his ass back down into the seat and pouted his lower lip out. "I wanna talk to a lawyer. Why hasn't my lawyer showed up yet? This is a serious breach of justice!"

"We don't know where your lawyer is," Cole said earnestly. "As far as we know, he was supposed to arrive shortly after you used your one phone call to speak with him. If he decided it would be better for you to rot here, I can't say I disagree with him. The only downside to this is my boyfriend is getting tired and would like to go home before the weather makes that impossible."

Foleman looked over toward Joss at mention of the word "boyfriend." "You two funny for each other?" he spat.

"I wouldn't be pointing fingers," Cole retorted humorously. "Especially with your track record. Your golems kidnapped young boys for you and cooked them alive, then fed the remains to you through your cage. The bodies we were able to find looked like they'd been gnawed on."

Joss didn't look so confident now. Cole pretended not to notice and kept all his attention focused on Foleman, who didn't look so sure himself.

"I was starving," he mumbled, looking away. "There was nothing I could do. I told them I needed to get out of town, needed to find someplace safe to hide, but they misunderstood. They thought I was just leaving them."

"So they put you in a safe place," Cole said, piecing it together. "The safest place they could think of, and they brought some of your favorites to you."

Foleman's eyes sharpened. "I have nothing to say about that," he shot out quickly.

"You don't have to," Cole replied, shrugging. "A lesser man might feel sorry for you. You were being held hostage and desperate for nourishment."

Cole waited, and Foleman's eyes slowly rose to meet his. "I am a survivor, Foleman," he said in a deliberate voice. "I have done things for years, longer than your tiny brain can fathom, that I wasn't proud of. I'm even less proud of them now, but I did what I did to survive. I might sympathize with your situation some small bit, but Inspector Vallimun here doesn't."

Joss glanced at Cole and said nothing.

"At the end of the day, no matter how hungry you were, you ate children to stay alive. And those golems fed them to you thinking you would like it. Magic isn't the same as pushing buttons to get a result.

You had to pour some of yourself into those things to get the kind of reaction they had to you. They must have brought you children before, and since you needed food, that must have been the same thing in what passed for their minds. So they brought some of your favorite young boys to you as a snack to keep you alive."

Foleman was drawing into himself now, as though trying to retreat from Cole's words.

Cole did not let up. "I bet they tasted real good," he whispered. "Somewhere in your mind where you justify all your actions, their roasted bodies were sweet, just like when they were alive."

"Stop it!" Foleman hissed fiercely.

"Making excuses for your actions must be easy," Cole went on calmly. "You've done it for years now. I've lived a long time. I've heard humans left and right try to justify their actions. I've done things I wasn't proud of, and I've done things that I am outright ashamed of to this day, but they were decisions I made. In the end, I live with them rather than hiding behind a mask of lies."

"Shut up." Foleman's voice was little more than a grunt now, yet it carried a white-hot agony buried beneath those words. "No more."

"Humans will go to great lengths to preserve their self-esteem. You have, and so did all those people at the schools where you taught. They needed to save face, so you were swept out the back door quietly like something that smelled bad. You've been the dirty little secret of quite a few people over the years."

"You can't do this." Spittle flew from Foleman's mouth as he snarled at Cole. "I know my rights. Nothing was proven! You can't talk to me like this."

Cole stretched one arm over the back of his seat casually. His left leg rose to stretch out over the corner of the table. Cole might have been posing for a picture. Joss was waiting behind him, ready to jump in any second. Foleman looked like he wanted to break free from his bonds and wrap both hands around Cole's throat. His fingers were fat enough to cover all of one side. However, Cole thought Joss was preparing to protect Foleman from him.

Knowing what this would do to his love, Cole reined himself back in a little. He just hoped Joss didn't interfere yet. Foleman was nearly ready now, and it would only take a little bit more to break through. Drawing his power to him, Cole let it drift through the air across the table ever so slightly. The invisible threads of his glamour touched Foleman's face with their tips.

He flinched slightly.

"Tell me about them," Cole said, the magic coming out with his breath.

Foleman was clamming up again. Cole needed to break through the barrier he'd erected around himself to seize the truth hidden behind it. Steeling himself, he drew in a deep breath and struck home. "They want you dead. You thought I was with them when we found you in that cage. You said that I'd come to kill you, but you were wrong."

Foleman peeked out at that.

"I was never sent to kill you," Cole revealed. "Only find you. If I were to put the word out, though, they would find you here. That is what you've been so worried about all this time. There aren't many places to run inside a jail cell, and you have no means of working alchemy here to escape. All your supplies were confiscated."

Foleman trembled.

"They are going to find you," Cole told him confidently. "You know that and so do I. Sooner or later, they will find out how you were arrested and brought here. It will be simple for them to kill you. There are cops everywhere in this building, but you and I are from a different world than most people. We know there are ways to murder a man that the police will never catch sight of."

"Don't let them kill me."

Cole waited a moment before speaking. "Pardon?" he asked, tilting his head. "Would you mind repeating that?"

"Don't let them kill me," Foleman whispered. It sounded as though all the life were being sucked out of his voice. "I was just doing a job," he went on. "They said I would be paid well if I could figure it out for them. Money was tight after the Order had me blacklisted."

Cole's eyes narrowed. "The Order?"

Foleman shook his head. Clearly, he'd said too much. "They said that their employer wanted the code cracked, and he thought I would be able to do it. I was already given some in advance. The bakery barely made enough to pay for itself, and the house was in need of repairs. With what they were willing to dish out, though, I could move to a different town and start over."

"You were working on an experiment in alchemy for someone else."

Cole waited a moment, then risked brushing Foleman's mind gently with his glamour again. The contact made him jump hard this time.

Foleman looked around the room wildly. "What was that?" he demanded in a broken voice. "What did you just do to me?"

"Calm down," Joss said. "No one here is going to hurt you, Mr. Foleman."

Joss was trying to play the role of the good cop, but Foleman was having none of it. "First I get death threats and weird things following me wherever I go. Then two golems I made go berserk and hold me hostage. The cage was bad enough, but I refuse to be held prisoner here."

Foleman took a deep breath. "Help!"

Cole knew without a doubt that the interrogation was over. Foleman was screaming his head off, causing the noise to reverberate off the walls. A moment later, the door swung open, and several officers entered the room with guns drawn.

"Get me out of here!" Foleman demanded as he fought to free himself from his chair. "He's trying to kill me. They're doing something to my brain. They're making me say things I don't mean to. This is a violation of my rights. I want a lawyer. I want a lawyer!"

"Get him out of here," Joss barked, pointing. "Take him back to his cell."

Foleman struggled the whole way. With a thoughtful expression, Cole watched him being dragged off.

Joss, on the contrary, seemed relieved to be rid of him. "That went well," he mused sarcastically.

"A lot better than I had thought it would," Cole said, looking out the open door. "I don't suppose you were listening closely when he mentioned 'the Order'."

"I was. Does it mean anything?"

"It might," Cole said, not looking at him. "Although I hope I am wrong for once and it has no bearing whatsoever on this case. Can you do something for me?"

"What?" Joss took a seat near Cole and stared over the table at him. "What is the Order?"

"The Hermetic Order of the Golden Dawn," Cole said. "They are a group of practitioners that began in the 1800s. Most of them were already well off when the Order began, so it mainly consists of the elite and powerful seeking enlightenment. They hate the fey."

Cole remained deep in thought for a moment.

"What does it all mean?" Joss asked hesitatingly. "What do you need?"

Cole sighed. "If I am right, we are all in serious jeopardy. I need you to do some digging through the records of that school over on Staten. Suddenly, I have an idea as to why the mayor and chief of police were so keen on us solving the murder that occurred there."

"I'll get someone on it right away," Joss said. "Why do you think the Order is involved?"

Cole said nothing at first. When he did, finally, it was in a serious tone. "I think the Order may be tied into the school. You mentioned in your office that Foleman had been a teacher there briefly. He said that the Order blacklisted him. If the Order has control over the school, they might have had him banned to keep a scandal from going public."

"But what makes you think this Order is behind that particular school?"

"Because," Cole sighed. "I'm getting old. There was something about that place that was bothering me from the start. Different fey were being subjugated. That is right up the Order's alley. And that name...."

"Whose name?" Cole didn't answer again. "You're starting to worry me, MacColewyn. What does the Order have to do with you?"

Cole stood up. "Not here," he said. "Let's go somewhere else to talk first."

Joss stood with him. "Where?"

"My car," said Cole, already moving for the door. "Less chance we will be overheard there."

Cole kept his hands near both guns as they made their way out to the garage. Joss kept a safe distance away in case all hell broke loose. He wasn't sure what to expect at this point, but Cole was acting suspicious enough to put him on edge.

"All right," he said once they were safely inside Cole's new vehicle. "You said that this Order was made up of the rich and powerful and that they're looking for—"

"A bunch of amateur practitioners," Cole countered. "They like to think of themselves as hotshot wizards and sorcerers. For whatever the reason, they regard the fey as lesser beings. It's not so surprising, really, considering how the last few millennia have run in this realm. Lots of other creatures don't care for the fey in general."

Joss waited a moment for the sour disposition in Cole's face to fade slightly. "So Foleman was a member of the Order?"

"Most likely. Either that or he worked for them. I'm guessing after the incident at the school, they regarded him as a liability. His grandparents die and leave him the bakery and house, no doubt a small bit of good fortune, but neither one would support themselves. Someone came to him and offered the man a pile of cash if he would do a job for them."

"That was what caught my attention the most," Joss said, shifting more comfortably in his seat. "He said someone wanted him to do a job. We know he was experimenting with alchemy. Speaking of which, I could use the name of one of those experts you mentioned before."

"I'll call them later," Cole said. "Assuming they're interested, we might see them as early as tomorrow morning."

"Excellent. What will we do with Foleman in the meantime, though?"

Cole shrugged. "Keep him locked up and hope whoever wants him dead hasn't found him yet. At this point, I don't know if it was the Order who hired him or wanted him dead. It could be both."

"He thought you were with this Order?" Joss asked, sounding skeptical. "I thought you said they hate the fey."

"He thought I was their servant," Cole explained. "Most likely, anyway."

"The Order is behind the school," he affirmed a second later. "I should have recognized their logo on the windows in the two front doors. What they wanted with Foleman and why they want him dead now is anyone's guess, though."

Joss sighed long and deep. "When we step in it, there's no going back. Sometimes I wish I could just chuck this damn badge and walk away from it all."

Cole looked at him for a moment. "Why don't you?"

"I don't know," Joss confessed, looking forlorn. "I guess it's because if I didn't do it, nobody else would."

"Your compassion could spell the end of you," Cole warned playfully. "Or is it glory you're seeking?"

"Glory," Joss said flatly. "Without a doubt, glory."

The two stared out through the windshield. The parking garage was silent save for the sound of traffic moving sluggishly through the city streets beyond. Wind kicked up, blowing snow into the building.

"It sounds like the storm is getting worse," Joss noted.

"It always worsens before it gets better," Cole said. "Someone is enslaving my people, Joss. I can't let this continue."

Joss didn't answer. Instead, his hand snaked over to Cole's and entwined with it. Joss's fingers playfully stroked over the hairless knuckles of Cole's hand for a moment. Cole responded by giving the hand a squeeze, careful not to break his mortal lover's fingers. Neither one said anything. There was nothing left to do but sit and enjoy the quietness inside the car.

All too soon, it was time for it to be over. "Do you want me to give you a ride home?" Cole asked.

"One of the other guys agreed to give me a lift," Joss said, shaking his head. "I've still got some things to wrap up here first. Thanks for offering, though."

"Anytime." Cole gave Joss's hand one last gentle squeeze before releasing him. "Anytime."

It was a long, lonely drive back to the sithen. Cole felt like his heart weighed a ton in his chest as he located the garage. It had gone back to its former hiding place on Fifth Avenue. The garage door opened without any prompting from him. The car seemed to know he was out of sorts and drove itself the rest of the way in without a fuss.

Once inside, Cole climbed out and headed for the door to his home. All he wanted after the events of today was some peace and quiet. He would have liked to share it with Joss, but that hadn't been in the cards this time. Feeling miserable, he opened the door and cast out his wish to the sithen for it to take him to his room as quickly as possible.

Instead, Cole found himself standing in a narrow corridor next to the kitchen. Furthermore, a fight was going on. The kitchen was a shambles, and a fire had started on the stove. It smelled like something rotten had been boiling. A metal bowl missed his head by inches and clattered noisily against the wall.

Inside the kitchen, Boogaloo was screaming at Mal, who had split himself into twins again. Both were yelling at the wood goblin, who responded with his shrill cries and by flashing his claws in their faces. This did little to dissuade them, as Mal was neither truly flesh nor actually standing there in front of him. Being a part of the sithen, Mal formed a body for himself simply because it was convenient.

Cole didn't bother trying to work out why they were arguing. Silently, he drew out Jabberwock and pointed the gun skyward, then fired.

The noise cut through their yelling like a knife.

"I have had a very long day," Cole said, punctuating each word through gritted teeth. "It has not been easy going out into the snow-covered streets trying to find out exactly what is going on and who is responsible. I would like to think a former sorcerer and a wood goblin could occupy the same space while I'm gone without creating chaos all around them. I especially would think this after taking into consideration the fact that said space is theoretically infinite, and therefore capable of providing them with ample room, should they start to feel crowded."

Mal and Boogaloo looked toward one another tentatively.

"I am going to take a hot shower," Cole finished, putting his gun away. "Following that, I might look in on our other guest, the one who apparently hasn't made a mess all over this room. In the meantime, why don't both of you find something more constructive to do with your time before I decide to use each of you as target dummies."

With that having been said, Cole marched past them to the other side of the room, where the exit was. This time, the sithen showed him to a door Cole hadn't seen for a while. This brought him to his room, where the connecting bathroom was already open and lit.

Cole shed his clothes at once and went in. The shower turned on hot and ready for him. Cole let the day wash off his body as he thought of the last few times he'd stood in here with Joss next to him. Though the shower was spacious, their bodies had always managed to brush against each other. Cole was missing the inspector something fierce. It actually felt a little odd.

It took a long time before Cole felt clean. Afterward, however, he was in higher spirits as he toweled off and wrapped the fabric around his waist. The sidhe were not a modest bunch, but Cole had lived long enough among humans to consider such things. He wanted to check in on Jynx, and there was no way of knowing how she might react to his naked form. It was best to be prepared.

Mal, it turned out, had put her in a room far, far away from his. Whether this was foresight on the part of the former sorcerer or just the sithen taking Jynx's personal feelings into account Cole wasn't sure. The door was locked, and Cole had to knock three times before it clicked open. Jynx was standing on the other side wearing a pair of smoke-colored cargo pants several sizes too big for her. They were held up by a pair of suspenders stretched taut over her breasts, which were partially concealed by a velvet tank top.

Mal must have supplied the clothes for her.

"I wanted to see how you were doing," Cole said. "Everything okay?"

Jynx had already seized him by the hand and was dragging him inside. Cole wondered briefly if she was thinking of the same thing he was and whether the honorable thing to do was to turn around and leave. He was totally out of his element, having had no experience with changelings or the morals they adhered to.

It turned out to be a moot point. Jynx was leading him over to her bed, but for the purpose of showing him something. Cole noticed several boxes of crayons scattered all over it. There were sheets of construction paper that had been scribbled on. Light from a computer monitor in the corner spilled over them.

Cole looked down at one sheet in particular that Jynx seemed keen for him to see. "What is it?" he asked, picking it up.

The drawing was of Jynx. Now that Cole was holding it up and giving the paper his full attention, he could see she hadn't scribbled at all. Jynx had used the different crayons to capture her appearance.

It was breathtaking. "You did this?" he affirmed, feeling foolish for asking.

Jynx nodded enthusiastically nonetheless. Quickly, she snatched the paper out of his hand and pressed several others there. The first one was an overhead view of a grotto of trees. It was twilight, and a girl Cole thought was Jynx again was dancing in circles around a bonfire with a very young boy. The two appeared close, though Cole couldn't accurately explain why he thought that.

"Who is that?" he asked her, pointing to the boy.

Jynx's eyes grew darker as she showed him another picture. It was of a man dressed in robes befitting royalty. Around the man were dancing shadows whose leering faces gave Cole chills. Wolves had been added at the edges, keeping their heads down low.

Cole didn't need to ask. "The one who calls himself the Lord of All Fey," he said. "He's the one who used the black rings. You knew each other when he was a boy. That's what you were doing on that island."

Jynx nodded sadly.

"You were going to stop him," he whispered in a low voice. "You didn't want me hurting the wolves because you knew he was controlling them."

Jynx took the drawing on top away. Cole looked down and saw a close-up image of a black ring. It was drawn exactly as he remembered but with much finer detail. Now that he had a closer look, Cole could make out several things he'd missed. The inside of the ring, for instance, was covered in runes. Cole couldn't read the language, but it almost seemed like the runes were wired in with the ring's circuitry.

"Technology and magic," Cole realized. "That's why the Lord of All Fey can control lesser fey so easily. It isn't just magic that he's using against them. The fey have a harder time coping against human technology, so he combines it with magic to enslave them."

Cole turned to Jynx again. "But where did he learn to do this?"

Jynx responded by pulling the drawing out of the pile. Cole started to look down at it, but she quickly pulled another from farther down and laid it on top.

It was the shadows again. Cole counted twelve of them in all. They had formed a circle and captured the false lord. The figure's face was concealed. He had curled up into a frightened ball at the sight of them.

"I don't quite understand," Cole told her. "The Lord of All Fey… he's doing this because of something else? Who are these?"

Jynx frowned and shook her head. By her eyes, Cole could see she didn't know the answer any more than he did.

The next question that came to mind made him pause. "This friend of yours," Cole said, pointing to the other picture where the false lord was standing surrounded by laughing shadows and wolves. "Why didn't you stop him before all this?"

Jynx looked grief-stricken for a moment, but her eyes displayed none of the anger he'd been expecting. Instead, Jynx moved the picture on top away. Cole saw her there in the woods again, this time running from what looked like a fleet of giant cats with fire in their eyes. The look of terror on Jynx's face was palpable.

"Cait Sith," Cole said, understanding. "You were chased away by Cait Sith, the fey cats who serve the middle houses of nobility in Faerie. Were they the ones you escaped from?"

Jynx nodded.

"They must have found you," Cole went on, narrating the story on her behalf. "You had to run so he wouldn't get involved. It must have been difficult."

Jynx sat down on the bed, holding her hands tightly together. Cole put the pages aside and sat next to her. The fey, when lonely or upset, tended to touch one another. Humans had a whole different set of guidelines about such things, and he had no clue as to which ones Jynx might value now. Cautiously, he put an arm around her shoulder. When she drew toward him instead of away, Cole took that as a sign and pulled her in close.

"He was your friend," he said, piecing the story together at last. "You played together, but when the Cait Sith came, you had to leave.

They were going to drag you back to Faerie and probably would've taken him as well. By the time you'd escaped them and thought it was safe, your friend had grown up. The shadows, whoever they are, had done something to him."

Jynx wrapped her arms around Cole's neck and pulled him in closer. Cole nuzzled her neck and blew his sweet breath over her hair, causing the stray hairs to pull away and dance around one another. Slowly, he began to sing to her. Jynx closed her eyes and listened, wearing a sad smile as the words drifted through her. When he had finished, she pulled away to look at him.

Cole smiled and felt a shimmer in the air. Looking around Jynx, he saw Mal standing next to the computer wearing a surprised expression.

"I thought I would come and check how things were going," he stammered, eyes wide as dinner plates. "It would appear they are going fine, so I'll just leave."

"How's the kitchen looking?" Cole cut across sharply.

"Right." Mal nodded. "I'll see to that right away."

Jynx smiled, then turned her head back to Cole. Her eyes had gone from laughing to sorrowful in a split instant. Without words, Cole knew what she was asking. He could see it in the unshed tears that were threatening to spill down her cheeks. The Lord of All Fey had once been a friend to her. Jynx knew why he had gone all the way over to Staten Island and what he planned to do once the dawn came. She wasn't asking him to put a stop to the so-called Lord of All Fey.

She was asking for his help.

SUNRISE brought with it a new day in the epic struggle between Mother Nature's snowstorm and the denizens of New York. A truce had been declared for the moment, however, and the humans who called the labyrinth of glass and plastic home were out early, making the most of it. Snow was falling by the time Cole entered the fray of traffic, but it was such a light mist that most didn't bother giving it notice. The sun was even trying to grace Manhattan with its touch by piercing the blanket of clouds. It didn't last long, naturally, but Cole appreciated the moment, however brief.

No one said a word to Cole as he wandered through the precinct. He was used to the silent treatment by now, and it wasn't like he had made a lot of friends in the few years prior when he was a consultant. Cole just ignored his fellow officers and continued on to Joss's office. If the day ever came, he knew he wouldn't have them watching his back. It was a lonely truth to live with, but Cole had been living with harsh realities for as long as he could remember.

Joss was not in his office. The door wasn't locked, though, so Cole strode on in and took a seat behind the desk. He needed to use the phone, and since he'd forgotten to do so before leaving the sithen, now seemed as good a time as any. It sounded childish, but Cole rather fancied the idea of making an official police phone call from behind Joss's desk.

It took four rings before Rainette DuBois answered. Cole was expecting her to sound agitated. The witch didn't disappoint.

"Who is this?" she demanded in lieu of a greeting. "If this is about that hot water heater, you can just shove it. I've got better things to do right now."

"Greetings, Rainette," Cole said cheerily. "You seem to be taking to the early spring snow rather well. In fact, I would go as far as to say it's done wonders for your outlook."

Rainette was silent. "I know that voice," she mumbled to herself. "Cole, is this you?"

"It is," he said. "How have you been?"

"Lousy," she replied.

Cole thought he heard a man's voice in the background. "Yeah, get over it!" Rainette barked away from the receiver. "Sorry, that was my ex. He doesn't quite understand that we don't live together anymore. Anyway, I'm supposed to pass a message on to you. The other girls from Pagan Studies are pissed. None of us saw you at Katalina's funeral."

Cole swallowed the thick lump that had suddenly grown in his throat. "I was there," he assured her. "I just thought it would be better to stay out of sight during the ceremony. In case you'd forgotten, Katalina's family didn't approve of me much. Neither did you, now that

I think about it. It seemed like the honorable thing."

Rainette grew quiet. "I looked for you," she said softly. "None of us thought you would skip out on it. We all knew how much she meant to you."

"She meant the world to me," Cole said. A moment later, he added, "I failed her."

Rainette snorted. "No one blamed you, stupid. This is New York, and even the home of a former sidhe noble is at a high risk of being burglarized. Katalina just had the rotten luck of being home at the time."

"They were looking for me," he confessed. "She was killed because they had come there looking for me."

Rainette wasn't dissuaded. "Rotten luck," she repeated. "It happens. Katalina would have your hide if she knew you were beating yourself up over her dying. I heard she went out with a bang."

The compassion from Rainette caught Cole by surprise. It took a moment to sink in, and even then, the sensation settled into his belly like a lead weight. Rainette had never shown anything but contempt for him before. Her defending him in the face of their mutual friend's death was not something he'd anticipated.

Cole wasn't sure he wanted it, either.

"So, to what do I owe the honor of this call?" she went on. "It can't be because you missed being the recipient of my charm and winning smile. Since Katalina isn't here to referee, that must mean you're in some serious trouble."

"What made you think that?" Cole wondered curiously.

"You're desperate enough to call me," Rainette pointed out. "Either you've dug yourself into a hole from which China is visible or the world is getting ready to tear itself apart like in that movie we watched together."

"Actually I was wondering if you would be willing to come downtown to Precinct 1021. We've come across a case where this wacko was working on some kind of alchemy experiment. That was always more your expertise than mine, so I was hoping you'd be willing to decode the perp's papers. I can't make sense of it."

"So you're still working as a police consultant," Rainette mused. "That's a surprise."

"As a matter of fact, I'm a cop now."

The silence on the other end of the line was one normally reserved for the split second after a shot had been fired. Cole thought briefly that Rainette might have suffered a heart attack until she spoke again.

"Could you repeat that?" she asked slowly. "I didn't hear you correctly."

"I'm a special detective for Section Thirteen," Cole elaborated. "We're an undercover branch of the NYPD that works at solving occult crimes and murders involving the supernatural. James Corhagen is also a member, if you recall him."

Rainette was quiet again for a moment. "Excuse me," she said, putting the phone down. "I'll be right back."

Cole sighed impatiently and waited as the sounds of Rainette's hysterical laughter drifted through the other receiver and to his end. Several minutes went by with no end in sight. Finally, Rainette picked the phone up again, gasping. It sounded as though she'd been hyperventilating. "I'm fine," she assured him. "I'm fine."

Cole rolled his eyes.

"So," Rainette continued. "You're a cop now. How did this happen? Were the NYPD really that desperate?"

"It seems so," he retorted. "Would you be willing to help or not?"

Rainette took a long time coming to her decision. "I have to be at work soon," she said. "It isn't like I can just drop everything for you at a moment's notice."

Cole sighed yet again. "Come down to the station and have a look at the research papers. You know more about this stuff than any of Katalina's friends. Do this, and I'll see what I can do about getting you put in the computer as a consultant. That way, you're getting paid. You'll get a consultant's fee for decoding this guy's work and won't be behind on your rent."

Rainette had always had trouble paying rent on time. The promise of extra cash along with a little flattery was enough to tip her over the edge. "I'll call in sick at work," she said, fumbling around with something. "What time do you need me there?"

"As soon as possible," Cole told her. "I'll have someone waiting for you at the front door. They can take you to where the research was stored away so you can have a look at it. Better yet, I'll have it brought up to Joss's office. He's the one in charge of Section Thirteen."

"Got it," Rainette said. "Be there as soon as I can."

Cole hung up and pushed the chair away from the desk. Now all he had to do was figure out how to go about getting Rainette approved as a consultant and find someone willing to bring those boxes of research papers up here. Joss would probably know how to get Rainette approved, assuming his phone was turned on. Cole started to pull his out when his eyes caught sight of someone passing by the open door.

Jumping up, Cole ran out into the hallway. "Hey!" he called out, feeling stupid for not knowing the officer's name. "Hold up."

The officer stopped and turned around. It was the same guy that had helped them search Foleman's place.

"Officer...." Cole had to get closer to him in order to read the name on his badge. It was in much tinier print than usual. "Staffelbach?"

"That's me," the guy said, giving Cole a nod. "Can I help you?"

Before Cole could open his mouth, an alarm blared through the hallway, cutting him off. "Code 10-32 in holding cell area!" a woman's voice shouted over the PA system. "Code 10-32 in holding cell. All available officers respond immediately!"

The call continued alongside the noise of the alarm. Cole didn't waste time racking his brain to remember what the code meant. The way Staffelbach's face paled before he took off in the direction of the holding cells below was more than enough. Cole charged after him and had caught up in seconds. Officer Staffelbach already had his baton out and ready. Cole drew Bandersnatch and Jabberwock as they hit the stairs.

Down below in the holding cells, it was pure pandemonium. Something, and Cole had a vague impression as to what it was, had busted right through the concrete wall as though it were toilet paper. Injured officers were scattered everywhere. Some of them looked dead.

Up ahead, the doors leading to the cells had been ripped right off. Cole charged through them without hesitation. To his great shock, however, Staffelbach was right behind him.

"Get back," he warned. "If what I think did this is still here, you won't be able to handle it."

Staffelbach pointed to his badge in answer and ran right past him. Short of stature though he might have been, the man was nothing but pure balls in the face of danger. Cole couldn't help but admire that, though it was certain to get the poor bastard torn to shreds in a moment.

Sure enough, Cole spotted the ogre up ahead a second later. The stench it'd left behind in its wake was overpowering now. Staffelbach was standing boldly in front of it, gripping his baton tight enough to turn his knuckles pale. The ogre's skin was elm green with spots of pine that could have been freckles. Its orange eyes stared at Staffelbach as it swung the head of Richard Foleman around in a circle.

"There goes the taxpayers' money that would have been spent on a trial," Cole mused, taking aim with his guns. "And people say the police aren't doing their part to conserve during the economic crisis."

Cole fired, but neither bullet hit its mark. The ogre was moving around too much, and Officer Staffelbach had made the incredibly poor choice of getting right in front of the creature. The ogre was using the head of Richard Foleman like a small club, swinging it around. Staffelbach managed to duck out of the way, but the ogre was advancing with each swing, and there was just enough of the officer's small frame to block any decent shot Cole might have had.

That wasn't to say Staffelbach was doing nothing. Each time the ogre swung at him and took a step forward, Staffelbach ducked down and jabbed the beast in the knee with his baton. So far, it had had the effect of making the beast mad. Cole kept both guns ready in case a clear shot became available. As the ogre moved in closer, however, he happened to step into a patch of sunlight coming through a barred window. The light reflected off something on the ogre's arm, and Cole's eyes were fast enough to catch what it was.

Holstering both guns, Cole drew out Aed Deigh instead and brought forth the red-hot blade of fire. "Staffelbach," he barked, preparing to spring, "bring him this way!"

Staffelbach kept taking jabs at the ogre's knees every chance he got even as he backed away toward the direction of Cole's voice.

"Freeze!" someone behind Cole shouted.

Cole turned around to find the cavalry had arrived. It was perfect timing in the worst possible way. Sweeping his blade around, Cole summoned forth a wall of fire that blocked the entire hallway. Both he and the ogre vanished from the other officers' sight under the intensity of the blaze. From behind it, several men cried out in surprise at the unexpected wave of heat.

Turning back to the more pressing issue, Cole waited for the ogre to take one more pivotal step. Guns weren't such a good idea in this case, since the target was so small. Having an entire hallway filled with bullets would only make things worse. Cole took a chance and leaped just as Staffelbach managed to dodge out of the way. Instead of leaping at the ogre, however, Cole jumped up onto the wall as the flames behind him started to die down.

One of the officers shouted as he rebounded off it and hurled himself toward the beast's frame. Staffelbach was knocked out of the way just as Cole swiped at the black ring fitted tightly around the ogre's arm. Aed Deigh sliced the device off cleanly, cutting into the flesh and muscle of the creature in the process. The ogre howled from the pain, then abruptly fell silent.

Cole stepped back out of the way, snatching Staffelbach off the floor as well as the ogre fell forward and passed out against the solid wall.

"Are you alive?" he asked the brave, if incredibly foolish, officer. "On second thought, my first question is what gave you the idea that attacking an ogre was a good idea? Once you've answered that, feel free to tell me whether you lived through it or not."

"I'm alive," Staffelbach said, laughing painfully. "A little banged up, but I'll recover. Did you just call that thing an ogre?"

"It is an ogre," Cole said. "Wait here. I want to go see if this poor fellow killed anyone else during his rampage."

"How do you know it's a he?" Staffelbach called out as Cole marched around the turn in the corridor and out of sight.

"Look between his legs," Cole yelled back. Just barely, he could hear the officer reply.

"Oh, I see."

For all the havoc the ogre had caused, the damage seemed to be located primarily around the entrance to lockup. Cole couldn't see any signs that the ogre under the black ring's influence had been there to attack any prisoners other than Foleman. The rest had taken cover behind mattresses pressed up against the walls as makeshift shields. One peeked his head out as Cole walked past.

"Hey, sugar!" he teased, making kissing noises.

Cole flipped Aed Deigh around in a practiced move and shot a blade made of solid ice out the opposite end. The projectile shattered on impact against the wall just inches above where the man's head had been. In a flash, he took cover behind the mattress once again, as if that could provide him with sufficient protection.

Cole found what he was looking for up ahead. It was worse than he'd pictured, though not nearly as bad as it could have been. While controlled by the black ring, the ogre had torn the bars of the cell clean off and warped them. Foleman's body was still inside the cell, minus a head, of course. Next to him was….

Cole felt the world tilt underneath him. Something foul rose up from his belly into his mouth, choking him. It took a moment to swallow it back down, but the gruesome image did not fade away.

Joss was lying on his side near the wall, unconscious. Blood had puddled all around him from the stump on his right side where the ogre had torn his arm off. The limb, or more accurately, what was left of it, had been flung to the side. The ogre had apparently crushed it under his feet after killing Foleman. It almost looked like an afterthought.

There was movement from farther down the hall. Cole smelled more people, presumably officers, but he didn't care. He couldn't will enough strength to drag himself over to Joss's side. The footsteps stopped just a few feet from him.

"Hold it right there!"

The sound of bullets falling into their chambers snapped him out of it. Cole came to attention then and found himself staring down a wall of NYPD's finest. Each of them was pointing a gun at his head.

"Drop the weapon and put your hands behind your head," a man in a suit ordered, holding a badge up. "Internal Affairs. You are under arrest."

Chapter *Seven*

"INTERNAL Affairs has been monitoring Section Thirteen since the moment it was re-formed."

Special Agent Dickson was a short man with very dark hair that slicked back naturally. His hairline, however, was stretched a little too high up, indicating he was in the early stages of going bald. Dickson's partner, Special Agent Rockard, stood almost as tall as Cole would have if they hadn't handcuffed him to the chair after ushering him inside an unused interrogation room and stripping him of his badge.

In contrast, Rockard had very light blond hair that showed no signs whatsoever of disappearing any time soon. The only real flaw to his physical features was that his nose seemed a little bit too large for his face. He was also thin, to the point that it gave the impression he was unhealthy. Both men watched Cole as though he could leap up somehow and bite their heads off.

Of course, being that Cole wasn't human, that very well could have happened. He was just more interested in learning what the two were snooping around for at the present time.

Special Agent Dickson leaned forward under the flickering overhead light to stare into Cole's face. "We've been monitoring your activities since the Bowling Green Park incident over a month ago. Care to shed some light on that subject for us, Mr. MacColewyn?"

Cole suspected the special agent was trying to appear dominant by leaving off his newly acquired title of "detective." "I'd be thrilled to," he said in an eerily calm voice. "Which part would you like to know about first? The fifty-foot geyser that seemingly shot up out of solid concrete or the micro-tornado that was reported moments later?"

Dickson's mouth puckered like he'd tasted something sour. Rockard was looking away as though he were coughing. Cole could hear the snicker, though.

"Or," he added, "how about the reports of jaywalkers dressed in soldier fatigues marching into the park and never coming out? Or all the dead bodies tabloid reporters said had to be carted off back to the morgues that they'd gone missing from?"

"Funny," Dickson said, rising. His face was still contorted into a sour expression. "Internal Affairs investigated those events. Which, I might add, occurred before you were brought in to Section Thirteen as a special detective in charge of occult matters. Before that, you had worked for the NYPD as a consultant alongside Detective James Corhagen. We couldn't find anything in the files dealing with those incidents that suggested you were present. Care to tell us how you know all that?"

Cole shrugged. "I live under Bowling Green Park. It's not so odd when you think about it."

Rockard didn't try to conceal his smile this time. Dickson didn't notice, as he'd gone back to staring into Cole's face.

"Mr. MacColewyn, are you aware of the seriousness of your situation?"

Cole looked back toward Rockard before meeting Dickson's eyes. "You're both with Internal Affairs," he said, still utterly calm. "As I understand it, you are the police that policemen fear. No one in police departments nationwide is more hated than you. Have I left anything out?"

"We aren't trying to hurt you, Mr. MacColewyn," Special Agent Rockard said quickly, leaping away from the wall. "But you must understand that the circumstances are suspicious. Adding to this fact, Section Thirteen has always carried a strange and unusual history."

"Section Thirteen investigates crimes involving the occult and supernatural deaths," Cole said, watching the man more closely now. "Are you saying it comes as a surprise that some of the reports filed are different than those of homicide or assault and battery?"

The men looked to one another. A silent communication passed between them that Cole was sure he wasn't meant to understand. Sighing, he tried to shift to a more comfortable position as Special Agent Dickson took over again.

"We've spent a lot of time trying to dig up information about you," he said in a low, threatening tone. "You're almost like a ghost. The name MacColewyn comes up a lot if you go back far enough in this city's criminal history, and what few descriptions we found all say the same thing: tall with long hair past the shoulders, pale skin, and the most interestingly colored eyes."

Cole remained perfectly still. Dickson saw this and moved in for the kill. "They say you can't be real," he hissed close to Cole's ear. "We showed photographs of you to this one woman who claimed to have rented a room out to you back in the fifties. She swore to us on a stack of Bibles in front of her that you were the same man. There's talk among some of the other officers that you tell people you aren't human. What kind of scam are you running here, huh?"

Rockard came up from behind and stood on Cole's other side. "We know something is happening in this city," he said, leaning in almost as close to Cole as his partner was. "We're not blind, but you can't expect us to believe that ogres and monsters are responsible. So why don't you tell us who you really are?"

Cole raised his head and faced forward. "Who am I, gentlemen?"

Slowly, slow enough that both men could see, Cole raised his arms. He could only bring them up so high because of the handcuffs and because the two of them were so close, but it was high enough. With a single snapping movement, the cuffs broke apart. Cole grabbed each bracelet, one after the other, and snapped it off his wrists before the Internal Affairs officers had time to react. Reaching down between his legs, he grabbed the final chain that bound him to the chair and yanked it away.

Placing the scraps in a neat pile on the table in front of them, Cole folded his hands in his lap and waited. "Who I am, gentlemen, is someone very short on patience."

Dickson and Rockard backed away from him slightly. "You're strong," Dickson acknowledged skeptically. "But I've seen circus performers with a similar gimmick. It isn't going to work here."

"Fair enough." Cole stood, the movement itself like flowing water, and swung a karate chop down into the table, breaking it cleanly in half. Walking around the chair past Rockard, who by now was giving Cole an awful lot of breathing space, he then stood in front of the wall where the special agent had been standing only moments ago. Cole swung a punch at it and caused pieces of stone to go flying. An impression of his fist, several inches deep, was left behind.

Cole walked back over to the IA agents, holding his bleeding knuckles up for them to see. He had barely licked the blood off the surface before the skin started to knit itself back together.

On a counter not far away, next to a coffee pot, Cole spotted his guns, badge, and Aed Deigh. Neither agent moved to stop him as he picked each one up and stuck it back on his body in its proper place.

Aed Deigh he saved for last. "I hear three officers tried to pick this up after I dropped it, even though I told them not to," Cole said. "All of them had to be taken to a hospital, the first two for third-degree burns. The last one had to see a specialist because her hands were frostbitten."

"No one said you could take those!"

Dickson started to move, and suddenly Cole was standing in front of him and Rockard. Before they could draw their guns, his hand was in front of their faces. Both men went slack as their hands felt limply to their sides.

"Joss always tells me I shouldn't do things like this," Cole said with quiet fury. "He tries to do things the right way, the way humans are supposed to behave. I'm not human, but I humor him. Currently, however, Joss Vallimun is lying barely alive in a hospital bed after some crackpot slapped a control device on a poor bastard ogre's arm and sent him to stomp all over my lover's severed arm. Taking that into account, there is no one here at this police station to tell me what to do or how things are supposed to be done. With that in mind, I am going to make both of you forget the last half hour or so and walk out of that door now."

Neither mortal responded.

"Good," said Cole. "If either of you share a brain cell between your thick skulls, you won't come bothering me again."

The door was locked, but all it took was one swift kick to smash it open. Both IA agents stayed right where they were as he left and headed down the hall. His gut told him Staffelbach was somewhere close by. Sure enough, he caught a whiff of the officer coming from a door several feet down on his left. Cole didn't bother checking to see if this door was locked. He simply forced it open with his foot and stepped in.

Staffelbach looked at him with a wide-eyed expression.

"I thought you might like to take a breather from all this excitement for a moment and come with me," Cole said, tossing the younger officer his badge and gun. "You handled yourself pretty well against that controlled ogre. I haven't seen anyone do that before, not and live."

Staffelbach strapped his gun under his armpit before he answered. "When you're short, everyone else tends to look bigger. It stops being intimidating after a while. Where are we going?"

"Internal Affairs is busy contemplating their navels for the time being. I thought you might like to come help me sort out this whole business behind who sent that ogre to attack the holding cells and murder that man. Or you could stay here and wait for those two dumb fucks to come out of the trance they're in and try to pin the blame on you."

Staffelbach clipped his badge onto his belt. "I'm ready."

Cole's next stop was to the damaged holding cell area itself. A tarp had been fastened over the gaping hole where the ogre had burst through. Paramedics had cleared away the scattered bodies to either the ER or a morgue. No one tried to stop Cole as he marched under the police tape. None of the other prisoners had been taken away just yet. He had witnessed the ogre being placed in a cell by himself as Dickson and Rockard had led him through earlier.

Said cell was being guarded by two heavily armed officers. The ogre was sitting quietly on a bunk, trying to look inconspicuous. Bits of trash and puddles of what smelled like human urine were scattered all around the floor near him. Cole eyed them for a second before considering the two guards.

"Have the others been throwing trash at him for very long?" he asked.

"Since they stuck it in here," one replied, snickering. "The brass still doesn't know if they should get him a lawyer or animal control."

"Let me guess." Cole's voice lowered to the same chilling calm tone he'd used on the two special agents while being interrogated. "Neither of you did anything about it."

Both men shrugged. "It's not like it feels anything."

Cole nodded. "I see. You mean like this?"

Both of Cole's fists connected with their abdomens in a flicker of movement. His knuckles came close to their spines before he drew back. There would be internal bleeding, perhaps even organ damage. The thought made him smile.

"Your name?" he asked the ogre while fishing the keys to the cell out of the unconscious guard's pocket.

The ogre glanced up nervously. "Marcel."

Cole paused. "Marcel," he repeated. "Seriously?"

Marcel the ogre shrugged. "My family was from France originally before immigrating here. They might have lived elsewhere before that, but I never asked. Are you here to execute me?"

"Not quite," Cole said, opening the cell. "Maybe later. You might not remember, but while that black ring was on your arm, you tore the arm off of my boyfriend and stepped on it. They'll not be able to reattach it, I think, because of how extensive the damage was."

Marcel bent his head low. "I'm so sorry," he said remorsefully. "My memory is still fuzzy."

"I can imagine," Cole said, leaning against the side of the cell. "Someone tried to put me under with one of those damned things. I know what it is like. That is the only reason I haven't pumped your brains full of lead."

Marcel drew himself up with as much dignity as an ogre could while reeking of human piss. "Why are you here, then?"

"Because I need your help," said Cole. "I could use someone as strong as you, and you owe me something for cutting that ring off instead of just killing you when I had the chance. Anyone else here would have shot first and never asked questions. They tried to, in fact. I was the one who held them off."

Marcel brushed his thumb over the cut on his arm that still hadn't healed. "Did you have to cut me so deep?" he asked, sounding petulant for a moment. "It still hurts."

"You were moving around too much," Cole said, moving out of the cell. "Are you coming, or would you prefer to sit here and wait for something worse to happen, because I don't think a lawyer is coming."

"They can't hold him here without giving him a lawyer," Staffelbach said as Marcel squeezed through the opening. "It's illegal."

"Right," Cole replied flippantly. "Because that sort of thing has never happened before."

Cole stopped just before they reached the police tape and pulled a set of cuffs out of Staffelbach's back pocket.

"Easy," the officer warned cheekily. "I used to charge for that sort of thing."

"Put these on you," Cole instructed the ogre. "They won't fit, but so long as no one notices they aren't clasped shut, you should be all right. I don't think anyone will be pleased that we're releasing a cop-killer back into the streets so soon."

"Why are we doing this?" Staffelbach asked as Marcel reluctantly complied.

"I'm formally deputizing him," Cole said. "Inspector Vallimun is out of the game and may not be coming back. Right now, that only leaves myself and Detective Corhagen, whom I haven't been able to locate in the Section. With you both, that brings the number up to four, assuming you are still on board."

"I'm in," Staffelbach assured him, taking Marcel gently by an arm without flinching. "But neither of us can deputize a criminal."

"He isn't a criminal," Cole explained. "That black ring I cut off his arm is a control device built to enslave members of the fey. He wasn't responsible for his actions. I can vouch for it, but in the meantime, we need to get him out of here and to a place where he can shower before someone decides civil rights are for humans and puts a bullet in his skull."

"It has happened before," Marcel informed them. "I survived."

"There are a lot of angry cops in this building right now," Cole reminded him. "And they are armed."

Marcel lowered his head in submission. "Good point."

Cole tried to keep some of the stares from the other cops away, but it wasn't easy. Everyone was shaken by the assault, and their anger burned at the glamour he threw at them. Not all of them noticed immediately, and it was much easier than he might have found it a year or two ago, but they still noticed in the end. With Marcel seemingly in handcuffs, however, they didn't ask questions. Some looked positively relieved to see him being escorted away.

Cole found Corhagen in Joss's office, along with Rainette, of all people. During the excitement, Cole had totally forgotten about her. She didn't look happy with him at the moment. Her naturally chestnut-colored skin glowed even under the florescent lights. It set off the mane of dark curls surrounding her head while framing those deep black eyes at the same time. Rainette's aura always seemed to hum with irritation whenever he was near. Now was no exception.

"Someone said she was here to speak with you," Corhagen explained. "I brought her up here, but they said you had been arrested and were being held by Internal Affairs."

There was no trace of hostility or reproach from Corhagen now. Cole decided to drop their animosity for the time being. Removing the cuffs from Marcel, he pointed at a chair and moved over to a wall, where he stood by himself.

"I heard about what happened to Vallimun," Corhagen said gently. "They think he's going to make it, but the next few hours will be touch and go. It doesn't look like his arm can be reattached. They said there was way too much damage done to it."

Cole didn't speak.

"What next?" Corhagen finally asked. "Is this the same guy they said busted up the holding area?"

"He was under the control of a black ring," Cole replied. "His name is Marcel. His family was originally from France, and he's here to help us out."

"How is that?"

"Marcel had a black ring put on him," Cole said pointedly. "His memory is fuzzy, but he had to have been on Staten Island for that to happen. Either that, or the false Lord of All Fey is branching out. Regardless, he can be a big help to us, and we are currently shorthanded."

"Excuse me," Rainette interrupted, raising a hand. "I don't mean to sound rude, but am I still going to be decoding those files you told me about? I did blow off work to come here and help."

Cole looked at her. "This is how it is going to go," he said, looking around the room. "As of right now, we are officially deputizing you all into Section Thirteen. The situation is dire, and our commander has just been swept off the board. Rainette, you're a practicing witch with experience in alchemy studies. Marcel's strength should prove useful. Also, for those who don't know yet, this is Officer Staffelbach. While Marcel was still under the ring's control, Staffelbach took him on with just a baton and lived to tell about it."

Corhagen smiled and gave the officer a nod. Even Rainette looked impressed. Soon, though, she raised a hand.

"Assuming I go along with this, will I get to shoot people?"

"At some point, I'm going to be counting on it," Cole answered.

Rainette didn't lower her hand. "Do I get a badge?"

"Later," he said. "Anything else?"

"Am I still getting paid? You said that I would get paid for helping with those files. Will I get paid more this way?"

Corhagen looked at her for a moment. "Are you sure this is a good idea?" he asked Cole, who was busy pressing two fingers to his forehead.

"We'll work out the details once things have slowed down," he said. "Assuming all of you decide to stay on, you'll be made official members of Section Thirteen. That will include a new badge, plus a benefits package for those who weren't already getting one."

"Screw the library, in that case," Rainette said happily. "I'd much rather be a cop."

"Wonderful." Cole turned to Corhagen. "Find out which evidence locker those papers were taken to and have them brought up here so she can start going through them. Also…." Cole looked to Staffelbach next.

"I'd like for you to see where Internal Affairs took that black ring. It didn't explode like the others, so it's probably still in the building. I want Rainette to see what she can make of it as well while she's here."

"Internal Affairs probably has it stored away in their own private evidence room," Corhagen said, pulling his mouth away from the receiver in his hand. "We'll never get it back from there."

"I'll go, then," Cole said. "Staffelbach, bring the papers up here once Corhagen locates them. In the meantime, Marcel, you don't leave this room until Corhagen can find you a deputy badge to wear. We don't want anyone outside trying to avenge their fallen comrades."

"That probably won't stop many of them," Corhagen protested. "But I'll see if I can't scrounge one up from somewhere."

Marcel looked toward the door anxiously. "I'm not scared," he denied upon noticing that the others were looking at him. "I just don't enjoy it when people shoot at me."

"There is a lot of that going around," Cole retorted as he went out the door. "I should be back soon."

"You know," Corhagen said, stopping him, "the chief is going to shit bricks of gold when he learns you did all this. It could cost you your badge."

"I'll shove it down his throat and make him pull it out of his ass," Cole responded, turning to look at Corhagen. "The chief isn't the one who spent the last month and a half running his ass all over Manhattan trying to hold it in one piece while looking for a certifiable lunatic with godlike powers over the weather and a serial kidnapping hobby. If the chief has a problem with the way this Section is handling a situation that has gotten out of control due to a lack of support from the brass and obfuscating stupidity, the chief can politely go fuck himself. The chief—"

Cole froze. "—is right behind me, isn't he?"

Everyone turned to face the door at the same time. Rainette had to peek around Cole to see. "There's no one there," she told him.

Cole turned around. "Are you sure?"

The doorframe was vacant. "Sorry, guy," Rainette said in a phony sympathetic voice. "You're losing it."

Cole stared at the blank spot for a moment nevertheless. "I could have sworn…," he began. "Never mind. Corhagen, while you're at it, I wanted you to look up something on Wikipedia."

Rainette snorted as Cole leaned over Corhagen, who was busy typing in the URL. "So this is how the NYPD does it," she chided. "Just go to Wikipedia where all the questions are magically solved."

"Just one," Cole replied, ignoring her tone for the moment. "I wanted to know about Frances North, the man that academy was named for."

"Not much here," Corhagen told him. "Just some stuff about him being a royalist with an uncommon sense of integrity."

"Try Google," Staffelbach suggested. "There's probably one or two sites out there with more information."

"What are you looking for?" Rainette asked, moving in closer now.

"Something that connects this Sir Francis North to what has been happening on Staten Island," Cole said. "The late Foleman hinted that a bigger player is involved, but until I find out who, I won't be satisfied."

Cole glanced down at the screen. "Wait, go back!" he yelled, pointing. "Right there. That link."

"The one about witchcraft in the 1600s?"

"It says he was the defender of an elderly woman accused of witchcraft," Rainette read. "And deeply critical of the prosecution during that time. His derision of it helped end the witch hunts of that period."

Rainette rose wearing a satisfied smile. "Good for him."

"That's it," Cole said, rising up as well. "That is what ties it all together."

"I'm lost," Corhagen said.

"So am I," Staffelbach admitted, moving over to the desk.

"I'm not," Rainette insisted, looking shifty-eyed.

"I am," said Marcel, though he remained seated. "How does a human defending witches a few centuries back make a difference to what has been happening to my kind?"

"And mine," Cole reminded him. "Everything, in fact. I'll explain once I've returned from getting that black ring away from Internal Affairs. There is a high chance they might try to meddle with it. If that happens, it could explode, and there would go our best chance to solve this case."

Cole made for the door without another word. As he turned down the hallway, he was nearly blindsided by a strange man wearing a long beard and tugging a young boy along by the arm. Ignoring them, Cole continued toward where he'd last seen Dickson and Rockard. They were about to prove useful to him.

BOTH men were eager to know more about the black ring. Cole had been betting on that, and it turned out to be a wise wager. Casting glamour inside a metal building with man-made concrete was difficult, and holding two grown minds for an extended period of time was even worse. However, both really wanted another look at the device, so it was simple to just tweak that urge and guide them. As far as explaining his presence, each man had an ego the size of Texas. Cole was supposed to be with them. They needed him to explain what the device did, and who else would know but him? He was obviously behind it all in some way. They'd already deduced that much. It was very clever of them to link the broken pieces together so that they pointed in Cole's direction. They were both very smart and incredibly good-looking men.

It was so easy Cole nearly felt bad for them.

Nearly.

The black ring, it turned out, was being stored in one of the evidence rooms downstairs. Cole figured they must have been using it for private storage until they were ready to transfer it to their main branch. The ring was being kept in a thick black box so no one else would see it or tamper with it. The IA was as paranoid as Cole had already heard.

Now he had the ring. The only problem left was ditching these two without drawing too much attention to himself or getting shot. Cole waited as Rockard opened the box and held the ring up inside a plastic evidence bag. His eyes drifted over to Dickson, who was staring at his partner as though transfixed. An idea began to form in his head.

"Thank you," Cole said, taking the bag out of Rockard's hand. "I'll get right on this."

Cole brushed a finger through the air, swiping it over where Rockard and Dickson stood looking at him. Slowly, almost against their wills, they turned to face each other. Cole allowed the glamour a moment to settle in. It was really more about showing people what they really wanted instead of forcing them, like so many humans tried to believe. The want was there, buried deep under human social norms and fear fueled by years of being policemen.

Now, Cole poured his essence into it. He hadn't been raised to be human. The sidhe shared few views in common with humans. Love was natural, and if love blossomed between two males, it was meant to be shared. These acts were sacred and cherished within the eyes of Danu and her Consort, the Horned One.

Cole pushed his belief down into the crevice where their secrets had been shoved away. It devoured every errant thought both men had ever had about why it was wrong. Within seconds, they were all over each other.

Cole hadn't expected it to happen so fast. In fact, he was caught slightly off guard when Rockard literally tore Dickson's shirt off him and tossed the remains over his shoulder.

He allowed himself a moment to watch as the two Internal Affairs agents stripped away both the façades of their ranks and their carefully projected machismo. It was like watching trees bloom in the sunlight. Soon they were naked, running hands over each other's bodies, exploring with the passion of a spring that had yet to fully show her face outside. Cole felt his power growing as a result of their passion. His own cock stiffened in his leather pants.

Idly, he stroked it. There was work to do, Cole reminded himself. He needed to get going. Their actions weren't fueled by the glamour anymore. Something else had taken its place. He sensed another's actions in this, and it gave him pause. It could be an enemy, yet he felt no real reason to draw his guns. Sniffing the air, Cole thought he recognized the trace. It was similar to what he'd felt down in the pit of the sithen. Cole had tried going back there after Naryssa's escape, but it had disappeared. Or, more likely, it was no longer available to him.

It was the Goddess whose presence filled the room now. Cole felt his heart clench as he slowly backed away. Dickson was going to town on Rockard's fat cock, sucking it like a Hoover vacuum. The sounds were practically echoing off the wall. The Goddess's presence grew stronger by the second. Cole could no longer remain and quietly ducked out through the door.

His heart was pounding like a drum. Cole wasn't sure if his skin was glowing. Going by his bare arms, it didn't look like it, yet he felt the same sensation as all the other times when fey magic was rising up around him. Cole hurried back to Joss's office and had just reached the door with the bagged ring in hand when he heard it.

So did everyone else, for that matter.

It could have been mistaken for another explosion, but the sound was gradual. All the new members of Section Thirteen spilled out into the hallway in front of him as someone from around the corner screamed.

Just around said corner, the top of a pine tree was breaking through the floor. Another one was coming through near the wall, splitting it apart as it reached upward for the sun, which was still another two floors away. The screaming officer had gathered the attention of others just in time to spot the third and final one breaking through a little farther down.

A sinking feeling developed in the pit of Cole's stomach as he counted down the floors and realized the evidence room where he'd left Dickson and Rockard was somewhere underfoot. Turning around, he motioned for the others to follow and took the long way down, a flight of stairs that ended on the northern end of the building.

A crowd was already gathered around ground zero. There was nothing left of what had been the evidence room. It and the surrounding area had been transformed into a grove surrounded by three towering loblolly pines. The fragrance was filling the area, making the humans feel woozy. From inside the center, over everyone's frightened whispers, Cole could hear sounds of frantic lovemaking. Someone was fucking up a storm inside it, and he had a good idea as to who they were.

"MacColewyn!"

Cole turned around to find the precinct captain himself bearing down on him from the other end of what was left of the hallway. Several small birds that had appeared overhead scattered as his voice echoed shrilly.

"What do you call this?" Captain Hawkins demanded, pointing at the mess around them.

"A pine grove," Cole answered at once in a bored voice. "A rather minor one, but still a pine grove all the same."

"I see," the captain said, barely holding his anger in check. "And what happened to the evidence room that used to be right over there?"

"Gone." Cole shouldn't have been enjoying himself, but it was hilarious to see the ever-so-reserved Captain Hawkins having a conniption. "Probably destroyed."

Captain Hawkins glanced around, noticing that they were far from alone, and grabbed Cole by the arm. Cole had to fight down the urge to beat the man senseless for handling him so and reluctantly complied by trailing after him.

"This is supposed to be your area of expertise," Captain Hawkins hissed in a low voice. "How could this have happened?"

Before Cole could answer, the captain was launching into a tirade. "First some circus freak breaks into the holding area and murders a man, then trees start bursting out of the concrete. And to top it all off, two members of Internal Affairs were found inside humping each other like a couple of fag hounds. I've just watched two grown men become fudgepackers because of this crap."

Cole waited for the captain to calm down. "Do you need another moment?" he asked. "Or should I begin?"

"Please!"

Cole chose his words carefully. "It's something divine," he said. "That's all I can tell you for right now."

"Divine?" The captain was confused, though understandably for once. "Like an act of God or something?"

"No god that humans remember did this," Cole amended, then thought better of it as Rainette came into his line of sight. "For the most part, anyway. All I can tell you is it had nothing to do with the disturbance earlier."

Captain Hawkins looked suspicious now. "How are you so sure about that?"

"Because of this," Cole said, holding the bag with the black ring in it up. "This is what caused the disturbance before. I found others like it on Staten Island while Section Thirteen was investigating the murder of that teacher near the private academy. I think the two incidents are related to each other."

The captain studied the ring for a moment before looking Cole squarely in the eye. "I've had the mayor riding my ass about that," he said softly. "Care to explain that statement further?"

Captain Hawkins then noticed Marcel standing off to the side away from the crowd. The poor ogre was doing his best to remain inconspicuous.

"What's he doing out of his cell?" Hawkins demanded.

"He is with Section Thirteen now," Cole quickly explained. "Marcel was under the control of this black ring. Someone used him as a pawn to assassinate Foleman in his cell. Marcel has agreed to work with us to help locate the perpetrator behind all of this. I've formally deputized him," Cole added as the captain studied the ogre a moment.

"What about the rest of them?" Hawkins inquired, looking each one over. "Are they civilians too?"

"Officer Staffelbach was the one who helped me take Marcel down while he was under the ring's influence," Cole said. "He has potential and is willing to give working in the Section a try. Rainette is a witch whom I've known for a while. She was the sole keeper of records for the occult section of the New York library. Alchemy is one of her fields."

The captain didn't look pleased as he gave them a once-over. "Inspector Vallimun was in charge of Section Thirteen," he said carefully after a moment. "I heard what happened to him. Shouldn't Detective Corhagen be the one leading you all now?"

Cole met the mortal's stare. "You tell me, sir," he replied. "Who has more experience with these things, Corhagen or myself?"

The captain didn't look as though he wanted to answer at first. "Fine," he said at last through gritted teeth. "Get over to Staten and fix this mess. I don't like the idea of you being in charge of anything. I didn't agree with Vallimun when he pulled those strings to get you into the NYPD. I especially don't like the fact that you boys set up shop in my yard. The brass has had its eyes on us ever since, and the shit will hit the fan once word gets out about this, if it hasn't already."

"We're leaving now," Cole said.

"Hold your horses," the mortal insisted. "What are we supposed to do about this mess?"

"Just leave it, I'm afraid." Two other officers had gone into the grove in an attempt to drag Dickson and Rockard out. The moment they got close, the power of the grove overtook them, and they wound up naked and fucking away right alongside. "It should wear off soon," Cole said. "Until then, keep everyone away from it. I doubt you want word of an unplanned orgy erupting all over the front pages of the tabloids."

That got the captain distracted enough for Cole to slip away.

Staffelbach was watching the action with mirth smeared all over his face like cream on a cat's whiskers. "Internal Affairs will never recover from this," he said gleefully. "I don't know what did this, but I thank them for it."

"You're welcome," Cole replied. "Now let's get out of here."

"Where are we going?" Corhagen asked. "What did the captain want?"

"To tell me how much he's grown fond of me," Cole said sarcastically. "We're going out to Staten Island now. I can feel a storm coming, and it will be one for the books."

Cole's powers weren't nearly as effective against the metal and plastic surrounding him, but a storm of that magnitude would have been hard to ignore. He wished he could have gone to the hospital first to visit Joss and check up on him, but the humming in his veins said he should go now. The storm was slowing down for no one, and once it struck, there was a high chance all means of travel would stop.

It was at times like this Cole wished he had something witty to say to lighten the mood. There wasn't time to run by the sithen and check on Jynx and Boogaloo. The sithen had a phone. Cole knew that much, but his head was too preoccupied with what had occurred in the last few hours to remember the number. It was a humbling situation. He just had to trust that Mal could keep them busy until this was over.

Somehow, that thought hurt worse than knowing Joss was in the hospital sans an arm, but only a little.

SURE enough, the snow was really starting to come down before they made it to the bridge. Corhagen had agreed to drive Rainette and Marcel with him, since Cole's vehicle was too small for the ogre to fit. It had taken some doing, but in the end Hawkins consented to let them sign out an old Ford Transit that had been seized during a raid. Marcel fit nicely in the back without complaining once. Rainette, on the other hand, didn't look happy until Cole reminded her of the long drive ahead that she could be spending alone in a vehicle with him.

That had shut her up.

They had to show their badges before crossing the toll. Officers were directing traffic and didn't look keen on letting them through. Cole found this suspicious, but when the man in charge got a look at his shield, he waved them on through without a word. Cole had already given the others directions to meet up with him at the Staten Island police station. Since Corhagen knew the way, he wasn't worried about them getting lost.

Staffelbach had been quiet during the ride thus far. Not the most enthusiastic conversationalist, yet Cole found the human's presence tolerable. The vehicle born of the wild hunt serving as their transportation seemed to take the slick roads as a challenge, so the squealing of tires filled the air quite often to brush away the awkward silence.

"I haven't seen snow this bad in a long time," Staffelbach commented. "It almost makes me wish I was back in Miami."

"You're from Miami?" Cole asked, turning the wheel sharply.

"I lived there for a few years," he said. "Up until I graduated high school. Believe it or not, I'm an Alabama boy born and raised. My mom left me with my dad in Florida when I was thirteen. I decided to come to New York and become a cop like on TV."

"You don't sound like you are from that part of the world," Cole noted. "I've met a handful of people from there, and you don't carry the accent."

"I know." Staffelbach grinned, laughing. "When I moved to Miami, people there made fun of me for my accent, so I trained myself to talk without it. My mom gave me a hard time over it, since she thought I was tossing away my roots, but I'm glad I did it regardless. I can't imagine how much worse it would have been if I'd come all the way up here with a Southern drawl."

Cole thought on that for a moment, then nodded. "So you became a police officer because of the television shows you watched?"

Staffelbach nodded back. "Dumb decision, I know. It's nothing at all like how I expected, but once I was through with police academy, I didn't want to give up. It took two tries to get through. I failed the first time because I didn't make the weight requirements."

"I see."

Staffelbach was watching him closely now. "You don't sound like you're from around here," he noted. "Where did you come from originally?"

"You wouldn't believe me if I told you," Cole replied. "But I've lived in New York for a number of years. This isn't the worst storm I've seen, incidentally."

"How long have you lived in New York, then?"

"Almost ninety years." Cole gave the answer without thinking. When he realized his mistake, he turned to check Staffelbach's reaction.

"You saw me wield Aed Deigh," Cole said when Staffelbach showed no outward surprise. "You don't seem bothered by Marcel, even though it must be obvious by now that he isn't human. Does it seem odd that I could have lived that long?"

"You look amazing for your age," he joked in reply before turning serious. "I... don't really know what to make of what I've seen so far today. I've read a bunch of stuff that made me wonder if there wasn't more to the world than what meets the eye. Still, it's a lot to accept in such a short amount of time."

"I guess I could understand that," Cole remarked. "Still, you seem far more accepting than how most humans react."

Staffelbach shrugged around the seat belt. "It might sound cheesy," he said, "but I try not to base too many judgments on what I see initially. I never bought into the idea they tried feeding us at the academy that one quick glance tells you everything about a person."

"Humans aren't that complex," Cole countered.

"You think so?" Staffelbach seemed poised to issue a challenge. "What would you say about me based on what you've seen so far?"

Cole thought a moment. "I saw you jump in front of an out-of-control ogre earlier today," he said. "You took him on with just a stick in your hand and were able to hold him off. That is something men from a whole different era wouldn't have tried. Your balls are either visible from a space platform, or you were trying to die in the most gruesome manner possible. Just in case it is the latter, I would recommend standing on a set of train tracks instead. Ogres have been known to suck the marrow from the bones of their prey while they are still alive."

Staffelbach glanced shakily back at the Transit that was following them across the bridge. "And now he's carrying a badge? Are you sure that was a good idea?"

"Marcel was under someone else's control," Cole reminded him. "Besides, if he comes to work for the NYPD, our salaries might not get docked. They can take it out of his paycheck."

That made Staffelbach sit back. "In that case, finish your assessment of me."

"You like excitement," Cole stated. "You were hoping the NYPD could provide you with that, so you became a cop. Finding out that wasn't the case was a huge letdown for you, but you stayed on anyway. You have a devoted streak in you even when it's not in your best interests. Also, I suspect you have some private reason for going out of your way to not make Marcel feel uncomfortable because of his appearance."

Staffelbach looked at Cole for a moment. "I'm gay," he stated, and kept right on looking as if expecting a reaction.

Cole glanced toward Staffelbach before looking back to the road. "I understand that means you prefer having sex with other men instead of women." Cole paused as they reached a line of traffic near the end of the bridge. "Was there something in particular I should have gleaned from that statement?" he asked, slowly putting on the brakes. "Or have I misunderstood and you were just mentioning it in passing?"

Staffelbach smiled. "You really aren't human," he said. "I don't think I've ever met anyone who took it that way. You sound genuinely confused and totally at ease all at the same time."

"I was not raised human," Cole replied calmly. "I am a sidhe, and we value the beauty in all things. I understand that this is something most people don't accept or refuse outright to understand. Either way, it does not matter to me."

"You don't care either way, then?"

"Inspector Vallimun and I are lovers," Cole said in lieu of an explanation. "He was the reason I consented to join Section Thirteen and become a cop. If it had been anyone else, I might have turned them down. I also know how 'being gay', as it is called, is viewed in the NYPD. You took a risk by telling me that."

"You took a risk telling me about you and the inspector," Staffelbach replied. "I was there when they brought him out on the stretcher. I'm so sorry."

Cole returned to staring out the window even though the line of traffic wasn't letting up just yet. "I'll deal with that once this is over with. Otherwise, I might not make it through the night."

"I understand. Sorry if I was babbling. I was trying to stay quiet so I wouldn't do that. It's a bad habit of mine."

"I didn't tell you to shut up," Cole pointed out.

Snow was hammering the island by the time they had navigated through the icy streets. The February blizzard had transformed the quaint isolated town into a winter wonderland right off a post card. At least, it would have been except for the bleak feeling of doom in the air. Cole could sense it the moment the wheels of his car left the asphalt of the bridge. Something had taken hold of the town in the short time since he'd left.

The wind was really starting to whip up as Cole pulled up to the police station. Captain Hawkins had agreed to phone ahead for them so that they would be expected, yet the building appeared deserted. More accurately, it looked abandoned. Cole didn't see any lights on through the windows. He wanted to tell himself that the windows were simply obscured by the snowfall. That was a human excuse, however. The snow wasn't falling thickly enough to blind him just yet. Corhagen was bringing the Transit to a stop alongside his vehicle as he climbed out.

Staffelbach emerged reluctantly and shivered. "It doesn't look like there's anyone home," he noted, rubbing both hands together.

"There isn't," Cole replied as Corhagen and the others joined them. "The building is empty."

"It's a police station," Corhagen pointed out obviously. "They wouldn't shut down just because of the weather."

"They probably didn't," Cole said. "But the fact remains that no one is inside."

"How do you know?" This was from Rainette, who seemed to have gotten over her squeamishness around Marcel and was taking refuge in his hulking shadow.

"A deserted building always feels a certain way," Cole said. "I can usually sense it, especially if the building is empty and shouldn't be. The police are gone."

Everyone turned to stare at the structure with a dawning sense of horror. "What does it mean, though?" Staffelbach shouted over the wind that suddenly kicked up.

"It means the Lord of All Fey has just staged a coup d'état," Cole said gravely. "And everyone on this island has been taken hostage, including us."

CHAPTER 8

"YOU were right." Corhagen didn't sound happy as he reentered the room. "The whole place looks like it was abandoned. Also, the station is pitch-black. The power must have gone out at some point."

Cole watched as Corhagen stopped short of him. "The good news is that it happened recently. I found some Styrofoam cups filled with warm coffee in the break area. There was more than one half-eaten donut there too."

"They've got donuts?" Rainette jumped off the counter she'd been using as a seat and made tracks for the back.

Cole watched her leave, shaking his head. "Go team," he groaned. "If the place was abandoned within the last few hours, there are probably still weapons and other equipment we can use."

"What about the rest of New York?" Staffelbach asked. "Won't they get curious after a while?"

"The academy principal picked an excellent time to try and seize this island as his own private country," Cole replied. "There is a major storm brewing out there. In a few hours, it will be overpowering all of Manhattan and the surrounding areas. The local government will be too busy trying to deal with the situation to notice. The lack of communication can be blamed on it also. Their next step will likely be to take out the bridge. That way, the island stays cut off from the rest of the world."

"Whu izh kee duking fizz?" Rainette grunted, coming through the door with a glazed donut in each hand and one in her mouth.

"Try that again," Cole suggested. "More slowly this time and with less baked good."

"I said," Rainette began after she'd spat the donut in her mouth onto an available napkin, "why is he doing this? I can't wrap my head around a school principal going through something so far-fetched. This sounds like the sort of thing you'd read about happening in one of those dumb kids' books."

"Like the one where they can shapeshift into animals?" Staffelbach offered.

"Exactly," she replied. "I hated those damn things." Ignoring the look on Staffelbach's face, she went on, "My high school principal was a jerk, but even he wouldn't have attempted something this huge."

"He may have delusions of grandeur," Corhagen pointed out.

"Why he is doing this has become irrelevant at this point," Cole broke in. "It has become our responsibility to stop him. I say the first thing we do is gather up any weapons in this place. We didn't come prepared to face an army, and that could be what we wind up fighting."

Rainette froze. "Army?"

"Yes," Cole said, avoiding her look. "And if that bothers you, feel free to walk back through several miles of snow drifts and take a swim in the below-freezing New York Bay."

"Are you out of your mind?" Rainette looked indignant as she dropped a piece of her donut. "That water is filthy."

"Marcel," Cole began, ignoring her completely now, "go with Corhagen and check the back areas. Staffelbach, watch the front with Rainette. I want to have a look around in the main office to see if someone left a clue. We still don't know why all the officers in this building left."

"That is weird," Rainette was saying as they split up. "Why take out the police, anyway?"

"You take out the muscle that protects a country before taking it over," Cole replied. "That is basic military protocol for an overthrow."

"Staten is an island," Rainette countered, shouting after him. "Not a nation."

"It's a start," Cole replied. "And every tyrant has to start somewhere."

Cole found nothing in the main office or any of the other rooms in his section of the police station. There was nothing to suggest a struggle had taken place. For all intents and purposes, it really did look as though each and every member of the police and any prisoners being held here had simply got up and left. Cole reasoned the Lord of All Fey could have done this with enough lesser fey who were skilled at glamour. He had seen pixies do it before, though with fewer people.

"We found more donuts," Corhagen informed him when he came back to the front. "I skipped lunch."

"These are good," Marcel noted, stuffing a whole one down his throat. "Very chewy."

Cole felt like throwing his hands up in surrender right then. "I'm so glad I elected myself leader of this outfit," he mumbled. "Next time, the only bunch I want to ride into battle with are circus midgets or the Power Rangers."

"You're not supposed to call them midgets anymore," Rainette said loftily. "They are 'little people' now."

Cole's head snapped up sharply. "Did anyone else hear that?" Bandersnatch and Jabberwock were drawn before anyone could answer.

"I didn't hear anything," Corhagen said after swallowing.

"Neither did I," replied Staffelbach, though he got down off the table he was on regardless.

"I did," Marcel said, standing up. "It came from the back where we were a moment ago. It sounded like a window being forced open."

Cole nodded and began directing them to take cover. With his size, Marcel would have a hard time hiding in the corridors, however, and Cole was sure he wouldn't be able to shoot around his oversized frame without killing him.

So they waited instead. Whoever had broken in wasn't doing a very good job of keeping the noise down. By this point, all of them could hear it. Someone was grumbling now, and Cole thought the voice sounded familiar. Waiting with both guns at the ready, he watched as two short figures, one taller than the other, came through the door.

"Whoa!" Boogaloo cried out, holding his claws up high. "Hold ya fire there, sidhe! We cum smokin' peace pipe er whatevers."

Both guns slid back into their holsters smoothly. "What are you and Jynx doing here?" Cole demanded. "You were supposed to stay at the sithen."

"Nice ta see ya too," Boogaloo retorted. "Jynx 'ere wanted ta show ya more ah her fancy drawins and such. She insisted on cummin' along 'n' wouldn't stand ta listen ta sensible advice. So I tagged 'long ta make sure she didn't get up ta no good. That," he added as Jynx approached Cole with her drawings in hand, "an' ya stupid bumblin' butler was drivin' me bonkers."

Jynx had brought only two drawings with her. Cole marveled over the fact that they were in perfectly fine condition before their content registered with his brain.

"How'd you get over here?" Corhagen was asking.

"Stowed away on ah ferry tha' came loose from da docks," Boogaloo replied. "We saw da sidhe's ride outside ah here 'n' figured he wuz inside."

Cole was too busy looking over Jynx's drawings to pay the wood goblin much attention. The first drawing was beautiful. There were endless groves of trees and woodland animals playing about, ponds that shimmered in the moonlight, and the same two figures from the first drawing she had shown him standing in the center. They were happily holding each other's hands.

It looked like a paradise. Cole couldn't imagine how much time had gone into it. The next one gave him pause, though. As bright as the first one was, the second was just as grisly. It was hard to accurately describe what he was seeing. There was fire and shadows, both looking alive and stricken with madness. The longer he looked at it, the more Cole could make out. Pixies and other smaller fey were trapped within, writhing in agony. It made him sick to see it.

Jynx pulled the first drawing in front of Cole's face, then showed him the other. "Before and after?" he tried. "Or...?"

Jynx was shaking her head rapidly.

"First this one," he said, pointing at the depiction of paradise. "And then this. Are you saying...?"

Jynx was growing frustrated. Again, she showed Cole the first drawing, then placed the second one over it.

Cole thought on this for a moment. "This is what the Lord of All Fey originally planned to do," he said, bringing it all together.

Jynx nodded, holding the paradise picture up high.

"And this is what he's going to end up creating." Cole pulled the second drawing to the forefront. "The Lord of All Fey wanted to create a paradise for all the other lesser fey, but if he doesn't stop, this is what will end up happening."

Jynx nodded gravely.

"And he's going to use Staten Island?" Rainette called out from farther away. "He could have selected a better location. I would've gone with Greenwich Village myself."

"An island is isolated," Cole said softly. "And if properly defended, it could hold off an army."

Something in Jynx's eyes made Cole think he was within a footstep of the truth.

"This is what you two played together when he was a kid," he said, holding up the first drawing for her to see. "You wanted to make your own world together so you could play with each other all the time. He's decided to build that for you now, even though it's years too late."

Jynx nodded.

"He didn't understand why you left," Cole went on. "He thought that maybe you had abandoned him. So after all this time, he's decided to make the sort of world you always dreamed of having, and maybe you'd return. That was why you came here."

"To stop him?"

Cole shook his head at the same time that Jynx looked over at the detective. "To show him that it didn't matter," Cole answered for her. "And to explain why she had to leave the first time."

Rainette walked around the counter and stood behind Jynx, holding her tenderly by the shoulders. "That is an awful lot of trouble to go through for a guy," she chided. "When we get finished here, remind me to introduce you to a little something called AdultFriendFinder.com."

Cole rolled his eyes along with Staffelbach and even Corhagen. "How are we going to get out of here?" Corhagen asked. "The roads are getting worse, and I don't know if that Transit we signed for will survive."

Rainette raised a hand. "I'd like to go on record saying that I'm against walking in the snow."

"We all are," Corhagen replied. "It doesn't mean we won't do it if there is no other option."

Cole didn't have a solution, and the fact made him both doubtful and angry with himself. Gazing across the room at the entrance leading to the back area, Cole considered it for a long, ponderous moment, then pushed away from the counter. There had to be something in this place they could use. Blizzards beset the area regularly during the winter months. A small island like Staten was sure to have something that could cope.

His worries turned out to be for nothing. Cole managed to find the weapons cabinet in the back. It was a modest bounty, but beggars weren't supposed to be choosers. The real prize came when Cole happened to peek out a frosted-over window. There was a clear spot that resembled more a crack in the glass, and when Cole glanced through it on a whim, he grinned.

"Snowplow!" he yelled down the hall.

It brought Corhagen and Staffelbach momentarily. "Say what?" the younger officer asked.

"Snowplow," Cole repeated. "We can push our way through the snow."

"Wonder what it's doing here?" Corhagen asked, peeking at it through squinted eyes.

"It doesn't matter," Cole said. "The keys have got to be around here somewhere. Look for them while I get the others."

"That reminds me," Staffelbach said as he began searching through some cabinet drawers. "Where exactly are we taking this outfit, anyway?"

"The school," Cole answered, stopping in the doorway. "That was where this whole thing began. I think the Lord of All Fey made it his temporary headquarters."

"He's a principal," Corhagen reasoned, following suit beside

Staffelbach. "It makes a strange kind of sense, I guess. At least with the weather, the school is bound to be empty."

Rainette wasn't keen to leave the donuts behind. Marcel obediently followed, helping her to speed up every few steps. Jynx and Boogaloo were given instructions to remain at the station. Only the wood goblin seemed keen on the idea, so Cole left him in charge of keeping the changeling safe and away from the doors.

"I'll be back," he swore to her. "Don't worry. We're going to get this mess sorted out."

Jynx didn't look convinced, and Cole could feel her sad eyes watching him the whole time he walked away.

"I found them!" Staffelbach declared upon his return. "They were on a key rack in the next room."

"I was going to check there next," Corhagen grumbled in a teasing manner. "So what's our next move, boss?"

"Suit up," he told them. "There are weapons and vests in the back there. Put them on and be out front in ten minutes ready to start this show. Does anyone here know how to drive a snowplow?"

No one moved for a moment. Then Marcel tentatively raised his hand. "It was only for a week," he explained sheepishly. "Getting fired wasn't really my fault."

"Did you kill anyone with it?" Cole asked, holding the keys away.

"No."

Marcel caught the keys in midair.

"Try not to hit any houses on the way there. The rest of you, ten minutes. I'm going to go start the car."

Cole had entertained the idea of using his vehicle to try and plow through the snow on his own. It wasn't that the little guy wasn't capable of handling tough road conditions. It had already proven that it was, but Cole sensed the coach of the wild hunt was a relatively smaller power, a minor leaguer overall. The last thing he needed was to push it beyond what it was capable of and wind up getting them all killed. Besides that, having the snowplow in front of them meant much smoother sailing, even if it would be a bit slow at first.

No one was ready in ten minutes. At twenty, Cole started to lean on the horn. It was very likely he had just announced their presence, but after waiting with nothing to do but stare at erratic snowflakes melting on the windshield, Cole would have been more than happy for the Lord of All Fey to show up and save them a trip.

Twenty-seven minutes following his big announcement, they came running out of the building en masse. Rainette did not look happy.

"Officer Rainette was having some trouble getting her vest on," Corhagen explained, climbing into the back with her.

"I'm going to kill you for blowing the horn like that," she growled. "Just you wait and see. How come this thing is so itchy, by the way? I think whoever wore it last was sweating and didn't wash it. Ew!"

"I can't believe I'm actually saying this," Cole mumbled as Staffelbach adjusted the front seat to give her some more legroom, "but could you please try to maintain the facade of being an officer of the law?"

"You're right," Corhagen said after a moment's pause where Rainette merely flipped Cole off. "I can't believe that came from you either, Mr. Leather Pants."

"Before we go," Corhagen added.

"What?" Cole groaned.

"I just wanted to get everyone's names straight," Corhagen finished defensively. "I know Marcel. He's pretty hard to forget."

"Speaking of which, where is he?" Cole asked, peering through the curtain of snow.

"Bringing the snowplow around," Corhagen said. "Like I was saying, anyway, I know Marcel and Cole. What are your first names?"

Corhagen pointed at Staffelbach and Rainette. "Paul," Staffelbach answered at once. "Paul Staffelbach."

"Rainette DuBois," Rainette replied. "Nice to meet you. Please, no jokes. I am not now nor have I ever been a Southern Belle, and I couldn't show you Desire on a map if you highlighted it."

Marcel was bringing the snowplow around as Cole started the car. "Can we turn the heat up, please?" Rainette begged. "It's freezing in here."

THE Lord of All Fey had been a busy little bee. Houses all along the streets were coated in layers of snow, making them resemble frosted Christmas delicacies. The windows were dark and lifeless, however. The same presence Cole had felt before was still lingering in the air. If anything, it had grown more prominent. Even Rainette and the others appeared touched by it.

It was worse the closer they got to the school. The town was becoming more than simply cloaked by an ill omen. The residences in this area were positively abandoned. Even some doors had been left hanging open. Cole got the eerie impression that those doors had been left open because the families behind them had been dragged out. He had a sudden intuition as to what the police in the area had been up to since leaving their posts at the station.

The academy was just up ahead. It was the only building within two miles that still had electricity. The lights coming from it were almost a beacon, but rather than being warming, they gave off an ominous, foreboding glare.

There were police officers posted at the corners of the iron fence, as well as the front gate. Those two took aim the moment the snowplow came close. Marcel was smart enough to stop the plow and get out with his hands raised.

"Follow his lead," Cole said. "I have an idea."

The newly deputized members of Section Thirteen climbed out without a word, hands above their heads, and followed after Cole. Corhagen managed to catch up to him before they reached the gate.

"What's the plan?" he hissed in Cole's ear.

It made Cole shudder involuntarily. "We walk over and let them take us prisoner," he replied. "It's the easiest way to get in, and we won't be risking the uninitiated in a full-blown battle."

Corhagen sounded as though he wanted to protest. As they came up on the gates, however, he swallowed loudly and took a step back. "Good plan."

The policemen watching the gate were wearing red rings around their necks. They had been collared the same way the Cu Sith had been, but once Cole got a good look at them through the falling snow, he suspected the rings weren't as effective. Hiding behind each officer's neck was a pixie, each one collared with a miniature ring of their own. The pixies didn't appear at all happy to be there. The snow wasn't bothering them, but the rings themselves had an obvious effect on them.

The eyes of the policemen were dazed, as though they'd been bespelled. Cole smiled as he realized what must have happened and stopped just short of them opening fire. "We have come seeking asylum with the Lord of All Fey in his new kingdom," Cole shouted loudly above the storm. "We wish to speak with him personally so that we can pledge our unwavering loyalty to him."

It was a testament to how cold it was that Rainette said nothing in objection. Both officers stared past them into the distance for a moment as if they hadn't heard, then slowly glanced toward each other. At once, they shouldered their guns and motioned Cole forward.

"Wait here at the gate," the officer on the left said in a benign voice. "We will send for someone to escort you to see our master."

Cole motioned the others forward as well. He was careful not to touch the iron gates. Being so close to them was making him antsy, yet he couldn't resist taking a peek through them for some reason. It might have been telling as to how bad the snow was getting. Cole had to take several steps back to confirm what he'd glimpsed.

A spire shaped like an obelisk was thrusting skyward out of the academy building. Cole couldn't help but stare as the ill foreboding he'd sensed before returned in full force, leaving little doubt in his mind as to its source.

Someone was coming up along the path leading to the gates, which swung open as he drew close. It was a trow, Cole saw. The fey creature was only a little more than four feet tall with bluish-grey skin and yellow eyes. His hooked nose stuck out several inches away from the rest of his face, and though Cole had never laid eyes on the creature before, there was something oddly familiar about his smell.

"Come with me," the trow ordered, motioning with a finger. "The master wishes to speak with you."

The others hurried along after him, but Cole lingered a few steps back and continued to stare at the tower hanging over them. It was definitely radiating some kind of energy, and it looked to be the same shade of black as those rings controlling the pixies. The pieces were starting to come together in his mind as he crossed the threshold.

Inside, the building was warm, like a sauna.

"You may keep your weapons," the trow was telling them. "The master has no fear of them. He will see you all momentarily. I suggest you smarten yourselves up in the meantime."

Cole sniffed the air and felt the same sense of déjà vu as before. The scent was coming from the trow, and though Cole still couldn't place the face, there could be no mistaking it. Closing his eyes for a second, he wracked his brain for an answer. It only took a moment, perhaps due to the fact that the event in question had occurred just one room away. His eyes flew open just as the trow was walking off. It didn't make sense, yet he knew it to be true.

"Principal McGregor," he called out sharply.

"Yes," the trow replied in an irritated voice, turning back around. "What is it?"

Their eyes met, and the trow's forehead wrinkled up in frustration as defeat sagged his shoulders. Cole smiled knowingly.

"But how?" Rainette said, staring openly at him. "I thought you said that...."

"You were wearing a husk when Corhagen and Joss came to see you in your office," Cole explained. "Since this academy is under the control of the Hermetic Order of the Golden Dawn, you were taking a big risk working here. The real Lord of All Fey must have found out about you and used that information to force you into becoming his stalking horse."

"How'd you know?" the trow asked.

Cole tapped himself on the nose. "I have a keen sense of smell."

"So it is true, then," the trow stated, looking over at Cole reproachfully. "You were once one of Titania's most prized wolves. I wouldn't have bought it until now."

"Why help someone who is enslaving our people?" Cole asked seriously. "You could have left and started over somewhere else."

"You know what the Order is like," the trow barked back. "They hate all of us. Those blasted rings were made by the Order to capture us for study. The Lord of All Fey hacked into the Order's mainframe and stole their technology so he could use it against them."

"Impressive," Rainette said. "I didn't think anyone had the balls to break through the Hermetic Order's computer system and live to tell about it."

Corhagen looked at her. "Does everybody but me know about this Order thing?"

"I didn't," Staffelbach said.

"I did," replied Marcel behind him. "All fey know and fear the Order. You do not live in this city without hearing whispers of them if you are fey."

Rainette shrugged when Corhagen looked at her. "I read a lot," she replied defensively. "And it doesn't take a genius to figure out someone works behind the scenes in this town."

"Just a bunch of amateurs pretending to be gods," Cole said dismissively. "And this is the end result. Someone stole their research and made themselves the ruler of a nonexistent kingdom."

"Bold words coming from a fallen sidhe," the trow snapped, baring his teeth.

"None of this could have been done in just a couple of weeks," Cole said. "Why didn't anyone come to me?"

"You took jobs for money," the trow reminded him. "Not everyone can afford you, and then you sold yourself out to be the dog of a bunch of humans. No one trusts you anymore, sidhe, not that we ever did much to begin with."

Cole fell silent, meeting the trow's gaze without flinching. "We came here to put an end to what has been happening on this island," he said finally. "If you want to help, then tell us how we can shut down the Lord of All Fey's control over the others. Otherwise, take us to him."

McGregor the trow smiled sadly and raised the hem of his left pant leg. There, just above the ankle, was a black ring. It looked as though it had been there for a while and was even digging into the flesh a bit. Dried blood had crusted around the inside of it.

"I've made my choice," the trow replied, though he didn't sound happy at all. "There is no means for me to go back on it now."

Cole nodded and took the lead. "Then show us the way."

There were classrooms on both sides of the entrance hall. Some of the doors were cracked, and there were quite a few people gathered inside. Most of them were seated against the wall in rows. Both children and adults had been brought in. On the whole, from what little Cole could see, there were at least two adults for every child. All of them appeared shell-shocked.

The numbers quickly added up in his head. "You brought in the parents of children who attend the academy," he said to McGregor the trow. "Why? What do they have to do with any of this?"

The trow barely glanced back. "If the Lord of All Fey wishes for you to know, he will tell you himself. My place is not to question his will. I have been informed of that before. My advice to you is not to imply anything. He has ways of dealing with those that displease them."

Cole didn't have much sympathy. "Just like you said," he replied curtly. "You made your choice."

The hallway led into a chamber that connected with several other corridors leading off in different directions. As they drew up on it, Cole could feel the air humming with energy. Magic, human magic, to be precise, was being pulled in through the connecting hallways into a circle drawn at the center. Cole paused to study it a moment. It didn't look like a recent addition.

"Rainette," he said quietly.

"I see," she replied. "It was designed to convert and channel energy."

Rainette hesitated as she glanced around the open space. "This is hazarding a guess, but I suspect the halls are designed to be shaped like a unicursal hexagram. The corridors bring the energy from students to the circle. These kids are stuck in classrooms all day long. It gets hot; they have all this nervous energy being pent up, so it has to go somewhere. That place is the circle."

"So this was set up by the Order when the school was built?"

Rainette nodded. "That would be my guess."

"Yes," McGregor interrupted loudly. "It was, many years ago, in fact. The Lord of All Fey didn't make us do anything different to the circle itself. Merely add to it. The Lord of All Fey capitalized on the energy gathered to power his network of black rings."

"That is why the students and their parents are here," Cole said. "All that fear and uncertainty is going right into there."

"It is one reason," the trow answered calmly. "But we're wasting time here. Our master is waiting on us, and he hates delays."

"What's so special about that circle?" Corhagen asked as they continued on behind McGregor.

Both Staffelbach and Marcel were listening in closely. "The circle is channeling energy up into that obelisk at the top of the school. I think the Lord of All Fey is using it as fuel so he can control as many enslaved fey as possible. It would help him spread his reach out farther."

"We are seriously outnumbered here," Staffelbach groaned.

"Is it too late to announce my retirement?" Rainette asked. "I'd rather not die here today with all of you."

McGregor wound up taking them to a room at the very end of the hall. The sign outside the door said it was the recreation room.

"Wait here," McGregor told them. "Make yourselves comfortable while I inform the Lord that you are ready to see him." The trow shuffled away without another word.

Cole waited until he had taken several steps before closing the door. "While we have a moment," he said quickly, "let's get what we know together. There isn't time to check and see if the room has been bugged, so keep things concise."

"Right," everyone replied.

"The Lord of All Fey is probably a member of the Hermetic Order of the Golden Dawn," Cole continued, speaking very rapidly. "For those still in the dark, it is a secret order that was founded over a century ago by practitioners of human magic. Since then, they've kept a low profile, which is why I think this Lord is a renegade member."

"That feels right," Corhagen agreed. "And he's using those black rings to control different fey so they can be his private army and conquer an island to serve as his base."

"Did anyone else notice those red rings on the officers guarding the place?" Rainette asked.

"I did," Cole said.

Corhagen nodded. "I did too. This fey lord must be able to control humans now along with fey."

"I don't think so," Cole countered. "Not completely, anyway. If he could, why not put them on the arms of the people he took hostage? Why not just make more red rings and enslave the whole human population of Staten?"

Rainette frowned. "He's got a point, though I hate admitting it."

"There were pixies on the shoulders of those guards," Cole said. "Those red rings must not work very well. The pixie's glamour holds them in check."

"I hate to bring everyone down," Staffelbach said, looking grim, "but none of this stuff actually helps us with the problem at hand. We're about to go toe to toe with someone who can control people. How are we supposed to fight him, especially if he can just use innocent people as shields?"

"We don't," Cole said.

When the door eased itself back open, they were all facing it. McGregor stuck his head in and swept the room before looking directly at Cole.

"The master will speak with the fallen sidhe," he said neutrally. "But no one else."

"Ah," Cole said. "That's fine with me."

The trow backed away to let Cole pass first. "The others may wait here for you if they wish," he added, almost as an afterthought. "No harm will come to them for now."

"If harm comes to them while I am gone," Cole replied icily, "then they have my permission to retaliate in the most painful manner they can."

The others smiled as the door shut.

"You take a great risk in allowing mortals to follow you here," McGregor warned, leading the way again.

"I've lived with and alongside mortals for many years. If there is one thing to be counted on, it's that underestimating them will only lead to one's downfall."

"You are far too optimistic," the trow derided.

"I'll choose not to accept the advice of someone who threw away his freedom," Cole replied. "And to a mortal, no less. Whatever you think of me as a sidhe, it pales in comparison to what you have done."

The trow let out a sharp hiss. "Like I wanted to be this!" he snarled. "I didn't have a choice in the matter."

"Then leave," Cole said simply. "Cut the ring off your leg and walk out of here with your head held high."

"These things explode if you remove them!"

McGregor slammed the leg that had the ring attached against a row of lockers as if to illustrate his point. "If I try to take it off—"

"It would hurt," Cole agreed. "Badly, even, but you are not human. You are a trow, clever engineers and skilled magicians all. Your race carved some impressive things into Faerie history over the eons and won wars by fighting smarter instead of harder. If anyone could take that ring off your leg, it should be yourself."

McGregor froze in his tracks. A set of double doors stood just up ahead. Whatever lay beyond them was something he couldn't face. The trow kept his eyes squarely on the floor just beyond the tips of his bare feet.

"You have no one to blame for your situation but yourself," Cole stated. "This could have ended long before now, but I am the one sent in to clean it up. And I seriously doubt this Lord of All Fey could have gotten so far without someone to help things along. How much aid did you provide him with?"

McGregor began to shake. "He tortured me," the trow whispered. "He… I didn't want to at first, but he…."

Cole didn't really need a description. "I have been tortured before," Cole said. "After my father ejected me from his sanctuary. My mother was Summer Court. The power she passed on to me weakened him, and he was involved in a feud with a rival house. Titania offered to let me train to become one of her wolves, but Lord Oberon had a stipulation. I had to spend ten months in his private Citadel of Pain."

The trow shuddered. "I've heard stories. Was it as bad as everyone says?"

That was a rude question according to Faerie standards, but Cole answered it anyway. "I don't remember much," he admitted. "After a while, what was left of my mind just blanked everything out. My body rode the remaining months out, but it was a while before I could look at someone without screaming. It made the training that followed inconvenient."

McGregor the trow looked up at Cole's face. "You are a good man, I think," he said softly. "Different than I'd heard and better than the sidhe I've come across."

Cole shrugged. "I can't be all that great. None in Faerie wanted me, not even Queen Titania in the end."

McGregor gave a chuckle at that thought, then knelt down on the floor as if to tie his shoe, despite the fact that he was not wearing any. Cole watched as he raised his pant leg and began fiddling with the black ring. It took a moment, but the ring came free in the end. McGregor continued to handle it carefully, as though it were a bomb.

"I don't know how long until it explodes," McGregor warned. "It may not at all, but I'd rather not risk my fingers by holding it when it happens. There's an empty closet up ahead, so I'll dispose of it there. If you don't mind, after that, I'll be getting out of here. My former master is behind those double doors and to your right. You can't miss him."

Cole watched the trow leave, then disappeared himself through the double doors. There was a corridor just to the right, like McGregor had said. Down it and to the left was an open door with light spilling out of it. Surrounding the door were hobgoblins, collared and holding axes in one hand. Both took one look at Cole and sneered but made no move to block his path. Cole saluted the two mockingly before stepping inside the brightly lit room.

It was a teacher's lounge from the look of things, or had been at some point. Most of the furniture was gone. Tables and whatnot had been pushed up against the walls out of the way. Only the soda and snack machines held prominence. Someone had moved them to surround a single plush chair. It might have been the most comfortable chair in the whole place. And sitting in it…

…was an eleven-year-old boy.

With his feet propped up on a coffee table stretched out horizontally in front of him.

The boy had brown eyes and brown hair. Freckles dotted his cheeks below very bored eyes that matched the rest of his expression. He was dressed in something that might have come from somebody's idea of the nineteenth century or a theater department's wardrobe closet.

The boy had a gauntlet covering his left arm. It looked metallic and very complicated, something that had clearly taken hours of labor to create. Lights blinked on it, and the hand was glowing with a mystic circle with symbols that shone even under the florescent lights.

"Where's McGregor?" the boy wondered, glancing to either side of Cole. "He was supposed to come back with you."

"McGregor left," Cole answered.

Rather than looking alarmed or even upset, the boy just sighed, pressed a button on the gauntlet, and waited. After a moment, he jabbed the same button again. After the third try, Cole began to figure out what he was trying to accomplish.

"He isn't coming back," Cole explained. "He left for good, took the ring off his leg and walked out."

That got the boy's attention. "You're serious? He actually figured out how to take it off? That would explain why some of the wolves went missing, I guess."

Cole kept his mouth shut rather than explaining that just yet. His mind was still reeling on some level, taking in that a human child was behind everything he'd witnessed. Even in his bewilderment, however, much of it began to make sense. "You are the Lord of All Fey," he said, pointing.

"Yes," the boy replied, straightening himself up. "Are you the one everyone calls Cole? That's an odd name for somebody who's so pale."

"I get that," Cole replied. "Occasionally. I was expecting you to be a changeling. Then again, I expected you were McGregor at first. Do you have a name other than the Lord of All Fey?"

The boy, in reply, stabbed another button on his gauntlet. At once, the hobgoblins that had been standing guard by the door outside came in.

"Find McGregor and bring him back here," the boy instructed them. "Alive, but in a lot of pain."

Each hobgoblin merely nodded and left.

"I'm getting tired of this," the boy muttered. "What is the point of ruling a place if nobody ever does as they're told?"

"I'm sure a few of your teachers would share those same sentiments," Cole muttered.

The boy scowled at that. "Why are you here?"

Cole hesitated before answering. "I came seeking asylum on your island away from the humans. I brought a handful with me, however, and one ogre that I think you already made the acquaintance of. He was wearing one of your black rings, anyway."

The boy's eyes narrowed. "The one who attacked the precinct house?"

"It's called a police station, but yes." Cole waited another moment. "You didn't send him there to kill Foleman?"

"I should have," said the boy, and there was an unmistakable note of loathing in his voice. "One of my prototype rings went missing, and I finally was able to track it to that station." Emphasis was placed on that last word. "By the time I got there," he was saying, "the place was a total wreck. I had to sneak in with McGregor to see what was going on."

Cole frowned. "You were the boy outside Inspector Vallimun's office," he said, remembering. "That was McGregor?"

Before the boy could answer, Cole thought of it. "A husk," he said. "McGregor was wearing a husk. That is how he appears human during the day while he's the principal. He must have another one somewhere."

"He did," the boy said. "It was in his office. Unless he comes back for it, it belongs to me. I think I'll have it burned as punishment." The boy spoke as though he were talking about the weather.

"Do you know who would want Foleman dead?"

"Someone who hated him more than I did." The note of loathing was back in the boy's voice. "Though I find that hard to imagine. I did send the Cu Sith to kill Mr. Jagger, in case you were wondering about that."

"Why would I care about that?"

The boy shot Cole a glare in response. "I know you're a cop," he replied. "You were talking about Mr. Jagger's murder to Thorton and Higgins on the front steps yesterday."

Cole thought back. "You were in the line in front of them. They were pushing you."

"They always push me." The boy was glaring at Cole with hatred glowing in his eyes. "Why didn't you stop them from pushing me?"

"Was I supposed to?" When the boy said nothing, Cole tried again. "I guess I didn't think it was any of my business."

"It should have been the teacher's business," he said. "They always push me. They always do something to me, and whenever I complained or tried to fight back, the teacher punished me instead. No one ever does anything."

The boy pushed several more buttons on his gauntlet. "Come with me," he demanded, getting up off the chair. "I want to show you something."

"What?" Cole asked, moving aside slightly so he could pass.

"You came here to stop me," the boy answered, hitting another button. "I know that. I'm not stupid like all the other kids, no matter what they might have told you about me. You're probably wondering why I did all this. I want to show you."

Obediently, Cole followed the boy back out into the hallway the way he came. When they reached the double doors, the boy turned right and kept on going until he reached one of the occupied classrooms. Turning around, he waited for Cole to catch up.

"Your little legs move fast," Cole noted.

"When you have to stay several steps ahead of people, you learn how to move quickly," he replied. "Just so you know, two other hobgoblins are watching the rec room where your team is staying. If I push this button on my arm, they'll kill them." The boy pointed as if to illustrate.

"They'll fight back," Cole told him. "I told them to fight back if anything attacked them. The woman, Rainette, would have done it anyway. I don't think she would want to die inside a school, even if it wasn't hers. She had a long and painful history with the educational system, from what I hear."

"You're trying to be funny," the boy noted.

"I'm not," Cole said earnestly. "Show me what you wanted me to see."

The boy pointed at the narrow window in the door. "The fat lady wearing the floral print dress," he said. "She should be sitting at her desk at the front of the room. It always made her feel special."

Cole looked and saw her at once. "She's sitting on the floor next to a crying child," he replied. "I think she's been crying herself."

"I used to have her for first period when I was seven," the boy explained. "She put me in front of Fredrick Tatum. He used to kick the back of my desk through the whole period. I could never concentrate. I almost failed her class as a result, and my mother spanked me whenever I brought home a bad grade. Tatum did it loud enough for the whole room to hear, but she never stopped him. If I turned around to hit him, she made me stay in from recess."

Cole blinked. "She's crying again," he said. "The little girl is gone now, but she's crying by herself."

"She'll be crying a lot more when I'm done with her," the boy promised. "This way."

Cole followed him a little bit further down.

"That's Coach Williams in the corner," the boy said when Cole peeked into the classroom. "He likes to watch the other students from there."

"He's sitting at a desk doing card tricks," Cole told him. "Some of the kids are laughing."

In response, the Lord of All Fey narrowed his eyes in anger and brushed past Cole, kicking the door in, his gauntlet arm raised. All eyes turned to him as the blue circle on his gauntlet glowed brightly. The coach dropped the deck in his hands, causing the cards to scatter as lightning jumped out at him from the Lord of All Fey's hand.

The coach screamed, along with the rest of the class. Some students jumped out of their seats and moved back. The ones closest to the grown man dove for cover. Coach Williams let out an unearthly sound as the energy crackled along his skin, sending him flying away from the desk to the floor and into convulsions.

Still, the Lord of All Fey didn't let up. The coach's screams had become whimpers before he finally relented. Turning around, the boy stormed back out of the room to a dead silence that filled the air along with the stench of burned flesh.

"What did he do?" Cole asked calmly after the boy had slammed the door shut behind him.

"He used to be the gym teacher," the boy said. "We always had physical education with the bigger kids. He would make them gang up on me. One tackled me during dodgeball and sent me home with a black eye. My mother grounded me for it."

"He sounds like a wonderful person," Cole mused, watching through the window as several kids began helping the coach up.

"He always picks on the kids who don't have fathers," the boy explained. "Mine died when I was a baby. My mom remarried a few years ago, but he's never at home. My real father is the reason I go to this school."

The boy had to stand on his tiptoes to see inside. After a moment, he looked away as if angry about something and stormed off. "Come on," he called back after Cole. "There's one more thing."

The last stop took them up a whole flight of stairs and around two corners. Cole peeked in without being prompted this time and saw two human females inside being watched over by floating specters. The older one looked like a teacher, while the younger girl could have been the same age as the Lord of All Fey. Cole sensed there was a connection there, as one of the dark spirits swooped down near the girl, causing her to shriek.

The spirits seemed to enjoy that. "I never collared them," the boy explained, peeking in on his tiptoes. "Couldn't figure out a way to, since they don't have flesh. They just showed up on their own not long ago."

"They're fausts," Cole explained. "Dark spirits with a taste for human misery. They're attracted to places that have seen a lot of grief."

The boy snorted. "They'll really love this place, then. The girl is Angie Clayton, by the way. She was the favorite of Mrs. Hollins there for years. She sat behind me in class and would stick her pencil deep into the back of my neck. I still have the scars."

"Let me guess," Cole said. "No one believed you."

In answer, the Lord of All Fey turned around and lifted his shaggy hair away from his neck to show Cole the marks. "I think they're still there," he said. "It's been a while since I looked, though. Kind of hard to when you need at least three mirrors to see, and it isn't as though I really need anything to remind me."

Cole wasn't looking at the scars, though. They were visible, but what caught his eye was the strange symbol. It looked like a tattoo set against the pale marks where the skin had been burned away. Cole brushed a finger over it and immediately felt a shock go through him.

"I'm sorry about what happened to you for so long," he said softly. "I'm sorry so many bad things happened here and no one ever did anything about it. I know what it's like. Something tells me you won't believe that, but I've been where you are. The thing is, even back then, I never enslaved others to get revenge."

The boy turned around slowly. His eyes were barely slits as he stared up at Cole.

Cole wasn't intimidated by it, though. "I can understand you wanting to punish these people for what they did," he continued, keeping his guard up just in case. "In fact, if you had gone about it a different way, I might have stayed to help. I wouldn't have wanted you to kill any of these people, but they deserve something for what happened. You were right in that the teachers had a responsibility to protect you as much as anyone else."

"The rings were originally designed to do things far worse," the boy said defensively. "They were on an encrypted disk I found that had been my father's. He had been part of the Order and had a lot of data stored away about them. When I cracked the code, this stuff was there for me to pick through. It took years to get most of it."

"The dryad you tried to enslave died because one of those rings was placed around her tree," Cole said, holding his anger in check now. "I was there when she died."

The boy's eyes widened. "She wasn't supposed to die. I just thought—"

Cole cut him off by pulling Bandersnatch from its holster. He didn't take aim, not yet, but it was hard. "If you wanted revenge, you should have gotten it on your own. I'm putting a stop to this now. Whoever you are, you aren't the Lord of All Fey. I've met him, and he is a lot more powerful than you could ever hope to be."

The boy studied him for a moment. "I'm sorry," he said, looking down slightly. "You really ought to have pointed that gun at me when you had the chance."

The magic circle on his gauntlet glowed now. Cole began to raise his gun slowly as the kid hit a button, then raised his fist. "You should have killed me when you had the chance," the boy said. "Although I do apologize for putting the ring on you earlier. That looked like it hurt."

Cole flinched. "You were behind me in the basement," he said, thinking back. "How did you move where I wouldn't hear you?"

"A friend showed me how to," the boy replied, taking aim himself. "My only friend. The best friend I ever had. What happened with the ring won't be as bad as this, though."

With those words, the boy sent a current of electricity through the air, straight at Cole. It landed directly on his chest. Cole screamed as the current spread all through his body, making him drop Bandersnatch to the floor.

The boy's grin quickly turned to a frown, followed by wide-eyed horror as Cole arose wearing a smirk on his face. "Next time," he said cockily, "try dialing it up to eleven." Both blades extended out from Aed Deigh. "Let's dance, kid."

CHAPTER 9

THE first swipe chilled the air and froze part of the kid's gauntlet. Cole used this window of half a second to charge forward and seize him by the arm.

"Deadly to humans," he jeered, squeezing hard.

The boy jammed his thumb into the gauntlet's console. "Dodge this," he replied as the pentagram on the surface of his palm changed, then glowed orange. A ball of light formed inside the boy's fingers. Cole had a second to make his move before the kid released it at him. Bending back, he let the energy blast fly over him without loosening his grip.

Unfortunately, Cole forgot to close his legs.

Pain shot through him as the kid's boot connected with his two low-hangers. Cole loosened his grip without meaning to, and the boy was gone in a flash.

"I'm going to stop treating you like a kid in a moment," Cole wheezed angrily, willing the pain away. "Unless you cut this shit out."

Something struck Cole in the chest. The nonexistent gravity humans spoke of lost its hold on him, and he was lifted off his feet and into the air. When Cole landed, the tile floor did not make the most receptive cushion. The Lord of All Fey was advancing on him with a new glowing pentagram shining on his gauntlet arm. Cole flipped forward and brought his blade down. Aed Deigh was primed and ready to cut the metal device clear off his body. There was a blinding flash, though, and Cole found himself standing before a transparent shield.

"Shield ward," the boy told him confidently. "Blocks all physical attacks."

Cole leaped away and swung his blade around, striking at the shield several times in sequence. Each attack did nothing but send bursts of sparks to the side and coat the air in a light gray mist. The boy ducked when he brought the icy blade sideways at his head, then hit another button and let Cole have it again with another burst of electricity. This time, it actually stung.

"That's starting to hurt," Cole warned. "I'd advise you to cut it out."

Another pentagram appeared, this one scarlet red. "Try this one on for size, then," the boy crowed. With a snap of his fingers, the Lord of All Fey sent a wave of flames directly at Cole's face. Cole flipped out of the way and smelled his hair getting singed.

"Little boys shouldn't play with fire," he warned. "Don't adults teach their kids that anymore? And I would be having second thoughts about challenging me with flames right now if I were you. Let me show you how an expert does it."

Cole swung Aed Deigh, and the firebrand unleashed a volley of spike-shaped flames directly at the boy's head. The Lord of All Fey ducked as the spikes struck the stone wall behind him. Pieces flew as the flames exploded, leaving the Lord of All Fey with a few smoking hairs himself.

"Missed," he stated flatly.

Cole swung the blade again, sending another volley a little bit sharper to the left again. The boy dodged easily this time, and in just the right direction. Cole laughed as the flames struck, of all things, a fire extinguisher behind where the kid had stopped moving. The metal canister burst, spewing white foam everywhere. Most of the goop landed on the poor boy's head.

"Didn't miss that time," Cole retorted. "Not so easy, is it?"

Wiping his brow, the boy gritted his teeth and punched one of the buttons he had used earlier. The shield returned, much larger than before, and Cole had to steel himself for an attack as the Lord of All Fey charged him. The two traded blows for a moment, Cole's ancient weapon once again filling the hallway with sparks and fog. The boy was giving it his all this time, using the shield offensively and not just to block.

"Tell me something," Cole asked as their battle continued. "How does a kid like you get beaten up every day for years?"

"My mother said she would beat me within an inch of my life if she ever found out I was fighting other kids in school," the Lord of All Fey replied curtly, swinging the shield up at Cole's head. "That doesn't mean I didn't know how to."

"You've got some nice moves," Cole acknowledged as they tangoed down the hallway. "You can think fast on your feet, and you know how to make adjustments. You'd have made a fine sidhe warrior from what I can tell."

"Don't try to flatter me," the kid snapped back, growing angry. His eyes blazed as he sent a blast of lightning at Cole again, which he deflected using the heated edge of Aed Deigh. "Adults only flatter kids that they want to control or feel sorry for," he screamed. "I don't want you to pity me!"

"It wasn't pity," Cole insisted, getting in a few ice blasts near the kid's feet. "I was never an adult. I am not human, and in the realm of Faerie, pity is only given to weak fools for amusement. Do you think yourself that?"

"I am the Lord of All Fey," the boy declared, making Cole spin out of the way as orange energy balls flew from his palm. "No one else could have done what I have so far. Before this day is over with, no one will pity me ever again. They won't dare!"

The two went toe to toe against each other. There was a fire in the boy's eyes that contrasted with the bitterness and anguish etched into his face from years of abuse. Cole saluted it mentally as the boy's shield and his blade clashed against one another, sending a roar up through the hall.

"I'm quicker than you," the boy screamed. "Smarter than you and younger than you. What else have you got against me?"

"Something different," Cole said in a sad, calm voice. "Something that you can only get with time and experience."

"What?" he spat.

Cole retracted both blades into the hilt and stepped out of the line of fire. "I know how to wait."

The shot that was fired sounded like a cannon going off in the silence following Cole's words. The bullet struck the Lord of All Fey in the back on his right shoulder blade. His small body jerked as shock and pain contorted his face. Cole rushed forward at once, catching him before he hit the floor and at the same time tearing the metal gauntlet from his arm.

"I've got you," he whispered into the boy's ear. "Just close your eyes and relax."

Corhagen's footsteps echoed as he walked toward them. "I've been shot," the boy said weakly, noticing the blood pooling on the floor beside him.

"Yes, you were," Cole acknowledged. "That was a good battle you gave me, though. I will remember it for a long time."

"We heard fighting up here," Corhagen said, lowering his gun.

"But I came anyway," Rainette added, peeking out from behind Corhagen's frame. "Staffelbach and the ogre are downstairs checking people for injuries and helping them escape."

"That worked a lot better than last time in the park," Cole said, pressing down hard on the boy's wound. "And you didn't even need a bazooka. Did the collared fey give you much trouble?"

"A bit," Rainette replied. "Once they realized their master was busy doing something else, though, they pretty much turned tail and ran. The cops were the worst, though. They kept on fighting even after the pixies abandoned them. I think some of them might have mistaken us for crooks, but it got sorted out in the end."

"They stopped shooting when one of them heard me yelling that I was with the NYPD," Corhagen added.

"The most important thing is that I got to shoot at people today," Rainette cut in gleefully. "Best first day on the job ever!"

Cole was ignoring her in favor of holding the tip of Aed Deigh's red-hot edge to the open wound. The bullet hadn't gone in very deep, and Cole had been able to remove it while Rainette was rambling. The heat was causing the wound to close faster. Once that was done, he flipped the weapon around and soothed the wound using the icy edge.

The whole time, not a sound came out of the boy.

"A part of me still doesn't believe this is the perp we've been after this whole time," Corhagen said, looking down at the kid shrewdly.

"On the other hand, though, I'm really hoping you'll tell me it was so that I can fall asleep tonight knowing I didn't just shoot an innocent kid."

"You didn't," Cole said. "This is the Lord of All Fey. I still don't know his real name, but maybe we can work that out of him shortly. I think I've got the bleeding stopped now."

Corhagen stared. "This kid could've used a hobby," he said finally. "Don't they still make Nintendo games?"

Cole passed the gauntlet up to Rainette, who seemed reluctant to accept it, since some of the blood from the boy's bullet wound had gotten on it.

"Just take it," he insisted. "See if you can't figure out how to shut off those damned black rings on everyone."

"You need a special code," the boy answered weakly. "It's eleven, twelve, twenty, zero, four."

Nobody moved.

"That was helpful," she reasoned. "Did you arrest the wrong preteen by mistake?"

"They'll be coming for me," he whispered, coughing. "Once those collars come off, they'll want revenge."

Cole studied the boy for a moment. "That won't happen," he stated. "Not while I'm here."

"You won't be for long," the boy countered, looking into Cole's tri-colored eyes. "You all have to leave sometime, and the fey are known for being resourceful. If they want me dead, there's little you can do to stop them. The smallest fey are everywhere and in places most people don't think to look in. They might not look like much, but they can do serious damage. That was why I went for them first."

The boy grew quiet for a moment. "You have eyes like theirs. You're one of them, aren't you?"

Cole nodded. "Have you got a name?"

"Daniel Whittaker," the boy said, coughing again.

Corhagen's eyes lit up. "He's the kid from the file," the detective said. "The one who accused Foleman of sexual assault."

Cole shushed him. "I don't think that bullet hit anything serious," he said to Daniel. "You're just going to be hurting for a while."

Daniel didn't seem affected by Cole's words. "I've had worse."

Cole turned to Corhagen and Rainette, who were observing the exchange as though watching something fascinating. Both looked a little shell-shocked by the kid's responses. Though he was clearly in pain, the boy's facial expression looked almost resigned, like that of a man on death row.

"Get somebody up here with a first aid kit," Cole ordered. "We need to get him patched up. After that, before we take him away, Corhagen, I'd like a moment alone."

"How come?" Corhagen asked, a note of suspicion threading through his words.

"I just need to talk," Cole said. "Give me five minutes."

Corhagen turned around. "You've got until the ambulance arrives," he said. "I'm going downstairs to make the call right now. This kid needs to go to the hospital before we book him." Corhagen was shaking his head sadly as he walked off. "I still don't believe it."

Rainette looked down at Cole, who was glaring at her now. "Oh!" she exclaimed. "You were wanting me to go too, right?"

Cole nodded. Rainette took one look at the blood puddled on the floor near her feet and left without a murmur of protest. For all her talk about getting to shoot people, it didn't look as though she handled the aftermath all that well. He could remember Katalina mentioning once how Rainette had dropped out of nursing school after a semester. It looked like that mystery was solved.

Pushing Katalina out of his thoughts for the time being, Cole observed Daniel Whittaker carefully.

"She came," he said after a moment's deliberation. "It took her a long time to lose the Cait Sith that were chasing her, but Jynx came back to see you."

Daniel's eyes flickered to life for the first time. "She came back?"

"She was here for a while," Cole told him. "I don't know for how long, but she's been helping the Cu Sith and other fey get free of the collars."

"Oh," Daniel replied quietly, glancing away. "So that was who it was."

"I know where she is."

Daniel shook his head. "I don't want her to see me like this," he whispered, tears filling the corners of his eyes. "And it won't be long before one of the hobgoblins or the wolves hunt me down. No matter what cell you put me in, they'll find me."

"She was your friend," Cole said, as the mystery came together at last. "You played with her when you were younger, correct?"

It almost looked as though Daniel wasn't going to answer. After a moment, however, he nodded his head weakly. "She was my only friend. We played together in the woods every day. I used to dream about running away with her. Then she disappeared."

"The Cait Sith found her," Cole explained, holding him up. "They are the agents of the House that held her captive. She had to run so you wouldn't be hurt."

Daniel seemed to contemplate this. "Can I ask you a question?" Cole continued. "Off the record, as they say."

Daniel shrugged and winced as pain shot through him. "Okay," he mumbled, fighting back tears now for a different reason.

"Foleman," Cole began. "He used to teach school here a couple of years back, before the Order kicked him out. There were a lot of reports about him molesting students in different schools. No charges were formally brought against him, but I'm guessing that was why the Order had him evicted. He hurt one of the students, and they had to get rid of him to avoid a scandal."

Daniel went rigid. His body shook now with rage held in. The tears he had been holding back spilled over his cheeks at last.

"You said whoever murdered him, whoever put that collar on Marcel and forced him to kill Foleman, was someone who hated the man even more than you did."

Daniel closed his eyes and gripped the fabric of his pants.

"Foleman was thrown out of here for touching you," Cole finished, laying a hand on Daniel's unwounded shoulder. "They covered it up."

"No one had to cover up anything," Daniel replied in a quiet, shaking voice. "No one believed me. My parents...."

The word came out like Daniel was describing something disgusting. "My parents," he went on, "wouldn't believe me. They didn't care and neither did the school principal. But Foleman had a record, so they thought it was best to push him out the door quietly before word got out to the local papers and it spun out of control. Before he left, Foleman did it one last time just to prove he could get away with it. Right after that, the principal dragged me into his office and said that if I went public with my story, he would see to it that I failed."

"That was why you collared him," Cole said.

"I wanted him to feel helpless," Daniel spat bitterly. "To know what it felt like for another person to have power over you. It felt good holding his life hostage. I told him that if he tried to take the collar off his leg or spilled the truth to the Order, I would tell everyone how he was really a fey. The Order believe the fey are a threat. They wouldn't want one watching over their kids."

"How did you find out he was a trow?"

Daniel laughed softly then. "He was changing out of his husk one day when I had been sent to the office for smarting off to Mr. Jagger. The receptionist was out, and he couldn't get back into it in time. That was really when I started putting the whole idea together in my head."

Neither spoke for a moment.

"I found a CD that belonged to my dad," Daniel explained. He sounded eager to share with Cole now. "It had information about the Order he belonged to, and stuff about magic. It took me a long time, but I managed to decode the instructions on how spells work. The black rings were a lot harder to work out. For a while, I wasn't sure I could get them working, but the answer came to me while I was breaking into the Order's central mainframe. Things got easier after that."

Daniel swallowed, then winced. Apparently, his shoulder was still hurting. "I don't regret killing Mr. Jagger," he stated. "He was a psychopath, a complete monster, and nobody ever did anything to stop him. I should have done it myself, though."

Cole didn't know what to say. He had always believed it was better to do one's own killing, but this wasn't Faerie, where he had been raised, and the child wasn't a sidhe.

"It'll be a relief when they come for me," he was saying now. "I thought about killing myself before, but I couldn't make myself go through with it. Being killed by the people I hurt, though? That feels all right. It feels right to me."

Cole heard Corhagen's footsteps coming back. A few minutes later, he was coming up the hallway with a displeased expression on his face.

"The ambulance will be here in a minute," he said. "Everyone else has cleared out, so we've got the building to ourselves. The Staten police force will probably want to question people about what happened, but seeing as how they were too busy shooting at us earlier, we can leave it here for them to sort out."

"Sounds good to me," Cole said. "Help me take him downstairs so the medics won't have to come all the way up here with a stretcher."

Corhagen frowned. "He should really stay where he is."

"He went toe to toe against me wielding Aed Deigh," Cole countered. "I was holding back, but he still gave me a run for my money."

"You shouldn't have," Daniel said, cutting in. "I wasn't holding back for your sake."

Corhagen sighed and reached down to help Daniel Whittaker up. It didn't look as though he was being very gentle with the boy's damaged arm, but Whittaker didn't complain.

"What excuse did he feed you?" Corhagen asked, talking over Daniel's head like he wasn't there.

"What do you mean?" Cole asked.

"I know that look on your face," Corhagen said, gripping Whittaker tightly. "I've seen it before on cops who had to arrest a kid for the first time. He fed you some sob story, didn't he?"

"No."

There was an edge to the flat tone in Cole's voice, but it had nothing to do with the boy currently between them, who walked along with their help like the world around him didn't exist anymore.

"It isn't the first time I have confronted a young one with my blade," Cole informed him. "The others had excuses. This one, I feel, had a reason."

"It always sounds like a reason," Corhagen protested, still talking as though Daniel couldn't hear them. "That'll change sooner or later. After a while, it all begins to sound like one big excuse."

Cole opened his mouth to reply and was cut off by the sound of something like thunder ripping through the air. The windows actually shook slightly as, off in the distance, smoke rose up between the rows of buildings.

"That's where pillar seven was located," Daniel croaked, pointing to the site of the explosion.

"Pillar?" Cole asked.

"I had the pixies build me pillars and spread them over town," Daniel explained. "There are a total of thirteen in all. They help spread the signal farther over the island so I could control more fey with the black rings."

"We keep running into that number," Cole muttered. "Do you mean like the one on the roof?"

"It's the center pillar," Daniel said, nodding. "The entire system is based around the magic circle carved into the tile floor downstairs."

"Sounds like someone just blew it sky high," Corhagen noted. "But who?"

"Nominally, I would say us," Cole replied. "But we didn't bring any heavy explosives with us, and the others are supposed to be downstairs still."

"They are," Corhagen assured him, watching the smoke clear.

"Then let's get moving," Cole said, shuffling Daniel along. "I don't know what that was about, but it's given me a bad feeling. We should regroup now."

They were almost on the ground floor when another explosion was heard. This one wasn't quite as loud, coming through the solid walls. Cole stopped to listen carefully and gauged it to be farther away than the last. Corhagen looked down at Daniel when Cole told him of this.

"Sounds like someone is cleaning up your mess for you."

"Or getting ready to make a much bigger one," Cole warned. "Let's find the others. Something just doesn't feel right."

Staffelbach and Rainette were waiting in the main office along with Marcel. One of them had brewed a big pot of coffee. Cole had never cared much for the stuff, but at the moment, he wouldn't have said no to it.

"Where is the ambulance?" he asked, helping Daniel to a seat.

"It hasn't shown up yet," Rainette replied, setting her cup down. "Probably because of the snow. Thank Goddess it finally let up, or else we'd have been stuck in here for the rest of the day."

"I'm just glad this is over with," Corhagen said, shooting Daniel a glare. "I'll be looking forward to taking a day or two off after this."

"Not with Joss in the hospital," Cole reminded him darkly.

"Oh, yeah."

No one said anything for a moment. "I'm truly sorry," said Marcel. "There was nothing I could do."

"We know," Cole assured him. "None of this was your fault."

"We know whose fault it was," Corhagen reminded him, glancing toward Daniel again.

Daniel wasn't responding to Corhagen's taunts, however. Other than an occasional sniffle, he wasn't showing any signs that he was in the room with them. Cole watched him for a moment, and Daniel finally seemed to become aware that his tri-colored eyes were piercing through him. It took a moment, but the boy's eyes were dry when he turned to face the sidhe.

"Your friend, Joss, was hurt when Marcel broke into the precinct wearing the ring?" he asked.

Cole nodded. "He lost an arm in the scuffle. I still haven't heard how he is doing."

"I'm sorry," Daniel told him. "Someone really did steal the prototype ring. I didn't send anyone to the precinct to kill Foleman. I wish I had, but I didn't order your friend to be hurt."

"I believe you," Cole said.

"You still made the damn things," Corhagen pointed out. "Nobody said you had to."

Daniel ignored Corhagen. His attention seemed to be for Cole and nobody else at the moment. "Was he a good friend of yours?" Daniel asked.

"He is my lover," Cole stated matter-of-factly.

"Cole!" Corhagen spat.

Rainette was smiling. Staffelbach chuckled. "Our fearless leader doesn't beat around the bush, does he?"

Corhagen turned beet red. "He's not our leader," he grumbled.

Daniel looked back at Cole. "You're gay?" he asked, though not bothered by the subject matter, it seemed.

Cole shook his head. "My kind do not share the same hang-ups as your people do. There is no gay or straight among the sidhe. It's something Detective Corhagen has yet to grasp."

"I see," Daniel replied. "Whoever used the black ring to control Mr. Marcel would have been familiar with its technology. It's not impossible for someone to hack the signal and control someone remotely. You just have to understand how it works."

No one said anything, so Daniel went on. "I think the Hermetic Order of the Golden Dawn had something to do with Foleman's death. If they wanted him dead, it was because he knew something important."

Cole thought for a moment. "Could it have been because of what he did to you?"

Everyone looked up at that statement. Daniel noticed but paid them no mind. "I doubt it seriously," he said. "I was never important enough to risk exposure like that."

"No," Cole agreed sadly. "I think that was a loss on their part."

Daniel smiled then. It suited the boy, whose face was still twisted in pain, both physical and emotional. Cole reached out and bumped knuckles with him.

"MacColewyn," Corhagen said, pushing himself off the copy machine he'd been using as a prop, "step outside with me for a second. I need to talk with you."

Corhagen didn't wait for Cole to give an answer. The door was left open just a crack. Cole could feel the others watching him as he left and the room filling with what might as well have been gasoline fumes.

Cole made sure he closed the door all the way before joining the detective on the other side of the wall.

"Problems?" he asked coolly.

"I know you think you're doing the right thing by trying to befriend this kid," Corhagen said, "but trust me. I've seen this kind of stuff before. Odds are Staffelbach has too. You're just setting yourself up to take a great big fall in the end."

Cole waited a moment. "You've got your way of doing things, and I've got mine."

"Only your way isn't the right way," Corhagen warned, snatching Cole's arm as he tried to walk off. "You're still new to this. I went along with this cowboy cop thing of yours when the captain ordered us to come here because—"

Something caught Cole's eye. Shaking his arm free, he glanced out the window through the cross emblem and snow. A group of trucks had just pulled up into the street around the front gate, which somebody had left open. They weren't ambulances, either. Men wearing riot gear with "US Marshal" stamped on the back stormed out and came running up the front walkway. Cole had maybe two seconds to decide before the front door opened.

The men were armed, and one was already taking aim at them as the doors were kicked open. Cole seized James by the tie and yanked him back toward the main office door. "Save it for later," he said as the marshals opened fire.

Corhagen slammed up against the door. Cole had meant for him to go through it, but remembered his closing it all the way just a moment ago and had to settle for Corhagen ducking down as best he could against the frame. Most of the bullets went over his head, except for one, which caught Cole in the side. He felt a rib snap while the projectile ricocheted away. There was no cover for him to take refuge behind, so he made his own.

Drawing Aed Deigh, he slammed the frosted blade into the tile floor and spread his will through it. Power flared, and a wall of ice began rising up out of the floor as the marshals kept right on firing. The ice spread quickly, but the bullets were chipping away at it.

Taking this into account, Cole brought Aed Deigh up, stopping the rise of ice in the process, and swung the red-hot end around. Fire roared sideways in a wave across the gap between himself and the men armed with guns. There were cries of agony, and the one who'd shot him was clutching his eyes in pain from the flash burn. With them distracted, he swung the ice end forward, sending a few icicles their way. The frozen blades struck like razor-sharp daggers into their flesh, steaming from the heat of their blood. Only one managed to stay out of the way and unharmed. He was taking aim as Cole slammed Aed Deigh back down into the floor again, making the wall in front of him rise up all the way to the ceiling.

By the time it was thick enough to stop the bullets, he was nearly tapped out, magic-wise.

"What the hell is that?" Rainette yelled from the doorway around James's frame as bullets continued to slam into Cole's miniature glacier.

"US Marshals," Corhagen told her, getting up.

"Or a group of men dressed like them," Cole countered as something that sounded like a grenade exploded on the other side of the ice, causing it to shake ominously. "We should get out of here now."

"Don't have to tell me twice," Rainette said. "School's out, everyone. Move it!"

More explosions rocked the wall as Marcel brought up the rear. "That won't hold for long," he noted.

"Is there a back way out of here?" Corhagen demanded of Daniel, grabbing him.

"That way," the boy replied at once, pointing further down the hall. "Just keep going and you'll reach the end, but there's nothing back behind the building but a wall of solid concrete. The only way out of the school is through the front gate."

"And if they were smart," Cole said, leading them forward, "they would have posted men on the platform at the top of the wall to snipe at anyone coming through."

"So what do we do?" Rainette didn't sound happy. "And why are we going up to the second floor?"

Everyone took the stairs two at a time. "The school is our best bet right now," Cole explained. "We have someone who knows this place inside and out. Establish a post, and take them out one at a time."

Something crashed down below, followed by another explosion off in the distance. "Someone is taking out the towers," Daniel noted. "And that would be the side doors. They're coming from all around."

"Daniel, you go with Rainette. She'll keep you safe." Cole motioned for Daniel and the others to move on past him up to the second floor. "I'm going to stay here and hold this point. Find the other stairwells and take out anyone who tries to come up them."

"And on the off chance these really are US Marshals?" Corhagen challenged.

"They tried to kill us without giving us a chance to surrender or any sort of warning," Cole replied calmly. "This isn't an arrest, Corhagen. It's a scrub. My gold says this is the Order taking out any eyewitnesses. Now that the locals are out of the way, they just need to take care of any hanging threads."

Marcel nodded and pulled Corhagen along with him. Corhagen looked less than happy, but he was no match for the seven-foot-tall ogre. "All fey know and fear the Order," he explained quickly, dragging the detective along. "If a lesser fey goes missing, it's said that the Order had something to do with it."

"Not this time," Cole stated. "Marcel, take Corhagen and go."

Cole raised Aed Deigh once more and held the tip against the stairs. A trail of ice spread down, almost like flowing water. Cole's magic had restored itself some, but he didn't want to try anything major just yet. Keeping this set of stairs slick would deter anyone from trying to climb them.

Once he was sure the others had gone, he climbed up the remainder of the way and repeated the process for good measure. Turning around, he saw Staffelbach standing there with a smug look on his face.

"I knew you were up to something," the officer said cheekily.

"How?" Cole wondered.

"You figured some stuff out about me," he replied in an easy tone. "That works both ways sometimes. You prefer working alone, even though you're solid in a group. This isn't the first time you've led a team into a fight."

"It's been a while," Cole said. "Shouldn't you be guarding a post right now?"

Staffelbach shrugged. "I'd rather stick it out with you, if that's okay. Things are a lot more exciting. Plus, I get the feeling you have a plan for getting us out of here. On the off chance it works, you'll need someone guarding your back."

"Go," Cole ordered, gesturing with the hand holding Aed Deigh, but Staffelbach remained unmoving. Behind them, down the flight of stairs, they could hear men slipping and cursing angrily.

"You lead. I'll follow," Staffelbach said.

Cole shook his head. "Are all other officers in your rank this stubborn and in need of proving something?" he wondered. "In most movies, don't men like you wind up getting gunned down at the climax?"

"I watch superhero movies these days, mostly," Staffelbach replied, running after Cole. "In those, the cops all look the same."

Cole got maybe ten feet away from the stairs when something went through him. It wasn't pain, not exactly. It wasn't hurting him, yet his brain screamed that something had just gone incredibly wrong. His whole body went slack in the space of a second. The next thing he knew, Cole had a great view of the patterned ceiling and the ventilation duct directly overhead.

Staffelbach was kneeling over him. "Snap out of it!" he shouted, but it might as well have been coming to Cole's ears from underwater. "What happened?"

"Can'... t m... ove," Cole tried. His jaw felt gummed up with rubber cement. "Bo... dy fee... ls s... tiff."

The pressure was gone in a flash. Cole gasped like he hadn't taken a good deep breath in months. It was like rising up out of water, only the water retreated over his body and back down below. His head still felt like it was clogged with cotton.

"Something just happened on the floor below us." Talking felt weird, like he was out of practice. "I don't know how, but it has to do with that circle we found before."

"We need to find the others," Staffelbach said, helping Cole up.

"I know," Cole agreed. "Marcel and Rainette especially. I want to know what happened with them."

"Not going to happen."

Behind Cole and Staffelbach was a troop of armed guards surrounding one man in particular dressed in a suit and tie with wire-rim glasses. The man in question was wearing quite possibly the most condescending smirk Cole had laid eyes on in quite a while. The armed guards had ditched the US Marshal facade, it seemed, or had not arrived to the party dressed for the occasion to begin with.

"Several of my men are down, thanks to your comrades," the man was saying over a toothpick in his mouth. "But we managed to wrestle them into an agreement. The only reason we kept them alive up until now is so you, Tuulois MacColewyn, can bear witness to a new beginning with us."

Cole sighed. "I am getting really sick of humans sneaking up on me while I'm distracted," he grumbled before turning to Staffelbach. "What about you?"

FOR once, the others weren't waiting on Cole when he was dragged down to the nexus where the ground floor hallways intersected. It looked as though Rainette had given her escorts some trouble. Corhagen had a black eye and a swollen slip while Marcel had been knifed. He was still standing, and the bleeding didn't appear too bad. The ogres' well-earned reputation of being bred as warriors was holding up. Daniel looked pale, yet his back remained straight the whole time.

The business-suit man had them brought around to where they stood on one side of the circle together, all except for Cole.

"The Hermetic Order of the Golden Dawn has an entire dossier on you," the suit was telling Cole as minions stripped him of his gear. One had a thick piece of velvet cloth in his hands and was using it to handle Aed Deigh.

"Did you know that, Mr. MacColewyn? We've been following you around for many years now. It came as a surprise to learn that you had joined the NYPD. That was a rather drastic career change from someone who once worked as a mob enforcer and right hand of one of the most notorious gangsters of the 1920s."

"I know my own history," Cole replied. "A lesson in it isn't necessary."

The suit leered. "There are several blank spots in that dossier, however," he continued. "The Order has speculated for some time about where you were during those periods of several years. I seriously doubt you would tell us, though."

"You'd be right."

The suit smiled and turned to where the others had been lined up on the other side of the circle. "I'm sure you are wondering what that disturbance earlier was all about. The Order knew about young Whittaker's activities. An eleven-year-old simply doesn't break into our mainframe computers without our knowing it."

"Right," Cole jeered. "More than likely, he had been there for a while when one of you stumbled onto him by accident. Once you realized what he was doing, you decided to step back and see how it played out."

The suit was turning pink in the face. "Your speculations are your own," the suit said through clenched teeth. "My men have orders to open fire on your team if you perform even the slightest act of rebellion."

"Why me?" Cole wondered. "How come I am so special?"

"The world can only wonder," the suit replied. "You don't seem extraordinary by most sidhe standards, at least from what our records say, but events seem to fall around you as though you have the favor of a higher order, so to speak. It makes us wonder. In any case, I know better than to try and corner you without having an ace in the hole. One wrong move from you and they die."

The suit clapped his hands together. From different hallways came robed men wearing the Order's insignia on the front, the same cross that was stamped into the window of the academy's front door.

"We're performing a little experiment today," the suit went on as several robed figures brought in an armful each of what looked like metal trash. Cole felt his skin prickle at the sight of it and knew what it was.

"Cold iron," he said.

"Very old iron indeed," the suit agreed, nodding. "And very much cold. We kept it in storage out in the snow while we weren't using it, just to be on the safe side. Right there in the center, gentleman, just like before."

The robed men dropped what looked like a bunch of iron fire pokers, fire log tongs, and several shovels into the center of the circle.

"The circle was tied in with the pillar set on top of this academy," the suit explained. "We couldn't have planned that better ourselves, and it was all thanks to young Whittaker here."

"Blow yourself!" Daniel called out.

"Such language," the suit tsked. "We'll have to mark that down on your discipline record."

"You're going to use the circle to channel the frequency of iron through the network of pillars," Cole summarized, hoping to draw attention away from the kid. "The way churches long ago would ring iron bells to scare away unwanted fey from towns."

The suit nodded. "Only this will be much more powerful," he clarified. "The frequency will be like sending tiny but potent molecules of iron into the very air itself, poisoning it and rendering every last fey within a hundred miles or so dead. What you felt before was just a little test to see how much of the circle we had to modify. Turns out, the only thing required was a little adjustment on the boy's system."

"Excuse me, sir!" a single guard cut in, holding up a cell phone. "There's been a report. We just lost another one."

The suit turned immediately to Cole. "Those pillars all over the island have been dropping like flies for nearly an hour now. Order whoever is doing it to stop or watch someone in this hallway die right in front of you."

"It isn't us," Cole said, shrugging.

The suit didn't believe him and snapped his fingers. At once, two guards aimed their rifles at Rainette.

"Hey, don't shoot me!" she shouted.

"Well," Cole mused, rolling his eyes, "there is probably a downside to that I just don't see at the moment."

"Thanks a lot," Rainette spat at him.

"Would you prefer I shot another one?" the suit asked. "Perhaps the detective you worked with as a consultant for so long?"

One of the guards pointed his gun at James's chest.

"You don't do your homework, do you?" Cole said, laughing. "Oh well. The truth is none of us knows who has been blowing up the pillars. It wasn't a huge priority for me, since they were just cleaning up a big mess for us. Before you dragged us all down here and showed me that circle, I thought maybe you were doing it."

"Why would we want the pillars destroyed?" the man in the suit retorted.

Cole shook his head. "Someone took your technology or magic or whatever it was the kid was using. It would make you look bad to just leave it lying around."

That made the suit pause. "Good point," he admitted. "You are cleverer than you appear, just like they warned me."

The men in robes were gathering in closer now, taking their places along the edge of the circle. Rainette was blocked from Cole's view, and he could see her struggling against her handcuffs. The Order had used handcuffs to hold the other members of the Section in place. The irony was amusing, truthfully.

"Have you got a name?" Cole asked suddenly.

"Arron Rookwood," the suit answered. "Why do you ask?"

"So far I've just been thinking of you as a guy in a suit." Cole glanced up toward the ceiling as he said this. "It felt impersonal to be held at gunpoint by a man whose name I didn't know."

Arron Rookwood jerked his head upward at once to where Cole was staring. There was a sudden movement from behind the robed figure where Rainette stood. Something green and liquid splashed against his back, causing him to scream in pain. The monk dropped to the floor inside the circle as Rainette let another green orb fly. It caught the next robed figure in the face. The hood fell away as he collapsed to the floor, revealing the green sticky liquid to be eating away at his flesh. Already half of his face was gone, leaving nothing but the skull and a few bits of muscle tissue showing.

"Stop her!" Rookwood commanded.

Every armed guard in the area raised their guns and pointed them. Rainette held her hands up in surrender at once, only to form two more orbs out of the moisture in the air. There were nearly twenty armed men present, however. One cocked his gun.

Rainette just snorted. "That only sounds threatening in the movies," she derided. "Nobody does that anymore."

Instead of tossing the orbs at one of the men ready to shoot her, Rainette sent them at the circle near their feet. The orbs splattered, their acidic touch eating through the floor and destroying the design. The energy around them seemed to clench, as though gasping in pain, then fizzled out completely.

The spell was gone.

"That wasn't a very smart thing to do," Rookwood said, signaling one of the guards to shoot her.

Rainette kept her hands raised as she smirked knowingly. "So give me detention," the witch crowed.

"No one move," Rookwood ordered. "Take the witch and the ogre and get them out of here. I want guns aimed at these four at all times. If one of them so much as twitches, shoot to kill. In the meanwhile, get someone in here that can fix that circle for us. We need it."

"Sir." The guard who spoke looked like he'd rather give his pistol a blowjob than draw attention to himself. "We lost yet another one."

Rookwood stared. "How many are gone?"

"Five, sir," the guard said nervously. "We can still make the project work with eight, but there might be some problems getting the range the Order wanted. We might not touch all of Manhattan this way."

Rookwood grew silent. His eyes fixed squarely on Daniel for a moment as the wheels turned in his mind. Cole kept a close eye on the man the whole time.

"Bring the gauntlet," he said finally. "If the kid built those things, he can get the system working. We just need him to modify the network to do what we need for us."

"The circle can be repaired," one of the robed ones assured Rookwood. "It will take a few moments, though. We will need blood to reconsecrate it. The more potent the blood, the better."

Rookwood turned at once to where Cole was watching. "Not a problem," he said. "Get started."

CHAPTER 10

"TAKE my blood instead," Marcel insisted, offering his arm.

Cole was being led into the circle, surrounded on all sides by the men in robes. The iron tools had been taken out so he could approach, but a couple of them were handed to each of his guards. Rookwood apparently wanted reassurance that Cole would fall in line. The moment Marcel stretched his arm out, Cole quickly and discreetly shook his head.

Rookwood noticed anyway but didn't give it much consideration. "I think your blood is too common for our purposes," he said, looking the ogre over. "Wouldn't you agree, Mr. Tuulois?"

"My blood is the blood of a warrior," Marcel stated, growling now.

"And my blood is the blood of high magic," Cole jumped in, ending the discussion. "Which is exactly what they need."

Rookwood turned around and considered Cole for a moment. "Considering the welfare of your men to the very end," he commented shrewdly. "How very noble, or was there some other reason?"

"I am sidhe," Cole said. "If it is power you desire, my blood is where you will find it. My pride would not stand for you using something as simple as an ogre's blood."

"Ah." Rookwood nodded. "The ever-present sidhe pride. I might have guessed."

Cole shot Marcel a small smile that the ogre returned with the slightest of nods. He didn't look happy, but Cole reasoned that the ogre wasn't terribly offended, or else he would have simply snapped Cole's head off and let him bleed out everywhere. That would have saved the robed monks a lot of trouble on top of everything else.

One such man was approaching Cole now with a razor-sharp athame. Another closer to Cole grabbed him by the arm and held it out to be cut. Cole resisted just long enough, then allowed the blade to dig into his flesh. The athame was ceremonial, inscribed with runes he didn't recognize. The runes seemed to glow a little as blood ran down his arm onto the floor. Power began to rise up almost immediately.

"Exit the circle please, gentlemen," Rookwood warned, stepping away.

The circle was cleared very quickly. The guards that had stayed out of the way until now were moving in closer with their guns aimed. The robed monks still had the cold iron tools in hand as a safety measure. No one was giving Cole room to move. They were prepared for even the slightest hint of attack from him.

Which just proved that humans would board up the windows only to leave the back door open. Unwittingly, Rookwood had given him all he needed.

The sidhe did not use circles the way mortals did. Some fey were attracted to them when they occurred naturally, but a circle wasn't necessary for them to use magic. Only humans and a few other lowly creatures required such rudimentary implements. Nevertheless, Cole had spent a few years among mortals and lived with Katalina long enough to understand the principle behind them. Circles symbolized completeness and harmony with nature, as well as the various circles of power that the planet's energy was conducted through.

Some argued that blood was the oldest form of magic by lesser creatures. The circle had been consecrated in blood before, probably by a human. Now Cole was adding something much more to the power drifting in. For a moment, he could feel it echoing down through the hallways. The building was more or less empty save for the people present. This place was designed to conduct the tension and anxiety from students and channel it. Even with the building almost deserted, there were memories of days gone by and shadows of pain and suffering. All that came crashing through the hallways into the spot where he stood.

Humans had such a short lifespan compared to the sidhe. More than that, however, their minds couldn't wrap around anything beyond just a few short decades. Cole had lived far beyond mortal time already and would continue to go on for ages after. Thus, every last wisp of a ghost from the vacant classrooms to the nooks and crannies came rushing at him.

The fausts had cleared out already. Cole didn't sense any of them, at least, and it was just as well. He wouldn't have enjoyed dealing with them. What came next was bad enough. The halls were suddenly filled with howls of pain and empty despair as ghosts and shadows galloped down in a stampede into the open space, triggering a maelstrom.

Daniel started screaming. "Not again!" Cole heard clearly through the eye of the storm that was the circle. "Please, not again!"

Without thinking, he jumped out of the center and ran toward the boy's voice. Grabbing wildly, he found an arm and pulled. Someone resisted for a moment, then came forward. It was Corhagen, and his free arm was clutching someone else. Marcel came next, with Rainette and a shell-shocked Daniel in tow. Staffelbach was bringing up the rear with his hands clutching Rainette's hand tightly.

Seeing they were okay, Cole immediately turned his attention back to the circle. Outside it, Rookwood could be heard yelling unintelligibly. That probably meant they didn't have much time.

"We all grabbed hold when the shit hit," Corhagen was telling him. "What have you done?"

"This place is soaked to the bone with memories of painful events and dark thoughts," Cole explained. "And I'm older than this structure, so my blood can call everything here to me."

Daniel was curled up on the floor now. "Can someone see to him?" Cole asked. "I didn't realize triggering this effect would cause the poor kid to go blue screen of death on us."

Rainette started to move toward Daniel but was cut off when Staffelbach got there first. Satisfied that someone was taking care of that angle, Cole held his left hand out and began pushing his power into the circle, then outward to the spirits that had formed around them.

"What are you doing now?" Corhagen demanded, sounding panicked.

"Something that will hopefully get us out of here," Cole said.

Rather than getting more powerful, the maelstrom outside the circle quieted. As the storm subsided, the others could see what had been happening. It became clear why none of the guards had tried shooting at them. They had all dropped their guns and weren't doing much better than Daniel right now. They were all extremely pale, and one or two had begun sobbing uncontrollably.

"There," Cole said, satisfied, noticing Corhagen's free hands for the first time. "Wait, how did all of you get those handcuffs off?"

Rainette raised a hand. "The same way I did before."

"One question," Corhagen said, looking around. "What exactly did you do?"

Something intangible smashed what might have been a massive fist into the row of lockers not far behind them. A second later, part of the ceiling overhead caved in.

"That isn't a good sign," Rainette noted.

"We would not have guessed otherwise," Marcel quipped, picking Daniel up off the floor again. "What is going on?"

Everyone but Cole ducked automatically as the opposite row of lockers was crushed underneath a humongous invisible foot. "I may have made a slight miscalculation," Cole answered quietly.

"How slight?" Corhagen demanded to know.

"I modified what power was left in the circle to combine it with my own power over those long dead," Cole said as they all began marching backward very quickly. Rookwood was just getting to his feet as the invisible assailant knocked him flying down the hall away from them.

"Because I'm older than this building, all the forgotten memories and spirits of everything that has ever happened here surrounded the circle and formed together into one angry being. I just wasn't expecting a being quite this large or this angry."

Corhagen looked sick now. "Are you trying to tell me you just basically summoned up a poltergeist Hulk and gave it free rein?"

Cole stopped short. "Well, when put like that, I guess it does sound like a bad idea."

"That explains why so many people reacted that way to it,"

Rainette said, moving farther back than anyone else, as the entire circle was being ravaged now. "All those bad memories of high school just came rushing back all at once. No wonder I had a sudden urge to track down and hex all the members of my old school's pep squad."

"Is this really the time?" Staffelbach wondered, cutting her off.

Whole chunks of tile were being ripped up and tossed around. They hit he guards and robed figures who were still unconscious and couldn't get out of the way. The poltergeist was putting all of its force behind each movement, which resulted in one robed man losing a leg. The sight made Cole think of Joss.

"I can fix this," Cole assured them. "At least, I'm reasonably sure I can."

"Try not to sound so reassuring," Corhagen snapped. "It makes you look bad."

"If I had the circle still, this would be easy," Cole was saying, thinking out loud. "Rainette, could you make another one somewhere outside?"

"Not from memory," she said, ducking as a metal locker just barely missed taking her head off.

"It doesn't have to be elaborate," Cole assured her. "Just make it the best you can. Marcel, go with her and keep her safe while she works. We don't want any Order guards sneaking up and opening fire."

"Yeah," Rainette said as Marcel left Daniel in Staffelbach's hands. "Let's see if that warrior blood is good for something."

Marcel just snorted and ran after her for the front door. The poltergeist was becoming more visible now. The air around it shimmered each time it moved, like ripples on the surface of a pond. Cole almost thought he could see the space around its middle growing darker, like a tinted window. It was time for decisive action.

"We need to destroy the tower on top of the roof," Cole said, holding Aed Deigh out as the monster continued its rampage, taking most of its frustrations out on the building itself and any Order members within arm's reach.

"Why that one?" Corhagen asked. "Will that stop this thing?"

"No," Cole replied. "But it will prevent them from trying this again. The circle might still be repairable. We need to ensure they can't harm any of the other fey."

Corhagen looked at him. "You realize I'm not actually a fey, right? It won't hurt me one bit."

"Protect and serve," Cole reminded him. "You took an oath, remember?"

Daniel was slowly getting to his feet again with Staffelbach's help. "I can feel it," he whispered.

"What?" Cole asked, turning around.

A piece of concrete clipped his ear, making it bleed. "I can feel it," Daniel repeated as loud as he could. "That… thing. It feels like a part of me is inside it."

Cole thought very quickly. "Can you control it?"

"He's just a kid, Cole!" Corhagen yelled.

The poltergeist was really bringing down the house. "Run for it," Corhagen ordered. "We can't stay here with that thing bringing the whole place down around us. It's time to regroup."

Cole hesitated, then nodded and turned to go. Looking around, he spotted Daniel in the same spot as before. He hadn't moved an inch. The poltergeist had turned semi-corporeal by now. It was hard to describe something that only vaguely resembled human shape. Cole had seen all manner of beasts and creatures. The strange didn't shock him—shock was considered unbecoming of a sidhe—yet this thing boggled his mind.

It was a shadow, one with thin limbs and claws as long as his torso. The head, for it did have a head in some way, seemed to stretch and warp itself. There might have been some reason behind the madness there, but it changed too much for Cole to fully comprehend it. The most noticeable thing was the number of faces on it, for it was covered from head to toe in them. Each face was that of a child, probably a fragment left over from students long gone by. The faces were screaming, wailing, crying out. Cole could hear their cries for revenge, for validation, for help. It was a symphony of human suffering rolled into one massive creature fueled by rage.

And he'd created it, albeit unwittingly. Cole couldn't say he had formed the monstrosity to be this destructive, and Daniel was staring it down without so much as twitching.

The boy had serious brass.

Cole charged forward with Aed Deigh and swiped at a claw as it came close to touching Daniel. Drawing the boy behind him, Cole faced the poltergeist down as it reared back and considered the sidhe for a moment.

"Do you know who I am?" Cole asked. "I brought you here. It wasn't meant to be this way, but here you are."

Daniel tugged on the back of Cole's shirt. "Let me try," he offered. "If it's made of all that disappointment, some of me must have wound up in there too. I can feel it."

"Just stay behind me." Cole barely glanced back as the poltergeist creature began to advance again. "It might kill you."

"So?"

Cole threw the kid over his shoulder and ran as the monster struck at them, and raced like mad for the front door. His ribs had thankfully knitted back together by now. He could already hear the thing coming after them as his foot connected with the metal door, knocking it clear off its hinges.

At least it had stopped snowing.

"Slight problem," Cole said, passing a very surprised Staffelbach and slightly less so Corhagen. "Going to keep it distracted. You two might want to move away from the door."

Cole cleared the front steps in a single leap. Staffelbach and Corhagen jumped out of the way just in time as the entire front entrance was torn apart by the poltergeist charging through it.

"See what you can do about that tower!" Cole called out to them, stopping in the middle of the street.

"It will just keep following us," Daniel insisted, trying without success to get down from Cole's shoulder. "If you let it take me, there might be another way to stop all this."

"Don't throw your life away, kid," Cole barked, calling forth both ends of Aed Deigh. "We're going to get through this together. You and I are survivors."

Daniel actually laughed. "If I wanted to die, I could have put a gun into my mouth a long time ago. It would have been a lot simpler than what I tried doing today."

"You didn't want to take your own life," Cole said as the monster continued to advance. "That would have been cowardly, but dying heroically in battle is another thing. You thought whoever they sent to stop you would just burst in like the Order tried today and gun you down. The fey you imprisoned would be avenged and your life would be over."

Daniel's voice sounded thick when he spoke again. It was almost too soft to hear over the roars of the monster and its footsteps, which were making the asphalt crack. "You don't know anything about me," he insisted.

"I know a great deal," Cole countered. "I know you didn't really want to hurt anybody. I know you deliberately hurt those fey so they would turn against you at the first chance. I know you wanted someone to stop you, and hoped they'd kill you so you didn't have to go through all this anymore."

Cole was doing a good job keeping out of the monster's reach and drawing it away from the academy. He wouldn't be able to stay uninjured much longer, though. He knew there was no way to keep that up with an eleven-year-old human slung over his shoulder like a sack of potatoes.

"You're trying to lure it away from the school," Daniel whispered. "Ghosts need a place to haunt, and this one is no different. If it gets too far away, it will begin to dissipate."

"Exactly," Cole said. "You are a smart boy."

"I'm not," Daniel corrected. "I just know things."

The poltergeist slammed both clawed limbs into the ground just past Cole, missing him. Cole, however, knew what was coming and jumped high as they raked through the sheets of snow back toward him. Cole landed amid the wreckage, careful not to rattle Daniel, who sounded sick, too much. Cole loosened his hold on the boy, hoping that would help, but this turned out to be a mistake. Daniel threw his weight forward the moment he felt Cole's grip slacken. In a heartbeat, he had escaped and was down on the ground, rolling into a crouch.

Cole turned automatically and suffered for it by getting backhanded by the monster into someone's parked SUV. There was a loud crunching sound like a soda can being crushed, followed by multi-colored spots swimming in front of his eyes and the taste of blood in his mouth. When things finally cleared, Cole spotted Daniel just a few painful steps away, facing down the poltergeist creature with a totally blank expression.

"Don't," Cole gasped around the blood trickling out of his mouth. "You don't know—"

Daniel held his arms up, spread wide, offering himself in Cole's place. "Don't get the wrong idea," the boy called out in a normal, even tone. "A few years ago, I might have been doing this out of altruism. These days, I just see it as evening the score. Karma always comes back on us in the end."

The creature stopped just short of where Daniel stood waiting and considering him for a moment. The poltergeist monster almost looked confused, though it was hard for Cole to tell, what with the ringing in his ears. Shaking it off, he stood up and ignored the lancing pain traveling up through his vertebrae.

Then the monster struck. Cole saw claws the size of spears stab straight through the boy's small frame without leaving behind a trace of blood. The world around them held its breath for a moment as both Daniel and the monster remained perfectly still.

Looking back on it after it was all well and truly over, Cole had been expecting something grander. There was no whirlwind this time, no howling of voices or cries of the lost and lonely. No more than there were already, at least. Instead, Cole blinked, and the poltergeist was gone. Daniel was lying in the snow. It almost looked like he had been there for a minute or two. Cole winced even as his body began to heal itself from the injury. Being thrown against a vehicle meant his body had to contend with man-made materials. By the time he got to Daniel's limp form, some of the pain had gone, though it still hurt to move.

Disregarding this, Cole stood up with Daniel unconscious in his arms. He could smell the presence of the poltergeist all around them, and it was originating from Daniel's body. The creature had taken up residence inside him.

It took under two minutes to make it back to the academy. Cole should have arrived much sooner, but his body was still healing the damage he'd taken. Rainette was putting the finishing touches on the circle she had drawn in the snow. Staffelbach, Corhagen, and Marcel were all keeping watch over her with guns drawn. A few dead bodies lay nearby, all of them agents of the Order.

Cole stepped over the bodies like they were nothing and placed Daniel in the center of the circle without preamble.

"We need an exorcism," he told her. "The poltergeist is inside his body. Daniel jumped in front of it to stop it."

Rainette let out a long sigh. "You haven't asked for much today, you know," she groaned. "Exorcisms aren't exactly my thing. I get the basic theory, but that sort of stuff is best left up to high priestesses and so forth."

"You can do it," Cole insisted, growing impatient.

Rainette, however, adamantly shook her head. "I'm sorry," she said in earnest. "It isn't that I wouldn't. I mean, the kid obviously needs it bad, but I'm just not qualified."

"Some of the Order came out here trying to make trouble," Corhagen said, pointing at the dead bodies. "We ran them off, though. I guess they're back inside the school now, but my gut says they won't be there for too much longer. We should just take the kid and get out of here. This whole operation has gone south to hell."

Cole knelt down in the snow. "Cole," Rainette began, but he raised a hand to silence her.

Cole was thinking of Katalina and her dying inside a magic circle she had made to protect herself. The goons Naryssa had sent to his loft had pounded on the magic shield until it gave her a nosebleed and she passed out from exhaustion. Placing his hands on the ground on the edge of the circle Rainette had drawn, he prayed.

Cole wasn't sure why. Certainly the Lord and Lady both had better things to do than cater to his whims or listen to his pleading for the life of one mortal. Yet something compelled Cole to try anyway. It was a strange feeling, praying here and now in the snow. The thick clumps of powder were melting around him. His body was still healing even as he thought back to the events of over a month ago when he'd found that stone temple deep within the bowels of the sithen. He'd never been able to find that place since. Even Mal didn't know why.

He remembered how he had felt afterward, however. That same feeling lingered in his head and in his chest. Cole breathed in deeply and drew himself toward that sensation. He didn't know how he knew, but the answer lay there. Cole felt power flare, something unlike anything he'd ever felt before, save for when Consort had appeared to him and offered him a choice between the chalice and the athame. Consort had had him drink from the cup, then took him there on the stone table.

Cole cast that power out to the circle, feeling it trace the edges like a graceful dancer. The feeling intensified as the magic spilled over into the circle, surrounding Daniel.

Cole hadn't been paying attention when he placed Daniel Whittaker into the circle. Daniel was lying on his side, however, with his back turned toward Cole. Cole could see the tattoo he had found earlier. It was red instead of black and looked swollen. As the magic caressed the boy's still form, that tattoo sent a pulse through to Cole. Cole felt it touch him, and everything went dark.

He is our proxy. You cannot take him.

Daniel was lying ahead of Cole in the same position as before. His body looked much further away now. Cole looked up and found the source of the multiple voices speaking in unison. A swarm of shadows hovered overhead just above his and Daniel's bodies.

We could offer a trade. He could offer himself up in the boy's stead. That would make things much easier.

This was from at least two voices, a male and female. They each spoke at nearly the same time. "I'm not that noble," Cole said, gazing around at them.

They were just like the shadows in the picture Jynx had shown him.

"You corrupted Daniel," he said, the last few pieces falling together in his mind. "You needed him to enslave the fey on this island for some reason. That was why he did it."

The boy was already corrupted. The other humans saw to that. We merely showed him how he might exact vengeance on them.

This time it was two males. "What price would you accept in return for releasing him?" Cole asked. "And removing the creature he absorbed?"

The creature was the result of your tampering, not ours. All of them agreed on that. Cole thought they sounded pleased. *The boy chose to accept it into him without influence from us. He took the phantasm into his body of his own free will.*

"It must be getting crowded in there," Cole said thoughtfully.

Your seed.

It was two males again who spoke, though a different pair than before. "What?" Cole asked, looking around for the source.

Your seed. We desire your essence. Give it to us, and we will trouble neither you nor the boy any further. We only want what springs from your root. You may take the child and go afterward.

Cole watched as Daniel remained perfectly still. At least the boy was facing the other way. It would be very awkward if he were to regain consciousness right now. He could already hear the wild accusations James would make should he learn of this. Cole hesitated as he reached for the fly of his pants.

"You can do a lot with someone's essence," Cole pointed out, looking up. "What guarantee do I have that you won't use it to bring me harm?"

We said we would trouble you no further. Your physical well-being is of little concern for us. We merely want your essence.

"Swear by it," Cole challenged. "Swear by the Mother of Darkness herself that you will not use it to bring direct harm to me."

In unison, they spoke. *We swear by the Mother of Darkness herself that we will not use the essence from your root to bring direct harm to you.*

Satisfied for the time being, Cole reached for his fly again. When he hesitated a second time, a dark shadow fell over Daniel's body, engulfing him.

The boy is no longer a concern. Give us your seed now!

A wooden bowl appeared in front of Cole where he knelt. Cole undid his fly and pulled his swollen member out. He had no desire for the act now. His thoughts were purely motivated by his need to fix what had gone wrong with the boy he could no longer see. Strangely, this was enough, in the end.

His climax built quickly. Cole wasn't sure if it was the sense of urgency in the air that helped or the hand of something more, but he came in a second. Were the circumstances not what they were, he might have felt embarrassed. His seed spilled over into the bowl in a flood. Thick ropes of it covered the inside and the edges. Letting out a sigh, Cole stuffed himself back into his pants and moved the bowl away.

"Done," he declared. "Release the boy."

It is already finished.

The darkness was gone. The bowl Cole had left his seed in was gone, and so was the shadow that had engulfed Daniel. The boy was stretched out just as before, in front of him inside the circle. Light shined around them now. The sun was peeking out from behind the heavy blanket of clouds.

"Was there a reason for you doing that?" Rainette asked from somewhere out of his field of vision. "Because watching it was uncomfortable."

Cole looked around. "Doing what?"

Rainette looked at Cole like he was telling a very unfunny joke. "You just flogged Mr. Johnson into a wooden bowl that appeared out of nowhere and then vanished once you were through."

"I had to," Cole said. "It was the only way they would free Daniel from their influence. Where is Corhagen?"

Both she and Staffelbach, who was standing near her, pointed toward the fence. "He tried to grab you when you opened the fly of your pants," she explained. Corhagen was lying awkwardly in a heap many feet away. "I think he must have thought you were going to violate the kid or something. The minute he touched you, though, there was this sound like lightning striking up close and the smell of hair burning. Before we knew it, he had been flung twelve feet away."

"Who did you mean by 'they'?" Staffelbach asked, helping Cole up by his non-sticky hand.

"Someone was controlling the kid," he said. "Kind of egging him on, I guess. They wanted a sample of my seed in exchange for freeing him."

"Gross," Rainette said flatly.

The tattoo on Daniel's neck had vanished. There was nothing left but the scars he had spoken of earlier. Cole brushed a thumb over the place where it had been and felt nothing. It might as well never have been there in the first place.

The poltergeist spirit inside the boy, however, still remained.

"We need to get this boy some help," Cole said. "And finish what we came here to do. There is still the matter of that pillar on top of the academy."

"Speaking of the pillars," Rainette interrupted, "we've been hearing those explosions again. I think most of the ones out in the city are gone."

"Even better," Cole said. "We owe whoever was helping us a Coke."

"Make mine a Sprite if yer don' mind."

Boogaloo was baring his fangs as he grinned, waddling up the path with Jynx by his side. "Figured we'd find you slumps jus' layin' down on da job."

"Why do I have the suspicion we just solved the mystery of who was blowing up those other towers?" Rainette asked with narrowed eyes.

"Didn' ah ever tell ya?" Boogaloo replied, knowing full well he hadn't. "Us'ta work as part ah demolition team near Jersey. Fools dere t'ought I wuz a circus freak 'er sumthin'."

"Where did you get the explosives?" Cole wondered, smiling as Jynx came forward to hug him.

Boogaloo shrugged. "Ah few household chemicals from 'ere an t'ere, along wit sum modeling clay. Yer girlfriend there really leveled the field fer me. She could scale up dem t'ings like nobudies business. 'Course, we had us a little trouble after while. Some bozos came to shut us down, but we took care ah 'em."

"How about taking care of one more?" Cole offered, pointing to the obelisk still looming over them. "Then we can go home."

"Tha's whut we came here fer," Boogaloo replied. "We thought you'd be sittin' here on yer arse just pullin' on yer pud while we did the hard work."

"You missed that part," Rainette told him. "Sorry."

"Someone see to Corhagen," Cole said as Jynx disengaged from him to check on Daniel before following along after Boogaloo. "If he doesn't need a hospital, we can leave the rest of this mess for the locals and take the kid to a place in Manhattan. I don't want to linger here any longer than I have to with the Order still lurking about."

"Nobody is going anywhere!"

Rookwood's voice rattled through the trees, sending birds flying. "Everything is ruined because of you, Tuulois MacColewyn!" he yelled, waving a gun around like a madman with each word. "You are going to pay, do you hear me? You are going to—"

Cole drew Jabberwock in a flash and fired. The bullet settled right between Rookwood's eyes and sent him tumbling down the steps to a heap at the bottom.

"Anticlimactic," Boogaloo said grimly, just steps away from where Rookwood's bleeding corpse lay. "But effective."

CHAPTER 11

CORHAGEN came to just in time to watch the last obelisk, the thirteenth pillar in Daniel Whittaker's network, tip over onto the playground equipment and squash it flat. Minutes after it fell, the Staten Island police, several fire trucks, and a number of ambulances rolled up in sequence. None of the first responders looked happy, and they were even less pleased with the mess that had been made. Several of the officers on the scene were doing their best to keep the situation under control while simultaneously throwing the blame at Cole and the rest of the Section.

Cole barely gave them the time of day.

Since the Staten Island hospital was closer, they went there to get everyone checked out. Cole was reluctant, wanting to get back to Manhattan as fast as possible, but Daniel needed serious help. Cole wasn't sure how much the doctors would be able to do, but his shoulder needed examining, at the least.

Corhagen was suffering from what the nurses on hand were calling a very mild shock. It didn't look as though grabbing Cole while he was in the midst of his speaking with the enigmatic shadows had caused any permanent damage. Physically, he was in need of some styling mousse more than anything. After a quick once-over, James was released with the doctor giving him a mild prescription and advice to get some rest soon.

The doctors had wanted to get their hands on Cole as well, but he refused. Marcel declined treatment also and asked to be excused so he could return home. Cole bid the ogre farewell with a mention for him to show up at Joss's office tomorrow morning. Rainette and Staffelbach were going to spend the night in observation and be released in the morning. Jynx and Boogaloo rode back with him to the sithen, with Boogaloo eager to regale him with stories of their heroic adventure together.

The wood goblin and changeling had gotten the idea to go out together and take care of the pillars on their own shortly after the Section left. It turned out one had been placed off in the distance from the police station. Jynx had sneaked out to follow them and spotted it, then ran back inside to show it to Boogaloo. In the end, Boogaloo really was able to whip up some heavy explosives with chemicals he found lying around.

The hard part had been taking care of the ones closer to the academy, especially once the Order showed up. Some of them had been ordered to stand guard, so Jynx and the goblin had to take care of them first. That was what slowed everything down. When Cole had created the poltergeist, Rookwood was distracted long enough for them to finish the job and blow the whole lot away.

It still didn't make up for what had happened to Daniel, but Cole found some measure of peace in knowing it had helped bring an end to it all. Though he still felt terrible, all the same.

Boogaloo and Jynx spent another evening at the sithen with Cole. Mal had been livid to find the goblin chowing down like Pac-Man in the kitchen, but Cole couldn't have cared less. He hadn't even asked why the wood goblin needed to crash at his place. Getting to sleep seemed like the most important thing.

Sleep was a long way off, however.

Cole got Jynx settled in first just so he could put off doing what he had to do for a little while longer. The changeling appeared to be well by all rights. No physical harm had been done to her. During their stay at the hospital, however, she had lingered close to where Daniel had been taken. He never laid eyes on her once the whole time. It seemed as though she were waiting for something, but Cole didn't know what. Once he brought her to the room the sithen had created for her, she undressed immediately and crawled into bed. It was clear she was asking Cole to leave her be for now.

Cole obliged by closing the door on his way out.

His next stop was to inform Mal not to murder Boogaloo at any time during the night or tomorrow. Cole wasn't sure what to do with the goblin just yet. He wasn't keen on having Boogaloo as a permanent resident, but one night was tolerable. Cole didn't plan on spending much time at the sithen until the case was closed. There were still one or two things left on the table to handle.

Back when he had first moved in, Cole had requested Mal create a storage area far from his private chamber. When his loft had been destroyed, he'd taken anything from it that might have been useful. Some of that had included Katalina's things. Most of it was in the storage area now, specifically an old laptop she had give him years ago that he had barely used.

Cole dug it out eventually, holding his emotions back the whole time. He never once registered any of the things his hands picked through. They were all shapeless, nameless things that just happened to be in the way. As such, he almost missed finding the laptop at first. After digging it out, he rushed out of the storage area without looking back.

Next, he went to the garage and started the car. The snow was everywhere, but the garage opened out on a section of road on 8th Street where some of it had been cleared away. Traffic was steady but tolerable until he got to the main roadway. From there, he drove to the hospital where Inspector Joss Vallimun was being treated.

Visiting hours were over, but Cole showed the receptionist his badge and insisted the matter was urgent. Cole was here to guard the inspector after the attack and relieve anyone on duty who was already there. It turned out no one from the precinct had been sent to watch over his lover. They'd left him in the hospital unconscious and alone.

It figured.

The receptionist had a nurse show Cole the way. After she left, Cole turned to the bed and looked Joss over.

It was hard. Joss was hooked up to a drip and a heart monitor. His body was lying at an odd angle, since his right arm was missing, and a square patch lay over his left eye. Joss looked unusually pale as he slept there.

Cole sat down in a chair nearby, where the bed would be visible at all times, and unzipped his bag. The laptop was out and booted up soon enough. Once he had the program he needed, Cole began typing. For several hours, he sat in the chair typing out his report for the events that had taken place on Staten. Most of it would probably be dismissed outright, which was why Cole was preparing two separate reports.

When the first was completed, almost three hours had gone by. Cole felt weary, yet his senses were on high alert for even the slightest movement. He turned sharply at one point when someone hurried past on the other side of the door. Nervous, he stood up and stretched, then checked the hall under the guise of using the bathroom in the hallway. Feeling only a little better, he went back to Joss's room and finished the second report.

That one took another two hours. By that time, it was after two in the morning. Joss had barely moved once the whole time. Cole stood up, stretched again, and then began packing up. He could have e-mailed his reports to the precinct captain, but Cole wanted to deliver them in person. That could wait until morning, though. Gathering up a blanket, he stretched himself out on the couch across from Joss's bed and closed his eyes.

He still couldn't sleep, though. It was almost sunrise when Cole finally gave up and left the hospital to go in for work.

RAINETTE and Staffelbach would be released later on that morning. Cole called the hospital to confirm it, then saved the files from his laptop onto two different disks. After labeling them, he went in search of Captain Hawkins. Instead, what he found was Internal Affairs.

Specifically, it was Dickson and Rockard, and neither of them looked pleased.

"I'm surprised to see either of you here," Cole said, not slowing down. "How is that asshole of yours, Dickson? Rockard looked like he was packing serious heat behind his zipper. I'd still be limping if I were you."

Dickson looked ready to explode. Cole might have been forced to push his way through them, but each man was keeping a considerable distance from the other, enough that Cole passed between them with no trouble at all. Both agents stalked behind him as he headed down to

Hawkins's office, albeit at what he was sure they thought to be a safe distance. Cole noticed the agents were attracting many stares and even a few snickers.

It was the one thing that cheered him up.

Hawkins wasn't in his office when Cole arrived. The door had been left open, cracked slightly, no doubt due to the man having to leave suddenly. Cole had passed the area where the pine grove had sprung up. The trees were already gone, and it didn't look like they had been cut down. Cole didn't spot any wood chips or specks of sawdust on the floor. The magic had left the building, but the damage was done. It was the only time he managed to lose Dickson and Rockard for a bit. Both of them took a detour around the area. Cole saw them pass by the door as he sat down, looking left and right for him.

Hawkins showed up an hour and some later. "Detective," he said nervously.

Cole could smell the anxiety coming off the captain in waves. He wasn't comfortable being in the same room with him at all. Without a word, Cole held up both disks in their cases and placed them on his desk.

"What are these?" Captain Hawkins asked, glancing down at them.

"My report," Cole said. "Of what happened on Staten Island."

Hawkins waited a moment, still looking the disks over like they were hexed. "You needed two disks worth of space to fill out your report?"

"There are two reports," Cole explained. "One tells what really happened and the other tells you what everyone will want to hear. I thought I'd let you decide."

Hawkins did look at Cole then, and he wasn't thrilled. "Are you aware that lying on a police report is a serious offense?" he asked. "One that could cost you your badge?"

Cole smiled. "Is it really a lie if you tell people what they want to hear because they refuse to listen to the truth?"

Hawkins swallowed. "And you believe me to be one of those people?"

Cole stood up and prepared to leave. "I was told one of the conditions for Section Thirteen being brought back was that we had to find those missing children. The other was that our reports not read like hallucinations brought on by abusing foreign substances. Therefore, I decided to give you a choice. You can submit what happened or tell the brass a story that they want to hear to keep feeling safe."

"Your first report won't make us feel safe," Captain Hawkins stated.

Cole nodded. "I very much doubt it."

When Cole left the office, Dickson and Rockard were waiting for him in the hallway. "Come with us," Dickson ordered, stopping dead in his tracks when he realized Cole was coming toward them.

"Brave," Cole noted. "I'd rather not. There are still a few things I need to take care of."

"We've been asked to inform you that you are under suspension until further notice," Rockard said, getting in front of Cole, then backing up. He didn't look thrilled to be there.

"You are to turn in your badge along with your guns," Dickson added, keeping away.

"My guns were mine before I joined the force," Cole informed them. "You can have the badge, but they are my personal property."

"We were told to collect your badge and guns," Dickson insisted.

"Too bad." Cole passed his badge over to Rockard. "Anything else?"

"Until the matter is resolved," Rockard said, pocketing Cole's badge, "you are to have no contact with any member of Section Thirteen or have any involvement in whatever cases are assigned to them. Do you understand this?"

Cole didn't answer.

"You were assigned a gun when you joined the Section," Dickson cut in. "We were to collect it."

"I'll have to find it," Cole told him. "I never used any guns but my own. If you will excuse me, gentlemen, I have to be going. Enjoy the rest of your time together."

It looked like they both had quite a bit more to add, but neither said a word. Cole stepped around Rockard easily and walked to the stairs that would take him up to Joss's office. He had a feeling the others would be waiting on him there.

Corhagen was, and so was Marcel. The ogre lowered his head slightly when Cole entered the room and shut the door behind him.

"I've been suspended from the force," Cole announced softly.

Corhagen looked surprised, while Marcel looked worried. "How come?" Corhagen asked. "What happened?"

"Internal Affairs had something to do with it," he said. "I didn't ask questions. With me being given the ax and Vallimun seriously injured, it falls to you to keep Section Thirteen going. I suspect that has to do with why I'm being shuffled through the cracks in the floor."

"So that I can be put in charge?" Corhagen was confused now. "That doesn't make much sense. How is giving me the Section a good thing for Internal Affairs?"

"They probably see you as someone they can control better," Cole admitted. He hated saying it, since Corhagen had always taken the truth badly.

To Cole's surprise, however, Corhagen just nodded. "Vallimun wasn't going to let them intimidate him," the detective said, piecing it together. "And you couldn't care less what they think. That just leaves myself and Staffelbach as the officers with the most experience."

"And between the two of you, Staffelbach doesn't have enough field experience yet to qualify for Section Thirteen leadership."

Marcel hesitated, then raised his right hand slightly. "What will happen to the rest of us?" he asked.

"I don't know," Cole confessed. "I am sorry I dragged you into this."

"That isn't what concerns me," Marcel replied quickly, giving Cole an appreciative look. "You defended me after I murdered a man and offered me a second chance. I am still in your debt. What I'm asking now is how I can help make it right?"

Cole looked to Corhagen. "Stay with the Section for now," he said. "I need someone who can watch everyone's back and keep them alive. Will you do that for me?"

Marcel nodded. "As the sidhe commands."

Cole shook his head. "Don't say things like that," he replied. "You are a cop now, and a warrior first. We're all exiles in New York, so that makes us on equal ground whether we like it or not."

"I'll take care of things," Corhagen assured him.

Cole was still uncomfortable, though he tried to conceal it. "Keep an eye out for the Order," he instructed. "Look for anything suspicious that doesn't add up. They were behind this mess somehow, and the brass would like for us to take the fall in their place. That means the Order has someone up top in a tight grip. You have to move carefully from now on."

Already, Corhagen didn't look happy at being told how to do his job. Cole disregarded it as unimportant and stood up, offering his hand to Marcel first.

"Watch out for yourself," he said. "And the others."

"I will," Marcel said. "On the skulls of my ancestors' slain enemies, I vow to."

Corhagen frowned. "Do you have to make promises like that all the time?" he wondered. "Because it's a little gross."

"Ignore him," Cole advised. "I'll be leaving soon."

Corhagen followed Cole out the door. "Give my regards to the others," Cole said. "Also, I need one last favor from you."

"What?"

Cole checked to ensure they were alone. The last thing he needed was Dickson or Rockard or someone under their thumb to be snooping around nearby.

"Find out where Daniel Whittaker was taken," he said quietly. "He isn't at the hospital on Staten anymore. I asked the doctor after I called about Staffelbach and Rainette, and he said someone had ordered him to be airlifted out in the middle of the night."

Corhagen appeared reluctant but nodded his consent. "I will," he said. "Do I have to swear by the bones of my ancestors or something, though?"

Cole walked off without answering.

MAL was waiting for Cole when he got back. "What's wrong?" the sidhe asked at once, knowing by Mal's expression that something horrible had happened. "Did Boogaloo invite his cousins over or something?"

"She's gone," Mal said. "I looked all over the sithen and can't find her."

Cole didn't need to ask who Mal was talking about. "How long ago?"

"I first noticed she had gone missing about two hours or so ago," Mal replied. "She was sleeping in her room the last time I checked, but then suddenly was gone. I don't understand how she could just vanish like that, right out from under my nose."

"Jynx has made a career out of disappearing and making herself scarce," Cole said, moving through the sithen's halls. "It's how she escaped from Faerie and stayed one step ahead of her captors."

"Where do you think she's gone?" Mal asked, keeping up by reappearing alongside Cole every so often.

"To wherever Daniel Whittaker is being held," Cole said, stopping outside his room. "The Order had him airlifted out of the hospital last night. Corhagen is checking for me. Hopefully, he will be able to dig up a trail and find out where they were headed. Chances are Jynx will be there with him."

"What do we do in the meantime?"

"Wait," Cole told him. "I'm going to lay down for a bit. I'll keep my cell phone on in case Corhagen calls. Make sure the car is ready to roll out at a moment's notice."

"Right," Mal said, saluting as Cole shut the door to his room behind him.

Cole fell on top of his bed without the preamble of undressing. He didn't really intend to sleep. His mind was too busy racing to let him nod off.

That was the idea, at least. The next thing Cole remembered, his phone was ringing on the sheets next to him, causing him to wake up with a start. According to the clock, the whole day had gone by.

"Hello?" he mumbled.

There was a voice on the other end. It sounded like Corhagen, but Cole couldn't make out what he was saying. After several impatient seconds, he glared down at the phone and realized he'd been holding it upside down.

"Hello?" Cole tried again. "Corhagen?"

"It's me," Corhagen replied. "What was going on? I kept talking and it sounded like you were grumbling from far away."

"The phone woke me up," Cole told him. "Is something the matter?"

"You wanted to know where they took the Whittaker kid, right?"

Cole nodded, then remembered Corhagen couldn't see him. "I did," he said over a yawn. "Where did the Order take him?"

"A nurse over on Staten confided to me that a specialist was brought in not long after we both left. He examined the Whittaker boy and determined him to be suffering from dementia and megalomania. That part I agree with, at least. He's been shipped up to this exclusive mental trauma center in Maine. The paper trail was already disappearing when I locked on to it."

"Give me a name," Cole said, stumbling over to his computer. "I'll get directions from there."

"It's the Temperance Lloyd Center," Corhagen whispered. "Listen, I can't tell you any more than that. I had to wait until I was sure nobody would be listening in to make this call. The higher-ups are talking nonstop. Without Vallimun here to hold down the fort, things are going nuts. I'm being monitored constantly."

"Go, then," Cole told him. "I have to get to Maine."

"Cole," Corhagen warned, "you can't do anything stupid this time. Everyone's ass is on the line, and I can only do so much to hold the tide back."

"I have to go," Cole insisted. "Jynx has disappeared. I think she left to track Daniel and is going up to Maine where the Order is holding him. If I don't stop her, she might get herself hurt. Or even worse, she might try to break him out, and the Section will be stuck with the blame."

Corhagen swore loudly.

"That's a word I haven't heard you use in a while," Cole noted, smiling. "The stress must be getting to you."

"I don't know how Vallimun does it," Corhagen mumbled. "And puts up with you on top of everything else."

"I'm amazing in the sack," Cole replied, typing the name of the institution into Yahoo Maps. "It's a great stress relief. You should still remember."

"Bye, now." Corhagen hung up.

Cole had the address a moment later. The institution was located deep in the woods of Androscoggin County. It would take a couple of hours to get there for sure.

"Mal," Cole called out, summoning the former sorcerer.

"Yes, sir!" Mal appeared at once. "Has the boy been found?"

"The Order had him shipped up to a spot in Maine. I'm leaving right now. Can you pack me enough food for three?"

Mal's mouth contorted into a painful-looking frown. "I'll see if the goblin managed to spare something from his rampage."

"Make it fast," Cole told him, checking to make sure he had his car keys. "I need to leave now."

CHAPTER 12

THE drive up to Androscoggin County was long but uneventful. Cole took a handful of detours off the map he'd printed out to guide him in case the Order was tailing him. More than once during the journey, Cole had the suspicion someone was watching him from afar. It was hard not worrying. The Order was something other fey had told tales of from the moment he had arrived in New York City.

Still, he was inside a chariot of the wild hunt. It had taken the form of a modern car, but that was superficial. Deep down to the revving engine that throbbed mile after mile, Cole could sense the power hidden in it. He was surrounded on all sides not by metal and glass but a power for the ages. Even a small one was by no means something to take lightly. Cole took comfort in reminding himself of those things. The car wouldn't allow just anyone to spy on him. Fey magic was far, far older than any human spell.

The food Mal had packed for him was hardly touched. Cole was saving it for when he found his target. Soon, he came upon the place where his target was being held, deep in the woods behind a thick wall of pine trees.

The Sir Francis North Academy had looked like a prison from the outside, and that had been a school. Cole had imagined all manner of horrors waiting outside the Temperance Lloyd Center. He had seen photographs of asylums in the past where the mentally damaged and socially unacceptable were hidden away out of public sight. He was certain the Order would have the stuff of nightmares prepared for anyone who put their dirty secrets at risk of exposure.

The Temperance Lloyd Center looked like a resort. Cole might have suspected he had been led astray except for the words etched into the front gates. The place was surrounded by iron fencing, of course. Instead of pulling up to the door, Cole kept driving. It was past the hour for visitors, and he was sure the Order had marked his name off the list of permitted guests.

Cole drove two or three miles down, then found a small road and used it to loop back. When he drove past the gates to the center this time, it was much faster. Cole didn't want to risk alerting anyone to his presence, and just doing a second drive-by was risky enough.

There was an all-night convenience store not far away. Cole had taken note of it earlier when he'd driven past before reaching the center. Now he parked in a dimly lit area of the parking lot. His car blended in nicely with the shadows lying over the space near the brush at the edge of the concrete. Looking around, he gave a satisfied nod and tapped the vehicle on the roof twice.

"Don't let anyone do anything to you that I would," Cole told it, to which the car replied by locking itself.

Something in Cole's gut told him the car wasn't happy about being left behind. Hoping to soothe it, he brushed a hand lightly across the back while walking away. The lights behind him flickered once as the young chariot of the wild hunts bid him farewell, then fell silent.

It was a long walk back to the center grounds. Cole had traveled light. His shirt had been left on the passenger seat, and the heaviest thing he carried with him were the twin guns hanging below his belt on the holsters he always kept them in. Aed Deigh had been tucked away in the horizontal sheath in back of his leather pants. To any stranger, he certainly looked like a madman wandering around shirtless on the side of the road in this weather.

When he was halfway to his goal, an SUV with a woman at the wheel passed by him, slowing down as it approached. Cole gave it no notice until he saw it turn around in the middle of the road roughly a mile ahead. Soon it was pulling up alongside the curb just inches from where he walked. The window rolled down, revealing an irate-looking man in his late twenties. The man did not look happy to see Cole. It was the woman sitting behind the wheel and leaning over the man's legs who spoke.

"Sir?" she called out to him loudly.

The radio was playing a love song in the background. "Can I help you?" Cole asked, getting another nasty look from the man beside the window.

"We just saw you walking down the side of the road," the woman said, caught off her guard by Cole's casual tone. "Did your car break down?"

Cole opened his mouth to speak, then thought better of his answer. "Something like that," he answered vaguely instead.

"Aren't you cold?" the woman asked, her eyes lingering on his chest and abs for longer than was necessary even by sidhe standards.

"The cold doesn't bother me," he replied. "I was just on my way to see a friend." A thought occurred to him. "I assure you I am quite sober," he added.

"You have to be freezing," the strange woman insisted. "Why don't you get in the backseat? We can give you a lift."

The woman's companion didn't look happy at all now.

"I think that might not be a good idea," Cole said apologetically, noting the smug smile on the gentleman's face now. "But I thank you for your kindness."

"Please," she insisted, hitting a button on her door to open the back doors. "I insist."

Thinking it over, Cole got into the backseat. He had been counting on low traffic in this area, since it was so late. Accepting their offer was not a smart choice, but something made him reconsider. For a brief moment, Cole considered disposing of them. At one time, it would have been another facet of his work, but Cole was a police detective now. He could just picture the look of disapproval on Joss's face.

"My name is Ariella Thomas," the woman said, bringing the SUV around. "This is my husband, John. Where were you headed so late?"

"Just down the road a ways," Cole answered. "You don't have to take me very far. It really isn't necessary."

"I can't believe you aren't cold with the weather as bad as it is," Mrs. Thomas was saying, ignoring him. "How can you not be cold?"

Cole smiled. "Mother Nature and I are old friends. We get along quite well with one another."

"You from out of town?" the husband interjected suddenly.

Cole hesitated. "I live in New York. The state," he added to help cover his tracks. "But I've done some traveling over time."

"You sound like you have an accent," the husband went on almost accusingly. "Only not one I've heard before. I used to live in New York City. No one I ever met before talks like you do."

A chuckle escaped Cole's throat. "I hear that a lot."

"It's very nice," Ariella commented. Her face was growing slightly red as she looked Cole over through the rearview mirror. "Listen, it's very late. Whoever you were coming to visit is probably asleep by now."

"That's entirely possible," Cole said absentmindedly while looking out into the darkness.

"Stay with us for the night," Ariella blurted, jerking the wheel as her husband's glare cut through her. "I'm serious. It's freezing cold, and you could die from hypothermia without a shirt on out there. Our house is just up ahead, in fact."

Cole turned away from the window, intrigued now. "I didn't know there were many homes on this stretch of highway."

"We stay at a clinic," Ariella replied, already making the turn. "This is the gate to it, in fact. It's called the Temperance Lloyd Center, a place for troubled youth. I work as a doctor here, and my husband and I live on the grounds in one of the apartment lodgings. In fact," she added as the gates parted, "I got called away on business, and John didn't want me driving on the road at night all alone."

Cole didn't believe in coincidences. "You live at a home for troubled youth? Isn't that unusual?"

"This is one of the... better places," Ariella said hesitatingly. "They have lodgings for certain staff members so the patients can have round-the-clock care if they need it."

"I see." Cole said nothing further but lowered his head for a moment as the SUV wound around the snake-like path up to the main building and whispered a short word of thanks to the Lord and Lady for their aid. He had no answer for why they were helping him tonight. It seemed odd to Cole, almost to the point of being suspicious, but he wasn't about to look a gift horse in the mouth now, as the quaint human expression went.

The road ended in a cul-de-sac that encircled the entire main building of the complex. A number of subsidiary roads in the back stretched over to other facilities. The good doctor turned at the first one and sped up to an extended structure that looked like several small homes stuck together in a row.

"Home sweet home," Ariella said, climbing out. "Come inside quickly or you will catch your death of a cold."

Cole complied. Ariella went first with the keys in hand while her husband brought up the rear. Cole could feel the mortal's eyes drilling into his head with every step.

The inside of the house was warm. Someone had gone to great lengths trying to establish a sense of hominess, though it was clearly artificial. Cole had taken maybe two steps inside after wiping his feet when it hit him. Everything was placed just so, every frame on the wall arranged to project false coziness. It smelled sterile, like a hospital.

"Come on in," Ariella insisted, leading Cole over to the couch by the arm. "I'm afraid we don't have much room. It's only John and myself, but the couch is really comfortable."

"Whatever you have is fine," Cole said politely.

Her husband, John, kept a close eye on Cole the whole time. Ariella offered Cole food, drink, a blanket, and several brands of alcohol and wine they kept in the cabinet. Cole caught sight of the bottles when the doctor opened the door to show him, and it looked like at least half had been used. Each time Ariella spoke, her husband's eyes got slightly narrower.

"I'm fine," Cole insisted gently, taking his shoes off. "Thank you."

John didn't move at first when Ariella wished both of them goodnight and went upstairs. Cole didn't let the man's constant vigil bother him. He was a guest in the man's home, after all. Stretching out across the couch, which was in fact surprisingly comfortable, Cole closed his eyes and allowed his senses to relax. He wanted the facade of being off his guard to settle in John's mind so he would leave. It took longer than Cole would have liked, but eventually the mortal went upstairs to join his wife.

Cole, however, didn't fall asleep.

Though his eyes were shut, Cole was aware of everything around him. After a while, once he thought it was safe, Cole peeked out through a half-closed eyelid and quickly searched the room. Everything was as it had been before he lay down. Nothing moved or gave any sign that he was being watched. Satisfied, Cole quickly rose and reached for his shoes.

He was halfway through fitting the second one on when there was a noise on the stairway. Cole froze and kept his hands down around his boots, pretending to fiddle with the laces. A moment later, Dr. Ariella Thomas drifted down the steps in a lacy nightgown.

Even in the dark, Cole could tell the gown was practically see-through. The material barely covered her small hips as she descended the remainder of the stairs and came over to the couch. From his angle leaning down, Cole could see she had nothing on underneath. Ariella watched him tie his boots.

"Don't go," she whispered, and it sounded to him like the woman's heart was breaking.

Cole sighed. "I have to," he said. "There's something I need to do. I should never have come here with you."

Ariella grabbed his arm as he stood. "Please."

Cole gently shook her away. "Are you in the habit of offering yourself to strangers you picked up off the side of the road in front of your husband while he's asleep?"

Ariella flinched. Going by the look on her face, Cole might as well have slapped her.

"I'm sorry," he mumbled helplessly. "I just don't understand why you brought me here. What is it you want from me?"

Ariella stepped forward and put her arms around Cole. "I want to feel warm," she whispered. "John won't touch me anymore. You were walking out in the cold after it had just finished snowing. How can you be so warm?"

Cole could feel himself getting hard. He didn't want to be aroused by her. He tried thinking of Joss lying in the hospital. That helped, but the tightness in his groin didn't subside completely. It returned in full force when Ariella's hand began stroking the length of him through his pants.

"I've never been with a man who wore leather pants," she whispered in his ear. "How come they fit you so well?"

"They were tailor-made." Cole gritted his teeth and steeled himself, then pulled Ariella's hand away. "I can't do this."

Ariella reached for him with her other hand. "Why not?"

Cole grunted as she fumbled with the buckle of his belt. "I love someone," he said. "And right now, they're lying in a hospital bed."

Ariella stopped then. "Tell me."

"There is little to tell," Cole said, taking her other hand into his. "There was a... fight. He was badly injured, and somehow I keep thinking it was my fault."

Ariella squeezed his hand, then laced her fingers into his.

"The last time I saw him," Cole went on, "he was unconscious. He never woke up, not even to speak to me. I think they were keeping him sedated."

"So you're...." Ariella began.

Cole waited for her to finish. When she didn't, he asked, "I'm what?"

"You like men?" she pressed.

Cole realized where this was headed finally and shook his head. "It has nothing to do with like or dislike," he replied. "Where I was raised, such things didn't matter. Love is never something to be restrained by social norms like gender. If one loves another, little else matters. He and I are lovers, but it doesn't necessarily mean we prefer one gender over another."

"Ah, you're both bisexual, then."

"Call it what you will if you must," he said, shrugging. "I didn't reject you because you were a woman. Simply put, this doesn't feel right."

"How come?" Ariella asked, raising his hand up to cup her breast.

"As I said, my lover is lying in a hospital bed miles from here." Cole sighed again as he pulled his hand away, forcefully this time.

"Also, again, as stated before, your husband is upstairs. I might not have the same qualms as others about these matters, but infidelity is frowned upon where I am from. I might not live there anymore, but it is still how I was raised. If you want me, I suggest asking his permission first."

Ariella paused, then began laughing. "So that's it, then?"

Cole felt like he had just missed something. "Of course," he said. "What did you think it was?"

John Thomas appeared suddenly at the top of the stairs. Grinning broadly, he began clapping as he came down to them. With each clap, John took a step, and each time he stepped, he clapped faster.

"Bravo," he said in a friendly voice, still grinning from ear to ear.

"Can I pick them or what?" Ariella said, laughing still.

Cole reached for his guns.

Ariella saw him move and placed a reassuring hand on his bicep. "Don't worry," she told him. "Nobody here is going to hurt you. John, I think you might have been right the first time."

"He could still be a cop," John offered, reaching the last step. "Or a secret agent, though on that last one, I highly doubt a man like him could blend in easily."

"John thought you were a mercenary," Ariella explained. "I said cop, but he was right about a police officer not having guns like those. I've never seen any like them before."

"They were specially made," Cole said. "May I ask what is going on now?"

"John and I are married," Ariella said simply. "And we have an open relationship. One of our favorite games is picking out strangers and seeing if I can seduce them while he watches."

Cole looked at her. "So you are in the habit of picking up strange men and offering yourself to them."

"Not while John is asleep," she replied, going over to meet him. "We have rules."

"Forgive us," John said quickly when Cole looked at them with a practiced stare of emptiness. "It was my turn to pick the game, and I wanted to play the role of the jealous husband. It might surprise you to learn just how many guys fall for that."

"Actually," Ariella countered. "John used to be a stage actor. He was brilliant, but then he gave it all up to be with me. We like playing games with a third party. It helps make things interesting."

"I don't like being played," Cole stated.

"I suspected you might be angry if you found out," Ariella admitted. "I'm sorry for leading you on and hurting you. It wasn't my intention, but some people are nervous around us. They don't—"

"Approve," Cole finished. "I understand that, and what you do with your lives is none of my business. I just don't like being lied to. In my world, it can get you killed or worse."

Ariella looked Cole over for a moment. "You keep saying that," she said, meeting his eyes. "Things like 'my world' and 'where I'm from'. Are you really a secret agent?"

"In Maine?" Cole pointed out.

Her husband frowned. "He has a point, darling."

"I should go," Cole said, unlocking the front door. "I'm sorry, but I can't stay here. There was something I came here to do."

"So you are a mercenary, then," Ariella said before Cole could make his exit.

"If you go," John warned, "if you're here to do something illegal, we have a responsibility to report you."

Cole waited a second. "I know."

"What happened?" Ariella asked as Cole started to leave again. "Who paid you to come here?"

"No one," Cole told them before he could think better of it. "I came here on my own. This isn't about money."

For the third time, Cole started to close the door behind him. As he stepped out into the dark, however, a loud siren began to blare through the night. Cole froze to listen and could hear people shouting in the far distance. It almost sounded like the sort of alarm that went off during prison breaks.

Ariella opened the door behind him. "That's the alarm," Ariella confirmed.

"Thank you, honey," John said gently, coming up behind her. "I think our friend solved that on his own."

"What does it mean?" Cole asked. "I haven't done anything yet."

"It usually goes off during a major emergency," she explained, stepping down onto the mat beside him. "Like if there is a fire or if there is a major breakout in the confined wards."

Something occurred to Cole then, and it made his blood run cold. "Was a young boy around the age of eleven moved into the confined ward last night or early this morning? He might have been brought in by helicopter."

Ariella narrowed her eyes suspiciously as she looked at Cole. John was looking down at him as well. "Why do you ask that?" her husband pressed, folding his arms.

"Because I think that boy is named Daniel Whittaker," Cole replied. "And it's possible he's making an escape right now. Someone may be helping him."

"How do you know?" John asked.

Cole waited, biting his lower lip as the alarm continued to sound. "I'm a cop," he said finally. "I work for the NYPD. There was an incident on Staten Island yesterday that the Whittaker boy was involved in. Someone had him moved via helicopter out of the hospital to here. I got a tip that someone might be planning to break him out."

"I never would have guessed cop," Ariella said. "Are you supposed to be here?"

"No," Cole said. "And I'm well aware of the consequences of that, so please don't point them out. Right now, something is happening."

An explosion rocked the air throughout the compound just then. Ariella staggered back slightly due to the noise and had to be steadied by John, who put his hands on her shoulders reassuringly.

"I have to go help," Cole told them. "If it is what I think it is, we're in danger."

Another explosion rattled the skies. Cole felt this one harder than the last and had to catch Ariella before she fell over.

"This is embarrassing," she muttered as he set her back on her feet. "My feminist social group from college would kill me if they knew I had to be handled by a guy like this."

"I won't tell if you won't," Cole told them. "Good-bye."

"Hey!" Ariella called out. "Will you come back when this is all over?"

Cole shook his head, moving backward now. "Probably not," he told her. "I wasn't supposed to be here in the first place, but if you two are in New York when my boyfriend gets out of the hospital, look either one of us up. He might be willing to try something."

The words felt hollow to Cole, but it wasn't enough to slow him down. He made it to the main building in a minute's time. There were holes in the far side of it, each one big enough to drive a truck through. Voices could be heard, children and adults alike screaming in terror. Cole didn't bother staying concealed. With all the chaos, it would be something if people noticed his presence. Still, he threw a cloak of glamour over himself, just enough to make any memories of him vague and hard to pin down, then ran straight for the damaged side of the building.

Two figures were already being lowered down to the ground. It looked like the shadows all around them had come to life and offered a hand. This wasn't the surprising part to Cole. He had seen far wilder magics in his time. The surprising part was seeing Jynx standing next to a handsome young man at least a head taller than her, one who looked eerily familiar.

It seemed Daniel Whittaker had enjoyed a growth spurt recently. It took a moment for Cole to figure it out, but the resemblance was unmistakable. His hair was solid black now, as black as the sky above them. He watched with emerald green eyes as Cole ran up to meet them.

"Detective," Daniel said by way of greeting. "Long time no see."

"You've changed," Cole noted, coming to a stop.

Cole's mind was racing as it caught up to the situation. "It was my blood," he said. "The blood that went in the circle to consecrate it again. I used it to summon the creature of rage from the academy's memories. You bonded with it when it attacked you."

"And now I have fey in my blood," Daniel said, nodding. "Not a bad deal to end up with, all things considered, especially when it means she and I can finally be together."

"I won't try and stop you." Something occurred to Cole then. "You are still 'you', correct? The poltergeist isn't in control?"

Daniel shook his head. "I absorbed it," he explained, sending more shadows out. "I guess there was so much hate in me for so long, it found a home there."

Jynx looked in the direction of the shouting voices at the same time Cole did.

"It looks like we're about to have company," Daniel said. "Hold on."

Cole wasn't close enough to grab either of them, but it didn't matter. Shadows from all around them rose and enveloped the three within a cocoon of pure black. It felt like being underwater or standing in a wind tunnel. Cole's ears roared and ached with the pressure, but it was only for a moment or so. Without warning, the shadows peeled back, revealing a dense wood all around them.

"We're about half of a mile away," Daniel said, answering his unspoken question. "I think, at least. These new powers of mine take some getting used to. I hope there's not too big of a learning curve."

"You'll get the hang of it," Cole told him. "I still cannot believe this is you. Are you certain the poltergeist is gone?"

Daniel looked thoughtfully out in the distance for a moment. "I feel it," he said slowly. "But not as anything separate. It's like the monster is a part of me now. I feel it as if it were my arm or a leg."

Cole smiled as Jynx moved in closer. "You've lost several years," he noted. "Though, not everyone here seems to mind."

Daniel shook his head. "I was too mature for eleven. I had no desire to go home and face my family over what I had done and what they thought of it. I have power to protect myself now, and Jynx has agreed to come with me. Best of all, I'm no longer too young for her."

Jynx was giving Daniel a wry look but snuggled in close to him when he said the last part. "I want to stay with her," Daniel went on, and he seemed to be asking for Cole's permission now. "It's what I always wanted."

Cole smiled at them. "Do you need a ride?"

Daniel shook his head. "I need to start learning how to control my new abilities sooner than later," he pointed out. "Plus, you'd be aiding and abetting a known felon. I can't let you risk yourself for me twice."

"I'm not a cop anymore," Cole told him. "I was suspended indefinitely early this morning."

Daniel and Jynx both looked angry. "Why?" he asked.

Cole shook his head. "They need someone to blame. People like us are always the scapegoats for those in power. I'll be fine. Go," Cole told them when it looked like neither was going to be convinced. "You need to leave now before they figure out a way to track you. I need to get back to New York."

Jynx and Daniel looked like they wanted to protest on his behalf, but Cole wouldn't hear of it. "If you don't need a ride," he said, hoping to change the subject, "could I get a lift from you instead? My car is parked at a convenience store not far down the highway. I really don't feel like walking."

"Not a problem," Daniel said as the shadows gathered around them once more.

"Thanks," Cole told him, meaning it. "Strictly speaking, though, this isn't how I imagined things would go. I thought for certain I would be spending the rest of the night trying to break you out."

"Sorry I ruined your plans," Daniel replied, laughing, before the darkness enveloped them completely.

"You'll get over it," Cole told him as the shadows whisked them away.

CHAPTER 13

IT TOOK three days for Cole to find the gun Dickson had been harping on about. It had fallen to the floor and rolled underneath his bed somehow. That was where Cole found it, at least, but knowing the sithen, it could have been anywhere. He left it at the front desk of the precinct with a note attached for it to be delivered to Internal Affairs, then turned around and walked out without a word. Corhagen and the others hadn't been anywhere in sight at the time, but he hadn't wanted to jeopardize their lives, anyway.

Daniel had dropped him off just a little off the mark, in a ditch down from where his car still was. Cole asked him to wait while he went back and fetched the food Mal had prepared for him. His butler would have pitched a fit if he forgot, so Cole made sure to deliver it. Daniel and Jynx thanked them, each in their own way. Daniel bumped knuckles with him while Jynx leaned in and kissed him lightly on the cheek.

Then they were both gone.

He hadn't asked where they were going. It was best Cole didn't know, and they wouldn't stay very long in one place. Cole hoped Jynx would help take care of Daniel and keep him in line. He was still very fragile and in a position where revenge would be sorely tempting. Still, Cole knew deep in his heart that the changeling was more than up to the challenge.

He only wished he could say the same for himself.

Internal Affairs was having him followed wherever he went. Cole began to notice right after he came back from Maine. On his way back from the precinct when he'd turned in the gun, a car was tailing him. Cole managed to give it the slip, but it was there again when he went to the supermarket to buy food to replace what Boogaloo had eaten and get several boxes of donuts.

The wood goblin had wanted to crash with Cole for a little longer, but Mal had been adamant. Cole agreed and called on the goblin's cousins, Bugbear and Bugaboo, to take him back with them. It took three boxes of Krispy Kremes before they agreed. The Internal Affairs car had been there, as well. Cole had walked over to the car as calm as you please and offered each man inside a donut. Neither had seen him coming, and they drove off without accepting.

Cole had just laughed. He was going to have to get used to being followed for a little while at least, it seemed. This made his next criminal plan more difficult. Breaking Vallimun out of the hospital was going to be a lot harder now with him under surveillance and Joss under guard. These were just ordinary cops assigned for Joss's protection, at least. They had been placed right after Cole was officially suspended. The Order was most likely behind it. Cole had dodged them for years, but it looked like he was finally going to tangle with them.

Glamouring himself didn't work, for the officers had been given talismans to ward off fey magic. They recognized him on the spot and asked him to leave. Cole tried bespelling their minds just to see if it would work, but neither woman responded. That cinched it in his mind that the Order was prepared for him.

It had been said that a simple plan was always the best. While another snowstorm brewed over New York, Cole had spent his time holed up in the sithen, thinking of a way to bring Joss to him. Ultimately, however, any magic he tried would most likely either be detected by the officers who'd been prepared to deal with him or ineffective altogether. To that end, Cole decided on brute force.

He waited until after sundown, when the snowstorm was at its worst. After driving to the hospital, Cole parked his car in an alley where there was low visibility and little chance of being spotted by security cameras. Mal had helped him put his hair up in a bun. It was embarrassing, but he needed it that way so it would stay out of his face. Cole had left his guns and Aed Deigh behind. His body felt off-balance and naked without them, yet he couldn't risk being identified by their telltale presence.

He had dressed simply for the occasion: a pair of black jeans, black running shoes, and a black T-shirt. A ski hood completed the ensemble. Between his food bill and the outfit, he was going to have to watch his spending for a while, at least until he found work again.

Internal Affairs had put out an APB alert on him. Any vehicle matching his description was to be reported. He learned this via Rainette. To his great surprise, the witch had called him a few days ago to warn him about it despite knowing what it could feasibly do to her. She'd at least had the sense to not call from her cell phone. Cole had given her props for using a pay phone instead, though she'd chewed him out for implying a lack of stealth all the same.

Knowing that they were tracking him, Cole had asked Mal to have the sithen drop him out in an area with few police cars. He had stuck to the residential roads the entire drive, and there had been no signs of anyone following him.

Now he just had to get inside the hospital without being seen. Slipping his mask on, Cole wove a veil of glamour around his head, giving him the appearance of a young man in his twenties. He kept his footsteps at a slow, even pace, since his glamour tended to be fragile when it came to moving around a lot. The receptionist barely gave him notice. Clearly, his temporary face was nothing impressive.

Cole reached the elevator and swiftly ducked inside. The glamour faded for a second, and he had to waste several precious seconds fixing it while his thumb jabbed the button for Joss's floor.

When he got off, the coast was clear. Joss's room was just down from a nurse's station, which was currently manned by a woman in her thirties. Cole reached out with his hand and pushed down hard on the air. In his mind, he was shoving sleep down onto her. The woman's eyes blinked for a second as she struggled to make sense out of what was happening to her. After a moment more, his magic won out, and she laid her head down on the desk.

Neither officer noticed. There were two men guarding Joss's room this time, which made Cole feel a lot better. Assuming they had been given the same talismans as the ones before, neither would be fooled by his glamour disguise, though Cole was grateful, at least, that the trinkets didn't register glamour not cast on the holders themselves.

Both men were distracted. One was holding a cell phone close to his ear and trying to look inconspicuous while the other flipped casually through a magazine. Cole approached them without a problem, on the lookout the entire time for any personnel who might come wandering their way. Cole reached the man reading the magazine first and quickly struck him on the back of the head.

The second man was out cold before he could pull himself away from his phone. "I'm sorry," Cole said into the machine in a deliberately gruff voice. "He'll have to call you back."

Cole killed the power in the phone by swiping the battery and tossing it back to the unconscious figure in front of him. Ducking through the door, he found himself standing just a few feet away from Joss.

This time, the inspector was awake.

"Cole?" Joss's voice sounded exhausted. "What are you doing here, and why are you wearing that mask?"

Not bothering to wonder why Joss wasn't affected by his glamour, Cole tore the spell away and moved over to the side of the bed.

"I've come to get you," Cole told him. "We have to hurry, though. They wouldn't let me in to see you, so I had to sneak in."

"They said you were thrown off the force," Joss whispered. "Someone said you were going to be arrested."

"We were set up," Cole explained, linking his fingers with the only hand his lover had now. "The Section has taken a huge hit. Someone wants us out of the way, I think."

"Son of a bitch."

Joss tried to sit up and winced in pain. "I've had doctors in and out of here all afternoon," he said weakly. "Mostly just to dope me up. Nobody is telling me anything yet. Do they know what happened to my arm?"

Cole felt his chest seize up. "It was crushed," he said, giving Joss's hand a squeeze. "There was no way to repair it. I came here tonight to ask you something."

Joss looked up at Cole's worried face through his one good eye. His other was still taped over with a white cotton patch.

"What is it?" Joss asked, sounding nervous now.

"There may be a way for me to fix you," Cole told him, letting go of his hand. "I have never seen it work before, and I don't know if it is even possible. If you don't want me to try it, I won't. I was going to bring you to the sithen and do it without asking, but I can't. You should know what the risks are."

"Tell me."

Cole took a deep breath. "Deep down at the very bottom of the sithen is a circular stone chamber with a carved table in it. That is where the sithen sprang from. It has a connection to the Goddess and Consort. I saw Consort there personally when we fought Naryssa. That was where I wound up. Something happened to me while I was down there."

Cole looked into Joss's good eye. "It changed me. I haven't been able to figure out how just yet, but I can feel it. My powers over summer and winter have been getting stronger. I can shoot fire and ice projectiles with Aed Deigh now. At first I thought maybe it was just because I was living inside the sithen now, but that doesn't feel quite right. I don't think that's entirely it. It has to do with what Consort did to me."

"What did he do?" Joss asked, taking Cole by the hand again.

"He...." Cole hesitated at revealing the whole truth. Humans could be so unreasonable when it came to sex at times. "We coupled. It was before you and I were together."

Joss didn't seem bothered. "And afterward you began to notice a change?"

"Yes," Cole said. "Gradually, but looking back, it was there from the start."

"Okay." Joss had to swallow before he could speak again. "How will this help me?"

"I can take you there and speak with the Consort directly," Cole explained. "If he is willing, you might get your arm and eye back. I have called wild magic to me before, though I don't know why it happened. The first time was when we thought I had accidentally changed Corhagen into a sidhe. There are stories in the darker places of Faerie and here where mortals were healed via wild magic."

Joss thought for a long time. "What will happen to me?"

"I don't know," Cole admitted. "Wild magic affects each person it touches differently. For some, the transformation is merely a reflection of their own deep desires and wishes. They become more themselves, but that is also reflected in their physical appearance. Other stories tell of humans becoming grotesque monstrosities that had to be killed for everyone's safety."

A minute or two more went by as Joss debated in silence. "What is happening in the Section right now?" he asked.

Cole thought over what he knew so far. "Corhagen has been put in charge. Rainette, Staffelbach, and Marcel are all still there. They joined up right after you were hurt so we could raid the academy on Staten Island."

Cole realized Joss probably hadn't heard any of this, not if the hospital was keeping him under with medication. Quickly, he gave Joss a recap of what had gone down there. When he was finished, Joss looked ready to punch his fist through a wall.

"Fuck!" he swore. "The stupid motherfuckers!"

"I concur," Cole said, nodding. "Corhagen seems to be enjoying his new role as leader of the Section for the moment. If you recall, he always thought of it as his idea even though the real Section Thirteen had existed before he was born."

Joss acted as though he wasn't listening. "They've got to be planning something big," he said to himself. "This Order of Dawn or whatever. They wouldn't just have us shut down for the sake of it. This smells of a set-up. They need us out of the way for some reason."

"I think so too," Cole told him. "So what do you say?"

Joss looked Cole in the eye again. "Get me the fuck outta here!"

THE two officers were coming to when Cole peeked his head out the door to check. He gave them a quick brush against the side of their heads with his hand to make them nod off again. This had little effect, so Cole quickly dug into the pocket of the one on the right, thinking he might find the talisman they'd been issued. Something seared the tips of his fingers, making him jump back. Cole punched the cop upside the head to knock him out, then looked to see what he'd touched that hurt him so much.

Each cop had nails in his pocket. Furthermore, their shoes had been modified with tiny nails punching through the soles. They were hardly the size of thumbtacks, yet Cole knew both were made of pure iron.

"A simple plan," he muttered, finding a rag first so he could collect the nails and shoes without hurting himself. "It's usually the best kind."

Now the guards could be put to sleep. After that, Cole tracked down a wheelchair in the nurse's station. Another nurse had found the one he'd put to sleep and was attempting to wake her, so Cole was forced to put him to sleep as well. Cole hefted the body up and left it snoozing in a chair in the back, then grabbed the wheelchair and went back to Joss's room.

Soon they were on their way.

No alarms sounded as Cole wheeled Joss out the front door. The receptionist started to look up this time, but Cole was able to distract her by making the woman think she was speaking with her boss. From there, it was a simple matter of taking Joss out to his car.

"That was way too easy," Cole said, helping Joss into the seat.

"You think that was easy?" Joss countered. "I thought we were going to get caught about five times in the elevator alone."

"Would you have preferred taking the stairs?"

The garage was less than a block away. Once they were safely inside, Cole let himself breathe evenly while he retrieved the wheelchair from the trunk and once more helped Joss into it. Joss was moving a little more on his own now, though he still looked terrible.

"Mal!" Cole shouted. "Mal, I need you in here!"

Mal appeared next to Cole at once. "Sir, what…."

Whatever Mal had been planning to ask was lost as he looked over at Joss. "Open the lower chamber to the sithen, Mal," Cole ordered, grabbing the chair's handles. "I'm taking Joss down to see Consort."

Mal looked pale. "Sir, you don't—"

Cole wasn't in a mood to argue. "Now, Mal."

Mal hung his head in abashed silence and pointed to his right. "There," he told Cole. "You'll find the way through there. Please be careful, sir."

Cole wheeled Joss over to the door without another word. Upon closer inspection, the door turned out to be wooden sliding doors for an old-fashioned elevator. Cole hadn't seen one of this type in years.

The doors opened without prompting from either of them. Turning Joss around, Cole dragged his lover in backward. Mal was watching them leave with a somber look on his face. The former sorcerer waved good-bye as the doors closed, cutting them off.

There were no buttons to push, but neither of them needed one. The elevator was moving on its own now. It was quiet save for the sound of a motor pulling the cables, assuming the sithen had even bothered making those and wasn't just artificially producing the noise for aesthetic effect. Were that the case, Cole might have requested music instead.

Cole had been expecting a long trip. In his mind, the lower chamber was a place deep within the earth. They were in the elevator, surrounded by stone on all sides, for maybe two minutes when the shaft opened up into a massive stone chamber.

The cage slowed its descent just before it touched bottom. When the cage opened, Cole wheeled Joss out without a word, not even looking back when the cage began to rise. He knew the hole it had come through would disappear, having served its purpose.

Joss was clutching himself with his one arm now. "This place feels…."

"Amazing," Cole breathed. He had forgotten how potent the magic in this part of the sithen was.

"Scary," Joss finished. "And I don't use that word often."

Cole wasn't listening. Someone was waiting for them beside the stone table. It was the same as the last time Cole had come here, a slab that looked like it had been carved straight out of a mountain. Carvings had been painstakingly etched into every corner of it, and surrounding the table were four pillars.

The woman beside the table was nude save for a hooded robe that concealed her face. Cole couldn't see what she looked like underneath it, but he recognized her on sight.

"Danu." The name escaped his mouth like a baby's breath.

"Who?" Joss asked, looking up at Cole.

Cole looked down. "Can't you see her?" he asked.

Joss shook his head and turned in the direction Cole was staring. "Am I supposed to be seeing someone? I can see the table, but there isn't anyone there."

Cole shook his head. "She's there," he told Joss. "I can see her."

"You can see me now." Danu's voice rushed through the cavern like feathered wings. The whole chamber went still at once. "Consort has shown you who you truly are, though you've yet to realize it."

Cole moved away from Joss's wheelchair and approached cautiously. The Goddess gave no indication that she was bothered by this, so Cole kept walking until he was a few feet from her. There, he dropped to one knee and bowed low.

"My Lady," he addressed her.

The Goddess was looking past Cole at Joss sitting obliviously in his chair. "He is a fine one for you," she said. "I approve, if that means anything to you."

Cole wasn't sure what to say in response. "I came here to plead for his sake," he told her, voice shaking now. "Whatever I may have to offer up in exchange, you may take freely in return for sparing him the cruel fate he was handed."

Danu looked down at Cole. "Does this one mean so much to you? Have you not others you could share your body with instead?"

"Please." The word choked Cole. Lowering his head further, he placed both hands above the back of his head and folded them together in a show of total submission.

"Please," he asked again. "Save him. If you cannot do it, then allow me to make my case to Consort instead. I don't care who does it, just spare him for me."

The silence that followed was devastating.

"Place him on the table," Danu instructed. "I will show you what to do afterward."

Cole waited to see if the Goddess was joking. When she gave no indication, he jumped up off the ground and raced back to where Joss was waiting for him. Joss was wearing an expression like Cole was out of his mind, yet he didn't recoil when the sidhe stood to the left of him and bent down.

"Put your arm around my neck," Cole instructed. "I'm going to place you on the stone table."

Joss complied, and once he had a good grip, Cole lifted him out of the wheelchair and carried him over to the table effortlessly.

"Careful," Cole advised as Joss struggled to move himself onto the surface. "Do you need help?"

Joss shook his head. Once he was safely in place, Cole looked around. The Goddess had vanished from sight the moment he'd stood up. Once Joss lay back down, however, she was there in the chamber again right behind them.

"Remove his clothing," she told Cole. "For this, he cannot have anything touched by mankind weighing him down. Soon he will no longer be connected to that world. It will be your choice that determines which new world he inhabits."

Cole looked at her. "I don't understand."

Though he still couldn't see her face, Cole had the impression that Danu was smiling now. "You will know when the time comes," she replied. "Mysterious ways, remember?"

Cole removed the hospital gown Joss was wearing, along with the patch over his left eye. What was underneath was a mess. Cole left the dressings on what remained of his lover's arm, however, for fear of making it bleed again. Joss's face was frightfully pale now. Moving to the stone table had drained what little strength was left in his body. Cole knew the man couldn't take any more blood loss. Tossing the bandages and gown away, Cole quickly stripped out of his own clothes. Once he was naked, Danu motioned for him to climb on top of the stone table as well.

"It is time for you to enjoy your gifts, my son."

Cole stared at her in confusion. "Gifts?"

"One that you have used before," she went on. "And one that should have been yours before now."

Her voice was filled with sorrow as she spoke. "I will be with you always, my beloved son. Never forget that, and please do not forget about me."

With those words, she was gone.

Cole waited for a moment, watching the spot where she had stood in case the Goddess decided to return spontaneously.

"I suppose she does move in mysterious ways," he said.

"What now?" Joss asked as Cole stretched out. "Are we supposed to just lie here?"

Cole ran his eyes over the battle-scarred body of his lover. There were bruises everywhere, and the stump that had once been his right arm was impossible to ignore. Cole brushed his fingers through the hairs on Joss's chest, playing with them idly.

A voice whispered in his ear. "You chose the cup, my son," the Goddess's voice said. "You must heal him with your own flesh."

Joss was getting aroused. His horse-sized cock stretched out down the length of his thigh as if following a trail to Cole's crotch.

"That's the first time I've been hard since the attack in the holding cell," Joss noted. "At least some part of me is feeling better."

Cole seized Joss's shaft, gripping the thick tube of muscle in his fist and pumping it up and down slowly. Joss groaned at once, throwing his head back.

"Go easy on me," Joss hissed. "I've been in the hospital, after all."

"We have to do this," Cole said before sticking his tongue out to lick at the slit. "It is the only way to heal you."

Joss didn't argue, though the grunts he made lying back down on the stone slab weren't all pleasurable. Cole took this into account as he began taking the plum-sized head into his mouth while jacking his fist up and down. Joss was leaking precum within seconds as he breathed heavily. Cole rose up off the shaft abruptly and turned around so he could look Joss in the face. The inspector gazed up at Cole, smiling, his expression marred only slightly by the pain he was feeling.

Cole leaned in and kissed his lover on the mouth. He didn't intend to do it so forcefully, but the moment their mouths touched, Cole began to kiss Joss's face like a starved man. Joss tried to match Cole's pace, but it was impossible for him. Cole forced him back and began making a trail of kisses down the side of Joss's neck. Joss ran his fingers through Cole's hair as the sidhe moved lower, past his chest. Finding the bun there, Joss fumbled with it for a moment until he was able to free the long mane of snow-colored hair as Cole continued down.

Both of their manes spread out around them. Cole could feel Joss lovingly spinning the silky threads around his hand as he ran his tongue up the crevice of Joss's abs. From the mortal's bellybutton to the cleft between his pecs and back down, Cole left a trail of his saliva.

Cole moved forward for another kiss. In doing so, his body slid between Joss's spread legs. Joss wrapped both legs around Cole's waist as he felt the tip of Cole's thick cock push at the entrance hidden there. Cole was kissing him like mad again. It was as if the sidhe was trying to dig his way down inside. When Cole's dick pushed past the ring of muscle guarding Joss's asshole, the man moaned low and loud in the sidhe's mouth.

"I love you," Cole whispered fiercely.

Joss pulled away to stare at Cole's face.

"It's true," Cole insisted. "No matter what happens after this, even though you may not feel the same for me, know that I love you. I do this for you, Joss Vallimun."

Cole began to move inside of him. Joss felt every thrust like it was rattling the fillings of his teeth. Gradually, though, he began to feel something different. He couldn't put his finger on it, but the air around them felt charged now. Cole was moving faster than before, pulling his impressive cock nearly all the way out before brutally reentering.

The pain had diminished. In its place, Joss began to feel something warm and inviting spill through from the center of his chest. He thought Cole might have cum already, but the sidhe was still pounding away into his ass. Joss's breathing was becoming labored now. It was hard to focus on what was happening around them while Cole hammered him like a machine.

The air smelled of spring and flowers. Joss thought he recognized honeysuckle and roses mixed together with the scents of fresh pine and cedar. The chamber faded away as Cole's rhythm began to really take hold of him. Joss cursed and moaned, shouting obscenities that would have made a sailor blush as he felt Cole drilling him a new asshole. His pain was a distant memory now. Joss felt as though his body were made for fucking and nothing else.

Cole suddenly stopped moving and jerked himself out. Joss started to protest, but Cole was on the move before he could utter a word. Aiming Joss's bull shaft up, Cole lowered himself down onto it and let out a gasp as the first inch or so slid into his guts. Joss's lone eye bulged to twice its normal size as Cole took him without any lube. The pain was evident, yet Cole kept pushing himself down, determined to take the whole thing if it were the last thing he did.

Joss grabbed at Cole with his one arm, then froze. His right side was tingling like something was there. Joss had heard of phantom pain before, but it wasn't supposed to make him see his arm like it was transparent. The phantom appendage glowed like summer sunlight. It was his arm, and yet it was different.

Cole wasn't bothered by the sight of it. Taking hold of it, though there shouldn't have been anything more tangible there than morning mist, Cole gripped both hands in his as he forced himself all the way down. As his cheeks brushed the hairs surrounding Joss's balls, Cole threw his head back and let loose a howl that echoed all around them.

"*Fuck!*" he screamed.

Joss did precisely that. Bracing the heels of his feet on the stone table, he shoved his hips upward into Cole's ass like a rocket taking off for space. Cole howled again as his intestines stretched to accommodate the massive girth opening him wide. Joss could see through both eyes now. He was too caught up in the feel of being inside his lover to worry much over how that was possible. His arm was becoming more solid as well. Joss pulled the more substantial one free and gripped Cole's nipples, twisting them hard. Cole snarled in answer and raked his fingernails across Joss's backside.

The two moved as animals in the grips of a wild mating. Whatever injuries the mortal had sustained before were long gone. The phantom limb was solid now. Rather than sunshine, though, it now glowed silver like moonlight. There was a black tint to the underside, as though a shadow were woven into flesh.

Joss was using his arms to hold Cole in place as he furiously fucked the sidhe in his lap. Cole had wrapped both of his arms around Joss's neck to hold him close as he slammed down to meet each thrust that impaled him. When Cole had had enough, he shoved the mortal away forcefully and quickly yanked both of Joss's legs apart.

Joss fell backward as Cole bent his lover's body forward up to his shoulders and stuffed his dick all the way in. Joss had to grab onto what little of the table he could to keep from being pushed off. Cole was fucking him senseless now, his tri-colored eyes of copper, gold, and topaz shining along with the moonlight glow of his skin.

After a while, Cole consented to let Joss stretch him down on all fours and plow him from behind. The mortal draped his body over Cole's like a cloak. When they both came together, their seed sprayed the table's surface, painting it white.

Joss collapsed on top of Cole, his prick softening as the last few spurts of cum oozed out onto the sidhe's flesh. Cole muttered something, then moved to turn over onto his back. Joss started to move away, but Cole was quick to pull him close again. As he looked up into his newly whole lover's face, he spotted the change.

The left eye was blood red. It was no longer damaged but a solid orb of dark crimson. Looking closely, Cole saw a triple helix woven around in a circle. Overlaying the triple helix circle was a triquetra. There was no pupil, yet Joss was watching him through it.

Rather than asking, Joss cautiously probed the area around his eye. Cole pulled the hand away instead and held up Joss's new one. The newborn appendage was solid black like obsidian. Cole could almost see the muscles hidden underneath. Over the upper side of the arm was silver. It crept over the arm like something wicked and sinister. The fingers were black as well and tipped with claws.

As Cole observed this new creation with wonder, skin spilled down from the shoulder to coat it, concealing the arm from sight. Now it looked like any other human arm, matching the left one perfectly.

Joss's hair shone even though there was no sunlight. His face had regained a kind of youthful joy. Cole smiled up at him as his love flexed his new fingers.

"Welcome back," Cole said, bringing him down for a kiss.

Joss obliged, then pulled himself away. "Let's get to work."

Read the beginning of Cole's story

The Thirteenth Child

J.L. O'Faolain

J.L. O'FAOLAIN was born the youngest, with four older sisters, in the backwoods of the Deep South. Those that have braved getting to know him have attributed this to being the root of his growing insanity. A teased bibliophile in his youth, O'Faolain spent his years prior to getting published as a cook, laundry man, delivery boy, grease monkey, and retail stocker. He has a plethora of skills and abilities, none of which would work well on a job application. In his spare time, O'Faolain enjoys weightlifting, philosophy, deconstruction, reading, writing, porn, and the Internet in general. Aside from becoming a successfully published author, he would very much like to pilot a giant robot while Two-Mix's "Rhythm Emotion" is playing in the background. Either that, or travel the world in a dirigible. In short, the general consensus by all, including himself, is that he is a mighty strange fellow.

www.ingramcontent.com/pod-product-compliance
Lightning Source LLC
Chambersburg PA
CBHW050657290626
47170CB00015B/1072